I0784578

A. E. W. Mason

Detective Gabriel Hanaud: At the Villa Rose & The Affair at the Semiramis Hotel

OK Publishing 2021

*A. E. W. Mason*

# Detective Gabriel Hanaud: At the Villa Rose & The Affair at the Semiramis Hotel

Published by

## MUSAICUM

Books

- Advanced Digital Solutions & High-Quality book Formatting -

musaicumbooks@okpublishing.info

2021 OK Publishing

ISBN 978-80-272-7935-7

# Contents

# At the Villa Rose

# CHAPTER I

## SUMMER LIGHTNING

It was Mr. Ricardo's habit as soon as the second week of August came round to travel to Aix-les-Bains, in Savoy, where for five or six weeks he lived pleasantly. He pretended to take the waters in the morning, he went for a ride in his motor-car in the afternoon, he dined at the Cercle in the evening, and spent an hour or two afterwards in the baccarat-rooms at the Villa des Fleurs. An enviable, smooth life without a doubt, and it is certain that his acquaintances envied him. At the same time, however, they laughed at him and, alas with some justice; for he was an exaggerated person. He was to be construed in the comparative. Everything in his life was a trifle overdone, from the fastidious arrangement of his neckties to the feminine nicety of his little dinner-parties. In age Mr. Ricardo was approaching the fifties; in condition he was a widower —a state greatly to his liking, for he avoided at once the irksomeness of marriage and the reproaches justly levelled at the bachelor; finally, he was rich, having amassed a fortune in Mincing Lane, which he had invested in profitable securities.

Ten years of ease, however, had not altogether obliterated in him the business look. Though he lounged from January to December, he lounged with the air of a financier taking a holiday; and when he visited, as he frequently did, the studio of a painter, a stranger would have hesitated to decide whether he had been drawn thither by a love of art or by the possibility of an investment. His "acquaintances" have been mentioned, and the word is suitable. For while he mingled in many circles, he stood aloof from all. He affected the company of artists, by whom he was regarded as one ambitious to become a connoisseur; and amongst the younger business men, who had never dealt with him, he earned the disrespect reserved for the dilettante. If he had a grief, it was that he had discovered no great man who in return for practical favours would engrave his memory in brass. He was a Maecenas without a Horace, an Earl of Southampton without a Shakespeare. In a word, Aix-les-Bains in the season was the very place for him; and never for a moment did it occur to him that he was here to be dipped in agitations, and hurried from excitement to excitement. The beauty of the little town, the crowd of well-dressed and agreeable people, the rose-coloured life of the place, all made their appeal to him. But it was the Villa des Fleurs which brought him to Aix. Not that he played for anything more than an occasional louis; nor, on the other hand, was he merely a cold looker-on. He had a bank-note or two in his pocket on most evenings at the service of the victims of the tables. But the pleasure to his curious and dilettante mind lay in the spectacle of the battle which was waged night after night between raw nature and good manners. It was extraordinary to him how constantly manners prevailed. There were, however, exceptions.

For instance. On the first evening of this particular visit he found the rooms hot, and sauntered out into the little semicircular garden at the back. He sat there for half an hour under a flawless sky of stars watching the people come and go in the light of the electric lamps, and appreciating the gowns and jewels of the women with the eye of a connoisseur; and then into this starlit quiet there came suddenly a flash of vivid life. A girl in a soft, clinging frock of white satin darted swiftly from the rooms and flung herself nervously upon a bench. She could not, to Ricardo's thinking, be more than twenty years of age. She was certainly quite young. The supple slenderness of her figure proved it, and he had moreover caught a glimpse, as she rushed out, of a fresh and very pretty face; but he had lost sight of it now. For the girl wore a big black satin hat with a broad brim, from which a couple of white ostrich feathers curved over at the back, and in the shadow of that hat her face was masked. All that he could see was a pair of long diamond eardrops, which sparkled and trembled as she moved her head-and that she did constantly. Now she stared moodily at the ground; now she flung herself back; then she twisted nervously to the right, and then a moment afterwards to the left; and then again she stared in front of her, swinging a satin slipper backwards and forwards against the pavement with the petulance of a child. All her movements were spasmodic; she was on the verge of hysteria. Ricardo was expecting her to burst into tears, when she sprang up and as swiftly as she had come she hurried back into the rooms. "Summer lightning," thought Mr. Ricardo.

Near to him a woman sneered, and a man said, pityingly: "She was pretty, that little one. It is regrettable that she has lost."

A few minutes afterwards Ricardo finished his cigar and strolled back into the rooms, making his way to the big table just on the right hand of the entrance, where the play as a rule runs high. It was clearly running high to-night. For so deep a crowd thronged about the table that Ricardo could only by standing on tiptoe see the faces of the players. Of the banker he could not catch a glimpse. But though the crowd remained, its units were constantly changing, and it was not long before Ricardo found himself standing in the front rank of the spectators, just behind the players seated in the chairs. The oval green table was spread out beneath him littered with bank-notes. Ricardo turned his eyes to the left, and saw seated at the middle of the table the man who was holding the bank. Ricardo recognised him with a start of surprise. He was a young Englishman, Harry Wethermill, who, after a brilliant career at Oxford and at Munich, had so turned his scientific genius to account that he had made a fortune for himself at the age of twenty-eight.

He sat at the table with the indifferent look of the habitual player upon his cleanly chiselled face. But it was plain that his good fortune stayed at his elbow to-night, for opposite to him the croupier was arranging with extraordinary deftness piles of bank-notes in the order of their value. The bank was winning heavily. Even as Ricardo looked Wethermill turned up "a natural," and the croupier swept in the stakes from either side.

"Faites vos jeux, messieurs. Le jeu est fait?" the croupier cried, all in a breath, and repeated the words. Wethermill waited with his hand upon the wooden frame in which the cards were stacked. He glanced round the table while the stakes were being laid upon the cloth, and suddenly his face flashed from languor into interest. Almost opposite to him a small, white-gloved hand holding a five-louis note was thrust forward between the shoulders of two men seated at the table. Wethermill leaned forward and shook his head with a smile. With a gesture he refused the stake. But he was too late. The fingers of the hand had opened, the note fluttered down on to the cloth, the money was staked.

At once he leaned back in his chair.

"Il y a une suite," he said quietly. He relinquished the bank rather than play against that five-louis note. The stakes were taken up by their owners.

The croupier began to count Wethermill's winnings, and Ricardo, curious to know whose small, delicately gloved hand it was which had brought the game to so abrupt a termination, leaned forward. He recognised the young girl in the white satin dress and the big black hat whose nerves had got the better of her a few minutes since in the garden. He saw her now clearly, and thought her of an entrancing loveliness. She was moderately tall, fair of skin, with a fresh colouring upon her cheeks which she owed to nothing but her youth. Her hair was of a light brown with a sheen upon it, her forehead broad, her eyes dark and wonderfully clear. But there was something more than her beauty to attract him. He had a strong belief that somewhere, some while ago, he had already seen her. And this belief grew and haunted him. He was still vaguely puzzling his brains to fix the place when the croupier finished his reckoning.

"There are two thousand louis in the bank," he cried. "Who will take on the bank for two thousand louis?"

No one, however, was willing. A fresh bank was put up for sale, and Wethermill, still sitting in the dealer's chair, bought it. He spoke at once to an attendant, and the man slipped round the table, and, forcing his way through the crowd, carried a message to the girl in the black hat. She looked towards Wethermill and smiled; and the smile made her face a miracle of tenderness. Then she disappeared, and in a few moments Ricardo saw a way open in the throng behind the banker, and she appeared again only a yard or two away, just behind Wethermill. He turned, and taking her hand into his, shook it chidingly.

"I couldn't let you play against me, Celia," he said, in English; "my luck's too good to-night. So you shall be my partner instead. I'll put in the capital and we'll share the winnings."

The girl's face flushed rosily. Her hand still lay clasped in his. She made no effort to withdraw it.

"I couldn't do that," she exclaimed.

"Why not?" said he. "See!" and loosening her fingers he took from them the five-louis note and tossed it over to the croupier to be added to his bank. "Now you can't help yourself. We're partners."

The girl laughed, and the company at the table smiled, half in sympathy, half with amusement. A chair was brought for her, and she sat down behind Wethermill, her lips parted, her face joyous with excitement. But all at once Wethermill's luck deserted him. He renewed his bank three times, and had lost the greater part of his winnings when he had dealt the cards through. He took a fourth bank, and rose from that, too, a loser.

"That's enough, Celia," he said. "Let us go out into the garden; it will be cooler there."

"I have taken your good luck away," said the girl remorsefully. Wethermill put his arm through hers.

"You'll have to take yourself away before you can do that," he answered, and the couple walked together out of Ricardo's hearing.

Ricardo was left to wonder about Celia. She was just one of those problems which made Aix-les-Bains so unfailingly attractive to him. She dwelt in some street of Bohemia; so much was clear. The frankness of her pleasure, of her excitement, and even of her distress proved it. She passed from one to the other while you could deal a pack of cards. She was at no pains to wear a mask. Moreover, she was a young girl of nineteen or twenty, running about those rooms alone, as unembarrassed as if she had been at home. There was the free use, too, of Christian names. Certainly she dwelt in Bohemia. But it seemed to Ricardo that she could pass in any company and yet not be overpassed. She would look a little more picturesque than most girls of her age, and she was certainly a good deal more soignee than many, and she had the Frenchwoman's knack of putting on her clothes. But those would be all the differences, leaving out the frankness. Ricardo wondered in what street of Bohemia she dwelt. He wondered still more when he saw her again half an hour afterwards at the entrance to the Villa des Fleurs. She came down the long hall with Harry Wethermill at her side. The couple were walking slowly, and talking as they walked with so complete an absorption in each other that they were unaware of their surroundings. At the bottom of the steps a stout woman of fifty-five over-jewelled, and over-dressed and raddled with paint, watched their approach with a smile of good-humoured amusement. When they came near enough to hear she said in French:

"Well, Celie, are you ready to go home?"

The girl looked up with a start.

"Of course, madame," she said, with a certain submissiveness which surprised Ricardo. "I hope I have not kept you waiting."

She ran to the cloak-room, and came back again with her cloak.

"Good-bye, Harry," she said, dwelling upon his name and looking out upon him with soft and smiling eyes.

"I shall see you to-morrow evening," he said, holding her hand. Again she let it stay within his keeping, but she frowned, and a sudden gravity settled like a cloud upon her face. She turned to the elder woman with a sort of appeal.

"No, I do not think we shall be here, to-morrow, shall we, madame?" she said reluctantly.

"Of course not," said madame briskly. "You have not forgotten what we have planned? No, we shall not be here to-morrow; but the night after-yes."

Celia turned back again to Wethermill.

"Yes, we have plans for to-morrow," she said, with a very wistful note of regret in her voice; and seeing that madame was already at the door, she bent forward and said timidly, "But the night after I shall want you."

"I shall thank you for wanting me," Wethermill rejoined; and the girl tore her hand away and ran up the steps.

Harry Wethermill returned to the rooms. Mr. Ricardo did not follow him. He was too busy with the little problem which had been presented to him that night. What could that girl, he asked himself, have in common with the raddled woman she addressed so respectfully? Indeed, there had been a note of more than respect in her voice. There had been something of affection. Again Mr. Ricardo found himself wondering in what street in Bohemia Celia dwelt-and as he walked up to the hotel there came yet other questions to amuse him.

"Why," he asked, "could neither Celia nor madame come to the Villa des Fleurs to-morrow night? What are the plans they have made? And what was it in those plans which had brought the sudden gravity and reluctance into Celia's face?"

Ricardo had reason to remember those questions during the next few days, though he only idled with them now.


## CHAPTER II


## A CRY FOR HELP

It was on a Monday evening that Ricardo saw Harry Wethermill and the girl Celia together. On the Tuesday he saw Wethermill in the rooms alone and had some talk with him.

Wethermill was not playing that night, and about ten o'clock the two men left the Villa des Fleurs together.

"Which way do you go?" asked Wethermill.

"Up the hill to the Hotel Majestic," said Ricardo.

"We go together, then. I, too, am staying there," said the young man, and they climbed the steep streets together. Ricardo was dying to put some questions about Wethermill's young friend of the night before, but discretion kept him reluctantly silent. They chatted for a few moments in the hall upon indifferent topics and so separated for the night. Mr. Ricardo, however, was to learn something more of Celia the next morning; for while he was fixing his tie before the mirror Wethermill burst into his dressing-room. Mr. Ricardo forgot his curiosity in the surge of his indignation. Such an invasion was an unprecedented outrage upon the gentle tenor of his life. The business of the morning toilette was sacred. To interrupt it carried a subtle suggestion of anarchy. Where was his valet? Where was Charles, who should have guarded the door like the custodian of a chapel?

"I cannot speak to you for at least another half-hour," said Mr. Ricardo, sternly.

But Harry Wethermill was out of breath and shaking with agitation.

"I can't wait," he cried, with a passionate appeal. "I have got to see you. You must help me, Mr. Ricardo-you must, indeed!"

Ricardo spun round upon his heel. At first he had thought that the help wanted was the help usually wanted at Aix-les-Bains. A glance at Wethermills face, however, and the ringing note of anguish in his voice, told him that the thought was wrong. Mr. Ricardo slipped out of his affectations as out of a loose coat. "What has happened?" he asked quietly.

"Something terrible." With shaking fingers Wethermill held out a newspaper. "Read it," he said.

It was a special edition of a local newspaper, Le Journal de Savoie, and it bore the date of that morning.

"They are crying it in the streets," said Wethermill. "Read!"

A short paragraph was printed in large black letters on the first page, and leaped to the eyes.

"Late last night," it ran, "an appalling murder was committed at the Villa Rose, on the road to Lac Bourget. Mme. Camille Dauvray, an elderly, rich woman who was well known at Aix, and had occupied the villa every summer for the last few years, was discovered on the floor of her salon, fully dressed and brutally strangled, while upstairs, her maid, Helene Vauquier, was found in bed, chloroformed, with her hands tied securely behind her back. At the time of going to press she had not recovered consciousness, but the doctor, Emile Peytin, is in attendance upon her, and it is hoped that she will be able shortly to throw some light on this dastardly affair. The police are properly reticent as to the details of the crime, but the following statement may be accepted without hesitation:

"The murder was discovered at twelve o'clock at night by the sergent-de-ville Perrichet, to whose intelligence more than a word of praise is due, and it is obvious from the absence of all marks upon the door and windows that the murderer was admitted from within the villa. Meanwhile Mme. Dauvray's motor-car has disappeared, and with it a young Englishwoman who came to Aix with her as her companion. The motive of the crime leaps to the eyes. Mme. Dauvray was famous in Aix for her jewels, which she wore with too little prudence. The condition of the house shows that a careful search was made for them, and they have disappeared. It is anticipated that a description of the young Englishwoman, with a reward for her apprehension, will be issued immediately. And it is not too much to hope that the citizens of Aix, and indeed of France, will be cleared of all participation in so cruel and sinister a crime."

Ricardo read through the paragraph with a growing consternation, and laid the paper upon his dressing-table.

"It is infamous," cried Wethermill passionately.

"The young Englishwoman is, I suppose, your friend Miss Celia?" said Ricardo slowly.

Wethermill started forward.

"You know her, then?" he cried in amazement.

"No; but I saw her with you in the rooms. I heard you call her by that name."

"You saw us together?" exclaimed Wethermill. "Then you can understand how infamous the suggestion is."

But Ricardo had seen the girl half an hour before he had seen her with Harry Wethermill. He could not but vividly remember the picture of her as she flung herself on to the bench in the garden in a moment of hysteria, and petulantly kicked a satin slipper backwards and forwards against the stones. She was young, she was pretty, she had a charm of freshness, but-but-strive against it as he would, this picture in the recollection began more and more to wear a sinister aspect. He remembered some words spoken by a stranger. "She is pretty, that little one. It is regrettable that she has lost."

Mr. Ricardo arranged his tie with even a greater deliberation than he usually employed.

"And Mme. Dauvray?" he asked. "She was the stout woman with whom your young friend went away?"

"Yes," said Wethermill.

Ricardo turned round from the mirror.

"What do you want me to do?"

"Hanaud is at Aix. He is the cleverest of the French detectives. You know him. He dined with you once."

It was Mr. Ricardo's practice to collect celebrities round his dinner-table, and at one such gathering Hanaud and Wethermill had been present together.

"You wish me to approach him?"

"At once."

"It is a delicate position," said Ricardo. "Here is a man in charge of a case of murder, and we are quietly to go to him —"

To his relief Wethermill interrupted him.

"No, no," he cried; "he is not in charge of the case. He is on his holiday. I read of his arrival two days ago in the newspaper. It was stated that he came for rest. What I want is that he should take charge of the case."

The superb confidence of Wethermill shook Mr. Ricardo for a moment, but his recollections were too clear.

"You are going out of your way to launch the acutest of French detectives in search of this girl. Are you wise, Wethermill?"

Wethermill sprang up from his chair in desperation.

"You, too, think her guilty! You have seen her. You think her guilty-like this detestable newspaper, like the police."

"Like the police?" asked Ricardo sharply.

"Yes," said Harry Wethermill sullenly. "As soon as I saw that rag I ran down to the villa. The police are in possession. They would not let me into the garden. But I talked with one of them. They, too, think that she let in the murderers."

Ricardo took a turn across the room. Then he came to a stop in front of Wethermill.

"Listen to me," he said solemnly. "I saw this girl half an hour before I saw you. She rushed out into the garden. She flung herself on to a bench. She could not sit still. She was hysterical. You know what that means. She had been losing. That's point number one."

Mr. Ricardo ticked it off upon his finger.

"She ran back into the rooms. You asked her to share the winnings of your bank. She consented eagerly. And you lost. That's point number two. A little later, as she was going away, you asked her whether she would be in the rooms the next night-yesterday night-the night when the murder was committed. Her face clouded over. She hesitated. She became more than grave. There was a distinct impression as though she shrank from the contemplation of what it was proposed she should do on the next night. And then she answered you, 'No, we have other plans.' That's number three." And Mr. Ricardo ticked off his third point.

"Now," he asked, "do you still ask me to launch Hanaud upon the case?"

"Yes, and at once," cried Wethermill.

Ricardo called for his hat and his stick.

"You know where Hanaud is staying?" he asked.

"Yes," replied Wethermill, and he led Ricardo to an unpretentious little hotel in the centre of the town. Ricardo sent in his name, and the two visitors were immediately shown into a small sitting-room, where M. Hanaud was enjoying his morning chocolate. He was stout and broad-shouldered, with a full and almost heavy face. In his morning suit at his breakfast-table he looked like a prosperous comedian.

He came forward with a smile of welcome, extending both his hands to Mr. Ricardo.

"Ah, my good friend," he said, "it is pleasant to see you. And Mr. Wethermill," he exclaimed, holding a hand out to the young inventor.

"You remember me, then?" said Wethermill gladly.

"It is my profession to remember people," said Hanaud, with a laugh. "You were at that amusing dinner-party of Mr. Ricardo's in Grosvenor Square."

"Monsieur," said Wethermill, "I have come to ask your help."

The note of appeal in his voice was loud. M. Hanaud drew up a chair by the window and motioned to Wethermill to take it. He pointed to another, with a bow of invitation to Mr. Ricardo.

"Let me hear," he said gravely.

"It is the murder of Mme. Dauvray," said Wethermill.

Hanaud started.

"And in what way, monsieur," he asked, "are you interested in the murder of Mme. Dauvray?"

"Her companion," said Wethermill, "the young English girl-she is a great friend of mine."

Hanaud's face grew stern. Then came a sparkle of anger in his eyes.

"And what do you wish me to do, monsieur?" he asked coldly.

"You are upon your holiday, M. Hanaud. I wish you-no, I implore you," Wethermill cried, his voice ringing with passion, "to take up this case, to discover the truth, to find out what has become of Celia."

Hanaud leaned back in his chair with his hands upon the arms. He did not take his eyes from Harry Wethermill, but the anger died out of them.

"Monsieur," he said, "I do not know what your procedure is in England. But in France a detective does not take up a case or leave it alone according to his pleasure. We are only servants. This affair is in the hands of M. Fleuriot, the Juge d'instruction of Aix."

"But if you offered him your help it would be welcomed," cried Wethermill. "And to me that would mean so much. There would be no bungling. There would be no waste of time. Of that one would be sure."

Hanaud shook his head gently. His eyes were softened now by a look of pity. Suddenly he stretched out a forefinger.

"You have, perhaps, a photograph of the young lady in that card-case in your breast-pocket."

Wethermill flushed red, and, drawing out the card-case, handed the portrait to Hanaud. Hanaud looked at it carefully for a few moments.

"It was taken lately, here?" he asked.

"Yes; for me," replied Wethermill quietly.

"And it is a good likeness?"

"Very."

"How long have you known this Mlle. Celie?" he asked.

Wethermill looked at Hanaud with a certain defiance.

"For a fortnight."

Hanaud raised his eyebrows.

"You met her here?"

"Yes."

"In the rooms, I suppose? Not at the house of one of your friends?"

"That is so," said Wethermill quietly. "A friend of mine who had met her in Paris introduced me to her at my request."

Hanaud handed back the portrait and drew forward his chair nearer to Wethermill. His face had grown friendly. He spoke with a tone of respect.

"Monsieur, I know something of you. Our friend, Mr. Ricardo, told me your history; I asked him for it when I saw you at his dinner. You are of those about whom one does ask questions, and I know that you are not a romantic boy, but who shall say that he is safe from the appeal of beauty? I have seen women, monsieur, for whose purity of soul I would myself have stood security, condemned for complicity in brutal crimes on evidence that could not be gainsaid; and I have known them turn foul-mouthed, and hideous to look upon, the moment after their just sentence has been pronounced."

"No doubt, monsieur," said Wethermill, with perfect quietude. "But Celia Harland is not one of those women."

"I do not now say that she is," said Hanaud. "But the Juge d'Instruction here has already sent to me to ask for my assistance, and I refused. I replied that I was just a good bourgeois enjoying his holiday. Still it is difficult quite to forget one's profession. It was the Commissaire of Police who came to me, and naturally I talked with him for a little while. The case is dark, monsieur, I warn you."

"How dark?" asked Harry Wethermill.

"I will tell you," said Hanaud, drawing his chair still closer to the young man. "Understand this in the first place. There was an accomplice within the villa. Some one let the murderers in. There is no sign of an entrance being forced; no lock was picked, there is no mark of a thumb on any panel, no sign of a bolt being forced. There was an accomplice within the house. We start from that."

Wethermill nodded his head sullenly. Ricardo drew his chair up towards the others. But Hanaud was not at that moment interested in Ricardo.

"Well, then, let us see who there are in Mme. Dauvray's household. The list is not a long one. It was Mme. Dauvray's habit to take her luncheon and her dinner at the restaurants, and her maid was all that she required to get ready her 'petit dejeuner' in the morning and her 'sirop' at night. Let us take the members of the household one by one. There is first the chauffeur, Henri Servettaz. He was not at the villa last night. He came back to it early this morning."

"Ah!" said Ricardo, in a significant exclamation. Wethermill did not stir. He sat still as a stone, with a face deadly white and eyes burning upon Hanaud's face.

"But wait," said Hanaud, holding up a warning hand to Ricardo. "Servettaz was in Chambery, where his parents live. He travelled to Chambery by the two o'clock train yesterday. He was with them in the afternoon. He went with them to a cafe in the evening. Moreover, early this morning the maid, Helene Vauquier, was able to speak a few words in answer to a question. She said Servettaz was in Chambery. She gave his address. A telephone message was sent to the police in that town, and Servettaz was found in bed. I do not say that it is impossible that Servettaz was concerned in the crime. That we shall see. But it is quite clear, I think, that it was not he who opened the house to the murderers, for he was at Chambery in the evening, and the murder was already discovered here by midnight. Moreover-it is a small point-he lives, not in the house, but over the garage in a corner of the garden. Then besides the chauffeur there was a charwoman, a woman of Aix, who came each morning at seven and left in the evening at seven or eight. Sometimes she would stay later if the maid was alone in the house, for the maid is nervous. But she left last night before nine-there is evidence of that-and the murder did not take place until afterwards. That is also a fact, not a conjecture. We can leave the charwoman, who for the rest has the best of characters, out of our calculations. There remain then, the maid, Helene Vauquier, and" —he shrugged his shoulders —"Mlle. Celie."

Hanaud reached out for the matches and lit a cigarette.

"Let us take first the maid, Helene Vauquier. Forty years old, a Normandy peasant woman-they are not bad people, the Normandy peasants, monsieur-avaricious, no doubt, but on the whole honest and most respectable. We know something of Helene Vauquier, monsieur. See!" and he took up a sheet of paper from the table. The paper was folded lengthwise, written upon only on the inside. "I have some details here. Our police system is, I think, a little more complete than yours in England. Helene Vauquier has served Mme. Dauvray for seven years. She has been the confidential friend rather than the maid. And mark this, M. Wethermill! During those seven years how many opportunities has she had of conniving at last night's crime? She was found chloroformed and bound. There is no doubt that she was chloroformed. Upon that point Dr. Peytin is quite, quite certain. He saw her before she recovered consciousness. She was violently sick on awakening. She sank again into unconsciousness. She is only now in a natural sleep. Besides those people, there is Mlle. Celie. Of her, monsieur, nothing is known. You yourself know nothing of her. She comes suddenly to Aix as the companion of Mme. Dauvray —a young and pretty English girl. How did she become the companion of Mme. Dauvray?"

Wethermill stirred uneasily in his seat. His face flushed. To Mr. Ricardo that had been from the beginning the most interesting problem of the case. Was he to have the answer now?

"I do not know," answered Wethermill, with some hesitation, and then it seemed that he was at once ashamed of his hesitation. His accent gathered strength, and in a low but ringing voice, he added: "But I say this. You have told me, M. Hanaud, of women who looked innocent and were guilty. But you know also of women and girls who can live untainted and unspoilt amidst surroundings which are suspicious."

Hanaud listened, but he neither agreed nor denied. He took up a second slip of paper.

"I shall tell you something now of Mme. Dauvray," he said. "We will not take up her early history. It might not be edifying and, poor woman, she is dead. Let us not go back beyond her marriage seventeen years ago to a wealthy manufacturer of Nancy, whom she had met in Paris.

Seven years ago M. Dauvray died, leaving his widow a very rich woman. She had a passion for jewellery, which she was now able to gratify. She collected jewels. A famous necklace, a well-known stone-she was not, as you say, happy till she got it. She had a fortune in precious stones-oh, but a large fortune! By the ostentation of her jewels she paraded her wealth here, at Monte Carlo, in Paris. Besides that, she was kind-hearted and most impressionable. Finally, she was, like so many of her class, superstitious to the degree of folly."

Suddenly Mr. Ricardo started in his chair. Superstitious! The word was a sudden light upon his darkness. Now he knew what had perplexed him during the last two days. Clearly-too clearly-he remembered where he had seen Celia Harland, and when. A picture rose before his eyes, and it seemed to strengthen like a film in a developing-dish as Hanaud continued:

"Very well! take Mme. Dauvray as we find her-rich, ostentatious, easily taken by a new face, generous, and foolishly superstitious-and you have in her a living provocation to every rogue. By a hundred instances she proclaimed herself a dupe. She threw down a challenge to every criminal to come and rob her. For seven years Helene Vauquier stands at her elbow and protects her from serious trouble. Suddenly there is added to her-your young friend, and she is robbed and murdered. And, follow this, M. Wethermill, our thieves are, I think, more brutal to their victims than is the case with you."

Wethermill shut his eyes in a spasm of pain and the pallor of his face increased.

"Suppose that Celia were one of the victims?" he cried in a stifled voice.

Hanaud glanced at him with a look of commiseration.

"That perhaps we shall see," he said. "But what I meant was this. A stranger like Mlle. Celie might be the accomplice in such a crime as the crime of the Villa Rose, meaning only robbery. A stranger might only have discovered too late that murder would be added to the theft."

Meanwhile, in strong, clear colours, Ricardo's picture stood out before his eyes. He was startled by hearing Wethermill say, in a firm voice:

"My friend Ricardo has something to add to what you have said."

"I!" exclaimed Ricardo. How in the world could Wethermill know of that clear picture in his mind?

"Yes. You saw Celia Harland on the evening before the murder."

Ricardo stared at his friend. It seemed to him that Harry Wethermill had gone out of his mind. Here he was corroborating the suspicions of the police by facts-damning and incontrovertible facts.

"On the night before the murder," continued Wethermill quietly, "Celia Harland lost money at the baccarat-table. Ricardo saw her in the garden behind the rooms, and she was hysterical. Later on that same night he saw her again with me, and he heard what she said. I asked her to come to the rooms on the next evening-yesterday, the night of the crime-and her face changed, and she said, 'No, we have other plans for to-morrow. But the night after I shall want you.'"

Hanaud sprang up from his chair.

"And YOU tell me these two things!" he cried.

"Yes," said Wethermill. "You were kind enough to say to me I was not a romantic boy. I am not. I can face facts."

Hanaud stared at his companion for a few moments. Then, with a remarkable air of consideration, he bowed.

"You have won, monsieur," he said. "I will take up this case. But," and his face grew stern and he brought his fist down upon the table with a bang, "I shall follow it to the end now, be the consequences bitter as death to you."

"That is what I wish, monsieur," said Wethermill.

Hanaud locked up the slips of paper in his lettercase. Then he went out of the room and returned in a few minutes.

"We will begin at the beginning," he said briskly. "I have telephoned to the Depot. Perrichet, the sergent-de-ville who discovered the crime, will be here at once. We will walk down to the villa with him, and on the way he shall tell us exactly what he discovered and how he discovered it. At the villa we shall find Monsieur Fleuriot, the Juge d'instruction, who has already begun his examination, and the Commissaire of Police. In company with them we will inspect the villa. Except for the removal of Mme. Dauvray's body from the salon to her bedroom and the opening of the windows, the house remains exactly as it was."

"We may come with you?" cried Harry Wethermill eagerly.

"Yes, on one condition-that you ask no questions, and answer none unless I put them to you. Listen, watch, examine-but no interruptions!"

Hanaud's manner had altogether changed. It was now authoritative and alert. He turned to Ricardo.

"You will swear to what you saw in the garden and to the words you heard?" he asked. "They are important."

"Yes," said Ricardo.

But he kept silence about that clear picture in his mind which to him seemed no less important, no less suggestive.

The Assembly Hall at Leamington, a crowded audience chiefly of ladies, a platform at one end on which a black cabinet stood. A man, erect and with something of the soldier in his bearing, led forward a girl, pretty and fair-haired, who wore a black velvet dress with a long, sweeping train. She moved like one in a dream. Some half-dozen people from the audience climbed on to the platform, tied the girl's hands with tape behind her back, and sealed the tape. She was led to the cabinet, and in full view of the audience fastened to a bench. Then the door of the cabinet was closed, the people upon the platform descended into the body of the hall, and the lights were turned very low. The audience sat in suspense, and then abruptly in the silence and the darkness there came the rattle of a tambourine from the empty platform. Rappings and knockings seemed to flicker round the panels of the hall, and in the place where the door of the cabinet should be there appeared a splash of misty whiteness. The whiteness shaped itself dimly into the figure of a woman, a face dark and Eastern became visible, and a deep voice spoke in a chant of the Nile and Antony. Then the vision faded, the tambourines and cymbals rattled again. The lights were turned up, the door of the cabinet thrown open, and the girl in the black velvet dress was seen fastened upon the bench within.

It was a spiritualistic performance at which Julius Ricardo had been present two years ago. The young, fair-haired girl in black velvet, the medium, was Celia Harland.

That was the picture which was in Ricardo's mind, and Hanaud's description of Mme. Dauvray made a terrible commentary upon it. "Easily taken by a new face, generous, and foolishly superstitious, a living provocation to every rogue." Those were the words, and here was a beautiful girl of twenty versed in those very tricks of imposture which would make Mme. Dauvray her natural prey!

Ricardo looked at Wethermill, doubtful whether he should tell what he knew of Celia Harland or not. But before he had decided a knock came upon the door.

"Here is Perrichet," said Hanaud, taking up his hat. "We will go down to the Villa Rose."


## CHAPTER III


## PERRICHET'S STORY

Perrichet was a young, thick-set man, with a red, fair face, and a moustache and hair so pale in colour that they were almost silver. He came into the room with an air of importance.

"Aha!" said Hanaud, with a malicious smile. "You went to bed late last night, my friend. Yet you were up early enough to read the newspaper. Well, I am to have the honour of being associated with you in this case."

Perrichet twirled his cap awkwardly and blushed.

"Monsieur is pleased to laugh at me," he said. "But it was not I who called myself intelligent. Though indeed I would like to be so, for the good God knows I do not look it."

Hanaud clapped him on the shoulder.

"Then congratulate yourself! It is a great advantage to be intelligent and not to look it. We shall get on famously. Come!"

The four men descended the stairs, and as they walked towards the villa Perrichet related, concisely and clearly, his experience of the night.

"I passed the gate of the villa about half-past nine," he said. "The gate was closed. Above the wall and bushes of the garden I saw a bright light in the room upon the first floor which faces the road at the south-western corner of the villa. The lower windows I could not see. More than an hour afterwards I came back, and as I passed the villa again I noticed that there was now no light in the room upon the first floor, but that the gate was open. I thereupon went into the garden, and, pulling the gate, let it swing to and latch. But it occurred to me as I did so that there might be visitors at the villa who had not yet left, and for whom the gate had been set open. I accordingly followed the drive which winds round to the front door. The front door is not on the side of the villa which faces the road, but at the back. When I came to the open space where the carriages turn, I saw that the house was in complete darkness. There were wooden latticed doors to the long windows on the ground floor, and these were closed. I tried one to make certain, and found the fastenings secure. The other windows upon that floor were shuttered. No light gleamed anywhere. I then left the garden, closing the gate behind me. I heard a clock strike the hour a few minutes afterwards, so that I can be sure of the time. It was now eleven o'clock. I came round a third time an hour after, and to my astonishment I found the gate once more open. I had left it closed and the house shut up and dark. Now it stood open! I looked up to the windows and I saw that in a room on the second floor, close beneath the roof, a light was burning brightly. That room had been dark an hour before. I stood and watched the light for a few minutes, thinking that I should see it suddenly go out. But it did not: it burned quite steadily. This light and the gate opened and reopened aroused my suspicions. I went again into the garden, but this time with greater caution. It was a clear night, and, although there was no moon, I could see without the aid of my lantern. I stole quietly along the drive. When I came round to the front door, I noticed immediately that the shutters of one of the ground-floor windows were swung back, and that the inside glass window which descended to the ground stood open. The sight gave me a shock. Within the house those shutters had been opened. I felt the blood turn to ice in my veins and a chill crept along my spine. I thought of that solitary light burning steadily under the roof. I was convinced that something terrible had happened."

"Yes, yes. Quite so," said Hanaud. "Go on, my friend."

"The interior of the room gaped black," Perrichet resumed. "I crept up to the window at the side of the wall and flashed my lantern into the room. The window, however, was in a recess which opened into the room through an arch, and at each side of the arch curtains were draped. The curtains were not closed, but between them I could see nothing but a strip of the room. I stepped carefully in, taking heed not to walk on the patch of grass before the window. The light of my lantern showed me a chair overturned upon the floor, and to my right, below the middle one of the three windows in the right-hand side wall, a woman lying huddled upon the floor. It was Mme. Dauvray. She was dressed. There was a little mud upon her shoes, as though she had walked after the rain had ceased. Monsieur will remember that two heavy showers fell last evening between six and eight."

"Yes," said Hanaud, nodding his approval.

"She was quite dead. Her face was terribly swollen and black, and a piece of thin strong cord was knotted so tightly about her neck and had sunk so deeply into her flesh that at first I did not see it. For Mme. Dauvray was stout."

"Then what did you do?" asked Hanaud.

"I went to the telephone which was in the hall and rang up the police. Then I crept upstairs very cautiously, trying the doors. I came upon no one until I reached the room under the roof where the light was burning; there I found Helene Vauquier, the maid, snoring in bed in a terrible fashion."

The four men turned a bend in the road. A few paces away a knot of people stood before a gate which a sergent-de-ville guarded.

"But here we are at the villa," said Hanaud.

They all looked up and, from a window at the corner upon the first floor a man looked out and drew in his head.

"That is M. Besnard, the Commissaire of our police in Aix," said Perrichet.

"And the window from which he looked," said Hanaud, "must be the window of that room in which you saw the bright light at half-past nine on your first round?"

"Yes, m'sieur," said Perrichet; "that is the window."

They stopped at the gate. Perrichet spoke to the sergent-de-ville, who at once held the gate open. The party passed into the garden of the villa.


## CHAPTER IV


## AT THE VILLA

The drive curved between trees and high bushes towards the back of the house, and as the party advanced along it a small, trim, soldier-like man, with a pointed beard, came to meet them. It was the man who had looked out from the window, Louis Besnard, the Commissaire of Police.

"You are coming, then, to help us, M. Hanaud!" he cried, extending his hands. "You will find no jealousy here; no spirit amongst us of anything but good will; no desire except one to carry out your suggestions. All we wish is that the murderers should be discovered. Mon Dieu, what a crime! And so young a girl to be involved in it! But what will you?"

"So you have already made your mind up on that point!" said Hanaud sharply.

The Commissaire shrugged his shoulders.

"Examine the villa and then judge for yourself whether any other explanation is conceivable," he said; and turning, he waved his hand towards the house. Then he cried, "Ah!" and drew himself into an attitude of attention. A tall, thin man of about forty-five years, dressed in a frock coat and a high silk hat, had just come round an angle of the drive and was moving slowly towards them. He wore the soft, curling brown beard of one who has never used a razor on his chin, and had a narrow face with eyes of a very light grey, and a round bulging forehead.

"This is the Juge d'Instruction?" asked Hanaud.

"Yes; M. Fleuriot," replied Louis Besnard in a whisper.

M. Fleuriot was occupied with his own thoughts, and it was not until Besnard stepped forward noisily on the gravel that he became aware of the group in the garden.

"This is M. Hanaud, of the Surete in Paris," said Louis Besnard.

M. Fleuriot bowed with cordiality.

"You are very welcome, M. Hanaud. You will find that nothing at the villa has been disturbed. The moment the message arrived over the telephone that you were willing to assist us I gave instructions that all should be left as we found it. I trust that you, with your experience, will see a way where our eyes find none."

Hanaud bowed in reply.

"I shall do my best, M. Fleuriot. I can say no more," he said.

"But who are these gentlemen?" asked Fleuriot, waking, it seemed, now for the first time to the presence of Harry Wethermill and Mr. Ricardo.

"They are both friends of mine," replied Hanaud. "If you do not object I think their assistance may be useful. Mr. Wethermill, for instance, was acquainted with Celia Harland."

"Ah!" cried the judge; and his face took on suddenly a keen and eager look. "You can tell me about her perhaps?"

"All that I know I will tell readily," said Harry Wethermill.

Into the light eyes of M. Fleuriot there came a cold, bright gleam. He took a step forward. His face seemed to narrow to a greater sharpness. In a moment, to Mr. Ricardo's thought, he ceased to be the judge; he dropped from his high office; he dwindled into a fanatic.

"She is a Jewess, this Celia Harland?" he cried.

"No, M. Fleuriot, she is not," replied Wethermill. "I do not speak in disparagement of that race, for I count many friends amongst its members. But Celia Harland is not one of them."

"Ah!" said Fleuriot; and there was something of disappointment, something, too, of incredulity, in his voice. "Well, you will come and report to me when you have made your investigation." And he passed on without another question or remark.

The group of men watched him go, and it was not until he was out of earshot that Besnard turned with a deprecating gesture to Hanaud.

"Yes, yes, he is a good judge, M. Hanaud-quick, discriminating, sympathetic; but he has that bee in his bonnet, like so many others. Everywhere he must see l'affaire Dreyfus. He cannot get it out of his head. No matter how insignificant a woman is murdered, she must have letters in her possession which would convict Dreyfus. But you know! There are thousands like that-good, kindly, just people in the ordinary ways of life, but behind every crime they see the Jew."

Hanaud nodded his head.

"I know; and in a Juge d'Instruction it is very embarrassing. Let us walk on."

Half-way between the gate and the villa a second carriage-road struck off to the left, and at the entrance to it stood a young, stout man in black leggings.

"The chauffeur?" asked Hanaud. "I will speak to him."

The Commissaire called the chauffeur forward.

"Servettaz," he said, "you will answer any questions which monsieur may put to you."

"Certainly, M. le Commissaire," said the chauffeur. His manner was serious, but he answered readily. There was no sign of fear upon his face.

"How long have you been with Mme. Dauvray?" Hanaud asked.

"Four months, monsieur. I drove her to Aix from Paris."

"And since your parents live at Chambery you wished to seize the opportunity of spending a day with them while you were so near?"

"Yes, monsieur."

"When did you ask for permission?"

"On Saturday, monsieur."

"Did you ask particularly that you should have yesterday, the Tuesday?"

"No, monsieur; I asked only for a day whenever it should be convenient to madame."

"Quite so," said Hanaud. "Now, when did Mme. Dauvray tell you that you might have Tuesday?"

Servettaz hesitated. His face became troubled. When he spoke, he spoke reluctantly.

"It was not Mme. Dauvray, monsieur, who told me that I might go on Tuesday," he said.

"Not Mme. Dauvray! Who was it, then?" Hanaud asked sharply.

Servettaz glanced from one to another of the grave faces which confronted him.

"It was Mlle. Celie," he said, "who told me."

"Oh!" said Hanaud, slowly. "It was Mlle. Celie. When did she tell you?"

"On Monday morning, monsieur. I was cleaning the car. She came to the garage with some flowers in her hand which she had been cutting in the garden, and she said: 'I was right, Alphonse. Madame has a kind heart. You can go to-morrow by the train which leaves Aix at 1.52 and arrives at Chambery at nine minutes after two.'"

Hanaud started.

" 'I was right, Alphonse.' Were those her words? And 'Madame has a kind heart.' Come, come, what is all this?" He lifted a warning finger and said gravely, "Be very careful, Servettaz."

"Those were her words, monsieur."

" 'I was right, Alphonse. Madame has a kind heart'?"

"Yes, monsieur."

"Then Mlle. Celie had spoken to you before about this visit of yours to Chambery," said Hanaud, with his eyes fixed steadily upon the chauffeur's face. The distress upon Servettaz's face increased. Suddenly Hanaud's voice rang sharply. "You hesitate. Begin at the beginning. Speak the truth, Servettaz!"

"Monsieur, I am speaking the truth," said the chauffeur. "It is true I hesitate … I have heard this morning what people are saying … I do not know what to think. Mlle. Celie was always kind and thoughtful for me … But it is true" —and with a kind of desperation he went on —"yes, it is true that it was Mlle. Celie who first suggested to me that I should ask for a day to go to Chambery."

"When did she suggest it?"

"On the Saturday."

To Mr. Ricardo the words were startling. He glanced with pity towards Wethermill. Wethermill, however, had made up his mind for good and all. He stood with a dogged look upon his face, his chin thrust forward, his eyes upon the chauffeur. Besnard, the Commissaire, had made up his mind, too. He merely shrugged his shoulders. Hanaud stepped forward and laid his hand gently on the chauffeur's arm.

"Come, my friend," he said, "let us hear exactly how this happened!"

"Mlle. Celie," said Servettaz, with genuine compunction in his voice, "came to the garage on Saturday morning and ordered the car for the afternoon. She stayed and talked to me for a little while, as she often did. She said that she had been told that my parents lived at Chambery, and since I was so near I ought to ask for a holiday. For it would not be kind if I did not go and see them."

"That was all?"

"Yes, monsieur."

"Very well." And the detective resumed at once his brisk voice and alert manner. He seemed to dismiss Servettaz's admission from his mind. Ricardo had the impression of a man tying up an important document which for the moment he has done with, and putting it away ticketed in some pigeon-hole in his desk. "Let us see the garage!"

They followed the road between the bushes until a turn showed them the garage with its doors open.

"The doors were found unlocked?"

"Just as you see them."

Hanaud nodded. He spoke again to Servettaz. "What did you do with the key on Tuesday?"

"I gave it to Helene Vauquier, monsieur, after I had locked up the garage. And she hung it on a nail in the kitchen."

"I see," said Hanaud. "So any one could easily, have found it last night?"

"Yes, monsieur-if one knew where to look for it."

At the back of the garage a row of petrol-tins stood against the brick wall.

"Was any petrol taken?" asked Hanaud.

"Yes, monsieur; there was very little petrol in the car when I went away. More was taken, but it was taken from the middle tins-these." And he touched the tins.

"I see," said Hanaud, and he raised his eyebrows thoughtfully. The Commissaire moved with impatience.

"From the middle or from the end-what does it matter?" he exclaimed. "The petrol was taken."

Hanaud, however, did not dismiss the point so lightly.

"But it is very possible that it does matter," he said gently. "For example, if Servettaz had had no reason to examine his tins it might have been some while before he found out that the petrol had been taken."

"Indeed, yes," said Servettaz. "I might even have forgotten that I had not used it myself."

"Quite so," said Hanaud, and he turned to Besnard. "I think that may be important. I do not know," he said.

"But since the car is gone," cried Besnard, "how could the chauffeur not look immediately at his tins?"

The question had occurred to Ricardo, and he wondered in what way Hanaud meant to answer it. Hanaud, however, did not mean to answer it. He took little notice of it at all. He put it aside with a superb indifference to the opinion which his companions might form of him.

"Ah, yes," he said, carelessly. "Since the car is gone, as you say, that is so." And he turned again to Servettaz.

"It was a powerful car?" he asked.

"Sixty horse-power," said Servettaz.

Hanaud turned to the Commissaire.

"You have the number and description, I suppose? It will be as well to advertise for it. It may have been seen; it must be somewhere."

The Commissaire replied that the description had already been printed, and Hanaud, with a nod of approval, examined the ground. In front of the garage there was a small stone courtyard, but on its surface there was no trace of a footstep.

"Yet the gravel was wet," he said, shaking his head. "The man who fetched that car fetched it carefully."

He turned and walked back with his eyes upon the ground. Then he ran to the grass border between the gravel and the bushes.

"Look!" he said to Wethermill; "a foot has pressed the blades of grass down here, but very lightly-yes, and there again. Some one ran along the border here on his toes. Yes, he was very careful."

They turned again into the main drive, and, following it for a few yards, came suddenly upon a space in front of the villa. It was a small toy pleasure-house, looking on to a green lawn gay with flower-beds. It was built of yellow stone, and was almost square in shape. A couple of ornate pillars flanked the door, and a gable roof, topped by a gilt vane, surmounted it. To Ricardo it seemed impossible that so sordid and sinister a tragedy had taken place within its walls during the last twelve hours. It glistened so gaudily in the blaze of sunlight. Here and there the green outer shutters were closed; here and there the windows stood open to let in the air and light. Upon each side of the door there was a window lighting the hall, which was large; beyond those windows again, on each side, there were glass doors opening to the ground and protected by the ordinary green latticed shutters of wood, which now stood hooked back against the wall. These glass doors opened into rooms oblong in shape, which ran through towards the back of the house, and were lighted in addition by side windows. The room upon the extreme left, as the party faced the villa, was the dining-room, with the kitchen at the back; the room on the right was the salon in which the murder had been committed. In front of the glass door to this room a strip of what had once been grass stretched to the gravel drive. But the grass had been worn away by constant use, and the black mould showed through. This strip was about three yards wide, and as they approached they saw, even at a distance, that since the rain of last night it had been trampled down.

"We will go round the house first," said Hanaud, and he turned along the side of the villa and walked in the direction of the road. There were four windows just above his head, of which three lighted the salon, and the fourth a small writing-room behind it. Under these windows there was no disturbance of the ground, and a careful investigation showed conclusively that the only entrance used had been the glass doors of the salon facing the drive. To that spot, then, they returned. There were three sets of footmarks upon the soil. One set ran in a distinct curve from the drive to the side of the door, and did not cross the others.

"Those," said Hanaud, "are the footsteps of my intelligent friend, Perrichet, who was careful not to disturb the ground."

Perrichet beamed all over his rosy face, and Besnard nodded at him with condescending approval.

"But I wish, M. le Commissaire"—and Hanaud pointed to a blur of marks—"that your other officers had been as intelligent. Look! These run from the glass door to the drive, and, for all the use they are to us, a harrow might have been dragged across them."

Besnard drew himself up.

"Not one of my officers has entered the room by way of this door. The strictest orders were given and obeyed. The ground, as you see it, is the ground as it was at twelve o'clock last night."

Hanaud's face grew thoughtful.

"Is that so?" he said, and he stooped to examine the second set of marks. They were at the righthand side of the door. "A woman and a man," he said. "But they are mere hints rather than prints. One might almost think—" He rose up without finishing his sentence, and he turned to the third set and a look of satisfaction gleamed upon his face. "Ah! here is something more interesting," he said.

There were just three impressions; and, whereas the blurred marks were at the side, these three pointed straight from the middle of the glass doors to the drive. They were quite clearly defined, and all three were the impressions made by a woman's small, arched, high-heeled shoe. The position of the marks was at first sight a little peculiar. There was one a good yard from the window, the impression of the right foot, and the pressure of the sole of the shoe was more marked than that of the heel. The second, the impression of the left foot, was not quite so far from the first as the first was from the window, and here again the heel was the more lightly defined. But there was this difference-the mark of the toe, which was pointed in the first instance, was, in this, broader and a trifle blurred. Close beside it the right foot was again visible; only now the narrow heel was more clearly defined than the ball of the foot. It had, indeed, sunk half an inch into the soft ground. There were no further imprints. Indeed, these two were not merely close together, they were close to the gravel of the drive and on the very border of the grass.

Hanaud looked at the marks thoughtfully. Then he turned to the Commissaire.

"Are there any shoes in the house which fit those marks?"

"Yes. We have tried the shoes of all the women-Celie Harland, the maid, and even Mme. Dauvray. The only ones which fit at all are those taken from Celie Harland's bedroom."

He called to an officer standing in the drive, and a pair of grey suede shoes were brought to him from the hall.

"See, M. Hanaud, it is a pretty little foot which made those clear impressions," he said, with a smile; "a foot arched and slender. Mme. Dauvray's foot is short and square, the maid's broad and flat. Neither Mme. Dauvray nor Helene Vauquier could have worn these shoes. They were lying, one here, one there, upon the floor of Celie Harland's room, as though she had kicked them off in a hurry. They are almost new, you see. They have been worn once, perhaps, no more, and they fit with absolute precision into those footmarks, except just at the toe of that second one."

Hanaud took the shoes and, kneeling down, placed them one after the other over the impressions. To Ricardo it was extraordinary how exactly they covered up the marks and filled the indentations.

"I should say," said the Commissaire, "that Celie Harland went away wearing a new pair of shoes made on the very same last as those."

As those she had left carelessly lying on the floor of her room for the first person to notice, thought Ricardo! It seemed as if the girl had gone out of her way to make the weight of evidence against her as heavy as possible. Yet, after all, it was just through inattention to the small details, so insignificant at the red moment of crime, so terribly instructive the next day, that guilt was generally brought home.

Hanaud rose to his feet and handed the shoes back to the officer.

"Yes," he said, "so it seems. The shoemaker can help us here. I see the shoes were made in Aix."

Besnard looked at the name stamped in gold letters upon the lining of the shoes.

"I will have inquiries made," he said.

Hanaud nodded, took a measure from his pocket and measured the ground between the window and the first footstep, and between the first footstep and the other two.

"How tall is Mlle. Celie?" he asked, and he addressed the question to Wethermill. It struck Ricardo as one of the strangest details in all this strange affair that the detective should ask with confidence for information which might help to bring Celia Harland to the guillotine from the man who had staked his happiness upon her innocence.

"About five feet seven," he answered.

Hanaud replaced his measure in his pocket. He turned with a grave face to Wethermill.

"I warned you fairly, didn't I?" he said.

Wethermill's white face twitched.

"Yes," he said. "I am not afraid." But there was more of anxiety in his voice than there had been before.

Hanaud pointed solemnly to the ground.

"Read the story those footprints write in the mould there. A young and active girl of about Mlle. Celie's height, and wearing a new pair of Mlle. Celie's shoes, springs from that room where the murder was committed, where the body of the murdered woman lies. She is running. She is wearing a long gown. At the second step the hem of the gown catches beneath the point of her shoe. She stumbles. To save herself from falling she brings up the other foot sharply and stamps the heel down into the ground. She recovers her balance. She steps on to the drive. It is true the gravel here is hard and takes no mark, but you will see that some of the mould which has clung to her shoes has dropped off. She mounts into the motor-car with the man and the other woman and drives off-some time between eleven and twelve."

"Between eleven and twelve? Is that sure?" asked Besnard.

"Certainly," replied Hanaud. "The gate is open at eleven, and Perrichet closes it. It is open again at twelve. Therefore the murderers had not gone before eleven. No; the gate was open for them to go, but they had not gone. Else why should the gate again be open at midnight?"

Besnard nodded in assent, and suddenly Perrichet started forward, with his eyes full of horror.

"Then, when I first closed the gate," he cried, "and came into the garden and up to the house they were here-in that room? Oh, my God!" He stared at the window, with his mouth open.

"I am afraid, my friend, that is so," said Hanaud gravely.

"But I knocked upon the wooden door, I tried the bolts; and they were within-in the darkness within, holding their breath not three yards from me."

He stood transfixed.

"That we shall see," said Hanaud.

He stepped in Perrichet's footsteps to the sill of the room. He examined the green wooden doors which opened outwards, and the glass doors which opened inwards, taking a magnifying-glass from his pocket. He called Besnard to his side.

"See!" he said, pointing to the woodwork.

"Finger-marks!" asked Besnard eagerly.

"Yes; of hands in gloves," returned Hanaud. "We shall learn nothing from these marks except that the assassins knew their trade."

Then he stooped down to the sill, where some traces of steps were visible. He rose with a gesture of resignation.

"Rubber shoes," he said, and so stepped into the room, followed by Wethermill and the others. They found themselves in a small recess which was panelled with wood painted white, and here and there delicately carved into festoons of flowers. The recess ended in an arch, supported by two slender pillars, and on the inner side of the arch thick curtains of pink silk were hung. These were drawn back carelessly, and through the opening between them the party looked down the length of the room beyond. They passed within.


## CHAPTER V


## IN THE SALON

Julius Ricardo pushed aside the curtains with a thrill of excitement. He found himself standing within a small oblong room which was prettily, even daintily, furnished. On his left, close by the recess, was a small fireplace with the ashes of a burnt-out fire in the grate. Beyond the grate a long settee covered in pink damask, with a crumpled cushion at each end, stood a foot or two away from the wall, and beyond the settee the door of the room opened into the hall. At the end a long mirror was let into the panelling, and a writing-table stood by the mirror. On the right were the three windows, and between the two nearest to Mr. Ricardo was the switch of the electric light. A chandelier hung from the ceiling, an electric lamp stood upon the writing-table, a couple of electric candles on the mantel-shelf. A round satinwood table stood under the windows, with three chairs about it, of which one was overturned, one was placed with its back to the electric switch, and the third on the opposite side facing it.

Ricardo could hardly believe that he stood actually upon the spot where, within twelve hours, a cruel and sinister tragedy had taken place. There was so little disorder. The three windows on his right showed him the blue sunlit sky and a glimpse of flowers and trees; behind him the glass doors stood open to the lawn, where birds piped cheerfully and the trees murmured of summer. But he saw Hanaud stepping quickly from place to place, with an extraordinary lightness of step for so big a man, obviously engrossed, obviously reading here and there some detail, some custom of the inhabitants of that room.

Ricardo leaned with careful artistry against the wall.

"Now, what has this room to say to me?" he asked importantly. Nobody paid the slightest attention to his question, and it was just as well. For the room had very little information to give him. He ran his eye over the white Louis Seize furniture, the white panels of the wall, the polished floor, the pink curtains. Even the delicate tracery of the ceiling did not escape his scrutiny. Yet he saw nothing likely to help him but an overturned chair and a couple of crushed cushions on a settee. It was very annoying, all the more annoying because M. Hanaud was so uncommonly busy. Hanaud looked carefully at the long settee and the crumpled cushions, and he took out his measure and measured the distance between the cushion at one end and the cushion at the other. He examined the table, he measured the distance between the chairs. He came to the fireplace and raked in the ashes of the burnt-out fire. But Ricardo noticed a singular thing. In the midst of his search Hanaud's eyes were always straying back to the settee, and always with a look of extreme perplexity, as if he read there something, definitely something, but something which he could not explain. Finally he went back to it; he drew it farther away from the wall, and suddenly with a little cry he stooped and went down on his knees. When he rose he was holding some torn fragments of paper in his hand. He went over to the writing-table and opened the blotting-book. Where it fell open there were some sheets of note-paper, and one particular sheet of which half had been torn off. He compared the pieces which he held with that torn sheet, and seemed satisfied.

There was a rack for note-paper upon the table, and from it he took a stiff card.

"Get me some gum or paste, and quickly," he said. His voice had become brusque, the politeness had gone from his address. He carried the card and the fragments of paper to the round table. There he sat down and, with infinite patience, gummed the fragments on to the card, fitting them together like the pieces of a Chinese puzzle.

The others over his shoulders could see spaced words, written in pencil, taking shape as a sentence upon the card. Hanaud turned abruptly in his seat toward Wethermill.

"You have, no doubt, a letter written by Mlle. Celie?"

Wethermill took his letter-case from his pocket and a letter out of the case. He hesitated for a moment as he glanced over what was written. The four sheets were covered. He folded back the letter, so that only the two inner sheets were visible, and handed it to Hanaud. Hanaud compared it with the handwriting upon the card.

"Look!" he said at length, and the three men gathered behind him. On the card the gummed fragments of paper revealed a sentence:

"Je ne sais pas."

"'I do not know,'" said Ricardo; "now this is very important."

Beside the card Celia's letter to Wethermill was laid.

"What do you think?" asked Hanaud.

Besnard, the Commissaire of Police, bent over Hanaud's shoulder.

"There are strong resemblances," he said guardedly.

Ricardo was on the look-out for deep mysteries. Resemblances were not enough for him; they were inadequate to the artistic needs of the situation.

"Both were written by the same hand," he said definitely; "only in the sentence written upon the card the handwriting is carefully disguised."

"Ah!" said the Commissaire, bending forward again. "Here is an idea! Yes, yes, there are strong differences."

Ricardo looked triumphant.

"Yes, there are differences," said Hanaud. "Look how long the up stroke of the 'p' is, how it wavers! See how suddenly this 's' straggles off, as though some emotion made the hand shake. Yet this," and touching Wethermill's letter he smiled ruefully, "this is where the emotion should have affected the pen." He looked up at Wethermill's face and then said quietly:

"You have given us no opinion, monsieur. Yet your opinion should be the most valuable of all. Were these two papers written by the same hand?"

"I do not know," answered Wethermill.

"And I, too," cried Hanaud, in a sudden exasperation, "je ne sais pas. I do not know. It may be her hand carelessly counterfeited. It may be her hand disguised. It may be simply that she wrote in a hurry with her gloves on."

"It may have been written some time ago," said Mr. Ricardo, encouraged by his success to another suggestion.

"No; that is the one thing it could not have been," said Hanaud. "Look round the room. Was there ever a room better tended? Find me a little pile of dust in any one corner if you can! It is all as clean as a plate. Every morning, except this one morning, this room has been swept and polished. The paper was written and torn up yesterday."

He enclosed the card in an envelope as he spoke, and placed it in his pocket. Then he rose and crossed again to the settee. He stood at the side of it, with his hands clutching the lapels of his coat and his face gravely troubled. After a few moments of silence for himself, of suspense for all the others who watched him, he stooped suddenly. Slowly, and with extraordinary care, he pushed his hands under the head-cushion and lifted it up gently, so that the indentations of its surface might not be disarranged. He carried it over to the light of the open window. The cushion was covered with silk, and as he held it to the sunlight all could see a small brown stain.

Hanaud took his magnifying-glass from his pocket and bent his head over the cushion. But at that moment, careful though he had been, the down swelled up within the cushion, the folds and indentations disappeared, the silk covering was stretched smooth.

"Oh!" cried Besnard tragically. "What have you done?"

Hanaud's face flushed. He had been guilty of a clumsiness-even he.

Mr. Ricardo took up the tale.

"Yes," he exclaimed, "what have you done?"

Hanaud looked at Ricardo in amazement at his audacity.

"Well, what have I done?" he asked. "Come! tell me!"

"You have destroyed a clue," replied Ricardo impressively.

The deepest dejection at once overspread Hanaud's burly face.

"Don't say that, M. Ricardo, I beseech you!" he implored. "A clue! and I have destroyed it! But what kind of a clue? And how have I destroyed it? And to what mystery would it be a clue if I hadn't destroyed it? And what will become of me when I go back to Paris, and say in the Rue de Jerusalem, 'Let me sweep the cellars, my good friends, for M. Ricardo knows that I destroyed a clue. Faithfully he promised me that he would not open his mouth, but I destroyed a clue, and his perspicacity forced him into speech.'"

It was the turn of M. Ricardo to grow red.

Hanaud turned with a smile to Besnard.

"It does not really matter whether the creases in this cushion remain," he said, "we have all seen them." And he replaced the glass in his pocket.

He carried that cushion back and replaced it. Then he took the other, which lay at the foot of the settee, and carried it in its turn to the window. This was indented too, and ridged up, and just at the marks the nap of the silk was worn, and there was a slit where it had been cut. The perplexity upon Hanaud's face greatly increased. He stood with the cushion in his hands, no longer looking at it, but looking out through the doors at the footsteps so clearly defined-the foot-steps of a girl who had run from this room and sprung into a motor-car and driven away. He shook his head, and, carrying back the cushion, laid it carefully down. Then he stood erect, gazed about the room as though even yet he might force its secrets out from its silence, and cried, with a sudden violence:

"There is something here, gentlemen, which I do not understand."

Mr. Ricardo heard some one beside him draw a deep breath, and turned. Wethermill stood at his elbow. A faint colour had come back to his cheeks, his eyes were fixed intently upon Hanaud's face.

"What do you think?" he asked; and Hanaud replied brusquely:

"It's not my business to hold opinions, monsieur; my business is to make sure."

There was one point, and only one, of which he had made every one in that room sure. He had started confident. Here was a sordid crime, easily understood. But in that room he had read something which had troubled him, which had raised the sordid crime on to some higher and perplexing level.

"Then M. Fleuriot after all might be right?" asked the Commissaire timidly.

Hanaud stared at him for a second, then smiled.

"L'affaire Dreyfus?" he cried. "Oh la, la, la! No, but there is something else."

What was that something? Ricardo asked himself. He looked once more about the room. He did not find his answer, but he caught sight of an ornament upon the wall which drove the question from his mind. The ornament, if so it could be called, was a painted tambourine with a bunch of bright ribbons tied to the rim; and it was hung upon the wall between the settee and the fireplace at about the height of a man's head. Of course it might be no more than it seemed to be —a rather gaudy and vulgar toy, such as a woman like Mme. Dauvray would be very likely to choose in order to dress her walls. But it swept Ricardo's thoughts back of a sudden to the concert-hall at Leamington and the apparatus of a spiritualistic show. After all, he reflected triumphantly, Hanaud had not noticed everything, and as he made the reflection Hanaud's voice broke in to corroborate him.

"We have seen everything here; let us go upstairs," he said. "We will first visit the room of Mlle. Celie. Then we will question the maid, Helene Vauquier."

The four men, followed by Perrichet, passed out by the door into the hall and mounted the stairs. Celia's room was in the southwest angle of the villa, a bright and airy room, of which one window overlooked the road, and two others, between which stood the dressing-table, the garden. Behind the room a door led into a little white-tiled bathroom. Some towels were tumbled upon the floor beside the bath. In the bedroom a dark-grey frock of tussore and a petticoat were flung carelessly on the bed; a big grey hat of Ottoman silk was lying upon a chest of drawers in the recess of a window; and upon a chair a little pile of fine linen and a pair of grey silk stockings, which matched in shade the grey suede shoes, were tossed in a heap.

"It was here that you saw the light at half-past nine?" Hanaud said, turning to Perrichet.

"Yes, monsieur," replied Perrichet.

"We may assume, then, that Mlle. Celie was changing her dress at that time."

Besnard was looking about him, opening a drawer here, a wardrobe there.

"Mlle. Celie," he said, with a laugh, "was a particular young lady, and fond of her fine clothes, if one may judge from the room and the order of the cupboards. She must have changed her dress last night in an unusual hurry."

There was about the whole room a certain daintiness, almost, it seemed to Mr. Ricardo, a fragrance, as though the girl had impressed something of her own delicate self upon it. Wethermill stood upon the threshold watching with a sullen face the violation of this chamber by the officers of the police.

No such feelings, however, troubled Hanaud. He went over to the dressing-room and opened a few small leather cases which held Celia's ornaments. In one or two of them a trinket was visible; others were empty. One of these latter Hanaud held open in his hand, and for so long that Besnard moved impatiently.

"You see it is empty, monsieur," he said, and suddenly Wethermill moved forward into the room.

"Yes, I see that," said Hanaud dryly.

It was a case made to hold a couple of long ear-drops —those diamond ear-drops, doubtless, which Mr. Ricardo had seen twinkling in the garden.

"Will monsieur let me see?" asked Wethermill, and he took the case in his hands. "Yes," he said. "Mlle. Celie's ear-drops," and he handed the case back with a thoughtful air.

It was the first time he had taken a definite part in the investigation. To Ricardo the reason was clear. Harry Wethermill had himself given those ear-drops to Celia. Hanaud replaced the case and turned round.

"There is nothing more for us to see here," he said. "I suppose that no one has been allowed to enter the room?" And he opened the door.

"No one except Helene Vauquier," replied the Commissaire.

Ricardo felt indignant at so obvious a piece of carelessness. Even Wethermill looked surprised. Hanaud merely shut the door again.

"Oho, the maid!" he said. "Then she has recovered!"

"She is still weak," said the Commissaire. "But I thought it was necessary that we should obtain at once a description of what Celie Harland wore when she left the house. I spoke to M. Fleuriot about it, and he gave me permission to bring Helene Vauquier here, who alone could tell us. I brought her here myself just before you came. She looked through the girl's wardrobe to see what was missing."

"Was she alone in the room?"

"Not for a moment," said M. Besnard haughtily. "Really, monsieur, we are not so ignorant of how an affair of this kind should be conducted. I was in the room myself the whole time, with my eye upon her."

"That was just before I came," said Hanaud. He crossed carelessly to the open window which overlooked the road and, leaning out of it, looked up the road to the corner round which he and his friends had come, precisely as the Commissaire had done. Then he turned back into the room.

"Which was the last cupboard or drawer that Helene Vauquier touched?" he asked.

"This one."

Besnard stooped and pulled open the bottom drawer of a chest which stood in the embrasure of the window. A light-coloured dress was lying at the bottom.

"I told her to be quick," said Besnard, "since I had seen that you were coming. She lifted this dress out and said that nothing was missing there. So I took her back to her room and left her with the nurse."

Hanaud lifted the light dress from the drawer, shook it out in front of the window, twirled it round, snatched up a corner of it and held it to his eyes, and then, folding it quickly, replaced it in the drawer.

"Now show me the first drawer she touched." And this time he lifted out a petticoat, and, taking it to the window, examined it with a greater care. When he had finished with it he handed it to Ricardo to put away, and stood for a moment or two thoughtful and absorbed. Ricardo in his turn examined the petticoat. But he could see nothing unusual. It was an attractive petticoat, dainty with frills and lace, but it was hardly a thing to grow thoughtful over. He looked up in perplexity and saw that Hanaud was watching his investigations with a smile of amusement.

"When M. Ricardo has put that away," he said, "we will hear what Helene Vauquier has to tell us."

He passed out of the door last, and, locking it, placed the key in his pocket.

"Helene Vauquier's room is, I think, upstairs," he said. And he moved towards the staircase.

But as he did so a man in plain clothes, who had been waiting upon the landing, stepped forward. He carried in his hand a piece of thin, strong whipcord.

"Ah, Durette!" cried Besnard. "Monsieur Hanaud, I sent Durette this morning round the shops of Aix with the cord which was found knotted round Mme. Dauvray's neck."

Hanaud advanced quickly to the man.

"Well! Did you discover anything?"

"Yes, monsieur," said Durette. "At the shop of M. Corval, in the Rue du Casino, a young lady in a dark-grey frock and hat bought some cord of this kind at a few minutes after nine last night. It was just as the shop was being closed. I showed Corval the photograph of Celie Harland which M. le Commissaire gave me out of Mme. Dauvray's room, and he identified it as the portrait of the girl who had bought the cord."

Complete silence followed upon Durette's words. The whole party stood like men stupefied. No one looked towards Wethermill; even Hanaud averted his eyes.

"Yes, that is very important," he said awkwardly. He turned away and, followed by the others, went up the stairs to the bedroom of Helene Vauquier.


## CHAPTER VI


### HELENE VAUQUIER'S EVIDENCE

A nurse opened the door. Within the room Helene Vauquier was leaning back in a chair. She looked ill, and her face was very white. On the appearance of Hanaud, the Commissaire, and the others, however, she rose to her feet. Ricardo recognised the justice of Hanaud's description. She stood before them a hard-featured, tall woman of thirty-five or forty, in a neat black stuff dress, strong with the strength of a peasant, respectable, reliable. She looked what she had been, the confidential maid of an elderly woman. On her face there was now an aspect of eager appeal.

"Oh, monsieur!" she began, "let me go from here-anywhere-into prison if you like. But to stay here-where in years past we were so happy-and with madame lying in the room below. No, it is insupportable."

She sank into her chair, and Hanaud came over to her side.

"Yes, yes," he said, in a soothing voice. "I can understand your feelings, my poor woman. We will not keep you here. You have, perhaps, friends in Aix with whom you could stay?"

"Oh yes, monsieur!" Helene cried gratefully. "Oh, but I thank you! That I should have to sleep here to-night! Oh, how the fear of that has frightened me!"

"You need have had no such fear. After all, we are not the visitors of last night," said Hanaud, drawing a chair close to her and patting her hand sympathetically. "Now, I want you to tell these gentlemen and myself all that you know of this dreadful business. Take your time, mademoiselle! We are human."

"But, monsieur, I know nothing," she cried. "I was told that I might go to bed as soon as I had dressed Mlle. Celie for the seance."

"Seance!" cried Ricardo, startled into speech. The picture of the Assembly Hall at Leamington was again before his mind. But Hanaud turned towards him, and, though Hanaud's face retained its benevolent expression, there was a glitter in his eyes which sent the blood into Ricardo's face.

"Did you speak again, M. Ricardo?" the detective asked. "No? I thought it was not possible." He turned back to Helene Vauquier. "So Mlle. Celie practised seances. That is very strange. We will hear about them. Who knows what thread may lead us to the truth?"

Helene Vauquier shook her head.

"Monsieur, it is not right that you should seek the truth from me. For, consider this! I cannot speak with justice of Mlle. Celie. No, I cannot! I did not like her. I was jealous-yes, jealous. Monsieur, you want the truth —I hated her!" And the woman's face flushed and she clenched her hand upon the arm of her chair. "Yes, I hated her. How could I help it?" she asked.

"Why?" asked Hanaud gently. "Why could you not help it?"

Helene Vauquier leaned back again, her strength exhausted, and smiled languidly.

"I will tell you. But remember it is a woman speaking to you, and things which you will count silly and trivial mean very much to her. There was one night last June-only last June! To think of it! So little while ago there was no Mlle. Celie —" and, as Hanaud raised his hand, she said hurriedly, "Yes, yes; I will control myself. But to think of Mme. Dauvray now!"

And thereupon she blurted out her story and explained to Mr. Ricardo the question which had so perplexed him: how a girl of so much distinction as Celia Harland came to be living with a woman of so common a type as Mme. Dauvray.

"Well, one night in June," said Helene Vauquier, "madame went with a party to supper at the Abbaye Restaurant in Montmartre. And she brought home for the first time Mlle. Celie. But you should have seen her! She had on a little plaid skirt and a coat which was falling to pieces, and she was starving-yes, starving. Madame told me the story that night as I undressed her. Mlle. Celie was there dancing amidst the tables for a supper with any one who would be kind enough to dance with her."

The scorn of her voice rang through the room. She was the rigid, respectable peasant woman, speaking out her contempt. And Wethermill must needs listen to it. Ricardo dared not glance at him.

"But hardly any one would dance with her in her rags, and no one would give her supper except madame. Madame did. Madame listened to her story of hunger and distress. Madame believed it, and brought her home. Madame was so kind, so careless in her kindness. And now she lies murdered for a reward!" An hysterical sob checked the woman's utterances, her face began to work, her hands to twitch.

"Come, come!" said Hanaud gently, "calm yourself, mademoiselle."

Helene Vauquier paused for a moment or two to recover her composure. "I beg your pardon, monsieur, but I have been so long with madame-oh, the poor woman! Yes, yes, I will calm myself. Well, madame brought her home, and in a week there was nothing too good for Mlle. Celie. Madame was like a child. Always she was being deceived and imposed upon. Never she learnt prudence. But no one so quickly made her way to madame's heart as Mlle. Celie.

Mademoiselle must live with her. Mademoiselle must be dressed by the first modistes. Mademoiselle must have lace petticoats and the softest linen, long white gloves, and pretty ribbons for her hair, and hats from Caroline Reboux at twelve hundred francs. And madame's maid must attend upon her and deck her out in all these dainty things. Bah!"

Vauquier was sitting erect in her chair, violent, almost rancorous with anger. She looked round upon the company and shrugged her shoulders.

"I told you not to come to me!" she said, "I cannot speak impartially, or even gently of mademoiselle. Consider! For years I had been more than madame's maid-her friend; yes, so she was kind enough to call me. She talked to me about everything, consulted me about everything, took me with her everywhere. Then she brings home, at two o'clock in the morning, a young girl with a fresh, pretty face, from a Montmartre restaurant, and in a week I am nothing at all-oh, but nothing-and mademoiselle is queen."

"Yes, it is quite natural," said Hanaud sympathetically. "You would not have been human, mademoiselle, if you had not felt some anger. But tell us frankly about these seances. How did they begin?"

"Oh, monsieur," Vauquier answered, "it was not difficult to begin them. Mme. Dauvray had a passion for fortune-tellers and rogues of that kind. Any one with a pack of cards and some nonsense about a dangerous woman with black hair or a man with a limp-Monsieur knows the stories they string together in dimly lighted rooms to deceive the credulous-any one could make a harvest out of madame's superstitions. But monsieur knows the type."

"Indeed I do," said Hanaud, with a laugh.

"Well, after mademoiselle had been with us three weeks, she said to me one morning when I was dressing her hair that it was a pity madame was always running round the fortune-tellers, that she herself could do something much more striking and impressive, and that if only I would help her we could rescue madame from their clutches. Sir, I did not think what power I was putting into Mlle. Celie's hands, or assuredly I would have refused. And I did not wish to quarrel with Mlle. Celie; so for once I consented, and, having once consented, I could never afterwards refuse, for, if I had, mademoiselle would have made some fine excuse about the psychic influence not being en rapport, and meanwhile would have had me sent away. While if I had confessed the truth to madame, she would have been so angry that I had been a party to tricking her that again I would have lost my place. And so the seances went on."

"Yes," said Hanaud. "I understand that your position was very difficult. We shall not, I think," and he turned to the Commissaire confidently for corroboration of his words, "be disposed to blame you."

"Certainly not," said the Commissaire. "After all, life is not so easy."

"Thus, then, the seances began," said Hanaud, leaning forward with a keen interest. "This is a strange and curious story you are telling me, Mlle. Vauquier. Now, how were they conducted? How did you assist? What did Mlle. Celie do? Rap on the tables in the dark and rattle tambourines like that one with the knot of ribbons which hangs upon the wall of the salon?"

There was a gentle and inviting irony in Hanaud's tone. M. Ricardo was disappointed. Hanaud had after all not overlooked the tambourine. Without Ricardo's reason to notice it, he had none the less observed it and borne it in his memory.

"Well?" he asked.

"Oh, monsieur, the tambourines and the rapping on the table!" cried Helene. "That was nothing-oh, but nothing at all. Mademoiselle Celie would make spirits appear and speak!"

"Really! And she was never caught out! But Mlle. Celie must have been a remarkably clever girl."

"Oh, she was of an address which was surprising. Sometimes madame and I were alone. Sometimes there were others, whom madame in her pride had invited. For she was very proud, monsieur, that her companion could introduce her to the spirits of dead people. But never was Mlle. Celie caught out. She told me that for many years, even when quite a child, she had travelled through England giving these exhibitions."

"Oho!" said Hanaud, and he turned to Wethermill. "Did you know that?" he asked in English.

"I did not," he said. "I do not now."

Hanaud shook his head.

"To me this story does not seem invented," he replied. And then he spoke again in French to Helene Vauquier. "Well, continue, mademoiselle! Assume that the company is assembled for our seance."

"Then Mlle. Celie, dressed in a long gown of black velvet, which set off her white arms and shoulders well-oh, mademoiselle did not forget those little trifles," Helene Vauquier interrupted her story, with a return of her bitterness, to interpolate —"mademoiselle would sail into the room with her velvet train flowing behind her, and perhaps for a little while she would say there was a force working against her, and she would sit silent in a chair while madame gaped at her with open eyes. At last mademoiselle would say that the powers were favourable and the spirits would manifest themselves to-night. Then she would be placed in a cabinet, perhaps with a string tied across the door outside-you will understand it was my business to see after the string-and the lights would be turned down, or perhaps out altogether. Or at other times we would sit holding hands round a table, Mlle. Celie between Mme. Dauvray and myself. But in that case the lights would be turned out first, and it would be really my hand which held Mme. Dauvray's. And whether it was the cabinet or the chairs, in a moment mademoiselle would be creeping silently about the room in a little pair of soft-soled slippers without heels, which she wore so that she might not be heard, and tambourines would rattle as you say, and fingers touch the forehead and the neck, and strange voices would sound from corners of the room, and dim apparitions would appear-the spirits of great ladies of the past, who would talk with Mme. Dauvray. Such ladies as Mme. de Castiglione, Marie Antoinette, Mme. de Medici —I do not remember all the names, and very likely I do not pronounce them properly. Then the voices would cease and the lights be turned up, and Mlle. Celie would be found in a trance just in the same place and attitude as she had been when the lights were turned out. Imagine, messieurs, the effect of such seances upon a woman like Mme. Dauvray. She was made for them. She believed in them implicitly. The words of the great ladies from the past-she would remember and repeat them, and be very proud that such great ladies had come back to the world merely to tell her-Mme. Dauvray-about their lives. She would have had seances all day, but Mlle. Celie pleaded that she was left exhausted at the end of them. But Mlle. Celie was of an address! For instance-it will seem very absurd and ridiculous to you, gentlemen, but you must remember what Mme. Dauvray was-for instance, madame was particularly anxious to speak with the spirit of Mme. de Montespan. Yes, yes! She had read all the memoirs about that lady. Very likely Mlle. Celie had put the notion into Mme. Dauvray's head, for madame was not a scholar. But she was dying to hear that famous woman's voice and to catch a dim glimpse of her face. Well, she was never gratified. Always she hoped. Always Mlle. Celie tantalised her with the hope. But she would not gratify it. She would not spoil her fine affairs by making these treats too common. And she acquired-how should she not? —a power over Mme. Dauvray which was unassailable. The fortune-tellers had no more to say to Mme. Dauvray. She did nothing but felicitate herself upon the happy chance which had sent her Mlle. Celie. And now she lies in her room murdered!"

Once more Helene's voice broke upon the words. But Hanaud poured her out a glass of water and held it to her lips. Helene drank it eagerly.

"There, that is better, is it not?" he said.

"Yes, monsieur," said Helene Vauquier, recovering herself. "Sometimes, too," she resumed, "messages from the spirits would flutter down in writing on the table."

"In writing?" exclaimed Hanaud quickly.

"Yes; answers to questions. Mlle. Celie had them ready. Oh, but she was of an address altogether surprising.

"I see," said Hanaud slowly; and he added, "But sometimes, I suppose, the questions were questions which Mlle. Celie could not answer?"

"Sometimes," Helene Vauquier admitted, "when visitors were present. When Mme. Dauvray was alone-well, she was an ignorant woman, and any answer would serve. But it was not so when there were visitors whom Mlle. Celie did not know, or only knew slightly. These visitors might be putting questions to test her, of which they knew the answers, while Mlle. Celie did not."

"Exactly," said Hanaud. "What happened then?"

All who were listening understood to what point he was leading Helene Vauquier. All waited intently for her answer.

She smiled.

"It was all one to Mlle. Celie."

"She was prepared with an escape from the difficulty?"

"Perfectly prepared."

Hanaud looked puzzled.

"I can think of no way out of it except the one," and he looked round to the Commissaire and to Ricardo as though he would inquire of them how many ways they had discovered. "I can think of no escape except that a message in writing should flutter down from the spirit appealed to saying frankly," and Hanaud shrugged his shoulders, "'I do not know.'"

"Oh no no, monsieur," replied Helene Vauquier in pity for Hanaud's misconception, "I see that you are not in the habit of attending seances. It would never do for a spirit to admit that it did not know. At once its authority would be gone, and with it Mlle. Celie's as well. But on the other hand, for inscrutable reasons the spirit might not be allowed to answer."

"I understand," said Hanaud, meekly accepting the correction. "The spirit might reply that it was forbidden to answer, but never that it did not know."

"No, never that," said Helene. So it seemed that Hanaud must look elsewhere for the explanation of that sentence. "I do not know," Helene continued: "Oh, Mlle. Celie-it was not easy to baffle her, I can tell you. She carried a lace scarf which she could drape about her head, and in a moment she would be, in the dim light, an old, old woman, with a voice so altered that no one could know it. Indeed, you said rightly, monsieur-she was clever."

To all who listened Helene Vauquier's story carried its conviction. Mme. Dauvray rose vividly before their minds as a living woman. Celie's trickeries were so glibly described that they could hardly have been invented, and certainly not by this poor peasant-woman whose lips so bravely struggled with Medici, and Montespan, and the names of the other great ladies. How, indeed, should she know of them at all? She could never have had the inspiration to concoct the most convincing item of her story-the queer craze of Mme. Dauvray for an interview with Mme. de Montespan. These details were assuredly the truth.

Ricardo, indeed, knew them to be true. Had he not himself seen the girl in her black velvet dress shut up in a cabinet, and a great lady of the past dimly appear in the darkness? Moreover, Helene Vauquier's jealousy was so natural and inevitable a thing. Her confession of it corroborated all her story.

"Well, then," said Hanaud, "we come to last night. There was a seance held in the salon last night."

"No, monsieur," said Vauquier, shaking her head; "there was no seance last night."

"But already you have said —" interrupted the Commissaire; and Hanaud held up his hand.

"Let her speak, my friend."

"Yes, monsieur shall hear," said Vauquier.

It appeared that at five o'clock in the afternoon Mme. Dauvray and Mlle. Celie prepared to leave the house on foot. It was their custom to walk down at this hour to the Villa des Fleurs, pass an hour or so there, dine in a restaurant, and return to the Rooms to spend the evening. On this occasion, however, Mme. Dauvray informed Helene that they should be back early and bring with them a friend who was interested in, but entirely sceptical of, spiritualistic manifestations. "But we shall convince her to-night, Celie," she said confidently; and the two women then went out. Shortly before eight Helene closed the shutters both of the upstair and the downstair windows and of the glass doors into the garden, and returned to the kitchen, which was at the back of the house-that is, on the side facing the road. There had been a fall of rain at seven which had lasted for the greater part of the hour, and soon after she had shut the windows the rain fell again in a heavy shower, and Helene, knowing that madame felt the chill, lighted a small fire in the salon. The shower lasted until nearly nine, when it ceased altogether and the night cleared up.

It was close upon half-past nine when the bell rang from the salon. Vauquier was sure of the hour, for the charwoman called her attention to the clock.

"I found Mme. Dauvray, Mlle. Celie, and another woman in the salon," continued Helene Vauquier.

"Madame had let them in with her latchkey."

"Ah, the other woman!" cried Besnard. "Had you seen her before?"

"No, monsieur."

"What was she like?"

"She was sallow, with black hair and bright eyes like beads. She was short and about forty-five years old, though it is difficult to judge of these things. I noticed her hands, for she was taking her gloves off, and they seemed to me to be unusually muscular for a woman."

"Ah!" cried Louis Besnard. "That is important."

"Mme. Dauvray was, as she always was before a seance, in a feverish flutter. 'You will help Mlle. Celie to dress, Helene, and be very quick,' she said; and with an extraordinary longing she added, 'Perhaps we shall see her to-night.' Her, you understand, was Mme. de Montespan." And she turned to the stranger and said, "You will believe, Adele, after to-night."

"Adele!" said the Commissaire wisely. "Then Adele was the strange woman's name?"

"Perhaps," said Hanaud dryly.

Helene Vauquier reflected.

"I think Adele was the name," she said in a more doubtful tone. "It sounded like Adele."

The irrepressible Mr. Ricardo was impelled to intervene.

"What Monsieur Hanaud means," he explained, with the pleasant air of a man happy to illuminate the dark intelligence of a child, "is that Adele was probably a pseudonym."

Hanaud turned to him with a savage grin.

"Now that is sure to help her!" he cried. "A pseudonym! Helene Vauquier is sure to understand that simple and elementary word. How bright this M. Ricardo is! Where shall we find a new pin more bright? I ask you," and he spread out his hands in a despairing admiration.

Mr. Ricardo flushed red, but he answered never a word. He must endure gibes and humiliations like a schoolboy in a class. His one constant fear was lest he should be turned out of the room. The Commissaire diverted wrath from him however.

"What he means by pseudonym," he said to Helene Vauquier, explaining Mr. Ricardo to her as Mr. Ricardo had presumed to explain Hanaud, "is a false name. Adele may have been, nay, probably was, a false name adopted by this strange woman."

"Adele, I think, was the name used," replied Helene, the doubt in her voice diminishing as she searched her memory. "I am almost sure."

"Well, we will call her Adele," said Hanaud impatiently. "What does it matter? Go on, Mademoiselle Vauquier."

"The lady sat upright and squarely upon the edge of a chair, with a sort of defiance, as though she was determined nothing should convince her, and she laughed incredulously."

Here, again, all who heard were able vividly to conjure up the scene-the defiant sceptic sitting squarely on the edge of her chair, removing her gloves from her muscular hands; the excited Mme. Dauvray, so absorbed in the determination to convince; and Mlle. Celie running from the room to put on the black gown which would not be visible in the dim light.

"Whilst I took off mademoiselle's dress," Vauquier continued, "she said: 'When I have gone down to the salon you can go to bed, Helene. Mme. Adele' —yes, it was Adele —'will be fetched by a friend in a motorcar, and I can let her out and fasten the door again. So if you hear the car you will know that it has come for her.'"

"Oh, she said that!" said Hanaud quickly.

"Yes, monsieur."

Hanaud looked gloomily towards Wethermill. Then he exchanged a sharp glance with the Commissaire, and moved his shoulders in an almost imperceptible shrug. But Mr. Ricardo saw it, and construed it into one word. He imagined a jury uttering the word "Guilty."

Helene Vauquier saw the movement too.

"Do not condemn her too quickly, monsieur," she, said, with an impulse of remorse. "And not upon my words. For, as I say, I —hated her."

Hanaud nodded reassuringly, and she resumed:

"I was surprised, and I asked mademoiselle what she would do without her confederate. But she laughed, and said there would be no difficulty. That is partly why I think there was no seance held last night. Monsieur, there was a note in her voice that evening which I did not as yet understand. Mademoiselle then took her bath while I laid out her black dress and the slippers with the soft, noiseless soles. And now I tell you why I am sure there was no seance last night-why Mlle. Celie never meant there should be one."

"Yes, let us hear that," said Hanaud curiously, and leaning forward with his hands upon his knees.

"You have here, monsieur, a description of how mademoiselle was dressed when she went away." Helene Vauquier picked up a sheet of paper from the table at her side. "I wrote it out at the request of M. le Commissaire." She handed the paper to Hanaud, who glanced through it as she continued. "Well, except for the white lace coat, monsieur, I dressed Mlle. Celie just in that way. She would have none of her plain black robe. No, Mlle. Celie must wear her fine new evening frock of pale reseda-green chiffon over soft clinging satin, which set off her fair beauty so prettily. It left her white arms and shoulders bare, and it had a long train, and it rustled as she moved. And with that she must put on her pale green silk stockings, her new little satin slippers to match, with the large paste buckles-and a sash of green satin looped through another glittering buckle at the side of the waist, with long ends loosely knotted together at the knee. I must tie her fair hair with a silver ribbon, and pin upon her curls a large hat of reseda green with a golden-brown ostrich feather drooping behind. I warned mademoiselle that there was a tiny fire burning in the salon. Even with the fire-screen in front of it there would still be a little light upon the floor, and the glittering buckles on her feet would betray her, even if the rustle of her dress did not. But she said she would kick her slippers off. Ah, gentlemen, it is, after all, not so that one dresses for a seance," she cried, shaking her head. "But it is just so-is it not? —that one dresses to go to meet a lover."

The suggestion startled every one who heard it. It fairly took Mr. Ricardo's breath away. Wethermill stepped forward with a cry of revolt. The Commissaire exclaimed, admiringly, "But here is an idea!" Even Hanaud sat back in his chair, though his expression lost nothing of its impassivity, and his eyes never moved from Helene Vauquier's face.

"Listen!" she continued, "I will tell you what I think. It was my habit to put out some sirop and lemonade and some little cakes in the dining-room, which, as you know, is at the other side of the house across the hall. I think it possible, messieurs, that while Mlle. Celie was changing her dress Mme. Dauvray and the stranger, Adele, went into the dining-room. I know that Mlle. Celie, as soon as she was dressed, ran downstairs to the salon. Well, then, suppose Mlle. Celie had a lover waiting with whom she meant to run away. She hurries through the empty salon, opens the glass doors, and is gone, leaving the doors open. And the thief, an accomplice of Adele, finds the doors open and hides himself in the salon until Mme. Dauvray returns from the dining-room. You see, that leaves Mlle. Celie innocent."

Vauquier leaned forward eagerly, her white face flushing. There was a moment's silence, and then Hanaud said:

"That is all very well, Mlle. Vauquier. But it does not account for the lace coat in which the girl went away. She must have returned to her room to fetch that after you had gone to bed."

Helene Vauquier leaned back with an air of disappointment.

"That is true. I had forgotten the coat. I did not like Mlle. Celie, but I am not wicked —"

"Nor for the fact that the sirop and the lemonade had not been touched in the dining-room," said the Commissaire, interrupting her.

Again the disappointment overspread Vauquier's face.

"Is that so?" she asked. "I did not know —I have been kept a prisoner here."

The Commissaire cut her short with a cry of satisfaction.

"Listen! listen!" he exclaimed excitedly. "Here is a theory which accounts for all, which combines Vauquier's idea with ours, and Vauquier's idea is, I think, very just, up to a point. Suppose, M. Hanaud, that the girl was going to meet her lover, but the lover is the murderer. Then all becomes clear. She does not run away to him; she opens the door for him and lets him in."

Both Hanaud and Ricardo stole a glance at Wethermill. How did he take the theory? Wethermill was leaning against the wall, his eyes closed, his face white and contorted with a spasm of pain. But he had the air of a man silently enduring an outrage rather than struck down by the conviction that the woman he loved was worthless.

"It is not for me to say, monsieur," Helene Vauquier continued. "I only tell you what I know. I am a woman, and it would be very difficult for a girl who was eagerly expecting her lover so to act that another woman would not know it. However uncultivated and ignorant the other woman was, that at all events she would know. The knowledge would spread to her of itself, without a word. Consider, gentlemen!" And suddenly Helene Vauquier smiled. "A young girl tingling with excitement from head to foot, eager that her beauty just at this moment should be more fresh, more sweet than ever it was, careful that her dress should set it exquisitely off. Imagine it! Her lips ready for the kiss! Oh, how should another woman not know? I saw Mlle. Celie, her cheeks rosy, her eyes bright. Never had she looked so lovely. The pale-green hat upon her fair head heavy with its curls! From head to foot she looked herself over, and then she sighed-she sighed with pleasure because she looked so pretty. That was Mlle. Celie last night, monsieur. She gathered up her train, took her long white gloves in the other hand, and ran down the stairs, her heels clicking on the wood, her buckles glittering. At the bottom she turned and said to me:

"'Remember, Helene, you can go to bed.' That was it monsieur."

And now violently the rancour of Helene Vauquier's feelings burst out once more.

"For her the fine clothes, the pleasure, and the happiness. For me —I could go to bed!"

Hanaud looked again at the description which Helene Vauquier had written out, and read it through carefully. Then he asked a question, of which Ricardo did not quite see the drift.

"So," he said, "when this morning you suggested to Monsieur the Commissaire that it would be advisable for you to go through Mlle. Celie's wardrobe, you found that nothing more had been taken away except the white lace coat?"

"That is so."

"Very well. Now, after Mlle. Celie had gone down the stairs —"

"I put the lights out in her room and, as she had ordered me to do, I went to bed. The next thing that I remember-but no! It terrifies me too much to think of it."

Helene shuddered and covered her face spasmodically with her hands. Hanaud drew her hands gently down.

"Courage! You are safe now, mademoiselle. Calm yourself!"

She lay back with her eyes closed.

"Yes, yes; it is true. I am safe now. But oh! I feel I shall never dare to sleep again!" And the tears swam in her eyes. "I woke up with a feeling of being suffocated. Mon Dieu! There was the light burning in the room, and a woman, the strange woman with the strong hands, was holding me down by the shoulders, while a man with his cap drawn over his eyes and a little black moustache pressed over my lips a pad from which a horribly sweet and sickly taste filled my mouth. Oh, I was terrified! I could not scream. I struggled. The woman told me roughly to keep quiet. But I could not. I must struggle. And then with a brutality unheard of she dragged me up on to my knees while the man kept the pad right over my mouth. The man, with the arm which was free, held me close to him, and she bound my hands with a cord behind me. Look!"

She held out her wrists. They were terribly bruised. Red and angry lines showed where the cord had cut deeply into her flesh.

"Then they flung me down again upon my back, and the next thing I remember is the doctor standing over me and this kind nurse supporting me."

She sank back exhausted in her chair and wiped her forehead with her handkerchief. The sweat stood upon it in beads.

"Thank you, mademoiselle," said Hanaud gravely. "This has been a trying ordeal for you. I understand that. But we are coming to the end. I want you to read this description of Mlle. Celie through again to make sure that nothing is omitted." He gave the paper into the maid's hands. "It will be advertised, so it is important that it should be complete. See that you have left out nothing."

Helene Vauquier bent her head over the paper.

"No," said Helene at last. "I do not think I have omitted anything." And she handed the paper back.

"I asked you," Hanaud continued suavely, "because I understand that Mlle. Celie usually wore a pair of diamond ear-drops, and they are not mentioned here."

A faint colour came into the maid's face.

"That is true, monsieur. I had forgotten. It is quite true."

"Any one might forget," said Hanaud, with a reassuring smile. "But you will remember now. Think! think! Did Mlle. Celie wear them last night?" He leaned forward, waiting for her reply. Wethermill too, made a movement. Both men evidently thought the point of great importance. The maid looked at Hanaud for a few moments without speaking.

"It is not from me, mademoiselle, that you will get the answer," said Hanaud quietly.

"No, monsieur. I was thinking," said the maid, her face flushing at the rebuke.

"Did she wear them when she went down the stairs last night?" he insisted.

"I think she wore them," she said doubtfully. "Ye-es —yes," and the words came now firm and clear. "I remember well. Mlle. Celie had taken them off before her bath, and they lay on the dressing-table. She put them into her ears while I dressed her hair and arranged the bow of ribbon in it."

"Then we will add the earrings to your description," said Hanaud, as he rose from his chair with the paper in his hand, "and for the moment we need not trouble you any more about Mademoiselle Celie." He folded the paper up, slipped it into his letter-case, and put it away in his pocket. "Let us consider that poor Madame Dauvray! Did she keep much money in the house?"

"No, monsieur; very little. She was well known in Aix and her cheques were everywhere accepted without question. It was a high pleasure to serve madame, her credit was so good," said Helene Vauquier, raising her head as though she herself had a share in the pride of that good credit.

"No doubt," Hanaud agreed. "There are many fine households where the banking account is overdrawn, and it cannot be pleasant for the servants."

"They are put to so many shifts to hide it from the servants of their neighbours," said Helene. "Besides," and she made a little grimace of contempt, "a fine household and an overdrawn banking account-it is like a ragged petticoat under a satin dress. That was never the case with Madame Dauvray."

"So that she was under no necessity to have ready money always in her pocket," said Hanaud. "I understand that. But at times perhaps she won at the Villa des Fleurs?"

Helene Vauquier shook her head.

"She loved the Villa des Fleurs, but she never played for high sums and often never played at all. If she won a few louis, she was as delighted with her gains and as afraid to lose them again at the tables as if she were of the poorest, and she stopped at once. No, monsieur; twenty or thirty louis-there was never more than that in the house."

"Then it was certainly for her famous collection of jewellery that Madame Dauvray was murdered?"

"Certainly, monsieur."

"Now, where did she keep her jewellery?"

"In a safe in her bedroom, monsieur. Every night she took off what she had been wearing and locked it up with the rest. She was never too tired for that."

"And what did she do with the keys?"

"That I cannot tell you. Certainly she locked her rings and necklaces away whilst I undressed her. And she laid the keys upon the dressing-table or the mantel-shelf—anywhere. But in the morning the keys were no longer where she had left them. She had put them secretly away."

Hanaud turned to another point.

"I suppose that Mademoiselle Celie knew of the safe and that the jewels were kept there?"

"Oh yes! Mademoiselle indeed was often in Madame Dauvray's room when she was dressing or undressing. She must often have seen madame take them out and lock them up again. But then, monsieur, so did I."

Hanaud nodded to her with a friendly smile.

"Thank you once more, mademoiselle," he said. "The torture is over. But of course Monsieur Fleuriot will require your presence."

Helene Vauquier looked anxiously towards him.

"But meanwhile I can go from this villa, monsieur?" she pleaded, with a trembling voice.

"Certainly; you shall go to your friends at once."

"Oh, monsieur, thank you!" she cried, and suddenly she gave way. The tears began to flow from her eyes. She buried her face in her hands and sobbed. "It is foolish of me, but what would you?" She jerked out the words between her sobs. "It has been too terrible."

"Yes, yes," said Hanaud soothingly. "The nurse will put a few things together for you in a bag. You will not leave Aix, of course, and I will send some one with you to your friends."

The maid started violently.

"Oh, not a sergent-de-ville, monsieur, I beg of you. I should be disgraced."

"No. It shall be a man in plain clothes, to see that you are not hindered by reporters on the way."

Hanaud turned towards the door. On the dressing-table a cord was lying. He took it up and spoke to the nurse.

"Was this the cord with which Helene Vauquier's hands were tied?"

"Yes, monsieur," she replied.

Hanaud handed it to the Commissaire.

"It will be necessary to keep that," he said.

It was a thin piece of strong whipcord. It was the same kind of cord as that which had been found tied round Mme. Dauvray's throat. Hanaud opened the door and turned back to the nurse.

"We will send for a cab for Mlle. Vauquier. You will drive with her to her door. I think after that she will need no further help. Pack up a few things and bring them down. Mlle. Vauquier can follow, no doubt, now without assistance." And, with a friendly nod, he left the room.

Ricardo had been wondering, through the examination, in what light Hanaud considered Helene Vauquier. He was sympathetic, but the sympathy might merely have been assumed to deceive. His questions betrayed in no particular the colour of his mind. Now, however, he made himself clear. He informed the nurse, in the plainest possible way, that she was no longer to act as jailer. She was to bring Vauquier's things down; but Vauquier could follow by herself. Evidently Helene Vauquier was cleared.


## CHAPTER VII


## A STARTLING DISCOVERY

Harry Wethermill, however, was not so easily satisfied.

"Surely, monsieur, it would be well to know whither she is going," he said, "and to make sure that when she has gone there she will stay there-until we want her again?"

Hanaud looked at the young man pityingly.

"I can understand, monsieur, that you hold strong views about Helene Vauquier. You are human, like the rest of us. And what she has said to us just now would not make you more friendly. But-but —" and he preferred to shrug his shoulders rather than to finish in words his sentence. "However," he said, "we shall take care to know where Helene Vauquier is staying. Indeed, if she is at all implicated in this affair we shall learn more if we leave her free than if we keep her under lock and key. You see that if we leave her quite free, but watch her very, very carefully, so as to awaken no suspicion, she may be emboldened to do something rash-or the others may."

Mr. Ricardo approved of Hanaud's reasoning.

"That is quite true," he said. "She might write a letter."

"Yes, or receive one," added Hanaud, "which would be still more satisfactory for us-supposing, of course, that she has anything to do with this affair"; and again he shrugged his shoulders. He turned towards the Commissaire.

"You have a discreet officer whom you can trust?" he asked.

"Certainly. A dozen."

"I want only one."

"And here he is," said the Commissaire.

They were descending the stairs. On the landing of the first floor Durette, the man who had discovered where the cord was bought, was still waiting. Hanaud took Durette by the sleeve in the familiar way which he so commonly used and led him to the top of the stairs, where the two men stood for a few moments apart. It was plain that Hanaud was giving, Durette receiving, definite instructions. Durette descended the stairs; Hanaud came back to the others.

"I have told him to fetch a cab," he said, "and convey Helene Vauquier to her friends." Then he looked at Ricardo, and from Ricardo to the Commissaire, while he rubbed his hand backwards and forwards across his shaven chin.

"I tell you," he said, "I find this sinister little drama very interesting to me. The sordid, miserable struggle for mastery in this household of Mme. Dauvray-eh? Yes, very interesting. Just as much patience, just as much effort, just as much planning for this small end as a general uses to defeat an army-and, at the last, nothing gained. What else is politics? Yes, very interesting."

His eyes rested upon Wethermill's face for a moment, but they gave the young man no hope. He took a key from his pocket.

"We need not keep this room locked," he said. "We know all that there is to be known." And he inserted the key into the lock of Celia's room and turned it.

"But is that wise, monsieur?" said Besnard.

Hanaud shrugged his shoulders.

"Why not?" he asked.

"The case is in your hands," said the Commissaire. To Ricardo the proceedings seemed singularly irregular. But if the Commissaire was content, it was not for him to object.

"And where is my excellent friend Perrichet?" asked Hanaud; and leaning over the balustrade he called him up from the hall.

"We will now," said Hanaud, "have a glance into this poor murdered woman's room."

The room was opposite to Celia's. Besnard produced the key and unlocked the door. Hanaud took off his hat upon the threshold and then passed into the room with his companions. Upon the bed, outlined under a sheet, lay the rigid form of Mme. Dauvray. Hanaud stepped gently to the bedside and reverently uncovered the face. For a moment all could see it-livid, swollen, unhuman.

"A brutal business," he said in a low voice, and when he turned again to his companions his face was white and sickly. He replaced the sheet and gazed about the room.

It was decorated and furnished in the same style as the salon downstairs, yet the contrast between the two rooms was remarkable.

Downstairs, in the salon, only a chair had been overturned. Here there was every sign of violence and disorder. An empty safe stood open in one corner; the rugs upon the polished floor had been tossed aside; every drawer had been torn open, every wardrobe burst; the very bed had been moved from its position.

"It was in this safe that Madame Dauvray hid her jewels each night," said the Commissaire as Hanaud gazed about the room.

"Oh, was it so?" Hanaud asked slowly. It seemed to Ricardo that he read something in the aspect of this room too, which troubled his mind and increased his perplexity.

"Yes," said Besnard confidently. "Every night Mme. Dauvray locked her jewels away in this safe. Vauquier told us so this morning. Every night she was never too tired for that. Besides, here" —and putting his hand into the safe he drew out a paper —"here is the list of Mme. Dauvray's jewellery."

Plainly, however, Hanaud was not satisfied. He took the list and glanced through the items. But his thoughts were not concerned with it.

"If that is so," he said slowly, "Mme. Dauvray kept her jewels in this safe, why has every drawer been ransacked, why was the bed moved? Perrichet, lock the door-quietly-from the inside. That is right. Now lean your back against it."

Hanaud waited until he saw Perrichet's broad back against the door. Then he went down upon his knees, and, tossing the rugs here and there, examined with the minutest care the inlaid floor. By the side of the bed a Persian mat of blue silk was spread. This in its turn he moved quickly aside. He bent his eyes to the ground, lay prone, moved this way and that to catch the light upon the floor, then with a spring he rose upon his knees. He lifted his finger to his lips. In a dead silence he drew a pen-knife quickly from his pocket and opened it. He bent down again and inserted the blade between the cracks of the blocks. The three men in the room watched him with an intense excitement. A block of wood rose from the floor, he pulled it out, laid it noiselessly down, and inserted his hand into the opening.

Wethermill at Ricardo's elbow uttered a stifled cry. "Hush!" whispered Hanaud angrily. He drew out his hand again. It was holding a green leather jewel-case. He opened it, and a diamond necklace flashed its thousand colours in their faces. He thrust in his hand again and again and again, and each time that he withdrew it, it held a jewel-case. Before the astonished eyes of his companions he opened them. Ropes of pearls, collars of diamonds, necklaces of emeralds, rings of pigeon-blood rubies, bracelets of gold studded with opals-Mme. Dauvray's various jewellery was disclosed.

"But that is astounding," said Besnard, in an awe-struck voice.

"Then she was never robbed after all?" cried Ricardo.

Hanaud rose to his feet.

"What a piece of irony!" he whispered. "The poor woman is murdered for her jewels, the room's turned upside down, and nothing is found. For all the while they lay safe in this cache. Nothing is taken except what she wore. Let us see what she wore."

"Only a few rings, Helene Vauquier thought," said Besnard. "But she was not sure."

"Ah!" said Hanaud. "Well, let us make sure!" and, taking the list from the safe, he compared it with the jewellery in the cases on the floor, ticking off the items one by one. When he had finished he knelt down again, and, thrusting his hand into the hole, felt carefully about.

"There is a pearl necklace missing," he said. "A valuable necklace, from the description in the list and some rings. She must have been wearing them;" and he sat back upon his heels. "We will send the intelligent Perrichet for a bag," he said, "and we will counsel the intelligent Perrichet not to breathe a word to any living soul of what he has seen in this room. Then we will seal up in the bag the jewels, and we will hand it over to M. le Commissaire, who will convey it with the greatest secrecy out of this villa. For the list—I will keep it," and he placed it carefully in his pocket-book.

He unlocked the door and went out himself on to the landing. He looked down the stairs and up the stairs; then he beckoned Perrichet to him.

"Go!" he whispered. "Be quick, and when you come back hide the bag carefully under your coat."

Perrichet went down the stairs with pride written upon his face. Was he not assisting the great M. Hanaud from the Surete in Paris? Hanaud returned into Mme. Dauvray's room and closed the door. He looked into the eyes of his companions.

"Can't you see the scene?" he asked with a queer smile of excitement. He had forgotten Wethermill; he had forgotten even the dead woman shrouded beneath the sheet. He was absorbed. His eyes were bright, his whole face vivid with life. Ricardo saw the real man at this moment-and feared for the happiness of Harry Wethermill. For nothing would Hanaud now turn aside until he had reached the truth and set his hands upon the quarry. Of that Ricardo felt sure. He was trying now to make his companions visualise just what he saw and understood.

"Can't you see it? The old woman locking up her jewels in this safe every night before the eyes of her maid or her companion, and then, as soon as she was alone, taking them stealthily out of the safe and hiding them in this secret place. But I tell you-this is human. Yes, it is interesting just because it is so human. Then picture to yourselves last night, the murderers opening this safe and finding nothing-oh, but nothing! —and ransacking the room in deadly haste, kicking up the rugs, forcing open the drawers, and always finding nothing-nothing-nothing. Think of their rage, their stupefaction, and finally their fear! They must go, and with one pearl necklace, when they had hoped to reap a great fortune. Oh, but this is interesting-yes, I tell you —I, who have seen many strange things-this is interesting."

Perrichet returned with a canvas bag, into which Hanaud placed the jewel-cases. He sealed the bag in the presence of the four men and handed it to Besnard. He replaced the block of wood in the floor, covered it over again with the rug, and rose to his feet.

"Listen!" he said, in a low voice, and with a gravity which impressed them all. "There is something in this house which I do not understand. I have told you so. I tell you something more now. I am afraid—I am afraid." And the word startled his hearers like a thunderclap, though it was breathed no louder than a whisper, "Yes, my friends," he repeated, nodding his head, "terribly afraid." And upon the others fell a discomfort, an awe, as though something sinister and dangerous were present in the room and close to them. So vivid was the feeling, instinctively they drew nearer together. "Now, I warn you solemnly. There must be no whisper that these jewels have been discovered; no newspaper must publish a hint of it; no one must suspect that here in this room we have found them. Is that understood?"

"Certainly," said the Commissaire.

"Yes," said Mr. Ricardo.

"To be sure, monsieur," said Perrichet.

As for Harry Wethermill, he made no reply. His burning eyes were fixed upon Hanaud's face, and that was all. Hanaud, for his part, asked for no reply from him. Indeed, he did not look towards Harry Wethermill's face at all. Ricardo understood. Hanaud did not mean to be deterred by the suffering written there.

He went down again into the little gay salon lit with flowers and August sunlight, and stood beside the couch gazing at it with troubled eyes. And, as he gazed, he closed his eyes and shivered. He shivered like a man who has taken a sudden chill. Nothing in all this morning's investigations, not even the rigid body beneath the sheet, nor the strange discovery of the jewels, had so impressed Ricardo. For there he had been confronted with facts, definite and complete; here was a suggestion of unknown horrors, a hint, not a fact, compelling the imagination to dark conjecture. Hanaud shivered. That he had no idea why Hanaud shivered made the action still more significant, still more alarming. And it was not Ricardo alone who was moved by it. A voice of despair rang through the room. The voice was Harry Wethermill's, and his face was ashy white.

"Monsieur!" he cried, "I do not know what makes you shudder; but I am remembering a few words you used this morning."

Hanaud turned upon his heel. His face was drawn and grey and his eyes blazed.

"My friend, I also am remembering those words," he said. Thus the two men stood confronting one another, eye to eye, with awe and fear in both their faces.

Ricardo was wondering to what words they both referred, when the sound of wheels broke in upon the silence. The effect upon Hanaud was magical. He thrust his hands in his pockets.

"Helene Vauquier's cab," he said lightly. He drew out his cigarette-case and lighted a cigarette.

"Let us see that poor woman safely off. It is a closed cab I hope."

It was a closed landau. It drove past the open door of the salon to the front door of the house. In Hanaud's wake they all went out into the hall. The nurse came down alone carrying Helene Vauquier's bag. She placed it in the cab and waited in the doorway.

"Perhaps Helene Vauquier has fainted," she said anxiously: "she does not come." And she moved towards the stairs.

Hanaud took a singularly swift step forward and stopped her.

"Why should you think that?" he asked, with a queer smile upon his face, and as he spoke a door closed gently upstairs. "See," he continued, "you are wrong: she is coming."

Ricardo was puzzled. It had seemed to him that the door which had closed so gently was nearer than Helene Vauquier's door. It seemed to him that the door was upon the first, not the second landing. But Hanaud had noticed nothing strange; so it could not be. He greeted Helene Vauquier with a smile as she came down the stairs.

"You are better, mademoiselle," he said politely. "One can see that. There is more colour in your cheeks. A day or two, and you will be yourself again."

He held the door open while she got into the cab. The nurse took her seat beside her; Durette mounted on the box. The cab turned and went down the drive.

"Goodbye, mademoiselle," cried Hanaud, and he watched until the high shrubs hid the cab from his eyes. Then he behaved in an extraordinary way. He turned and sprang like lightning up the stairs. His agility amazed Ricardo. The others followed upon his heels. He flung himself at Celia's door and opened it He burst into the room, stood for a second, then ran to the window. He hid behind the curtain, looking out. With his hand he waved to his companions to keep back. The sound of wheels creaking and rasping rose to their ears. The cab had just come out into the road. Durette upon the box turned and looked towards the house. Just for a moment Hanaud leaned from the window, as Besnard, the Commissaire, had done, and, like Besnard again, he waved his hand. Then he came back into the room and saw, standing in front of him, with his mouth open and his eyes starting out of his head, Perrichet-the intelligent Perrichet.

"Monsieur," cried Perrichet, "something has been taken from this room."

Hanaud looked round the room and shook his head.

"No," he said.

"But yes, monsieur," Perrichet insisted. "Oh, but yes. See! Upon this dressing-table there was a small pot of cold cream. It stood here, where my finger is, when we were in this room an hour ago. Now it is gone."

Hanaud burst into a laugh.

"My friend Perrichet," he said ironically, "I will tell you the newspaper did not do you justice. You are more intelligent. The truth, my excellent friend, lies at the bottom of a well; but you would find it at the bottom of a pot of cold cream. Now let us go. For in this house, gentlemen, we have nothing more to do."

He passed out of the room. Perrichet stood aside, his face crimson, his attitude one of shame. He had been rebuked by the great M. Hanaud, and justly rebuked. He knew it now. He had wished to display his intelligence-yes, at all costs he must show how intelligent he was. And he had shown himself a fool. He should have kept silence about that pot of cream.


## CHAPTER VIII


## THE CAPTAIN OF THE SHIP

Hanaud walked away from the Villa Rose in the company of Wethermill and Ricardo.

"We will go and lunch," he said.

"Yes; come to my hotel," said Harry Wethermill. But Hanaud shook his head.

"No; come with me to the Villa des Fleurs," he replied. "We may learn something there; and in a case like this every minute is of importance. We have to be quick."

"I may come too?" cried Mr. Ricardo eagerly.

"By all means," replied Hanaud, with a smile of extreme courtesy. "Nothing could be more delicious than monsieur's suggestions"; and with that remark he walked on silently.

Mr. Ricardo was in a little doubt as to the exact significance of the words. But he was too excited to dwell long upon them. Distressed though he sought to be at his friend's grief, he could not but assume an air of importance. All the artist in him rose joyfully to the occasion. He looked upon himself from the outside. He fancied without the slightest justification that people were pointing him out. "That man has been present at the investigation at the Villa Rose," he seemed to hear people say. "What strange things he could tell us if he would!"

And suddenly, Mr. Ricardo began to reflect. What, after all, could he have told them?

And that question he turned over in his mind while he ate his luncheon. Hanaud wrote a letter between the courses. They were sitting at a corner table, and Hanaud was in the corner with his back to the wall. He moved his plate, too, over the letter as he wrote it. It would have been impossible for either of his guests to see what he had written, even if they had wished. Ricardo, indeed, did wish. He rather resented the secrecy with which the detective, under a show of openness, shrouded his thoughts and acts. Hanaud sent the waiter out to fetch an officer in plain clothes, who was in attendance at the door, and he handed the letter to this man. Then he turned with an apology to his guests.

"It is necessary that we should find out," he explained, "as soon as possible, the whole record of Mlle. Celie."

He lighted a cigar, and over the coffee he put a question to Ricardo.

"Now tell me what you make of the case. What M. Wethermill thinks-that is clear, is it not? Helene Vauquier is the guilty one. But you, M. Ricardo? What is your opinion?"

Ricardo took from his pocket-book a sheet of paper and from his pocket a pencil. He was intensely flattered by the request of Hanaud, and he proposed to do himself justice. "I will make a note here of what I think the salient features of the mystery"; and he proceeded to tabulate the points in the following way:

(1) Celia Harland made her entrance into Mme. Dauvray's household under very doubtful circumstances.

(2) By methods still more doubtful she acquired an extraordinary ascendency over Mme. Dauvray's mind.

(3) If proof were needed how complete that ascendency was, a glance at Celia Harland's wardrobe would suffice; for she wore the most expensive clothes.

(4) It was Celia Harland who arranged that Servettaz, the chauffeur, should be absent at Chambery on the Tuesday night-the night of the murder.

(5) It was Celia Harland who bought the cord with which Mme. Dauvray was strangled and Helene Vauquier bound.

(6) The footsteps outside the salon show that Celia Harland ran from the salon to the motor-car.

(7) Celia Harland pretended that there should be a seance on the Tuesday, but she dressed as though she had in view an appointment with a lover, instead of a spiritualistic seance.

(8) Celia Harland has disappeared.

These eight points are strongly suggestive of Celia Harland's complicity in the murder. But I have no clue which will enable me to answer the following questions:

(a) Who was the man who took part in the crime? (b) Who was the woman who came to the villa on the evening of the murder with Mme. Dauvray and Celia Harland?

(c) What actually happened in the salon? How was the murder committed?

(d) Is Helene Vauquier's story true?

(e) What did the torn-up scrap of writing mean? (Probably spirit writing in Celia Harland's hand.)

(f) Why has one cushion on the settee a small, fresh, brown stain, which is probably blood? Why is the other cushion torn?

Mr. Ricardo had a momentary thought of putting down yet another question. He was inclined to ask whether or no a pot of cold cream had disappeared from Celia Harland's bedroom; but he remembered that Hanaud had set no store upon that incident, and he refrained. Moreover, he had come to the end of his sheet of paper. He handed it across the table to Hanaud and leaned back in his chair, watching the detective with all the eagerness of a young author submitting his first effort to a critic.

Hanaud read it through slowly. At the end he nodded his head in approval.

"Now we will see what M. Wethermill has to say," he said, and he stretched out the paper towards Harry Wethermill, who throughout the luncheon had not said a word.

"No, no," cried Ricardo.

But Harry Wethermill already held the written sheet in his hand. He smiled rather wistfully at his friend.

"It is best that I should know just what you both think," he said, and in his turn he began to read the paper through. He read the first eight points, and then beat with his fist upon the table.

"No no," he cried; "it is not possible! I don't blame you, Ricardo. These are facts, and, as I said, I can face facts. But there will be an explanation-if only we can discover it."

He buried his face for a moment in his hands. Then he took up the paper again.

"As for the rest, Helene Vauquier lied," he cried violently, and he tossed the paper to Hanaud. "What do you make of it?"

Hanaud smiled and shook his head.

"Did you ever go for a voyage on a ship?" he asked.

"Yes; why?"

"Because every day at noon three officers take an observation to determine the ship's position-the captain, the first officer, and the second officer. Each writes his observation down, and the captain takes the three observations and compares them. If the first or second officer is out in his reckoning, the captain tells him so, but he does not show his own. For at times, no doubt, he is wrong too. So, gentlemen, I criticise your observations, but I do not show you mine."

He took up Ricardo's paper and read it through again.

"Yes," he said pleasantly. "But the two questions which are most important, which alone can lead us to the truth-how do they come to be omitted from your list, Mr. Ricardo?"

Hanaud put the question with his most serious air. But Ricardo was none the less sensible of the raillery behind the solemn manner. He flushed and made no answer.

"Still," continued Hanaud, "here are undoubtedly some questions. Let us consider them! Who was the man who took a part in the crime? Ah, if we only knew that, what a lot of trouble we should save ourselves! Who was the woman? What a good thing it would be to know that too! How clearly, after all, Mr. Ricardo puts his finger on the important points! What did actually happen in the salon?" And as he quoted that question the raillery died out of his voice. He leaned his elbows on the table and bent forward.

"What did actually happen in that little pretty room, just twelve hours ago?" he repeated. "When no sunlight blazed upon the lawn, and all the birds were still, and all the windows shuttered and the world dark, what happened? What dreadful things happened? We have not much to go upon. Let us formulate what we know. We start with this. The murder was not the work of a moment. It was planned with great care and cunning, and carried out to the letter of the plan. There must be no noise, no violence. On each side of the Villa Rose there are other villas; a few yards away the road runs past. A scream, a cry, the noise of a struggle-these sounds, or any one of them, might be fatal to success. Thus the crime was planned; and there WAS no scream, there WAS no struggle. Not a chair was broken, and only a chair upset. Yes, there were brains behind that murder. We know that. But what do we know of the plan? How far can we build it up? Let us see. First, there was an accomplice in the house-perhaps two."

"No!" cried Harry Wethermill.

Hanaud took no notice of the interruption.

"Secondly the woman came to the house with Mme. Dauvray and Mlle. Celie between nine and half-past nine. Thirdly, the man came afterwards, but before eleven, set open the gate, and was admitted into the salon, unperceived by Mme. Dauvray. That also we can safely assume. But what happened in the salon? Ah! There is the question." Then he shrugged his shoulders and said with the note of raillery once more in his voice:

"But why should we trouble our heads to puzzle out this mystery, since M. Ricardo knows?"

"I?" cried Ricardo in amazement.

"To be sure," replied Hanaud calmly. "For I look at another of your questions. 'WHAT DID THE TORN-UP SCRAP OF WRITING MEAN?' and you add: 'Probably spirit-writing.' Then there was a seance held last night in the little salon! Is that so?"

Harry Wethermill started. Mr. Ricardo was at a loss.

"I had not followed my suggestion to its conclusion," he admitted humbly.

"No," said Hanaud. "But I ask myself in sober earnest, 'Was there a seance held in the salon last night?' Did the tambourine rattle in the darkness on the wall?"

"But if Helene Vauquier's story is all untrue?" cried Wethermill, again in exasperation.

"Patience, my friend. Her story was not all untrue. I say there were brains behind this crime; yes, but brains, even the cleverest, would not have invented this queer, strange story of the seances and of Mme. de Montespan. That is truth. But yet, if there were a seance held, if the scrap of paper were spirit-writing in answer to some awkward question, why-and here I come to my first question, which M. Ricardo has omitted-why did Mlle. Celie dress herself with so much elegance last night? What Vauquier said is true. Her dress was not suited to a seance. A light-coloured, rustling frock, which would be visible in a dim light, or even in the dark, which would certainly be heard at every movement she made, however lightly she stepped, and a big hat-no no! I tell you, gentlemen, we shall not get to the bottom of this mystery until we know why Mlle. Celie dressed herself as she did last night."

"Yes," Ricardo admitted. "I overlooked that point." "Did she —" Hanaud broke off and bowed to Wethermill with a grace and a respect which condoned his words. "You must bear with me, my young friend, while I consider all these points. Did she expect to join that night a lover —a man with the brains to devise this crime? But if so-and here I come to the second question omitted from M. Ricardo's list-why, on the patch of grass outside the door of the salon, were the footsteps of the man and woman so carefully erased, and the footsteps of Mlle. Celie-those little footsteps so easily identified-left for all the world to see and recognise?"

Ricardo felt like a child in the presence of his schoolmaster. He was convicted of presumption. He had set down his questions with the belief that they covered the ground. And here were two of the utmost importance, not forgotten, but never even thought of.

"Did she go, before the murder, to join a lover? Or after it? At some time, you will remember, according to Vauquier's story, she must have run upstairs to fetch her coat. Was the murder committed during the interval when she was upstairs? Was the salon dark when she came down again? Did she run through it quickly, eagerly, noticing nothing amiss? And, indeed, how should she notice anything if the salon were dark, and Mme. Dauvray's body lay under the windows at the side?"

Ricardo leaned forward eagerly.

"That must be the truth," he cried; and Wethermill's voice broke hastily in:

"It is not the truth and I will tell you why. Celia Harland was to have married me this week."

There was so much pain and misery in his voice that Ricardo was moved as he had seldom been. Wethermill buried his face in his hands. Hanaud shook his head and gazed across the table at Ricardo with an expression which the latter was at no loss to understand. Lovers were impracticable people. But he-Hanaud-he knew the world. Women had fooled men before to-day.

Wethermill snatched his hands away from before his face.

"We talk theories," he cried desperately, "of what may have happened at the villa. But we are not by one inch nearer to the man and woman who committed the crime. It is for them we have to search."

"Yes; but except by asking ourselves questions, how shall we find them, M. Wethermill?" said Hanaud. "Take the man! We know nothing of him. He has left no trace. Look at this town of Aix, where people come and go like a crowd about the baccarat-table! He may be at Marseilles to-day. He may be in this very room where we are taking our luncheon. How shall we find him?"

Wethermill nodded his head in a despairing assent.

"I know. But it is so hard to sit still and do nothing," he cried.

"Yes, but we are not sitting still," said Hanaud; and Wethermill looked up with a sudden interest. "All the time that we have been lunching here the intelligent Perrichet has been making inquiries. Mme. Dauvray and Mlle. Celie left the Villa Rose at five, and returned on foot soon after nine with the strange woman. And there I see Perrichet himself waiting to be summoned."

Hanaud beckoned towards the sergent-de-ville.

"Perrichet will make an excellent detective," he said; "for he looks more bovine and foolish in plain clothes than he does in uniform."

Perrichet advanced in his mufti to the table.

"Speak, my friend," said Hanaud.

"I went to the shop of M. Corval. Mlle. Celie was quite alone when she bought the cord. But a few minutes later, in the Rue du Casino, she and Mme. Dauvray were seen together, walking slowly in the direction of the villa. No other woman was with them."

"That is a pity," said Hanaud quietly, and with a gesture he dismissed Perrichet.

"You see, we shall find out nothing-nothing," said Wethermill, with a groan.

"We must not yet lose heart, for we know a little more about the woman than we do about the man," said Hanaud consolingly.

"True," exclaimed Ricardo. "We have Helene Vauquier's description of her. We must advertise it."

Hanaud smiled.

"But that is a fine suggestion," he cried. "We must think over that," and he clapped his hand to his forehead with a gesture of self-reproach. "Why did not such a fine idea occur to me, fool that I am! However, we will call the head waiter."

The head waiter was sent for and appeared before them.

"You knew Mme. Dauvray?" Hanaud asked.

"Yes, monsieur-oh, the poor woman! And he flung up his hands.

"And you knew her young companion?"

"Oh yes, monsieur. They generally had their meals here. See, at that little table over there! I kept it for them. But monsieur knows well" —and the waiter looked towards Harry Wethermill —"for monsieur was often with them."

"Yes," said Hanaud. "Did Mme. Dauvray dine at that little table last night?"

"No, monsieur. She was not here last night."

"Nor Mlle. Celie?"

"No, monsieur! I do not think they were in the Villa des Fleurs at all."

"We know they were not," exclaimed Ricardo. "Wethermill and I were in the rooms and we did not see them."

"But perhaps you left early," objected Hanaud.

"No," said Ricardo. "It was just ten o'clock when we reached the Majestic."

"You reached your hotel at ten," Hanaud repeated. "Did you walk straight from here?"

"Yes."

"Then you left here about a quarter to ten. And we know that Mme. Dauvray was back at the villa soon after nine. Yes-they could not have been here last night," Hanaud agreed, and sat for a moment silent. Then he turned to the head waiter.

"Have you noticed any woman with Mme. Dauvray and her companion lately?"

"No, monsieur. I do not think so."

"Think! A woman, for instance, with red hair."

Harry Wethermill started forward. Mr. Ricardo stared at Hanaud in amazement. The waiter reflected.

"No, monsieur. I have seen no woman with red hair."

"Thank you," said Hanaud, and the waiter moved away.

"A woman with red hair!" cried Wethermill. "But Helene Vauquier described her. She was sallow; her eyes, her hair, were dark."

Hanaud turned with a smile to Harry Wethermill.

"Did Helene Vauquier, then, speak the truth?" he asked. "No; the woman who was in the salon last night, who returned home with Mme. Dauvray and Mlle. Celie, was not a woman with black hair and bright black eyes. Look!" And, fetching his pocket-book from his pocket, he unfolded a sheet of paper and showed them, lying upon its white surface a long red hair.

"I picked that up on the table-the round satinwood table in the salon. It was easy not to see it, but I did see it. Now, that is not Mlle. Celie's hair, which is fair; nor Mme. Dauvray's, which is dyed brown; nor Helene Vauquier's, which is black; nor the charwoman's, which, as I have taken the trouble to find out, is grey. It is therefore from the head of our unknown woman. And I will tell you more. This woman with the red hair-she is in Geneva."

A startled exclamation burst from Ricardo. Harry Wethermill sat slowly down. For the first time that day there had come some colour into his cheeks, a sparkle into his eye.

"But that is wonderful!" he cried. "How did you find that out?"

Hanaud leaned back in his chair and took a pull at his cigar. He was obviously pleased with Wethermill's admiration.

"Yes, how did you find it out?" Ricardo repeated.

Hanaud smiled.

"As to that," he said, "remember I am the captain of the ship, and I do not show you my observation." Ricardo was disappointed. Harry Wethermill, however, started to his feet.

"We must search Geneva, then," he cried. "It is there that we should be, not here drinking our coffee at the Villa des Fleurs."

Hanaud raised his hand.

"The search is not being overlooked. But Geneva is a big city. It is not easy to search Geneva and find, when we know nothing about the woman for whom we are searching, except that her hair is red, and that probably a young girl last night was with her. It is rather here, I think-in Aix-that we must keep our eyes wide open."

"Here!" cried Wethermill in exasperation. He stared at Hanaud as though he were mad.

"Yes, here; at the post office-at the telephone exchange. Suppose that the man is in Aix, as he may well be; some time he will wish to send a letter, or a telegram, or a message over the telephone. That, I tell you, is our chance. But here is news for us."

Hanaud pointed to a messenger who was walking towards them. The man handed Hanaud an envelope.

"From M. le Commissaire," he said; and he saluted and retired. "From M. le Commissaire?" cried Ricardo excitedly.

But before Hanaud could open the envelope Harry Wethermill laid a hand upon his sleeve.

"Before we pass to something new, M. Hanaud," he said, "I should be very glad if you would tell me what made you shiver in the salon this morning. It has distressed me ever since. What was it that those two cushions had to tell you?"

There was a note of anguish in his voice difficult to resist. But Hanaud resisted it. He shook his head.

"Again," he said gravely, "I am to remind you that I am captain of the ship and do not show my observation."

He tore open the envelope and sprang up from his seat.

"Mme. Dauvray's motor-car has been found," he cried. "Let us go!"

Hanaud called for the bill and paid it. The three men left the Villa des Fleurs together.


## CHAPTER IX


## MME. DAUVRAY'S MOTOR-CAR

They got into a cab outside the door. Perrichet mounted the box, and the cab was driven along the upward-winding road past the Hotel Bernascon. A hundred yards beyond the hotel the cab stopped opposite to a villa. A hedge separated the garden of the villa from the road, and above the hedge rose a board with the words "To Let" upon it. At the gate a gendarme was standing, and just within the gate Ricardo saw Louis Besnard, the Commissaire, and Servettaz, Mme. Dauvray's chauffeur.

"It is here," said Besnard, as the party descended from the cab, "in the coach-house of this empty villa."

"Here?" cried Ricardo in amazement.

The discovery upset all his theories. He had expected to hear that it had been found fifty leagues away; but here, within a couple of miles of the Villa Rose itself-the idea seemed absurd! Why take it away at all-unless it was taken away as a blind? That supposition found its way into Ricardo's mind, and gathered strength as he thought upon it; for Hanaud had seemed to lean to the belief that one of the murderers might be still in Aix. Indeed, a glance at him showed that he was not discomposed by their discovery.

"When was it found?" Hanaud asked.

"This morning. A gardener comes to the villa on two days a week to keep the grounds in order. Fortunately Wednesday is one of his days. Fortunately, too, there was rain yesterday evening. He noticed the tracks of the wheels which you can see on the gravel, and since the villa is empty he was surprised. He found the coach-house door forced and the motor-car inside it. When he went to his luncheon he brought the news of his discovery to the depot."

The party followed the Commissaire along the drive to the coach-house.

"We will have the car brought out," said Hanaud to Servettaz.

It was a big and powerful machine with a limousine body, luxuriously fitted and cushioned in the shade of light grey. The outside panels of the car were painted a dark grey. The car had hardly been brought out into the sunlight before a cry of stupefaction burst from the lips of Perrichet.

"Oh!" he cried, in utter abasement. "I shall never forgive myself-never, never!"

"Why?" Hanaud asked, turning sharply as he spoke.

Perrichet was standing with his round eyes staring and his mouth agape.

"Because, monsieur, I saw that car-at four o'clock this morning-at the corner of the road-not fifty yards from the Villa Rose."

"What!" cried Ricardo.

"You saw it!" exclaimed Wethermill.

Upon their faces was reflected now the stupefaction of Perrichet.

"But you must have made a mistake," said the Commissaire.

"No, no, monsieur," Perrichet insisted. "It was that car. It was that number. It was just after daylight. I was standing outside the gate of the villa on duty where M. le Commissaire had placed me. The car appeared at the corner and slackened speed. It seemed to me that it was going to turn into the road and come down past me. But instead the driver, as if he were now sure of his way, put the car at its top speed and went on into Aix."

"Was any one inside the car?" asked Hanaud.

"No, monsieur; it was empty."

"But you saw the driver!" exclaimed Wethermill.

"Yes; what was he like?" cried the Commissaire.

Perrichet shook his head mournfully.

"He wore a talc mask over the upper part of his face, and had a little black moustache, and was dressed in a heavy great-coat of blue with a white collar."

"That is my coat, monsieur," said Servettaz, and as he spoke he lifted it up from the chauffeur's seat. "It is Mme. Dauvray's livery."

Harry Wethermill groaned aloud.

"We have lost him. He was within our grasp-he, the murderer! —and he was allowed to go!"

Perrichet's grief was pitiable.

"Monsieur," he pleaded, "a car slackens its speed and goes on again-it is not so unusual a thing. I did not know the number of Mme. Dauvray's car. I did not even know that it had disappeared"; and suddenly tears of mortification filled his eyes. "But why do I make these excuses?" he cried. "It is better, M. Hanaud, that I go back to my uniform and stand at the street corner. I am as foolish as I look."

"Nonsense, my friend," said Hanaud, clapping the disconsolate man upon the shoulder. "You remembered the car and its number. That is something-and perhaps a great deal," he added gravely. "As for the talc mask and the black moustache, that is not much to help us, it is true." He looked at Ricardo's crestfallen face and smiled. "We might arrest our good friend M. Ricardo upon that evidence, but no one else that I know."

Hanaud laughed immoderately at his joke. He alone seemed to feel no disappointment at Perrichet's oversight. Ricardo was a little touchy on the subject of his personal appearance, and bridled visibly. Hanaud turned towards Servettaz.

"Now," he said, "you know how much petrol was taken from the garage?"

"Yes, monsieur."

"Can you tell me, by the amount which has been used, how far that car was driven last night?" Hanaud asked.

Servettaz examined the tank.

"A long way, monsieur. From a hundred and thirty to a hundred and fifty kilometres, I should say."

"Yes, just about that distance, I should say," cried Hanaud.

His eyes brightened, and a smile, a rather fierce smile, came to his lips. He opened the door, and examined with a minute scrutiny the floor of the carriage, and as he looked, the smile faded from his face. Perplexity returned to it. He took the cushions, looked them over and shook them out.

"I see no sign —" he began, and then he uttered a little shrill cry of satisfaction. From the crack of the door by the hinge he picked off a tiny piece of pale green stuff, which he spread out upon the back of his hand.

"Tell me, what is this?" he said to Ricardo.

"It is a green fabric," said Ricardo very wisely.

"It is green chiffon," said Hanaud. "And the frock in which Mlle. Celie went away was of green chiffon over satin. Yes, Mlle. Celie travelled in this car."

He hurried to the driver's seat. Upon the floor there was some dark mould. Hanaud cleaned it off with his knife and held some of it in the palm of his hand. He turned to Servettaz.

"You drove the car on Tuesday morning before you went to Chambery?"

"Yes, monsieur."

"Where did you take up Mme. Dauvray and Mlle. Celie?"

"At the front door of the Villa Rose."

"Did you get down from the seat at all?"

"No, monsieur; not after I left the garage."

Hanaud returned to his companions.

"See!" And he opened his hand. "This is black soil-moist from last night's rain-soil like the soil in front of Mme. Dauvray's salon. Look, here is even a blade or two of the grass"; and he turned the mould over in the palm of his hand. Then he took an empty envelope from his pocket and poured the soil into it and gummed the flap down. He stood and frowned at the motor-car.

"Listen," he said, "how I am puzzled! There was a man last night at the Villa Rose. There were a man's blurred footmarks in the mould before the glass door. That man drove madame's car for a hundred and fifty kilometres, and he leaves the mould which clung to his boots upon the floor of his seat. Mlle. Celie and another woman drove away inside the car. Mlle. Celie leaves a fragment of the chiffon tunic of her frock which caught in the hinge. But Mlle. Celie made much clearer impressions in the mould than the man. Yet on the floor of the carriage there is no trace of her shoes. Again I say there is something here which I do not understand." And he spread out his hands with an impulsive gesture of despair.

"It looks as if they had been careful and he careless," said Mr. Ricardo, with the air of a man solving a very difficult problem.

"What a mind!" cried Hanaud, now clasping his hands together in admiration. "How quick and how profound!"

There was at times something elephantinely elfish in M. Hanaud's demeanour, which left Mr. Ricardo at a loss. But he had come to notice that these undignified manifestations usually took place when Hanaud had reached a definite opinion upon some point which had perplexed him.

"Yet there is perhaps, another explanation," Hanaud continued. "For observe, M. Ricardo. We have other evidence to show that the careless one was Mlle. Celie. It was she who left her footsteps so plainly visible upon the grass, not the man. However, we will go back to M. Wethermill's room at the Hotel Majestic and talk this matter over. We know something now. Yes, we know-what do we know, monsieur?" he asked, suddenly turning with a smile to Ricardo, and, as Ricardo paused: "Think it over while we walk down to M. Wethermill's apartment in the Hotel Majestic."

"We know that the murderer has escaped," replied Ricardo hotly.

"The murderer is not now the most important object of our search. He is very likely at Marseilles by now. We shall lay our hands on him, never fear," replied Hanaud, with a superb gesture of disdain. "But it was thoughtful of you to remind me of him. I might so easily have clean forgotten him, and then indeed my reputation would have suffered an eclipse." He made a low, ironical bow to Ricardo and walked quickly down the road.

"For a cumbersome man he is extraordinarily active," said Mr. Ricardo to Harry Wethermill, trying to laugh, without much success. "A heavy, clever, middle-aged man, liable to become a little gutter-boy at a moment's notice."

Thus he described the great detective, and the description is quoted. For it was Ricardo's best effort in the whole of this business.

The three men went straight to Harry Wethermill's apartment, which consisted of a sitting-room and a bedroom on the first floor. A balcony ran along outside. Hanaud stepped out on to it, looked about him, and returned.

"It is as well to know that we cannot be overheard," he said.

Harry Wethermill meanwhile had thrown himself into a chair. The mask he had worn had slipped from its fastenings for a moment. There was a look of infinite suffering upon his face. It was the face of a man tortured by misery to the snapping-point.

Hanaud, on the other hand, was particularly alert. The discovery of the motor-car had raised his spirits. He sat at the table.

"I will tell you what we have learnt," he said, "and it is of importance. The three of them-the man, the woman with the red hair, and Mlle. Celie-all drove yesterday night to Geneva. That is only one thing we have learnt."

"Then you still cling to Geneva?" said Ricardo.

"More than ever," said Hanaud.

He turned in his chair towards Wethermill.

"Ah, my poor friend!" he said, when he saw the young man's distress.

Harry Wethermill sprang up with a gesture as though to sweep the need of sympathy away. "What can I do for you?" he asked.

"You have a road map, perhaps?" said Hanaud.

"Yes," said Wethermill, "mine is here. There it is"; and crossing the room he brought it from a sidetable and placed it in front of Hanaud.

Hanaud took a pencil from his pocket.

"One hundred and fifty kilometres was about the distance which the car had travelled. Measure the distances here, and you will see that Geneva is the likely place. It is a good city to hide in. Moreover the car appears at the corner at daylight. How does it appear there? What road is it which comes out at that corner? The road from Geneva. I am not sorry that it is Geneva, for the Chef de la Surete is a friend of mine."

"And what else do we know?" asked Ricardo.

"This," said Hanaud. He paused impressively. "Bring up your chair to the table, M. Wethermill, and consider whether I am right or wrong"; and he waited until Harry Wethermill had obeyed. Then he laughed in a friendly way at himself.

"I cannot help it," he said; "I have an eye for dramatic effects. I must prepare for them when I know they are coming. And one, I tell you, is coming now."

He shook his finger at his companions. Ricardo shifted and shuffled in his chair. Harry Wethermill kept his eyes fixed on Hanaud's face, but he was quiet, as he had been throughout the long inquiry.

Hanaud lit a cigarette and took his time.

"What I think is this. The man who drove the car into Geneva drove it back, because-he meant to leave it again in the garage of the Villa Rose."

"Good heavens!" cried Ricardo, flinging himself back. The theory so calmly enunciated took his breath away.

"Would he have dared?" asked Harry Wethermill.

Hanaud leaned across and tapped his fingers on the table to emphasise his answer.

"All through this crime there are two things visible-brains and daring; clever brains and extraordinary daring. Would he have dared? He dared to be at the corner close to the Villa Rose at daylight. Why else should he have returned except to put back the car? Consider! The petrol is taken from tins which Servettaz might never have touched for a fortnight, and by that time he might, as he said, have forgotten whether he had not used them himself. I had this possibility in my mind when I put the questions to Servettaz about the petrol which the Commissaire thought so stupid. The utmost care is taken that there shall be no mould left on the floor of the carriage. The scrap of chiffon was torn off, no doubt, when the women finally left the car, and therefore not noticed, or that, too, would have been removed. That the exterior of the car was dirty betrayed nothing, for Servettaz had left it uncleaned."

Hanaud leaned back and, step by step, related the journey of the car.

"The man leaves the gate open; he drives into Geneva the two women, who are careful that their shoes shall leave no marks upon the floor. At Geneva they get out. The man returns. If he can only leave the car in the garage he covers all traces of the course he and his friends have taken. No one would suspect that the car had ever left the garage. At the corner of the road, just as he is turning down to the villa, he sees a sergent-de-ville at the gate. He knows that the murder is discovered. He puts on full speed and goes straight out of the town. What is he to do? He is driving a car for which the police in an hour or two, if not now already, will be surely watching. He is driving it in broad daylight. He must get rid of it, and at once, before people are about to see it, and to see him in it. Imagine his feelings! It is almost enough to make one pity him. Here he is in a car which convicts him as a murderer, and he has nowhere to leave it. He drives through Aix. Then on the outskirts of the town he finds an empty villa. He drives in at the gate, forces the door of the coach-house, and leaves his car there. Now, observe! It is no longer any use for him to pretend that he and his friends did not disappear in that car. The murder is already discovered, and with the murder the disappearance of the car. So he no longer troubles his head about it. He does not remove the traces of mould from the place where his feet rested, which otherwise, no doubt, he would have done. It no longer matters. He has to run to earth now before he is seen. That is all his business. And so the state of the car is explained. It was a bold step to bring that car back-yes, a bold and desperate step. But a clever one. For, if it had succeeded, we should have known nothing of their movements-oh, but nothing-nothing. Ah! I tell you this is no ordinary blundering affair. They are clever people who devised this crime-clever, and of an audacity which is surprising."

Then Hanaud lit another cigarette.

Mr. Ricardo, on the other hand, could hardly continue to smoke for excitement.

"I cannot understand your calmness," he exclaimed.

"No?" said Hanaud. "Yet it is so obvious. You are the amateur, I am the professional-that is all."

He looked at his watch and rose to his feet.

"I must go" he said and as he turned towards the door a cry sprang from Mr. Ricardo's lips "It is true. I am the amateur. Yet I have knowledge, Monsieur Hanaud which the professional would do well to obtain."

Hanaud turned a guarded face towards Ricardo. There was no longer any raillery in his manner. He spoke slowly, coldly.

"Let me have it then!"

"I have driven in my motor-car from Geneva to Aix," Ricardo cried excitedly. "A bridge crosses a ravine high up amongst the mountains. At the bridge there is a Custom House. There-at the Pont de la Caille-your car is stopped. It is searched. You must sign your name in a book. And there is no way round. You would find sure and certain proof whether or no Madame Dauvray's car travelled last night to Geneva. Not so many travellers pass along that road at night. You would find certain proof too of how many people were in the car. For they search carefully at the Pont de la Caille."

A dark flush overspread Hanaud's face. Ricardo was in the seventh Heaven. He had at last contributed something to the history of this crime. He had repaired an omission. He had supplied knowledge to the omniscient. Wethermill looked up drearily like one who has lost heart.

"Yes, you must not neglect that clue," he said.

Hanaud replied testily:

"It is not a clue. M. Ricardo tells that he travelled from Geneva into France and that his car was searched. Well, we know already that the officers are particular at the Custom Houses of France. But travelling from France into Switzerland is a very different affair. In Switzerland, hardly a glance, hardly a word." That was true. M. Ricardo crestfallen recognized the truth. But his spirits rose again at once. "But the car came back from Geneva into France!" he cried.

"Yes, but when the car came back, the man was alone in it," Hanaud answered. "I have more important things to attend to. For instance I must know whether by any chance they have caught our man at Marseilles." He laid his hand on Wethermill's shoulder. "And you, my friend, I should counsel you to get some sleep. We may need all our strength to-morrow. I hope so." He was speaking very bravely. "Yes, I hope so."

Wethermill nodded.

"I shall try," he said.

"That's better," said Hanaud cheerfully. "You will both stay here this evening; for if I have news, I can then ring you up."

Both men agreed, and Hanaud went away. He left Mr. Ricardo profoundly disturbed. "That man will take advice from no one," he declared. "His vanity is colossal. It is true they are not particular at the Swiss Frontier. Still the car would have to stop there. At the Custom House they would know something. Hanaud ought to make inquiries." But neither Ricardo nor Harry Wethermill heard a word more from Hanaud that night.


## CHAPTER X


## NEWS FROM GENEVA

The next morning, however, before Mr. Ricardo was out of his bed, M. Hanaud was announced. He came stepping gaily into the room, more elephantinely elfish than ever.

"Send your valet away," he said. And as soon as they were alone he produced a newspaper, which he flourished in Mr. Ricardo's face and then dropped into his hands.

Ricardo saw staring him in the face a full description of Celia Harland, of her appearance and her dress, of everything except her name, coupled with an intimation that a reward of four thousand francs would be paid to any one who could give information leading to the discovery of her whereabouts to Mr. Ricardo, the Hotel Majestic, Aix-les-Bains!

Mr. Ricardo sat up in his bed with a sense of outrage.

"You have done this?" he asked.

"Yes."

"Why have you done it?" Mr. Ricardo cried.

Hanaud advanced to the bed mysteriously on the tips of his toes.

"I will tell you," he said, in his most confidential tones. "Only it must remain a secret between you and me. I did it-because I have a sense of humour."

"I hate publicity," said Mr. Ricardo acidly.

"On the other hand you have four thousand francs," protested the detective. "Besides, what else should I do? If I name myself, the very people we are seeking to catch-who, you may be sure, will be the first to read this advertisement-will know that I, the great, the incomparable Hanaud, am after them; and I do not want them to know that. Besides" —and he spoke now in a gentle and most serious voice —"why should we make life more difficult for Mlle. Celie by telling the world that the police want her? It will be time enough for that when she appears before the Juge d'Instruction."

Mr. Ricardo grumbled inarticulately, and read through the advertisement again.

"Besides, your description is incomplete," he said. "There is no mention of the diamond earrings which Celia Harland was wearing when she went away."

"Ah! so you noticed that!" exclaimed Hanaud. "A little more experience and I should be looking very closely to my laurels. But as for the earrings —I will tell you. Mlle. Celie was not wearing them when she went away from the Villa Rose."

"But-but," stammered Ricardo, "the case upon the dressing-room table was empty."

"Still, she was not wearing them, I know," said Hanaud decisively.

"How do you know?" cried Ricardo, gazing at Hanaud with awe in his eyes. "How could you know?"

"Because" —and Hanaud struck a majestic attitude, like a king in a play —"because I am the captain of the ship."

Upon that Mr. Ricardo suffered a return of his ill-humour.

"I do not like to be trifled with," he remarked, with as much dignity as his ruffled hair and the bed-clothes allowed him. He looked sternly at the newspaper, turning it over, and then he uttered a cry of surprise.

"But this is yesterday's paper!" he said.

"Yesterday evening's paper," Hanaud corrected.

"Printed at Geneva!"

"Printed, and published and sold at Geneva," said Hanaud.

"When did you send the advertisement in, then?"

"I wrote a letter while we were taking our luncheon," Hanaud explained. "The letter was to Besnard, asking him to telegraph the advertisement at once."

"But you never said a word about it to us," Ricardo grumbled.

"No. And was I not wise?" said Hanaud, with complacency. "For you would have forbidden me to use your name."

"Oh, I don't go so far as that," said Ricardo reluctantly. His indignation was rapidly evaporating. For there was growing up in his mind a pleasant perception that the advertisement placed him in the limelight.

He rose from his bed.

"You will make yourself comfortable in the sitting-room while I have my bath."

"I will, indeed," replied Hanaud cheerily. "I have already ordered my morning chocolate. I have hopes that you may have a telegram very soon. This paper was cried last night through the streets of Geneva."

Ricardo dressed for once in a way with some approach to ordinary celerity, and joined Hanaud.

"Has nothing come?" he asked.

"No. This chocolate is very good; it is better than that which I get in my hotel."

"Good heavens!" cried Ricardo, who was fairly twittering with excitement. "You sit there talking about chocolate while my cup shakes in my fingers."

"Again I must remind you that you are the amateur, I the professional, my friend."

As the morning drew on, however, Hanaud's professional quietude deserted him. He began to start at the sound of footsteps in the corridor, to glance every other moment from the window, to eat his cigarettes rather than to smoke them. At eleven o'clock Ricardo's valet brought a telegram into the room. Ricardo seized it.

"Calmly, my friend," said Hanaud.

With trembling fingers Ricardo tore it open. He jumped in his chair. Speechless, he handed the telegram to Hanaud. It had been sent from Geneva, and it ran thus:

"Expect me soon after three. —MARTHE GOBIN."

Hanaud nodded his head.

"I told you I had hopes." All his levity had gone in an instant from his manner. He spoke very quietly.

"I had better send for Wethermill?" asked Ricardo.

Hanaud shrugged his shoulders.

"As you like. But why raise hopes in that poor man's breast which an hour or two may dash for ever to the ground? Consider! Marthe Gobin has something to tell us. Think over those eight points of evidence which you drew up yesterday in the Villa des Fleurs, and say whether what she has to tell us is more likely to prove Mlle. Celie's innocence than her guilt. Think well, for I will be guided by you, M. Ricardo," said Hanaud solemnly. "If you think it better that your friend should live in torture until Marthe Gobin comes, and then perhaps suffer worse torture from the news she brings, be it so. You shall decide. If, on the other hand, you think it will be best to leave M. Wethermill in peace until we know her story, be it so. You shall decide."

Ricardo moved uneasily. The solemnity of Hanaud's manner impressed him. He had no wish to take the responsibility of the decision upon himself. But Hanaud sat with his eyes strangely fixed upon Ricardo, waiting for his answer.

"Well," said Ricardo, at length, "good news will be none the worse for waiting a few hours. Bad news will be a little the better."

"Yes," said Hanaud; "so I thought you would decide." He took up a Continental Bradshaw from a bookshelf in the room. "From Geneva she will come through Culoz. Let us see!" He turned over the pages. "There is a train from Culoz which reaches Aix at seven minutes past three. It is by that train she will come. You have a motor-car?"

"Yes."

"Very well. Will you pick me up in it at three at my hotel? We will drive down to the station and see the arrivals by that train. It may help us to get some idea of the person with whom we have to deal. That is always an advantage. Now I will leave you, for I have much to do. But I will look in upon M. Wethermill as I go down and tell him that there is as yet no news."

He took up his hat and stick, and stood for a moment staring out of the window. Then he roused himself from his reverie with a start.

"You look out upon Mont Revard, I see. I think M. Wethermill's view over the garden and the town is the better one," he said, and went out of the room.

At three o'clock Ricardo called in his car, which was an open car of high power, at Hanaud's hotel, and the two men went to the station. They waited outside the exit while the passengers gave up their tickets. Amongst them a middle-aged, short woman, of a plethoric tendency, attracted their notice. She was neatly but shabbily dressed in black; her gloves were darned, and she was obviously in a hurry. As she came out she asked a commissionaire:

"How far is it to the Hotel Majestic?"

The man told her the hotel was at the very top of the town, and the way was steep.

"But madame can go up in the omnibus of the hotel," he suggested.

Madame, however, was in too much of a hurry. The omnibus would have to wait for luggage. She hailed a closed cab and drove off inside it.

"Now, if we go back in the car, we shall be all ready for her when she arrives," said Hanaud.

They passed the cab, indeed, a few yards up the steep hill which leads from the station. The cab was moving at a walk.

"She looks honest," said Hanaud, with a sigh of relief. "She is some good bourgeoise anxious to earn four thousand francs."

They reached the hotel in a few minutes.

"We may need your car again the moment Marthe Gobin has gone," said Hanaud.

"It shall wait here," said Ricardo.

"No," said Hanaud; "let it wait in the little street at the back of my hotel. It will not be so noticeable there. You have petrol for a long journey?"

Ricardo gave the order quietly to his chauffeur, and followed Hanaud into the hotel. Through a glass window they could see Wethermill smoking a cigar over his coffee.

"He looks as if he had not slept," said Ricardo.

Hanaud nodded sympathetically, and beckoned Ricardo past the window.

"But we are nearing the end. These two days have been for him days of great trouble; one can see that very clearly. And he has done nothing to embarrass us. Men in distress are apt to be a nuisance. I am grateful to M. Wethermill. But we are nearing the end. Who knows? Within an hour or two we may have news for him."

He spoke with great feeling, and the two men ascended the stairs to Ricardo's rooms. For the second time that day Hanaud's professional calm deserted him. The window overlooked the main entrance to the hotel. Hanaud arranged the room, and, even while he arranged it, ran every other second and leaned from the window to watch for the coming of the cab.

"Put the bank-notes upon the table," he said hurriedly. "They will persuade her to tell us all that she has to tell. Yes, that will do. She is not in sight yet? No."

"She could not be. It is a long way from the station," said Ricardo, "and the whole distance is uphill."

"Yes, that is true," Hanaud replied. "We will not embarrass her by sitting round the table like a tribunal. You will sit in that arm-chair."

Ricardo took his seat, crossed his knees, and joined the tips of his fingers.

"So! not too judicial!" said Hanaud; "I will sit here at the table. Whatever you do, do not frighten her." Hanaud sat down in the chair which he had placed for himself. "Marthe Gobin shall sit opposite, with the light upon her face. So!" And, springing up, he arranged a chair for her. "Whatever you do, do not frighten her," he repeated. "I am nervous. So much depends upon this interview." And in a second he was back at the window.

Ricardo did not move. He arranged in his mind the interrogatory which was to take place. He was to conduct it. He was the master of the situation. All the limelight was to be his. Startling facts would come to light elicited by his deft questions. Hanaud need not fear. He would not frighten her. He would be gentle, he would be cunning. Softly and delicately he would turn this good woman inside out, like a glove. Every artistic fibre in his body vibrated to the dramatic situation.

Suddenly Hanaud leaned out of the window.

"It comes! it comes!" he said in a quick, feverish whisper. "I can see the cab between the shrubs of the drive."

"Let it come!" said Mr. Ricardo superbly.

Even as he sat he could hear the grating of wheels upon the drive. He saw Hanaud lean farther from the window and stamp impatiently upon the floor.

"There it is at the door," he said; and for a few seconds he spoke no more. He stood looking downwards, craning his head, with his back towards Ricardo.

Then, with a wild and startled cry, he staggered back into the room. His face was white as wax, his eyes full of horror, his mouth open.

"What is the matter?" exclaimed Ricardo, springing to his feet.

"They are lifting her out! She doesn't move! They are lifting her out!"

For a moment he stared into Ricardo's face-paralysed by fear. Then he sprang down the stairs. Ricardo followed him.

There was confusion in the corridor. Men were running, voices were crying questions. As they passed the window they saw Wethermill start up, aroused from his lethargy. They knew the truth before they reached the entrance of the hotel. A cab had driven up to the door from the station; in the cab was an unknown woman stabbed to the heart.

"She should have come by the omnibus," Hanaud repeated and repeated stupidly. For the moment he was off his balance.

# CHAPTER XI

## THE UNOPENED LETTER

The hall of the hotel had been cleared of people. At the entrance from the corridor a porter barred the way.

"No one can pass," said he.

"I think that I can," said Hanaud, and he produced his card. "From the Sureté at Paris."

He was allowed to enter, with Ricardo at his heels. On the ground lay Marthe Gobin; the manager of the hotel stood at her side; a doctor was on his knees. Hanaud gave his card to the manager.

"You have sent word to the police?"

"Yes," said the manager.

"And the wound?" asked Hanaud, kneeling on the ground beside the doctor. It was a very small wound, round and neat and clean, and there was very little blood. "It was made by a bullet," said Hanaud —"some tiny bullet from an air-pistol."

"No," answered the doctor.

"No knife made it," Hanaud asserted.

"That is true," said the doctor. "Look!" and he took up from the floor by his knee the weapon which had caused Marthe Gobin's death. It was nothing but an ordinary skewer with a ring at one end and a sharp point at the other, and a piece of common white firewood for a handle. The wood had been split, the ring inserted and spliced in position with strong twine. It was a rough enough weapon, but an effective one. The proof of its effectiveness lay stretched upon the floor beside them.

Hanaud gave it to the manager of the hotel.

"You must be very careful of this, and give it as it is to the police."

Then he bent once more over Marthe Gobin.

"Did she suffer?" he asked in a low voice.

"No; death must have been instantaneous," said the doctor.

"I am glad of that," said Hanaud, as he rose again to his feet.

In the doorway the driver of the cab was standing.

"What has he to say?" Hanaud asked.

The man stepped forward instantly. He was an old, red-faced, stout man, with a shiny white tall hat, like a thousand drivers of cabs.

"What have I to say, monsieur?" he grumbled in a husky voice. "I take up the poor woman at the station and I drive her where she bids me, and I find her dead, and my day is lost. Who will pay my fare, monsieur?"

"I will," said Hanaud. "There it is," and he handed the man a five-franc piece. "Now, answer me! Do you tell me that this woman was murdered in your cab and that you knew nothing about it?"

"But what should I know? I take her up at the station, and all the way up the hill her head is every moment out of the window, crying, 'Faster, faster!' Oh, the good woman was in a hurry! But for me I take no notice. The more she shouts, the less I hear; I bury my head between my shoulders, and I look ahead of me and I take no notice. One cannot expect cab-horses to run up these hills; it is not reasonable."

"So you went at a walk," said Hanaud. He beckoned to Ricardo, and said to the manager: "M. Besnard will, no doubt, be here in a few minutes, and he will send for the Juge d'Instruction. There is nothing that we can do."

He went back to Ricardo's sitting-room and flung himself into a chair. He had been calm enough downstairs in the presence of the doctor and the body of the victim. Now, with only Ricardo for a witness, he gave way to distress.

"It is terrible," he said. "The poor woman! It was I who brought her to Aix. It was through my carelessness. But who would have thought —?" He snatched his hands from his face and stood up. "I should have thought," he said solemnly. "Extraordinary daring-that was one of the qualities of my criminal. I knew it, and I disregarded it. Now we have a second crime."

"The skewer may lead you to the criminal," said Mr. Ricardo.

"The skewer!" cried Hanaud. "How will that help us? A knife, yes-perhaps. But a skewer!"

"At the shops-there will not be so many in Aix at which you can buy skewers-they may remember to whom they sold one within the last day or so."

"How do we know it was bought in the last day or so?" cried Hanaud scornfully. "We have not to do with a man who walks into a shop and buys a single skewer to commit a murder with, and so hands himself over to the police. How often must I say it!"

The violence of his contempt nettled Ricardo.

"If the murderer did not buy it, how did he obtain it?" he asked obstinately.

"Oh, my friend, could he not have stolen it? From this or from any hotel in Aix? Would the loss of a skewer be noticed, do you think? How many people in Aix to-day have had rognons a la brochette for their luncheon! Besides, it is not merely the death of this poor woman which troubles me. We have lost the evidence which she was going to bring to us. She had something to tell us about Celie Harland which now we shall never hear. We have to begin all over again, and I tell you we have not the time to begin all over again. No, we have not the time. Time will be lost, and we have no time to lose." He buried his face again in his hands and groaned aloud. His grief was so violent and so sincere that Ricardo, shocked as he was by the murder of Marthe Gobin, set himself to console him.

"But you could not have foreseen that at three o'clock in the afternoon at Aix —"

Hanaud brushed the excuse aside.

"It is no extenuation. I OUGHT to have foreseen. Oh, but I will have no pity now," he cried, and as he ended the words abruptly his face changed. He lifted a trembling forefinger and pointed. There came a sudden look of life into his dull and despairing eyes.

He was pointing to a side-table on which were piled Mr. Ricardo's letters.

"You have not opened them this morning?" he asked.

"No. You came while I was still in bed. I have not thought of them till now."

Hanaud crossed to the table, and, looking down at the letters, uttered a cry.

"There's one, the big envelope," he said, his voice shaking like his hand. "It has a Swiss stamp."

He swallowed to moisten his throat. Ricardo sprang across the room and tore open the envelope. There was a long letter enclosed in a handwriting unknown to him. He read aloud the first lines of the letter:

"I write what I saw and post it to-night, so that no one may be before me with the news. I will come over to-morrow for the money."

A low exclamation from Hanaud interrupted the words.

"The signature! Quick!"

Ricardo turned to the end of the letter.

"Marthe Gobin."

"She speaks, then! After all she speaks!" Hanaud whispered in a voice of awe. He ran to the door of the room, opened it suddenly, and, shutting it again, locked it. "Quick! We cannot bring that poor woman back to life; but we may still —" He did not finish his sentence. He took the letter unceremoniously from Ricardo's hand and seated himself at the table. Over his shoulder Mr. Ricardo, too, read Marthe Gobin's letter.

It was just the sort of letter, which in Ricardo's view, Marthe Gobin would have written —a long, straggling letter which never kept to the point, which exasperated them one moment by its folly and fired them to excitement the next.

It was dated from a small suburb of Geneva, on the western side of the lake, and it ran as follows:

"The suburb is but a street close to the lake-side, and a tram runs into the city. It is quite respectable, you understand, monsieur, with a hotel at the end of it, and really some very good houses. But I do not wish to deceive you about the social position of myself or my husband. Our house is on the wrong side of the street-definitely-yes. It is a small house, and we do not see the water from any of the windows because of the better houses opposite. M. Gobin, my husband, who was a clerk in one of the great banks in Geneva, broke down in health in the spring, and for the last three months has been compelled to keep indoors. Of course, money has not been plentiful, and I could not afford a nurse. Consequently I myself have been compelled to nurse him. Monsieur, if you were a woman, you would know what men are when they are ill-how fretful, how difficult. There is not much distraction for the woman who nurses them. So, as I am in the house most of the day, I find what amusement I can in watching the doings of my neighbours. You will not blame me.

"A month ago the house almost directly opposite to us was taken furnished for the summer by a Mme. Rossignol. She is a widow, but during the last fortnight a young gentleman has come several times in the afternoon to see her, and it is said in the street that he is going to marry her. But I cannot believe it myself. Monsieur is a young man of perhaps thirty, with smooth, black hair. He wears a moustache, a little black moustache, and is altogether captivating. Mme. Rossignol is five or six years older, I should think —a tall woman, with red hair and a bold sort of coarse beauty. I was not attracted by her. She seemed not quite of the same world as that charming monsieur who was said to be going to marry her. No; I was not attracted by Adele Rossignol."

And when he had come to that point Hanaud looked up with a start.

"So the name was Adele," he whispered.

"Yes," said Ricardo. "Helene Vauquier spoke the truth."

Hanaud nodded with a queer smile upon his lips.

"Yes, there she spoke the truth. I thought she did."

"But she said Adele's hair was black," interposed Mr. Ricardo.

"Yes, there she didn't," said Hanaud drily, and his eyes dropped again to the paper.

"I knew her name was Adele, for often I have heard her servant calling her so, and without any 'Madame' in front of the name. That is strange, is it not, to hear an elderly servant-woman calling after her mistress, 'Adele,' just simple 'Adele'? It was that which made me think monsieur and madame were not of the same world. But I do not believe that they are going to be married. I have an instinct about it. Of course, one never knows with what extraordinary women the nicest men will fall in love. So that after all these two may get married. But if they do, I do not think they will be happy.

"Besides the old woman there was another servant, a man, Hippolyte, who served in the house and drove the carriage when it was wanted —a respectable man. He always touched his hat when Mme. Rossignol came out of the house. He slept in the house at night, although the stable was at the end of the street. I thought he was probably the son of Jeanne, the servant-woman. He was young, and his hair was plastered down upon his forehead, and he was altogether satisfied with himself and a great favorite amongst the servants in the street. The carriage and the horse were hired from Geneva. That is the household of Mme. Rossignol."

So far, Mr. Ricardo read in silence. Then he broke out again.

"But we have them! The red-haired woman called Adele; the man with the little black moustache. It was he who drove the motor-car!"

Hanaud held up his hand to check the flow of words, and both read on again:

"At three o'clock on Tuesday afternoon madame was driven away in the carriage, and I did not see it return all that evening. Of course, it may have returned to the stables by another road. But it was not unusual for the carriage to take her into Geneva and wait a long time. I went to bed at eleven, but in the night M. Gobin was restless, and I rose to get him some medicine. We slept in the front of the house, monsieur, and while I was searching for the matches upon the table in the middle of the room I heard the sound of carriage wheels in the silent street.

I went to the window, and, raising a corner of the curtains, looked out. M. Gobin called to me fretfully from the bed to know why I did not light the candle and get him what he wanted. I have already told you how fretful sick men can be, always complaining if just for a minute one distracts oneself by looking out of the window. But there! One can do nothing to please them. Yet how right I was to raise the blind and look out of the window! For if I had obeyed my husband I might have lost four thousand francs. And four thousand francs are not to be sneezed at by a poor woman whose husband lies in bed.

"I saw the carriage stop at Mme. Rossignol's house. Almost at once the house door was opened by the old servant, although the hall of the house and all the windows in the front were dark. That was the first thing that surprised me. For when madame came home late and the house was dark, she used to let herself in with a latchkey. Now, in the dark house, in the early morning, a servant was watching for them. It was strange.

"As soon as the door of the house was opened the door of the carriage opened too, and a young lady stepped quickly out on to the pavement. The train of her dress caught in the door, and she turned round, stooped, freed it with her hand, and held it up off the ground. The night was clear, and there was a lamp in the street close by the door of Mme. Rossignol's house. As she turned I saw her face under the big green hat. It was very pretty and young, and the hair was fair. She wore a white coat, but it was open in front and showed her evening frock of pale green. When she lifted her skirt I saw the buckles sparkling on her satin shoes. It was the young lady for whom you are advertising, I am sure. She remained standing just for a moment without moving, while Mme. Rossignol got out. I was surprised to see a young lady of such distinction in Mme. Rossignol's company. Then, still holding her skirt up, she ran very lightly and quickly across the pavement into the dark house. I thought, monsieur, that she was very anxious not to be seen. So when I saw your advertisement I was certain that this was the young lady for whom you are searching.

"I waited for a few moments and saw the carriage drive off towards the stable at the end of the street. But no light went up in any of the rooms in front of the house. And M. Gobin was so fretful that I dropped the corner of the blind, lit the candle, and gave him his cooling drink. His watch was on the table at the bedside, and I saw that it was five minutes to three. I will send you a telegram to-morrow, as soon as I am sure at what hour I can leave my husband. Accept, monsieur, I beg you, my most distinguished salutations.

"MARTHE GOBIN."

Hanaud leant back with an extraordinary look of perplexity upon his face. But to Ricardo the whole story was now clear. Here was an independent witness, without the jealousy or rancours of Helene Vauquier. Nothing could be more damning than her statement; it corroborated those footmarks upon the soil in front of the glass door of the salon. There was nothing to be done except to set about arresting Mlle. Celie at once.

"The facts work with your theory, M. Hanaud. The young man with the black moustache did not return to the house at Geneva. For somewhere upon the road close to Geneva he met the carriage. He was driving back the car to Aix —" And then another thought struck him: "But no!" he cried. "We are altogether wrong. See! They did not reach home until five minutes to three."

Five minutes to three! But this demolished the whole of Hanaud's theory about the motor-car. The murderers had left the villa between eleven and twelve, probably before half-past eleven. The car was a machine of sixty horse-power, and the roads were certain to be clear. Yet the travellers only reached their home at three. Moreover, the car was back in Aix at four. It was evident they did not travel by the car.

"Geneva time is an hour later than French time," said Hanaud shortly. It seemed as if the corroboration of this letter disappointed him. "A quarter to three in Mme. Gobin's house would be a quarter to two by our watches here."

Hanaud folded up the letter, and rose to his feet.

"We will go now, and we will take this letter with us." Hanaud looked about the room, and picked up a glove lying upon a table. "I left this behind me," he said, putting it into his pocket. "By the way, where is the telegram from Marthe Gobin?"

"You put it in your letter-case."

"Oh, did I?"

Hanaud took out his letter-case and found the telegram within it. His face lightened.

"Good!" he said emphatically. "For, since we have this telegram, there must have been another message sent from Adele Rossignol to Aix saying that Marthe Gobin, that busybody, that inquisitive neighbour, who had no doubt seen M. Ricardo's advertisement, was on her way hither. Oh it will not be put as crudely as that, but that is what the message will mean. We shall have him." And suddenly his face grew very stern. "I MUST catch him, for Marthe Gobin's death I cannot forgive. A poor woman meaning no harm, and murdered like a sheep under our noses. No, that I cannot forgive."

Ricardo wondered whether it was the actual murder of Marthe Gobin or the fact that he had been beaten and outwitted which Hanaud could not forgive. But discretion kept him silent.

"Let us go," said Hanaud. "By the lift, if you please; it will save time."

They descended into the hall close by the main door. The body of Marthe Gobin had been removed to the mortuary of the town. The life of the hotel had resumed its course.

"M. Besnard has gone, I suppose?" Hanaud asked of the porter; and, receiving an assent, he walked quickly out of the front door.

"But there is a shorter way," said Ricardo, running after him: "across the garden at the back and down the steps."

"It will make no difference now," said Hanaud.

They hurried along the drive and down the road which circled round the hotel and dipped to the town.

Behind Hanaud's hotel Ricardo's car was waiting.

"We must go first to Besnard's office. The poor man will be at his wits' end to know who was Mme. Gobin and what brought her to Aix. Besides, I wish to send a message over the telephone."

Hanaud descended and spent a quarter of an hour with the Commissaire. As he came out he looked at his watch.

"We shall be in time, I think," he said. He climbed into the car. "The murder of Marthe Gobin on her way from the station will put our friends at their ease. It will be published, no doubt, in the evening papers, and those good people over there in Geneva will read it with amusement. They do not know that Marthe Gobin wrote a letter yesterday night. Come, let us go!"

"Where to?" asked Ricardo.

"Where to?" exclaimed Hanaud. "Why, of course, to Geneva."


## CHAPTER XII


## THE ALUMINIUM FLASK

"I have telephoned to Lemerre, the Chef de la Surete at Geneva," said Hanaud, as the car sped out of Aix along the road to Annecy. "He will have the house watched. We shall be in time. They will do nothing until dark."

But though he spoke confidently there was a note of anxiety in his voice, and he sat forward in the car, as though he were already straining his eyes to see Geneva.

Ricardo was a trifle disappointed. They were on the great journey to Geneva. They were going to arrest Mlle. Celie and her accomplices. And Hanaud had not come disguised. Hanaud, in Ricardo's eyes, was hardly living up to the dramatic expedition on which they had set out. It seemed to him that there was something incorrect in the great detective coming out on the chase without a false beard.

"But, my dear friend, why shouldn't I?" pleaded Hanaud. "We are going to dine together at the Restaurant du Nord, over the lake, until it grows dark. It is not pleasant to eat one's soup in a false beard. Have you tried it? Besides, everybody stares so, seeing perfectly well that it is false. Now, I do not want to-night that people should know me for a detective; so I do not go disguised."

"Humorist!" said Mr. Ricardo.

"There! you have found me out!" cried Hanaud, in mock alarm. "Besides, I told you this morning that that is precisely what I am."

Beyond Annecy, they came to the bridge over the ravine. At the far end of it, the car stopped. A question, a hurried glance into the body of the car, and the officers of the Customs stood aside.

"You see how perfunctory it is," said Hanaud and with a jerk the car moved on. The jerk threw Hanaud against Mr. Ricardo. Something hard in the detective's pocket knocked against his companion.

"You have got them?" he whispered.

"What?"

"The handcuffs."

Another disappointment awaited Ricardo. A detective without a false beard was bad enough, but that was nothing to a detective without handcuffs. The paraphernalia of justice were sadly lacking. However, Hanaud consoled Mr. Ricardo by showing him the hard thing; it was almost as thrilling as the handcuffs, for it was a loaded revolver.

"There will be danger, then?" said Ricardo, with a tremor of excitement. "I should have brought mine."

"There would have been danger, my friend," Hanaud objected gravely, "if you had brought yours."

They reached Geneva as the dusk was falling, and drove straight to the restaurant by the side of the lake and mounted to the balcony on the first floor. A small, stout man sat at a table alone in a corner of the balcony. He rose and held out his hands.

"My friend, M. Lemerre, the Chef de la Surete of Geneva," said Hanaud, presenting the little man to his companion.

There were as yet only two couples dining in the restaurant, and Hanaud spoke so that neither could overhear him. He sat down at the table.

"What news?" he asked.

"None," said Lemerre. "No one has come out of the house, no one has gone in."

"And if anything happens while we dine?"

"We shall know," said Lemerre. "Look, there is a man loitering under the trees there. He will strike a match to light his pipe."

The hurried conversation was ended.

"Good," said Hanaud. "We will dine, then, and be gay."

He called to the waiter and ordered dinner. It was after seven when they sat down to dinner, and they dined while the dusk deepened. In the street below the lights flashed out, throwing a sheen on the foliage of the trees at the water's side. Upon the dark lake the reflections of lamps rippled and shook. A boat in which musicians sang to music, passed by with a cool splash of oars. The green and red lights of the launches glided backwards and forwards. Hanaud alone of the party on the balcony tried to keep the conversation upon a light and general level. But it was plain that even he was overdoing his gaiety. There were moments when a sudden contraction of the muscles would clench his hands and give a spasmodic jerk to his shoulders. He was waiting uneasily, uncomfortably, until darkness should come.

"Eat," he cried —"eat, my friends," playing with his own barely tasted food.

And then, at a sentence from Lemerre, his knife and fork clattered on his plate, and he sat with a face suddenly grown white.

For Lemerre said, as though it was no more than a matter of ordinary comment:

"So Mme. Dauvray's jewels were, after all, never stolen?"

Hanaud started.

"You know that? How did you know it?"

"It was in this evening's paper. I bought one on the way here. They were found under the floor of the bedroom."

And even as he spoke a newsboy's voice rang out in the street below them. Lemerre was alarmed by the look upon his friend's face.

"Does it matter, Hanaud?" he asked, with some solicitude.

"It matters —" and Hanaud rose up abruptly.

The boy's voice sounded louder in the street below. The words became distinct to all upon that balcony.

"The Aix murder! Discovery of the jewels!"

"We must go," Hanaud whispered hoarsely. "Here are life and death in the balance, as I believe, and there" —he pointed down to the little group gathering about the newsboy under the trees —"there is the command which way to tip the scales."

"It was not I who sent it," said Ricardo eagerly.

He had no precise idea what Hanaud meant by his words; but he realised that the sooner he exculpated himself from the charge the better.

"Of course it was not you. I know that very well," said Hanaud. He called for the bill. "When is that paper published?"

"At seven," said Lemerre.

"They have been crying it in the streets of Geneva, then, for more than half an hour."

He sat drumming impatiently upon the table until the bill should be brought.

"By Heaven, that's clever!" he muttered savagely. "There's a man who gets ahead of me at every turn. See, Lemerre, I take every care, every precaution, that no message shall be sent. I let it be known, I take careful pains to let it be known, that no message can be sent without detection following, and here's the message sent by the one channel I never thought to guard against and stop. Look!"

The murder at the Villa Rose and the mystery which hid its perpetration had aroused interest. This new development had quickened it. From the balcony Hanaud could see the groups thickening about the boy and the white sheets of the newspapers in the hands of passers-by.

"Every one in Geneva or near Geneva will know of this message by now."

"Who could have told?" asked Ricardo blankly, and Hanaud laughed in his face, but laughed without any merriment.

"At last!" he cried, as the waiter brought the bill, and just as he had paid it the light of a match flared up under the trees.

"The signal!" said Lemerre.

"Not too quickly," whispered Hanaud.

With as much unconcern as each could counterfeit, the three men descended the stairs and crossed the road. Under the trees a fourth man joined them-he who had lighted his pipe.

"The coachman, Hippolyte," he whispered, "bought an evening paper at the front door of the house from a boy who came down the street shouting the news. The coachman ran back into the house."

"When was this?" asked Lemerre.

The man pointed to a lad who leaned against the balustrade above the lake, hot and panting for breath.

"He came on his bicycle. He has just arrived."

"Follow me," said Lemerre.

Six yards from where they stood a couple of steps led down from the embankment on to a wooden landing-stage, where boats were moored. Lemerre, followed by the others, walked briskly down on to the landing-stage. An electric launch was waiting. It had an awning and was of the usual type which one hires at Geneva. There were two sergeants in plain clothes on board, and a third man, whom Ricardo recognised.

"That is the man who found out in whose shop the cord was bought," he said to Hanaud.

"Yes, it is Durette. He has been here since yesterday."

Lemerre and the three who followed him stepped into it, and it backed away from the stage and, turning, sped swiftly outwards from Geneva. The gay lights of the shops and the restaurants were left behind, the cool darkness enveloped them; a light breeze blew over the lake, a trail of white and tumbled water lengthened out behind and overhead, in a sky of deepest blue, the bright stars shone like gold.

"If only we are in time!" said Hanaud, catching his breath.

"Yes," answered Lemerre; and in both their voices there was a strange note of gravity.

Lemerre gave a signal after a while, and the boat turned to the shore and reduced its speed. They had passed the big villas. On the bank the gardens of houses-narrow, long gardens of a street of small houses-reached down to the lake, and to almost each garden there was a rickety landing-stage of wood projecting into the lake. Again Lemerre gave a signal, and the boat's speed was so much reduced that not a sound of its coming could be heard. It moved over the water like a shadow, with not so much as a curl of white at its bows.

Lemerre touched Hanaud on the shoulder and pointed to a house in a row of houses. All the windows except two upon the second floor and one upon the ground floor were in absolute darkness, and over those upper two the wooden shutters were closed. But in the shutters there were diamond-shaped holes, and from these holes two yellow beams of light, like glowing eyes upon the watch, streamed out and melted in the air.

"You are sure that the front of the house is guarded?" asked Hanaud anxiously.

"Yes," replied Lemerre.

Ricardo shivered with excitement. The launch slid noiselessly into the bank and lay hidden under its shadow. Hanaud turned to his associates with his finger to his lips. Something gleamed darkly in his hand. It was the barrel of his revolver. Cautiously the men disembarked and crept up the bank. First came Lemerre, then Hanaud; Ricardo followed him, and the fourth man, who had struck the match under the trees, brought up the rear. The other three officers remained in the boat.

Stooping under the shadow of the side wall of the garden, the invaders stole towards the house. When a bush rustled or a tree whispered in the light wind, Ricardo's heart jumped to his throat. Once Lemerre stopped, as though his ears heard a sound which warned him of danger. Then cautiously he crept on again. The garden was a ragged place of unmown lawn and straggling bushes. Behind each one Mr. Ricardo seemed to feel an enemy. Never had he been in so strait a predicament. He, the cultured host of Grosvenor Square, was creeping along under a wall with Continental policemen; he was going to raid a sinister house by the Lake of Geneva. It was thrilling. Fear and excitement gripped him in turn and let him go, but always he was sustained by the pride of the man doing an out-of-the-way thing. "If only my friends could see me now!" The ancient vanity was loud in his bosom. Poor fellows, they were upon yachts in the Solent or on grouse-moors in Scotland, or on golf-links at North Berwick. He alone of them all was tracking malefactors to their doom by Leman's Lake.

From these agreeable reflections Ricardo was shaken. Lemerre stopped. The raiders had reached the angle made by the side wall of the garden and the house. A whisper was exchanged, and the party turned and moved along the house wall towards the lighted window on the ground floor. As Lemerre reached it he stooped. Then slowly his forehead and his eyes rose above the sill and glanced this way and that into the room. Mr. Ricardo could see his eyes gleaming as the light from the window caught them. His face rose completely over the sill. He stared into the room without care or apprehension, and then dropped again out of the reach of the light. He turned to Hanaud.

"The room is empty," he whispered.

Hanaud turned to Ricardo.

"Pass under the sill, or the light from the window will throw your shadow upon the lawn."

The party came to the back door of the house. Lemerre tried the handle of the door, and to his surprise it yielded. They crept into the passage. The last man closed the door noiselessly, locked it, and removed the key. A panel of light shone upon the wall a few paces ahead. The door of the lighted room was open. As Ricardo stepped silently past it, he looked in. It was a parlour meanly furnished. Hanaud touched him on the arm and pointed to the table.

Ricardo had seen the objects at which Hanaud pointed often enough without uneasiness; but now, in this silent house of crime, they had the most sinister and appalling aspect. There was a tiny phial half full of a dark-brown liquid, beside it a little leather case lay open, and across the case, ready for use or waiting to be filled, was a bright morphia needle. Ricardo felt the cold creep along his spine, and shivered.

"Come," whispered Hanaud.

They reached the foot of a flight of stairs, and cautiously mounted it. They came out in a passage which ran along the side of the house from the back to the front. It was unlighted, but they were now on the level of the street, and a fan-shaped glass window over the front door admitted a pale light. There was a street lamp near to the door, Ricardo remembered. For by the light of it Marthe Gobin had seen Celia Harland run so nimbly into this house.

For a moment the men in the passage held their breath. Some one strode heavily by on the pavement outside-to Mr. Ricardo's ear a most companionable sound. Then a clock upon a church struck the half-hour musically, distantly. It was half-past eight. And a second afterwards a tiny bright light shone. Hanaud was directing the light of a pocket electric torch to the next flight of stairs.

Here the steps were carpeted, and once more the men crept up. One after another they came out upon the next landing. It ran, like those below it, along the side of the house from the back to the front, and the doors were all upon their left hand. From beneath the door nearest to them a yellow line of light streamed out.

They stood in the darkness listening. But not a sound came from behind the door. Was this room empty, too? In each one's mind was the fear that the birds had flown. Lemerre carefully took the handle of the door and turned it. Very slowly and cautiously he opened the door. A strong light beat out through the widening gap upon his face. And then, though his feet did not move, his shoulders and his face drew back. The action was significant enough. This room, at all events, was not empty. But of what Lemerre saw in the room his face gave no hint. He opened the door wider, and now Hanaud saw. Ricardo, trembling with excitement, watched him. But again there was no expression of surprise, consternation, or delight. He stood stolidly and watched. Then he turned to Ricardo, placed a finger on his lips, and made room. Ricardo crept on tiptoe to his side. And now he too could look in. He saw a brightly lit bedroom with a made bed. On his left were the shuttered windows overlooking the lake. On his right in the partition wall a door stood open. Through the door he could see a dark, windowless closet, with a small bed from which the bedclothes hung and trailed upon the floor, as though some one had been but now roughly dragged from it. On a table, close by the door, lay a big green hat with a brown ostrich feather, and a white cloak. But the amazing spectacle which kept him riveted was just in front of him. An old hag of a woman was sitting in a chair with her back towards them. She was mending with a big needle the holes in an old sack, and while she bent over her work she crooned to herself some French song. Every now and then she raised her eyes, for in front of her, under her charge, Mlle. Celie, the girl of whom Hanaud was in search, lay helpless upon a sofa. The train of her delicate green frock swept the floor. She was dressed as Helene Vauquier had described. Her gloved hands were tightly bound behind her back, her feet were crossed so that she could not have stood, and her ankles were cruelly strapped together.

Over her face and eyes a piece of coarse sacking was stretched like a mask, and the ends were roughly sewn together at the back of her head. She lay so still that, but for the labouring of her bosom and a tremor which now and again shook her limbs, the watchers would have thought her dead. She made no struggle of resistance; she lay quiet and still. Once she writhed, but it was with the uneasiness of one in pain, and the moment she stirred the old woman's hand went out to a bright aluminium flask which stood on a little table at her side.

"Keep quiet, little one!" she ordered in a careless, chiding voice, and she rapped with the flask peremptorily upon the table. Immediately, as though the tapping had some strange message of terror for the girl's ear, she stiffened her whole body and lay rigid.

"I am not ready for you yet, little fool," said the old woman, and she bent again to her work.

Ricardo's brain whirled. Here was the girl whom they had come to arrest, who had sprung from the salon with so much activity of youth across the stretch of grass, who had run so quickly and lightly across the pavement into this very house, so that she should not be seen. And now she was lying in her fine and delicate attire a captive, at the mercy of the very people who were her accomplices.

Suddenly a scream rang out in the garden —a shrill, loud scream, close beneath the windows. The old woman sprang to her feet. The girl on the sofa raised her head. The old woman took a step towards the window, and then she swiftly turned towards the door. She saw the men upon the threshold. She uttered a bellow of rage. There is no other word to describe the sound. It was not a human cry; it was the bellow of an angry animal. She reached out her hand towards the flask, but before she could grasp it Hanaud seized her. She burst into a torrent of foul oaths. Hanaud flung her across to Lemerre's officer, who dragged her from the room.

"Quick!" said Hanaud, pointing to the girl, who was now struggling helplessly upon the sofa. "Mlle. Celie!"

Ricardo cut the stitches of the sacking. Hanaud unstrapped her hands and feet. They helped her to sit up. She shook her hands in the air as though they tortured her, and then, in a piteous, whimpering voice, like a child's, she babbled incoherently and whispered prayers. Suddenly the prayers ceased. She sat stiff, with eyes fixed and staring. She was watching Lemerre, and she was watching him fascinated with terror. He was holding in his hand the large, bright aluminium flask. He poured a little of the contents very carefully on to a piece of the sack; and then with an exclamation of anger he turned towards Hanaud. But Hanaud was supporting Celia; and so, as Lemerre turned abruptly towards him with the flask in his hand, he turned abruptly towards Celia too. She wrenched herself from Hanaud's arms, she shrank violently away. Her white face flushed scarlet and grew white again. She screamed loudly, terribly; and after the scream she uttered a strange, weak sigh, and so fell sideways in a swoon. Hanaud caught her as she fell. A light broke over his face.

"Now I understand!" he cried. "Good God! That's horrible."


## CHAPTER XIII


## IN THE HOUSE AT GENEVA

It was well, Mr. Ricardo thought, that some one understood. For himself, he frankly admitted that he did not. Indeed, in his view the first principles of reasoning seemed to be set at naught. It was obvious from the solicitude with which Celia Harland was surrounded that every one except himself was convinced of her innocence. Yet it was equally obvious that any one who bore in mind the eight points he had tabulated against her must be convinced of her guilt. Yet again, if she were guilty, how did it happen that she had been so mishandled by her accomplices? He was not allowed, however, to reflect upon these remarkable problems. He had too busy a time of it. At one moment he was running to fetch water wherewith to bathe Celia's forehead. At another, when he had returned with the water, he was distracted by the appearance of Durette, the inspector from Aix, in the doorway.

"We have them both," he said —"Hippolyte and the woman. They were hiding in the garden."

"So I thought," said Hanaud, "when I saw the door open downstairs, and the morphia-needle on the table."

Lemerre turned to one of the officers.

"Let them be taken with old Jeanne in cabs to the depot."

And when the man had gone upon his errand Lemerre spoke to Hanaud.

"You will stay here to-night to arrange for their transfer to Aix?"

"I will leave Durette behind," said Hanaud. "I am needed at Aix. We will make a formal application for the prisoners." He was kneeling by Celia's side and awkwardly dabbing her forehead with a wet handkerchief. He raised a warning hand. Celia Harland moved and opened her eyes. She sat up on the sofa, shivering, and looked with dazed and wondering eyes from one to another of the strangers who surrounded her. She searched in vain for a familiar face.

"You are amongst good friends, Mlle. Celie," said Hanaud with great gentleness.

"Oh, I wonder! I wonder!" she cried piteously.

"Be very sure of it," he said heartily, and she clung to the sleeve of his coat with desperate hands.

"I suppose you ARE friends," she said; "else why —?" and she moved her numbed limbs to make certain that she was free. She looked about the room. Her eyes fell upon the sack and widened with terror.

"They came to me a little while ago in that cupboard there-Adele and the old woman Jeanne. They made me get up. They told me they were going to take me away. They brought my clothes and dressed me in everything I wore when I came, so that no single trace of me might be left behind. Then they tied me." She tore off her gloves and showed them her lacerated wrists. "I think they meant to kill me-horribly." And she caught her breath and whimpered like a child. Her spirit was broken.

"My poor girl, all that is over," said Hanaud. And he stood up.

But at the first movement he made she cried incisively, "No," and tightened the clutch of her fingers upon his sleeve.

"But, mademoiselle, you are safe," he said, with a smile. She stared at him stupidly. It seemed the words had no meaning for her. She would not let him go. It was only the feel of his coat within the clutch of her fingers which gave her any comfort.

"I want to be sure that I am safe," she said, with a wan little smile.

"Tell me, mademoiselle, what have you had to eat and drink during the last two days?"

"Is it two days?" she asked. "I was in the dark there. I did not know. A little bread, a little water."

"That's what is wrong," said Hanaud. "Come, let us go from here!"

"Yes, yes!" Celia cried eagerly. She rose to her feet, and tottered. Hanaud put his arm about her. "You are very kind," she said in a low voice, and again doubt looked out from her face and disappeared. "I am sure that I can trust you."

Ricardo fetched her cloak and slipped it on her shoulders. Then he brought her hat, and she pinned it on. She turned to Hanaud; unconsciously familiar words rose to her lips.

"Is it straight?" she asked. And Hanaud laughed outright, and in a moment Celia smiled herself.

Supported by Hanaud she stumbled down the stairs to the garden. As they passed the open door of the lighted parlour at the back of the house Hanaud turned back to Lemerre and pointed silently to the morphia-needle and the phial. Lemerre nodded his head, and going into the room took them away. They went out again into the garden. Celia Harland threw back her head to the stars and drew in a deep breath of the cool night air.

"I did not think," she said in a low voice, "to see the stars again."

They walked slowly down the length of the garden, and Hanaud lifted her into the launch. She turned and caught his coat.

"You must come too," she said stubbornly.

Hanaud sprang in beside her.

"For to-night," he said gaily, "I am your papa!"

Ricardo and the others followed, and the launch moved out over the lake under the stars. The bow was turned towards Geneva, the water tumbled behind them like white fire, the night breeze blew fresh upon their faces. They disembarked at the landing-stage, and then Lemerre bowed to Celia and took his leave. Hanaud led Celia up on to the balcony of the restaurant and ordered supper. There were people still dining at the tables.

One party indeed sitting late over their coffee Ricardo recognised with a kind of shock. They had taken their places, the very places in which they now sat, before he and Hanaud and Lemerre had left the restaurant upon their expedition of rescue. Into that short interval of time so much that was eventful had been crowded.

Hanaud leaned across the table to Celia and said in a low voice:

"Mademoiselle, if I may suggest it, it would be as well if you put on your gloves; otherwise they may notice your wrists."

Celia followed his advice. She ate some food and drank a glass of champagne. A little colour returned to her cheeks.

"You are very kind to me, you and monsieur your friend," she said, with a smile towards Ricardo. "But for you —" and her voice shook.

"Hush!" said Hanaud —"all that is over; we will not speak of it."

Celia looked out across the road on to the trees, of which the dark foliage was brightened and made pale by the lights of the restaurant. Out on the water some one was singing.

"It seems impossible to me," she said in a low voice, "that I am here, in the open air, and free."

Hanaud looked at his watch.

"Mlle. Celie, it is past ten o'clock. M. Ricardo's car is waiting there under the trees. I want you to drive back to Aix. I have taken rooms for you at an hotel, and there will be a nurse from the hospital to look after you."

"Thank you, monsieur," she said; "you have thought of everything. But I shall not need a nurse."

"But you will have a nurse," said Hanaud firmly. "You feel stronger now-yes, but when you lay your head upon your pillow, mademoiselle, it will be a comfort to you to know that you have her within call. And in a day or two," he added gently, "you will perhaps be able to tell us what happened on Tuesday night at the Villa Rose?"

Celia covered her face with her hands for a few moments. Then she drew them away and said simply:

"Yes, monsieur, I will tell you."

Hanaud bowed to her with a genuine deference.

"Thank you, mademoiselle," he said, and in his voice there was a strong ring of sympathy.

They went downstairs and entered Ricardo's motor car.

"I want to send a telephone message," said Hanaud, "if you will wait here."

"No!" cried Celia decisively, and she again laid hold of his coat, with a pretty imperiousness, as though he belonged to her.

"But I must," said Hanaud with a laugh.

"Then I will come too," said Celia, and she opened the door and set a foot upon the step.

"You will not, mademoiselle," said Hanaud, with a laugh. "Will you take your foot back into that car? That is better. Now you will sit with your friend, M. Ricardo, whom, by the way, I have not yet introduced to you. He is a very good friend of yours, mademoiselle, and will in the future be a still better one."

Ricardo felt his conscience rather heavy within him, for he had come out to Geneva with the fixed intention of arresting her as a most dangerous criminal. Even now he could not understand how she could be innocent of a share in Mme. Dauvray's murder. But Hanaud evidently thought she was. And since Hanaud thought so, why, it was better to say nothing if one was sensitive to gibes. So Ricardo sat and talked with her while Hanaud ran back into the restaurant. It mattered very little, however, what he said, for Celia's eyes were fixed upon the doorway through which Hanaud had disappeared. And when he came back she was quick to turn the handle of the door.

"Now, mademoiselle, we will wrap you up in M. Ricardo's spare motor-coat and cover your knees with a rug and put you between us, and then you can go to sleep."

The car sped through the streets of Geneva. Celia Harland, with a little sigh of relief, nestled down between the two men.

"If I knew you better," she said to Hanaud, "I should tell you-what, of course, I do not tell you now-that I feel as if I had a big Newfoundland dog with me."

"Mlle. Celie," said Hanaud, and his voice told her that he was moved, "that is a very pretty thing which you have said to me."

The lights of the city fell away behind them. Now only a glow in the sky spoke of Geneva; now even that was gone and with a smooth continuous purr the car raced through the cool darkness. The great head lamps threw a bright circle of light before them and the road slipped away beneath the wheels like a running tide. Celia fell asleep. Even when the car stopped at the Pont de La Caille she did not waken. The door was opened, a search for contraband was made, the book was signed, still she did not wake. The car sped on.

"You see, coming into France is a different affair," said Hanaud.

"Yes," replied Ricardo.

"Still, I will own it, you caught me napping yesterday.

"I did?" exclaimed Ricardo joyfully.

"You did," returned Hanaud. "I had never heard of the Pont de La Caille. But you will not mention it? You will not ruin me?"

"I will not," answered M. Ricardo, superb in his magnanimity. "You are a good detective."

"Oh, thank you! thank you!" cried Hanaud in a voice which shook-surely with emotion. He wrung Ricardo's hand. He wiped an imaginary tear from his eye.

And still Celia slept. M. Ricardo looked at her. He said to Hanaud in a whisper:

"Yet I do not understand. The car, though no serious search was made, must still have stopped at the Pont de La Caille on the Swiss side. Why did she not cry for help then? One cry and she was safe. A movement even was enough. Do you understand?"

Hanaud nodded his head.

"I think so," he answered, with a very gentle look at Celia. "Yes, I think so."

When Celia was aroused she found that the car had stopped before the door of an hotel, and that a woman in the dress of a nurse was standing in the doorway.

"You can trust Marie," said Hanaud. And Celia turned as she stood upon the ground and gave her hands to the two men.

"Thank you! Thank you both!" she said in a trembling voice. She looked at Hanaud and nodded her head. "You understand why I thank you so very much?"

"Yes," said Hanaud. "But, mademoiselle" —and he bent over the car and spoke to her quietly, holding her hand —"there is ALWAYS a big Newfoundland dog in the worst of troubles-if only you will look for him. I tell you so —I, who belong to the Surete in Paris. Do not lose heart!" And in his mind he added: "God forgive me for the lie." He shook her hand and let it go; and gathering up her skirt she went into the hall of the hotel.

Hanaud watched her as she went. She was to him a lonely and pathetic creature, in spite of the nurse who bore her company.

"You must be a good friend to that young girl, M. Ricardo," he said. "Let us drive to your hotel."

"Yes," said Ricardo. And as they went the curiosity which all the way from Geneva had been smouldering within him burst into flame.

"Will you explain to me one thing?" he asked. "When the scream came from the garden you were not surprised. Indeed, you said that when you saw the open door and the morphia-needle on the table of the little room downstairs you thought Adele and the man Hippolyte were hiding in the garden."

"Yes, I did think so."

"Why? And why did the publication that the jewels had been discovered so alarm you?"

"Ah!" said Hanaud. "Did not you understand that? Yet it is surely clear and obvious, if you once grant that the girl was innocent, was a witness of the crime, and was now in the hands of the criminals. Grant me those premises, M. Ricardo, for a moment, and you will see that we had just one chance of finding the girl alive in Geneva. From the first I was sure of that. What was the one chance? Why, this! She might be kept alive on the chance that she could be forced to tell what, by the way, she did not know, namely, the place where Mme. Dauvray's valuable jewels were secreted. Now, follow this. We, the police, find the jewels and take charge of them. Let that news reach the house in Geneva, and on the same night Mlle. Celie loses her life, and not-very pleasantly. They have no further use for her. She is merely a danger to them. So I take my precautions-never mind for the moment what they were. I take care that if the murderer is in Aix and gets wind of our discovery he shall not be able to communicate his news."

"The Post Office would have stopped letters or telegrams," said Ricardo. "I understand."

"On the contrary," replied Hanaud. "No, I took my precautions, which were of quite a different kind, before I knew the house in Geneva or the name of Rossignol. But one way of communication I did not think of. I did not think of the possibility that the news might be sent to a newspaper, which of course would publish it and cry it through the streets of Geneva. The moment I heard the news I knew we must hurry. The garden of the house ran down to the lake. A means of disposing of Mlle. Celie was close at hand. And the night had fallen. As it was, we arrived just in time, and no earlier than just in time. The paper had been bought, the message had reached the house, Mlle. Celie was no longer of any use, and every hour she stayed in that house was of course an hour of danger to her captors."

"What were they going to do?" asked Ricardo.

Hanaud shrugged his shoulders.

"It is not pretty-what they were going to do. We reach the garden in our launch. At that moment Hippolyte and Adele, who is most likely Hippolyte's wife, are in the lighted parlour on the basement floor. Adele is preparing her morphia-needle. Hippolyte is going to get ready the rowing-boat which was tied at the end of the landing-stage. Quietly as we came into the bank, they heard or saw us. They ran out and hid in the garden, having no time to lock the garden door, or perhaps not daring to lock it lest the sound of the key should reach our ears. We find that door upon the latch, the door of the room open; on the table lies the morphia-needle. Upstairs lies Mlle. Celie-she is helpless, she cannot see what they are meaning to do."

"But she could cry out," exclaimed Ricardo. "She did not even do that!"

"No, my friend, she could not cry out," replied Hanaud very seriously. "I know why. She could not. No living man or woman could. Rest assured of that!"

Ricardo was mystified; but since the captain of the ship would not show his observation, he knew it would be in vain to press him.

"Well, while Adele was preparing her morphia-needle and Hippolyte was about to prepare the boat, Jeanne upstairs was making her preparation too. She was mending a sack. Did you see Mlle. Celie's eyes and face when first she saw that sack? Ah! she understood! They meant to give her a dose of morphia, and, as soon as she became unconscious, they were going perhaps to take some terrible precaution —" Hanaud paused for a second. "I only say perhaps as to that. But certainly they were going to sew her up in that sack, row her well out across the lake, fix a weight to her feet, and drop her quietly overboard. She was to wear everything which she had brought with her to the house. Mlle. Celie would have disappeared for ever, and left not even a ripple upon the water to trace her by!"

Ricardo clenched his hands.

"But that's horrible!" he cried; and as he uttered the words the car swerved into the drive and stopped before the door of the Hotel Majestic.

Ricardo sprang out. A feeling of remorse seized hold of him. All through that evening he had not given one thought to Harry Wethermill, so utterly had the excitement of each moment engrossed his mind.

"He will be glad to know!" cried Ricardo. "To-night, at all events, he shall sleep. I ought to have telegraphed to him from Geneva that we and Miss Celia were coming back." He ran up the steps into the hotel.

"I took care that he should know," said Hanaud, as he followed in Ricardo's steps.

"Then the message could not have reached him, else he would have been expecting us," replied Ricardo, as he hurried into the office, where a clerk sat at his books.

"Is Mr. Wethermill in?" he asked.

The clerk eyed him strangely.

"Mr. Wethermill was arrested this evening," he said.

Ricardo stepped back.

"Arrested! When?"

"At twenty-five minutes past ten," replied the clerk shortly.

"Ah," said Hanaud quietly. "That was my telephone message."

Ricardo stared in stupefaction at his companion.

"Arrested!" he cried. "Arrested! But what for?"

"For the murders of Marthe Gobin and Mme. Dauvray," said Hanaud. "Good-night."


## CHAPTER XIV


## MR. RICARDO IS BEWILDERED

Ricardo passed a most tempestuous night. He was tossed amongst dark problems. Now it was Harry Wethermill who beset him. He repeated and repeated the name, trying to grasp the new and sinister suggestion which, if Hanaud were right, its sound must henceforth bear. Of course Hanaud might be wrong. Only, if he were wrong, how had he come to suspect Harry Wethermill? What had first directed his thoughts to that seemingly heart-broken man? And when? Certain recollections became vivid in Mr. Ricardo's mind-the luncheon at the Villa Rose, for instance. Hanaud had been so insistent that the woman with the red hair was to be found in Geneva, had so clearly laid it down that a message, a telegram, a letter from Aix to Geneva, would enable him to lay his hands upon the murderer in Aix. He was isolating the house in Geneva even so early in the history of his investigations, even so soon he suspected Harry Wethermill. Brains and audacity-yes, these two qualities he had stipulated in the criminal. Ricardo now for the first time understood the trend of all Hanaud's talk at that luncheon. He was putting Harry Wethermill upon his guard, he was immobilising him, he was fettering him in precautions; with a subtle skill he was forcing him to isolate himself. And he was doing it deliberately to save the life of Celia Harland in Geneva. Once Ricardo lifted himself up with the hair stirring on his scalp. He himself had been with Wethermill in the baccarat-rooms on the very night of the murder. They had walked together up the hill to the hotel. It could not be that Harry Wethermill was guilty. And yet, he suddenly remembered, they had together left the rooms at an early hour. It was only ten o'clock when they had separated in the hall, when they had gone, each to his own room. There would have been time for Wethermill to reach the Villa Rose and do his dreadful work upon that night before twelve, if all had been arranged beforehand, if all went as it had been arranged. And as he thought upon the careful planning of that crime, and remembered Wethermill's easy chatter as they had strolled from table to table in the Villa des Fleurs, Ricardo shuddered. Though he encouraged a taste for the bizarre, it was with an effort. He was naturally of an orderly mind, and to touch the eerie or inhuman caused him a physical discomfort. So now he marvelled in a great uneasiness at the calm placidity with which Wethermill had talked, his arm in his, while the load of so dark a crime to be committed within the hour lay upon his mind. Each minute he must have been thinking, with a swift spasm of the heart, "Should such a precaution fail-should such or such an unforeseen thing intervene," yet there had been never a sign of disturbance, never a hint of any disquietude.

Then Ricardo's thoughts turned as he tossed upon his bed to Celia Harland, a tragic and a lonely figure. He recalled the look of tenderness upon her face when her eyes had met Harry Wethermill's across the baccarat-table in the Villa des Fleurs. He gained some insight into the reason why she had clung so desperately to Hanaud's coat-sleeve yesterday. Not merely had he saved her life. She was lying with all her world of trust and illusion broken about her, and Hanaud had raised her up. She had found some one whom she trusted-the big Newfoundland dog, as she expressed it. Mr. Ricardo was still thinking of Celia Harland when the morning came. He fell asleep, and awoke to find Hanaud by his bed.

"You will be wanted to-day," said Hanaud.

Ricardo got up and walked down from the hotel with the detective. The front door faces the hillside of Mont Revard, and on this side Mr. Ricardo's rooms looked out. The drive from the front door curves round the end of the long building and joins the road, which then winds down towards the town past the garden at the back of the hotel. Down this road the two men walked, while the supporting wall of the garden upon their right hand grew higher and higher above their heads. They came to a steep flight of steps which makes a short cut from the hotel to the road, and at the steps Hanaud stopped.

"Do you see?" he said. "On the opposite side there are no houses; there is only a wall. Behind the wall there are climbing gardens and the ground falls steeply to the turn of the road below. There's a flight of steps leading down which corresponds with the flight of steps from the garden. Very often there's a SERJENT-DE-VILLE stationed on the top of the steps. But there was not one there yesterday afternoon at three. Behind us is the supporting wall of the hotel garden. Well, look about you. We cannot be seen from the hotel. There's not a soul in sight-yes, there's some one coming up the hill, but we have been standing here quite long enough for you to stab me and get back to your coffee on the verandah of the hotel."

Ricardo started back.

"Marthe Gobin!" he cried. "It was here, then?"

Hanaud nodded.

"When we returned from the station in your motor-car and went up to your rooms we passed Harry Wethermill sitting upon the verandah over the garden drinking his coffee. He had the news then that Marthe Gobin was on her way."

"But you had isolated the house in Geneva. How could he have the news?" exclaimed Ricardo, whose brain was whirling.

"I had isolated the house from him, in the sense that he dared not communicate with his accomplices. That is what you have to remember. He could not even let them know that they must not communicate with him. So he received a telegram. It was carefully worded. No doubt he had arranged the wording of any message with the care which was used in all the preparations. It ran like this" —and Hanaud took a scrap of paper from his pocket and read out from it a copy of the telegram: "'Agent arrives Aix 3.7 to negotiate purchase of your patent.' The telegram was handed in at Geneva station at 12.45, five minutes after the train had left which carried Marthe Gobin to Aix. And more, it was handed in by a man strongly resembling Hippolyte Tace-that we know."

"That was madness," said Ricardo.

"But what else could they do over there in Geneva? They did not know that Harry Wethermill was suspected. Harry Wethermill had no idea of it himself. But, even if they had known, they must take the risk. Put yourself into their place for a moment. They had seen my advertisement about Celie Harland in the Geneva paper. Marthe Gobin, that busybody who was always watching her neighbours, was no doubt watched herself. They see her leave the house, an unusual proceeding for her with her husband ill, as her own letter tells us. Hippolyte follows her to the station, sees her take her ticket to Aix and mount into the train. He must guess at once that she saw Celie Harland enter their house, that she is travelling to Aix with the information of her whereabouts. At all costs she must be prevented from giving that information. At all risks, therefore, the warning telegram must be sent to Harry Wethermill."

Ricardo recognised the force of the argument.

"If only you had heard of the telegram yesterday in time!" he cried.

"Ah, yes!" Hanaud agreed. "But it was only sent off at a quarter to one. It was delivered to Wethermill and a copy was sent to the Prefecture, but the telegram was delivered first."

"When was it delivered to Wethermill?" asked Ricardo.

"At three. We had already left for the station. Wethermill was sitting on the verandah. The telegram was brought to him there. It was brought by a waiter in the hotel who remembers the incident very well. Wethermill has seven minutes and the time it will take for Marthe Gobin to drive from the station to the Majestic. What does he do? He runs up first to your rooms, very likely not yet knowing what he must do. He runs up to verify his telegram."

"Are you sure of that?" cried Ricardo. "How can you be? You were at the station with me. What makes you sure?"

Hanaud produced a brown kid glove from his pocket.

"This."

"That is your glove; you told me so yesterday."

"I told you so," replied Hanaud calmly; "but it is not my glove. It is Wethermill's; there are his initials stamped upon the lining-see? I picked up that glove in your room, after we had returned from the station. It was not there before. He went to your rooms. No doubt he searched for a telegram. Fortunately he did not examine your letters, or Marthe Gobin would never have spoken to us as she did after she was dead."

"Then what did he do?" asked Ricardo eagerly; and, though Hanaud had been with him at the entrance to the station all this while, he asked the question in absolute confidence that the true answer would be given to him.

"He returned to the verandah wondering what he should do. He saw us come back from the station in the motor-car and go up to your room. We were alone. Marthe Gobin, then, was following. There was his chance. Marthe Gobin must not reach us, must not tell her news to us. He ran down the garden steps to the gate. No one could see him from the hotel. Very likely he hid behind the trees, whence he could watch the road. A cab comes up the hill; there's a woman in it-not quite the kind of woman who stays at your hotel, M. Ricardo. Yet she must be going to your hotel, for the road ends. The driver is nodding on his box, refusing to pay any heed to his fare lest again she should bid him hurry. His horse is moving at a walk. Wethermill puts his head in at the window and asks if she has come to see M. Ricardo. Anxious for her four thousand francs, she answers 'Yes.' Perhaps he steps into the cab, perhaps as he walks by the side he strikes, and strikes hard and strikes surely. Long before the cab reaches the hotel he is back again on the verandah."

"Yes," said Ricardo, "it's the daring of which you spoke which made the crime possible-the same daring which made him seek your help. That was unexampled."

"No," replied Hanaud. "There's an historic crime in your own country, monsieur. Cries for help were heard in a by-street of a town. When people ran to answer them, a man was found kneeling by a corpse. It was the kneeling man who cried for help, but it was also the kneeling man who did the murder. I remembered that when I first began to suspect Harry Wethermill."

Ricardo turned eagerly.

"And when-when did you first begin to suspect Harry Wethermill?"

Hanaud smiled and shook his head.

"That you shall know in good time. I am the captain of the ship." His voice took on a deeper note. "But I prepare you. Listen! Daring and brains, those were the property of Harry Wethermill-yes. But it is not he who is the chief actor in the crime. Of that I am sure. He was no more than one of the instruments."

"One of the instruments? Used, then, by whom?" asked Ricardo.

"By my Normandy peasant-woman, M. Ricardo," said Hanaud. "Yes, there's the dominating figure-cruel, masterful, relentless-that strange woman, Helene Vauquier. You are surprised? You will see! It is not the man of intellect and daring; it's my peasant-woman who is at the bottom of it all."

"But she's free!" exclaimed Ricardo. "You let her go free!"

"Free!" repeated Ricardo. "She was driven straight from the Villa Rose to the depot. She has been kept AU SECRET ever since."

Ricardo stared in amazement.

"Already you knew of her guilt?"

"Already she had lied to me in her description of Adele Rossignol. Do you remember what she said —a black-haired woman with beady eyes; and I only five minutes before had picked up from the table-this."

He opened his pocket-book, and took from an envelope a long strand of red hair.

"But it was not only because she lied that I had her taken to the depot. A pot of cold cream had disappeared from the room of Mlle. Celie."

"Then Perrichet after all was right."

"Perrichet after all was quite wrong-not to hold his tongue. For in that pot of cold cream, as I was sure, were hidden those valuable diamond earrings which Mlle. Celie habitually wore."

The two men had reached the square in front of the Etablissement des Bains. Ricardo dropped on to a bench and wiped his forehead.

"But I am in a maze," he cried. "My head turns round. I don't know where I am."

Hanaud stood in front of Ricardo, smiling. He was not displeased with his companion's bewilderment; it was all so much of tribute to himself.

"I am the captain of the ship," he said.

His smile irritated Ricardo, who spoke impatiently.

"I should be very glad," he said, "if you would tell me how you discovered all these things. And what it was that the little salon on the first morning had to tell to you? And why Celia Harland ran from the glass doors across the grass to the motor-car and again from the carriage into the house on the lake? Why she did not resist yesterday evening? Why she did not cry for help? How much of Helene Vauquier's evidence was true and how much false? For what reason Wethermill concerned himself in this affair? Oh! and a thousand things which I don't understand."

"Ah, the cushions, and the scrap of paper, and the aluminium flask," said Hanaud; and the triumph faded from his face. He spoke now to Ricardo with a genuine friendliness. "You must not be angry with me if I keep you in the dark for a little while. I, too, Mr. Ricardo, have artistic inclinations. I will not spoil the remarkable story which I think Mlle. Celie will be ready to tell us. Afterwards I will willingly explain to you what I read in the evidences of the room, and what so greatly puzzled me then. But it is not the puzzle or its solution," he said modestly, "which is most interesting here. Consider the people. Mme. Dauvray, the old, rich, ignorant woman, with her superstitions and her generosity, her desire to converse with Mme. de Montespan and the great ladies of the past, and her love of a young, fresh face about her; Helene Vauquier, the maid with her six years of confidential service, who finds herself suddenly supplanted and made to tend and dress in dainty frocks the girl who has supplanted her; the young girl herself, that poor child, with her love of fine clothes, the Bohemian who, brought up amidst trickeries and practising them as a profession, looking upon them and upon misery and starvation and despair as the commonplaces of life, keeps a simplicity and a delicacy and a freshness which would have withered in a day had she been brought up otherwise; Harry Wethermill, the courted and successful man of genius.

"Just imagine if you can what his feelings must have been, when in Mme. Dauvray's bedroom, with the woman he had uselessly murdered lying rigid beneath the sheet, he saw me raise the block of wood from the inlaid floor and take out one by one those jewel cases for which less than twelve hours before he had been ransacking that very room. But what he must have felt! And to give no sign! Oh, these people are the interesting problems in this story. Let us hear what happened on that terrible night. The puzzle-that can wait." In Mr. Ricardo's view Hanaud was proved right. The extraordinary and appalling story which was gradually unrolled of what had happened on that night of Tuesday in the Villa Rose exceeded in its grim interest all the mystery of the puzzle. But it was not told at once.

The trouble at first with Mlle. Celie was a fear of sleep. She dared not sleep-even with a light in the room and a nurse at her bedside. When her eyes were actually closing she would force herself desperately back into the living world. For when she slept she dreamed through again that dark and dreadful night of Tuesday and the two days which followed it, until at some moment endurance snapped and she woke up screaming. But youth, a good constitution, and a healthy appetite had their way with her in the end.

She told her share of the story-she told what happened. There was apparently one terrible scene when she was confronted with Harry Wethermill in the office of Monsieur Fleuriot, the Juge d'instruction, and on her knees, with the tears streaming down her face, besought him to confess the truth. For a long while he held out. And then there came a strange and human turn to the affair. Adele Rossignol-or, to give her real name, Adele Tace, the wife of Hippolyte-had conceived a veritable passion for Harry Wethermill. He was of a not uncommon type, cold and callous in himself, yet with the power to provoke passion in women. And Adele Tace, as the story was told of how Harry Wethermill had paid his court to Celia Harland, was seized with a vindictive jealousy. Hanaud was not surprised. He knew the woman-criminal of his country-brutal, passionate, treacherous. The anonymous letters in a woman's handwriting which descend upon the Rue de Jerusalem, and betray the men who have committed thefts, had left him no illusions upon that figure in the history of crime. Adele Rossignol ran forward to confess, so that Harry Wethermill might suffer to the last possible point of suffering. Then at last Wethermill gave in and, broken down by the ceaseless interrogations of the magistrate, confessed in his turn too. The one, and the only one, who stood firmly throughout and denied the crime was Helene Vauquier. Her thin lips were kept contemptuously closed, whatever the others might admit. With a white, hard face, quietly and respectfully she faced the magistrate week after week. She was the perfect picture of a servant who knew her place. And nothing was wrung from her. But without her help the story became complete. And Ricardo was at pains to write it out.


## CHAPTER XV


## CELIA'S STORY

The story begins with the explanation of that circumstance which had greatly puzzled Mr. Ricardo-Celia's entry into the household of Mme. Dauvray.

Celia's father was a Captain Harland, of a marching regiment, who had little beyond good looks and excellent manners wherewith to support his position. He was extravagant in his tastes, and of an easy mind in the presence of embarrassments. To his other disadvantages he added that of falling in love with a pretty girl no better off than himself. They married, and Celia was born. For nine years they managed, through the wife's constant devotion, to struggle along and to give their daughter an education. Then, however, Celia's mother broke down under the strain and died. Captain Harland, a couple of years later, went out of the service with discredit, passed through the bankruptcy court, and turned showman. His line was thought-reading; he enlisted the services of his daughter, taught her the tricks of his trade, and became "The Great Fortinbras" of the music-halls. Captain Harland would move amongst the audience, asking the spectators in a whisper to think of a number or of an article in their pockets, after the usual fashion, while the child, in her short frock, with her long fair hair tied back with a ribbon, would stand blind-folded upon the platform and reel off the answers with astonishing rapidity. She was singularly quick, singularly receptive.

The undoubted cleverness of the performance, and the beauty of the child, brought to them a temporary prosperity. The Great Fortinbras rose from the music-halls to the assembly rooms of provincial towns. The performance became genteel, and ladies flocked to the matinees.

The Great Fortinbras dropped his pseudonym and became once more Captain Harland.

As Celia grew up, he tried a yet higher flight-he became a spiritualist, with Celia for his medium. The thought-reading entertainments became thrilling seances, and the beautiful child, now grown into a beautiful girl of seventeen, created a greater sensation as a medium in a trance than she had done as a lightning thought-reader.

"I saw no harm in it," Celia explained to M. Fleuriot, without any attempt at extenuation. "I never understood that we might be doing any hurt to any one. People were interested. They were to find us out if they could, and they tried to and they couldn't. I looked upon it quite simply in that way. It was just my profession. I accepted it without any question. I was not troubled about it until I came to Aix."

A startling exposure, however, at Cambridge discredited the craze for spiritualism, and Captain Harland's fortunes declined. He crossed with his daughter to France and made a disastrous tour in that country, wasted the last of his resources in the Casino at Dieppe, and died in that town, leaving Celia just enough money to bury him and to pay her third-class fare to Paris.

There she lived honestly but miserably. The slimness of her figure and a grace of movement which was particularly hers obtained her at last a situation as a mannequin in the show-rooms of a modiste. She took a room on the top floor of a house in the Rue St. Honore and settled down to a hard and penurious life.

"I was not happy or contented-no," said Celia frankly and decisively. "The long hours in the close rooms gave me headaches and made me nervous. I had not the temperament. And I was very lonely-my life had been so different. I had had fresh air, good clothes, and freedom. Now all was changed. I used to cry myself to sleep up in my little room, wondering whether I would ever have friends. You see, I was quite young-only eighteen-and I wanted to live."

A change came in a few months, but a disastrous change. The modiste failed. Celia was thrown out of work, and could get nothing to do. Gradually she pawned what clothes she could spare; and then there came a morning when she had a single five-franc piece in the world and owed a month's rent for her room. She kept the five-franc piece all day and went hungry, seeking for work. In the evening she went to a provision shop to buy food, and the man behind the counter took the five-franc piece. He looked at it, rung it on the counter, and, with a laugh, bent it easily in half.

"See here, my little one," he said, tossing the coin back to her, "one does not buy good food with lead."

Celia dragged herself out of the shop in despair. She was starving. She dared not go back to her room. The thought of the concierge at the bottom of the stairs, insistent for the rent, frightened her. She stood on the pavement and burst into tears. A few people stopped and watched her curiously, and went on again. Finally a sergent-de-ville told her to go away.

The girl moved on with the tears running down her cheeks. She was desperate, she was lonely.

"I thought of throwing myself into the Seine," said Celia simply, in telling her story to the Juge d'Instruction. "Indeed, I went to the river. But the water looked so cold, so terrible, and I was young. I wanted so much to live. And then-the night came, and the lights made the city bright, and I was very tired and-and —"

And, in a word, the young girl went up to Montmartre in desperation, as quickly as her tired legs would carry her. She walked once or twice timidly past the restaurants, and, finally, entered one of them, hoping that some one would take pity on her and give her some supper. She stood just within the door of the supper-room. People pushed past her-men in evening dress, women in bright frocks and jewels. No one noticed her. She had shrunk into a corner, rather hoping not to be noticed, now that she had come. But the novelty of her surroundings wore off. She knew that for want of food she was almost fainting. There were two girls engaged by the management to dance amongst the tables while people had supper-one dressed as a page in blue satin, and the other as a Spanish dancer. Both girls were kind. They spoke to Celia between their dances. They let her waltz with them. Still no one noticed her. She had no jewels, no fine clothes, no CHIC-the three indispensable things. She had only youth and a pretty face.

"But," said Celia, "without jewels and fine clothes and CHIC these go for nothing in Paris. At last, however, Mme. Dauvray came in with a party of friends from a theatre, and saw how unhappy I was, and gave me some supper. She asked me about myself, and I told her. She was very kind, and took me home with her, and I cried all the way in the carriage. She kept me a few days, and then she told me that I was to live with her, for often she was lonely too, and that if I would she would some day find me a nice, comfortable husband and give me a marriage portion. So all my troubles seemed to be at an end," said Celia, with a smile.

Within a fortnight Mme. Dauvray confided to Celia that there was a new fortune-teller come to Paris, who, by looking into a crystal, could tell the most wonderful things about the future. The old woman's eyes kindled as she spoke. She took Celia to the fortune-teller's rooms next day, and the girl quickly understood the ruling passion of the woman who had befriended her. It took very little time then for Celia to notice how easily Mme. Dauvray was duped, how perpetually she was robbed. Celia turned the problem over in her mind.

"Madame had been very good to me. She was kind and simple," said Celia, with a very genuine affection in her voice. "The people whom we knew laughed at her, and were ungenerous. But there are many women whom the world respects who are worse than ever was poor Mme. Dauvray. I was very fond of her, so I proposed to her that we should hold a seance, and I would bring people from the spirit world I knew that I could amuse her with something much more clever and more interesting than the fortune-tellers. And at the same time I could save her from being plundered. That was all I thought about."

That was all she thought about, yes. She left Helene Vauquier out of her calculations, and she did not foresee the effect of her steances upon Mme. Dauvray. Celia had no suspicions of Helene Vauquier. She would have laughed if any one had told her that this respectable and respectful middle-aged woman, who was so attentive, so neat, so grateful for any kindness, was really nursing a rancorous hatred against her. Celia had sprung from Montmartre suddenly; therefore Helene Vauquier despised her. Celia had taken her place in Mme. Dauvray's confidence, had deposed her unwittingly, had turned the confidential friend into a mere servant; therefore Helene Vauquier hated her. And her hatred reached out beyond the girl, and embraced the old, superstitious, foolish woman, whom a young and pretty face could so easily beguile. Helene Vauquier despised them both, hated them both, and yet must nurse her rancour in silence and futility. Then came the seances, and at once, to add fuel to her hatred, she found herself stripped of those gifts and commissions which she had exacted from the herd of common tricksters who had been wont to make their harvest out of Mme. Dauvray. Helene Vauquier was avaricious and greedy, like so many of her class. Her hatred of Celia, her contempt for Mme. Dauvray, grew into a very delirium. But it was a delirium she had the cunning to conceal. She lived at white heat, but to all the world she had lost nothing of her calm.

Celia did not foresee the hatred she was arousing; nor, on the other hand, did she foresee the overwhelming effect of these spiritualistic seances on Mme. Dauvray. Celia had never been brought quite close to the credulous before.

"There had always been the row of footlights," she said. "I was on the platform; the audience was in the hall; or, if it was at a house, my father made the arrangements. I only came in at the last moment, played my part, and went away. It was never brought home to me that some amongst these people really and truly believed. I did not think about it. Now, however, when I saw Mme. Dauvray so feverish, so excited, so firmly convinced that great ladies from the spirit world came and spoke to her, I became terrified. I had aroused a passion which I had not suspected. I tried to stop the seances, but I was not allowed. I had aroused a passion which I could not control. I was afraid that Mme. Dauvray's whole life-it seems absurd to those who did not know her, but those who did will understand-yes, her whole life and happiness would be spoilt if she discovered that what she believed in was all a trick."

She spoke with a simplicity and a remorse which it was difficult to disbelieve. M. Fleuriot, the judge, now at last convinced that the Dreyfus affair was for nothing in the history of this crime, listened to her with sympathy.

"That is your explanation, mademoiselle," he said gently. "But I must tell you that we have another."

"Yes, monsieur?" Celia asked.

"Given by Helene Vauquier," said Fleuriot.

Even after these days Celia could not hear that woman's name without a shudder of fear and a flinching of her whole body. Her face grew white, her lips dry.

"I know, monsieur, that Helene Vauquier is not my friend," she said. "I was taught that very cruelly."

"Listen, mademoiselle, to what she says," said the judge, and he read out to Celia an extract or two from Hanaud's report of his first interview with Helene Vauquier in her bedroom at the Villa Rose.

"You hear what she says. 'Mme. Dauvray would have had seances all day, but Mlle. Celie pleaded that she was left exhausted at the end of them. But Mlle. Celie was of an address.' And again, speaking of Mme. Dauvray's queer craze that the spirit of Mme. de Montespan should be called up, Helene Vauquier says: 'She was never gratified. Always she hoped. Always Mlle. Celie tantalised her with the hope. She would not spoil her fine affairs by making these treats too common.' Thus she attributes your reluctance to multiply your experiments to a desire to make the most profit possible out of your wares, like a good business woman."

"It is not true, monsieur," cried Celia earnestly. "I tried to stop the seances because now for the first time I recognised that I had been playing with a dangerous thing. It was a revelation to me. I did not know what to do. Mme. Dauvray would promise me everything, give me everything, if only I would consent when I refused. I was terribly frightened of what would happen. I did not want power over people. I knew it was not good for her that she should suffer so much excitement. No, I did not know what to do. And so we all moved to Aix."

And there she met Harry Wethermill on the second day after her arrival, and proceeded straightway for the first time to fall in love. To Celia it seemed that at last that had happened for which she had so longed. She began really to live as she understood life at this time. The day, until she met Harry Wethermill, was one flash of joyous expectation; the hours when they were together a time of contentment which thrilled with some chance meeting of the hands into an exquisite happiness. Mme. Dauvray understood quickly what was the matter, and laughed at her affectionately.

"Celie, my dear," she said, "your friend, M. Wethermill —'Arry, is it not? See, I pronounce your tongue-will not be as comfortable as the nice, fat, bourgeois gentleman I meant to find for you. But, since you are young, naturally you want storms. And there will be storms, Celie," she concluded, with a laugh.

Celia blushed.

"I suppose there will," she said regretfully. There were, indeed, moments when she was frightened of Harry Wethermill, but frightened with a delicious thrill of knowledge that he was only stern because he cared so much.

But in a day or two there began to intrude upon her happiness a stinging dissatisfaction with her past life. At times she fell into melancholy, comparing her career with that of the man who loved her. At times she came near to an extreme irritation with Helene Vauquier. Her lover was in her thoughts. As she put it herself:

"I wanted always to look my best, and always to be very good."

Good in the essentials of life, that is to be understood. She had lived in a lax world. She was not particularly troubled by the character of her associates; she was untouched by them; she liked her fling at the baccarat-tables. These were details, and did not distress her. Love had not turned her into a Puritan. But certain recollections plagued her soul. The visit to the restaurant at Montmartre, for instance, and the seances. Of these, indeed, she thought to have made an end. There were the baccarat-rooms, the beauty of the town and the neighbourhood to distract Mme. Dauvray. Celia kept her thoughts away from seances. There was no seance as yet held in the Villa Rose. And there would have been none but for Helene Vauquier.

One evening, however, as Harry Wethermill walked down from the Cercle to the Villa des Fleurs, a woman's voice spoke to him from behind.

"Monsieur!"

He turned and saw Mme. Dauvray's maid. He stopped under a street lamp, and said:

"Well, what can I do for you?"

The woman hesitated.

"I hope monsieur will pardon me," she said humbly. "I am committing a great impertinence. But I think monsieur is not very kind to Mlle. Celie."

Wethermill stared at her.

"What on earth do you mean?" he asked angrily.

Helene Vauquier looked him quietly in the face.

"It is plain, monsieur, that Mlle. Celie loves monsieur. Monsieur has led her on to love him. But it is also plain to a woman with quick eyes that monsieur himself cares no more for mademoiselle than for the button on his coat. It is not very kind to spoil the happiness of a young and pretty girl, monsieur."

Nothing could have been more respectful than the manner in which these words were uttered. Wethermill was taken in by it. He protested earnestly, fearing lest the maid should become an enemy.

"Helene, it is not true that I am playing with Mlle. Celie. Why should I not care for her?"

Helene Vauquier shrugged her shoulders. The question needed no answer.

"Why should I seek her so often if I did not care?"

And to this question Helene Vauquier smiled —a quiet, slow, confidential smile.

"What does monsieur want of Mme. Dauvray?" she asked. And the question was her answer.

Wethermill stood silent. Then he said abruptly:

"Nothing, of course; nothing." And he walked away.

But the smile remained on Helene Vauquier's face. What did they all want of Mme. Dauvray? She knew very well. It was what she herself wanted-with other things. It was money-always money. Wethermill was not the first to seek the good graces of Mme. Dauvray through her pretty companion. Helene Vauquier went home. She was not discontented with her conversation. Wethermill had paused long enough before he denied the suggestion of her words. She approached him a few days later a second time and more openly. She was shopping in the Rue du Casino when he passed her. He stopped of his own accord and spoke to her. Helene Vauquier kept a grave and respectful face. But there was a pulse of joy at her heart. He was coming to her hand.

"Monsieur," she said, "you do not go the right way." And again her strange smile illuminated her face. "Mlle. Celie sets a guard about Mme. Dauvray. She will not give to people the opportunity to find madame generous."

"Oh," said Wethermill slowly. "Is that so?" And he turned and walked by Helene Vauquier's side.

"Never speak of Mme. Dauvray's wealth, monsieur, if you would keep the favour of Mlle. Celie. She is young, but she knows her world."

"I have not spoken of money to her," replied Wethermill; and then he burst out laughing. "But why should you think that I —I, of all men-want money?" he asked.

And Helene answered him again enigmatically.

"If I am wrong, monsieur, I am sorry, but you can help me too," she said, in her submissive voice. And she passed on, leaving Wethermill rooted to the ground.

It was a bargain she proposed-the impertinence of it! It was a bargain she proposed-the value of it! In that shape ran Harry Wethermill's thoughts. He was in desperate straits, though to the world's eye he was a man of wealth. A gambler, with no inexpensive tastes, he had been always in need of money. The rights in his patent he had mortgaged long ago. He was not an idler; he was no sham foisted as a great man on an ignorant public. He had really some touch of genius, and he cultivated it assiduously. But the harder he worked, the greater was his need of gaiety and extravagance. Gifted with good looks and a charm of manner, he was popular alike in the great world and the world of Bohemia. He kept and wanted to keep a foot in each. That he was in desperate straits now, probably Helene Vauquier alone in Aix had recognised. She had drawn her inference from one simple fact. Wethermill asked her at a later time when they were better acquainted how she had guessed his need.

"Monsieur," she replied, "you were in Aix without a valet, and it seemed to me that you were of that class of men who would never move without a valet so long as there was money to pay his wages. That was my first thought. Then when I saw you pursue your friendship with Mlle. Celie-you, who so clearly to my eyes did not love her —I felt sure."

On the next occasion that the two met, it was again Harry Wethermill who sought Helene Vauquier. He talked for a minute or two upon indifferent subjects, and then he said quickly:

"I suppose Mme. Dauvray is very rich?"

"She has a great fortune in jewels," said Helene Vauquier.

Wethermill started. He was agitated that evening, the woman saw. His hands shook, his face twitched. Clearly he was hard put to it. For he seldom betrayed himself. She thought it time to strike.

"Jewels which she keeps in the safe in her bedroom," she added.

"Then why don't you —?" he began, and stopped.

"I said that I too needed help," replied Helene, without a ruffle of her composure.

It was nine o'clock at night. Helene Vauquier had come down to the Casino with a wrap for Mme. Dauvray. The two people were walking down the little street of which the Casino blocks the end. And it happened that an attendant at the Casino, named Alphonse Ruel, passed them, recognised them both, and-smiled to himself with some amusement. What was Wethermill doing in company with Mme. Dauvray's maid? Ruel had no doubt. Ruel had seen Wethermill often enough these recent days with Mme. Dauvray's pretty companion. Ruel had all a Frenchman's sympathy with lovers. He wished them well, those two young and attractive people, and hoped that the maid would help their plans.

But as he passed he caught a sentence spoken suddenly by Wethermill.

"Well, it is true; I must have money." And the agitated voice and words remained fixed in his memory. He heard, too, a warning "Hush!" from the maid. Then they passed out of his hearing. But he turned and saw that Wethermill was talking volubly. What Harry Wethermill was saying he was saying in a foolish burst of confidence.

"You have guessed it, Helene-you alone." He had mortgaged his patent twice over-once in France, once in England-and the second time had been a month ago. He had received a large sum down, which went to pay his pressing creditors. He had hoped to pay the sum back from a new invention.

"But Helene, I tell you," he said, "I have a conscience." And when she smiled he explained. "Oh, not what the priests would call a conscience; that I know. But none the less I have a conscience —a conscience about the things which really matter, at all events to me. There is a flaw in that new invention. It can be improved; I know that. But as yet I do not see how, and —I cannot help it —I must get it right; I cannot let it go imperfect when I know that it's imperfect, when I know that it can be improved, when I am sure that I shall sooner or later hit upon the needed improvement. That is what I mean when I say I have a conscience."

Helena Vauquier smiled indulgently. Men were queer fish. Things which were really of no account troubled and perplexed them and gave them sleepless nights. But it was not for her to object, since it was one of these queer anomalies which was giving her her chance.

"And the people are finding out that you have sold your rights twice over," she said sympathetically. "That is a pity, monsieur."

"They know," he answered; "those in England know."

"And they are very angry?"

"They threaten me," said Wethermill. "They give me a month to restore the money. Otherwise there will be disgrace, imprisonment, penal servitude."

Helene Vauquier walked calmly on. No sign of the intense joy which she felt was visible in her face, and only a trace of it in her voice.

"Monsieur will, perhaps, meet me to-morrow in Geneva," she said. And she named a small cafe in a back street. "I can get a holiday for the afternoon." And as they were near to the villa and the lights, she walked on ahead.

Wethermill loitered behind. He had tried his luck at the tables and had failed. And-and-he must have the money.

He travelled, accordingly, the next day to Geneva, and was there presented to Adele Tace and Hippolyte.

"They are trusted friends of mine," said Helene Vauquier to Wethermill, who was not inspired to confidence by the sight of the young man with the big ears and the plastered hair. As a matter of fact, she had never met them before they came this year to Aix.

The Tace family, which consisted of Adele and her husband and Jeanne, her mother, were practised criminals. They had taken the house in Geneva deliberately in order to carry out some robberies from the great villas on the lake-side. But they had not been fortunate; and a description of Mme. Dauvray's jewellery in the woman's column of a Geneva newspaper had drawn Adele Tace over to Aix. She had set about the task of seducing Mme. Dauvray's maid, and found a master, not an instrument.

In the small cafe on that afternoon of July Helene Vauquier instructed her accomplices, quietly and methodically, as though what she proposed was the most ordinary stroke of business. Once or twice subsequently Wethermill, who was the only safe go-between, went to the house in Geneva, altering his hair and wearing a moustache, to complete the arrangements. He maintained firmly at his trial that at none of these meetings was there any talk of murder.

"To be sure," said the judge, with a savage sarcasm. "In decent conversation there is always a reticence. Something is left to be understood."

And it is difficult to understand how murder could not have been an essential part of their plan, since —-But let us see what happened.


**CHAPTER XVI**

On the Friday before the crime was committed Mme. Dauvray and Celia dined at the Villa des Fleurs. While they were drinking their coffee Harry Wethermill joined them. He stayed with them until Mme. Dauvray was ready to move, and then all three walked into the baccarat rooms together. But there, in the throng of people, they were separated.

Harry Wethermill was looking carefully after Celia, as a good lover should. He had, it seemed, no eyes for any one else; and it was not until a minute or two had passed that the girl herself noticed that Mme. Dauvray was not with them.

"We will find her easily," said Harry.

"Of course," replied Celia.

"There is, after all, no hurry," said Wethermill, with a laugh; "and perhaps she was not un-willing to leave us together."

Celia dimpled to a smile.

"Mme. Dauvray is kind to me," she said, with a very pretty timidity.

"And yet more kind to me," said Wethermill in a low voice which brought the blood into Celia's cheeks.

But even while he spoke he soon caught sight of Mme. Dauvray standing by one of the tables; and near to her was Adele Tace. Adele had not yet made Mme. Dauvray's acquaintance; that was evident. She was apparently unaware of her; but she was gradually edging towards her. Wethermill smiled, and Celia caught the smile.

"What is it?" she asked, and her head began to turn in the direction of Mme. Dauvray.

"Why, I like your frock-that's all," said Wethermill at once; and Celia's eyes went down to it.

"Do you?" she said, with a pleased smile. It was a dress of dark blue which suited her well. "I am glad. I think it is pretty." And they passed on.

Wethermill stayed by the girl's side throughout the evening. Once again he saw Mme. Dau-vray and Adele Tace. But now they were together; now they were talking. The first step had been taken. Adele Tace had scraped acquaintance with Mme. Dauvray. Celia saw them almost at the same moment.

"Oh, there is Mme. Dauvray," she cried, taking a step towards her.

Wethermill detained the girl.

"She seems quite happy," he said; and, indeed, Mme. Dauvray was talking volubly and with the utmost interest, the jewels sparkling about her neck. She raised her head, saw Celia, nodded to her affectionately, and then pointed her out to her companion. Adele Tace looked the girl over with interest and smiled contentedly. There was nothing to be feared from her. Her youth, her very daintiness, seemed to offer her as the easiest of victims.

"You see Mme. Dauvray does not want you," said Harry Wethermill. "Let us go and play CHEMIN-DE-FER"; and they did, moving off into one of the further rooms.

It was not until another hour had passed that Celia rose and went in search of Mme. Dauvray. She found her still talking earnestly to Adele Tace. Mme. Dauvray got up at once.

"Are you ready to go, dear?" she asked, and she turned to Adele Tace. "This is Celie, Mme. Rossignol," she said, and she spoke with a marked significance and a note of actual exultation in her voice.

Celia, however, was not unused to this tone. Mme. Dauvray was proud of her companion, and had a habit of showing her off, to the girl's discomfort. The three women spoke a few words, and then Mme. Dauvray and Celia left the rooms and walked to the entrance-doors. But as they walked Celia became alarmed.

She was by nature extraordinarily sensitive to impressions. It was to that quick receptivity that the success of "The Great Fortinbras" had been chiefly due. She had a gift of rapid compre-hension. It was not that she argued, or deducted, or inferred. But she felt. To take a metaphor from the work of the man she loved, she was a natural receiver. So now, although no word was spoken, she was aware that Mme. Dauvray was greatly excited-greatly disturbed; and she dreaded the reason of that excitement and disturbance.

While they were driving home in the motor-car she said apprehensively:

"You met a friend then, to-night, madame?"

"No," said Mme. Dauvray; "I made a friend. I had not met Mme. Rossignol before. A bracelet of hers came undone, and I helped her to fasten it. We talked afterwards. She lives in Geneva."

Mme. Dauvray was silent for a moment or two. Then she turned impulsively and spoke in a voice of appeal.

"Celie, we talked of things"; and the girl moved impatiently. She understood very well what were the things of which Mme. Dauvray and her new friend had talked. "And she laughed. ... I could not bear it."

Celia was silent, and Mme. Dauvray went on in a voice of awe:

"I told her of the wonderful things which happened when I sat with Helene in the dark-how the room filled with strange sounds, how ghostly fingers touched my forehead and my eyes. She laughed-Adele Rossignol laughed, Celie. I told her of the spirits with whom we held converse. She would not believe. Do you remember the evening, Celie, when Mme. de Castiglione came back an old, old woman, and told us how, when she had grown old and had lost her beauty and was very lonely, she would no longer live in the great house which was so full of torturing memories, but took a small APPARTEMENT near by, where no one knew her; and how she used to walk out late at night, and watch, with her eyes full of tears, the dark windows which had been once so bright with light? Adele Rossignol would not believe. I told her that I had found the story afterwards in a volume of memoirs. Adele Rossignol laughed and said no doubt you had read that volume yourself before the seance."

Celia stirred guiltily.

"She had no faith in you, Celie. It made me angry, dear. She said that you invented your own tests. She sneered at them. A string across a cupboard! A child, she said, could manage that; much more, then, a clever young lady. Oh, she admitted that you were clever! Indeed, she urged that you were far too clever to submit to the tests of some one you did not know. I replied that you would. I was right, Celie, was I not?"

And again the appeal sounded rather piteously in Mme. Dauvray's voice.

"Tests!" said Celia, with a contemptuous laugh. And, in truth, she was not afraid of them. Mme. Dauvray's voice at once took courage.

"There!" she cried triumphantly. "I was sure. I told her so. Celie, I arranged with her that next Tuesday —"

And Celia interrupted quickly.

"No! Oh, no!"

Again there was silence; and then Mme. Dauvray said gently, but very seriously:

"Celie, you are not kind."

Celia was moved by the reproach.

"Oh, madame!" she cried eagerly. "Please don't think that. How could I be anything else to you who are so kind to me?"

"Then prove it, Celie. On Tuesday I have asked Mme. Rossignol to come; and —" The old woman's voice became tremulous with excitement. "And perhaps-who knows? —perhaps SHE will appear to us."

Celia had no doubt who "she" was. She was Mme. de Montespan.

"Oh, no, madame!" she stammered. "Here, at Aix, we are not in the spirit for such things."

And then, in a voice of dread, Mme. Dauvray asked: "Is it true, then, what Adele said?"

And Celia started violently. Mme. Dauvray doubted.

"I believe it would break my heart, my dear, if I were to think that; if I were to know that you had tricked me," she said, with a trembling voice.

Celia covered her face with her hands. It would be true. She had no doubt of it. Mme. Dauvray would never forgive herself-would never forgive Celia. Her infatuation had grown so to engross her that the rest of her life would surely be embittered. It was not merely a passion-it was a creed as well. Celia shrank from the renewal of these seances. Every fibre in her was in revolt. They were so unworthy-so unworthy of Harry Wethermill, and of herself as she now herself wished to be. But she had to pay now; the moment for payment had come.

"Celie," said Mme. Dauvray, "it isn't true! Surely it isn't true?"

Celia drew her hands away from her face.

"Let Mme. Rossignol come on Tuesday!" she cried, and the old woman caught the girl's hand and pressed it with affection.

"Oh, thank you! thank you!" she cried. "Adele Rossignol laughs to-night; we shall convince her on Tuesday, Celie! Celie, I am so glad!" And her voice sank into a solemn whisper, pathetically ludicrous. "It is not right that she should laugh! To bring people back through the gates of the spirit-world —that is wonderful."

To Celia the sound of the jargon learnt from her own lips, used by herself so thoughtlessly in past times, was odious. "For the last time," she pleaded to herself. All her life was going to change; though no word had yet been spoken by Harry Wethermill, she was sure of it. Just for this one last time, then, so that she might leave Mme. Dauvray the colours of her belief, she would hold a seance at the Villa Rose.

Mme. Dauvray told the news to Helene Vauquier when they reached the villa.

"You will be present, Helene," she cried excitedly. "It will be Tuesday. There will be the three of us."

"Certainly, if madame wishes," said Helene submissively. She looked round the room. "Mlle. Celie can be placed on a chair in that recess and the curtains drawn, whilst we-madame and madame's friend and I —can sit round this table under the side windows."

"Yes," said Celia, "that will do very well."

It was Madame Dauvray's habit when she was particularly pleased with Celia to dismiss her maid quickly, and to send her to brush the girl's hair at night; and in a little while on this night Helene went to Celia's room. While she brushed Celia's hair she told her that Servettaz's parents lived at Chambery, and that he would like to see them.

"But the poor man is afraid to ask for a day," she said. "He has been so short a time with madame."

"Of course madame will give him a holiday if he asks," replied Celia with a smile. "I will speak to her myself to-morrow."

"It would be kind of mademoiselle," said Helene Vauquier. "But perhaps —" She stopped.

"Well," said Celia.

"Perhaps mademoiselle would do better still to speak to Servattaz himself and encourage him to ask with his own lips. Madame has her moods, is it not so? She does not always like it to be forgotten that she is the mistress."

On the next day accordingly Celia did speak to Servettaz, and Servettaz asked for his holiday.

"But of course," Mme. Dauvray at once replied. "We must decide upon a day."

It was then that Helene Vauquier ventured humbly upon a suggestion.

"Since madame has a friend coming here on Tuesday, perhaps that would be the best day for him to go. Madame would not be likely to take a long drive that afternoon."

"No, indeed," replied Mme. Dauvray. "We shall all three dine together early in Aix and return here."

"Then I will tell him he may go to-morrow," said Celia.

For this conversation took place on the Monday, and in the evening Mme. Dauvray and Celia went as usual to the Villa des Fleurs and dined there.

"I was in a bad mind," said Celia, when asked by the Juge d'Instruction to explain that attack of nerves in the garden which Ricardo had witnessed. "I hated more and more the thought of the seance which was to take place on the morrow. I felt that I was disloyal to Harry. My nerves were all tingling. I was not nice that night at all," she added quaintly. "But at dinner I determined that if I met Harry after dinner, as I was sure to do, I would tell him the whole truth about myself. However, when I did meet him I was frightened. I knew how stern he could suddenly look. I dreaded what he would think. I was too afraid that I should lose him. No, I could not speak; I had not the courage. That made me still more angry with myself, and so I —I quarrelled at once with Harry. He was surprised; but it was natural, wasn't it? What else should one do under such circumstances, except quarrel with the man one loved? Yes, I really quarrelled with him, and said things which I thought and hoped would hurt. Then I ran away from him lest I should break down and cry. I went to the tables and lost at once all the money I had except one note of five louis. But that did not console me. And I ran out into the garden, very unhappy. There I behaved like a child, and Mr. Ricardo saw me. But it was not the little money I had lost which troubled me; no, it was the thought of what a coward I was. Afterwards Harry and I made it up, and I thought, like the little fool I was, that he wanted to ask me to marry him. But I would not let him that night. Oh! I wanted him to ask me —I was longing for him to ask me-but not that night. Somehow I felt that the seance and the tricks must be all over and done with before I could listen or answer."

The quiet and simple confession touched the magistrate who listened to it with profound pity. He shaded his eyes with his hand. The girl's sense of her unworthiness, the love she had given so unstintingly to Harry Wethermill, the deep pride she had felt in the delusion that he loved her too, had in it an irony too bitter. But he was aroused to anger against the man.

"Go on, mademoiselle," he said. But in spite of himself his voice trembled.

"So I arranged with him that we should meet on Wednesday, as Mr. Ricardo heard."

"You told him that you would 'want him' on Wednesday," said the Judge quoting Mr. Ricardo's words.

"Yes," replied Celia. "I meant that the last word of all these deceptions would have been spoken. I should be free to hear what he had to say to me. You see, monsieur, I was so sure that I knew what it was he had to say to me —" and her voice broke upon the words. She recovered herself with an effort. "Then I went home with Mme. Dauvray."

On the morning of Tuesday, however, there came a letter from Adele Tace, of which no trace was afterwards discovered. The letter invited Mme. Dauvray and Celia to come out to Annecy and dine with her at an hotel there. They could then return together to Aix. The proposal fitted well with Mme. Dauvray's inclinations. She was in a feverish mood of excitement.

"Yes, it will be better that we dine quietly together in a place where there is no noise and no crowd, and where no one knows us," she said; and she looked up the time-table. "There is a train back which reaches Aix at nine o'clock," she said, "so we need not spoil Servettaz' holiday."

"His parents will be expecting him," Helene Vauquier added.

Accordingly Servettaz left for Chambery by the 1.50 train from Aix; and later on in the afternoon Mme. Dauvray and Celia went by train to Annecy. In the one woman's mind was the queer longing that "she" should appear and speak to-night; in the girl's there was a wish passionate as a cry. "This shall be the last time," she said to herself again and again —"the very last."

Meanwhile, Helene Vauquier, it must be held, burnt carefully Adele Taces letter. She was left in the Villa Rose with the charwoman to keep her company. The charwoman bore testimony that Helene Vauquier certainly did burn a letter in the kitchen-stove, and that after she had burned it she sat for a long time rocking herself in a chair, with a smile of great pleasure upon her face, and now and then moistening her lips with her tongue. But Helene Vauquier kept her mouth sealed.

## CHAPTER XVII

# THE AFTERNOON OF TUESDAY

Mme. Dauvray and Celia found Adele Rossignol, to give Adele Tace the name which she assumed, waiting for them impatiently in the garden of an hotel at Annecy, on the Promenade du Paquier. She was a tall, lithe woman, and she was dressed, by the purse and wish of Helene Vauquier, in a robe and a long coat of sapphire velvet, which toned down the coarseness of her good looks and lent something of elegance to her figure.

"So it is mademoiselle," Adele began, with a smile of raillery, "who is so remarkably clever."

"Clever?" answered Celia, looking straight at Adele, as though through her she saw mysteries beyond. She took up her part at once. Since for the last time it had got to be played, there must be no fault in the playing. For her own sake, for the sake of Mme. Dauvray's happiness, she must carry it off to-night with success. The suspicions of Adele Rossignol must obtain no verification. She spoke in a quiet and most serious voice. "Under spirit-control no one is clever. One does the bidding of the spirit which controls."

"Perfectly," said Adele in a malicious tone. "I only hope you will see to it, mademoiselle, that some amusing spirits control you this evening and appear before us."

"I am only the living gate by which the spirit forms pass from the realm of mind into the world of matter," Celia replied.

"Quite so," said Adele comfortably. "Now let us be sensible and dine. We can amuse ourselves with mademoiselle's rigmaroles afterwards."

Mme. Dauvray was indignant. Celia, for her part, felt humiliated and small. They sat down to their dinner in the garden, but the rain began to fall and drove them indoors. There were a few people dining at the same hour, but none near enough to overhear them. Alike in the garden and the dining-room, Adele Tace kept up the same note of ridicule and disbelief. She had been carefully tutored for her work. She was able to cite the stock cases of exposure —"LES FRERES Davenport," as she called them, Eusapia Palladino and Dr. Slade. She knew the precautions which had been taken to prevent trickery and where those precautions had failed. Her whole conversation was carefully planned to one end, and to one end alone. She wished to produce in the minds of her companions so complete an impression of her scepticism that it would seem the most natural thing in the world to both of them that she should insist upon subjecting Celia to the severest tests. The rain ceased, and they took their coffee on the terrace of the hotel. Mme. Dauvray had been really pained by the conversation of Adele Tace. She had all the missionary zeal of a fanatic.

"I do hope, Adele, that we shall make you believe. But we shall. Oh, I am confident we shall." And her voice was feverish.

Adele dropped for the moment her tone of raillery.

"I am not unwilling to believe," she said, "but I cannot. I am interested-yes. You see how much I have studied the subject. But I cannot believe. I have heard stories of how these manifestations are produced-stories which make me laugh. I cannot help it. The tricks are so easy. A young girl wearing a black frock which does not rustle-it is always a black frock, is it not, because a black frock cannot be seen in the dark? —carrying a scarf or veil, with which she can make any sort of headdress if only she is a little clever, and shod in a pair of felt-soled slippers, is shut up in a cabinet or placed behind a screen, and the lights are turned down or out —" Adele broke off with a comic shrug of the shoulders. "Bah! It ought not to deceive a child."

Celia sat with a face which WOULD grow red. She did not look, but none the less she was aware that Mme. Dauvray was gazing at her with a perplexed frown and some return of her suspicion showing in her eyes. Adele Tace was not content to leave the subject there.

"Perhaps," she said, with a smile, "Mlle. Celie dresses in that way for a seance?"

"Madame shall see to-night," Celia stammered, and Camille Dauvray rather sternly repeated her words.

"Yes, Adele shall see to-night. I myself will decide what you shall wear, Celie."

Adele Tace casually suggested the kind of dress which she would prefer.

"Something light in colour with a train, something which will hiss and whisper if mademoiselle moves about the room-yes, and I think one of mademoiselle's big hats," she said. "We will have mademoiselle as modern as possible, so that, when the great ladies of the past appear in the coiffure of their day, we may be sure it is not Mlle. Celie who represents them."

"I will speak to Helene," said Mme. Dauvray, and Adele Tace was content.

There was a particular new dress of which she knew, and it was very desirable that Mlle. Celie should wear it to-night. For one thing, if Celia wore it, it would help the theory that she had put it on because she expected that night a lover; for another, with that dress there went a pair of satin slippers which had just come home from a shoemaker at Aix, and which would leave upon soft mould precisely the same imprints as the grey suede shoes which the girl was wearing now.

Celia was not greatly disconcerted by Mme. Rossignol's precautions. She would have to be a little more careful, and Mme. de Montespan would be a little longer in responding to the call of Mme. Dauvray than most of the other dead ladies of the past had been. But that was all. She was, however, really troubled in another way. All through dinner, at every word of the conversation, she had felt her reluctance towards this seance swelling into a positive disgust. More than once she had felt driven by some uncontrollable power to rise up at the table and cry out to Adele:

"You are right! It IS trickery. There is no truth in it."

But she had mastered herself. For opposite to her sat her patroness, her good friend, the woman who had saved her. The flush upon Mme. Dauvray's cheeks and the agitation of her manner warned Celia how much hung upon the success of this last seance. How much for both of them!

And in the fullness of that knowledge a great fear assailed her. She began to be afraid, so strong was her reluctance, that she would not bring her heart into the task. "Suppose I failed to-night because I could not force myself to wish not to fail!" she thought, and she steeled herself against the thought. To-night she must not fail. For apart altogether from Mme. Dauvray's happiness, her own, it seemed, was at stake too.

"It must be from my lips that Harry learns what I have been," she said to herself, and with the resolve she strengthened herself.

"I will wear what you please," she said, with a smile. "I only wish Mme. Rossignol to be satisfied."

"And I shall be," said Adele, "if—" She leaned forward in anxiety. She had come to the real necessity of Helene Vauquier's plan. "If we abandon as quite laughable the cupboard door and the string across it; if, in a word, mademoiselle consents that we tie her hand and foot and fasten her securely in a chair. Such restraints are usual in the experiments of which I have read. Was there not a medium called Mlle. Cook who was secured in this way, and then remarkable things, which I could not believe, were supposed to have happened?"

"Certainly I permit it," said Celia, with indifference; and Mme. Dauvray cried enthusiastically:

"Ah, you shall believe to-night in those wonderful things!"

Adele Tace leaned back. She drew a breath. It was a breath of relief.

"Then we will buy the cord in Aix," she said.

"We have some, no doubt, in the house," said Mme. Dauvray.

Adele shook her head and smiled.

"My dear madame, you are dealing with a sceptic. I should not be content."

Celia shrugged her shoulders.

"Let us satisfy Mme. Rossignol," she said.

Celia, indeed, was not alarmed by this last precaution. For her it was a test less difficult than the light-coloured rustling robe. She had appeared upon so many platforms, had experienced too often the bungling efforts of spectators called up from the audience, to be in any fear. There were very few knots from which her small hands and supple fingers had not learnt long since to extricate themselves. She was aware how much in all these matters the personal equation counted. Men who might, perhaps, have been able to tie knots from which she could not get free were always too uncomfortable and self-conscious, or too afraid of hurting her white arms and wrists, to do it. Women, on the other hand, who had no compunctions of that kind, did not know how.

It was now nearly eight o'clock; the rain still held off.

"We must go," said Mme. Dauvray, who for the last half-hour had been continually looking at her watch.

They drove to the station and took the train. Once more the rain came down, but it had stopped again before the train steamed into Aix at nine o'clock.

"We will take a cab," said Mme. Dauvray: "it will save time."

"It will do us good to walk, madame," pleaded Adele. The train was full. Adele passed quickly out from the lights of the station in the throng of passengers and waited in the dark square for the others to join her. "It is barely nine. A friend has promised to call at the Villa Rose for me after eleven and drive me back in a motor-car to Geneva, so we have plenty of time."

They walked accordingly up the hill, Mme. Dauvray slowly, since she was stout, and Celia keeping pace with her. Thus it seemed natural that Adele Tace should walk ahead, though a passer-by would not have thought she was of their company. At the corner of the Rue du Casino Adele waited for them and said quickly:

"Mademoiselle, you can get some cord, I think, at the shop there," and she pointed to the shop of M. Corval. "Madame and I will go slowly on; you, who are the youngest, will easily catch us up." Celia went into the shop, bought the cord, and caught Mme. Dauvray up before she reached the villa.

"Where is Mme. Rossignol?" she asked.

"She went on," said Camille Dauvray. "She walks faster than I do."

They passed no one whom they knew, although they did pass one who recognised them, as Perrichet had discovered. They came upon Adele, waiting for them at the corner of the road, where it turns down toward the villa.

"It is near here-the Villa Rose?" she asked.

"A minute more and we are there."

They turned in at the drive, closed the gate behind them, and walked up to the villa.

The windows and the glass doors were closed, the latticed shutters fastened. A light burned in the hall.

"Helene is expecting us," said Mme. Dauvray, for as they approached she saw the front door open to admit them, and Helene Vauquier in the doorway. The three women went straight into the little salon, which was ready with the lights up and a small fire burning. Celia noticed the fire with a trifle of dismay. She moved a fire-screen in front of it.

"I can understand why you do that, mademoiselle," said Adele Rossignol, with a satirical smile. But Mme. Dauvray came to the girl's help.

"She is right, Adele. Light is the great barrier between us and the spirit-world," she said solemnly.

Meanwhile, in the hall Helene Vauquier locked and bolted the front door. Then she stood motionless, with a smile upon her face and a heart beating high. All through that afternoon she had been afraid that some accident at the last moment would spoil her plan, that Adele Tace had not learned her lesson, that Celie would take fright, that she would not return. Now all those fears were over. She had her victims safe within the villa. The charwoman had been sent home. She had them to herself. She was still standing in the hall when Mme. Dauvray called aloud impatiently:

"Helene! Helene!"

And when she entered the salon there was still, as Celia was able to recall, some trace of her smile lingering upon her face.

Adele Rossignol had removed her hat and was taking off her gloves. Mme. Dauvray was speaking impatiently to Celia.

"We will arrange the room, dear, while Helene helps you to dress. It will be quite easy. We shall use the recess."

And Celia, as she ran up the stairs, heard Mme. Dauvray discussing with her maid what frock she should wear. She was hot, and she took a hurried bath. When she came from her bathroom she saw with dismay that it was her new pale-green evening gown which had been laid out. It was the last which she would have chosen. But she dared not refuse it. She must still any suspicion. She must succeed. She gave herself into Helene's hands. Celia remembered afterwards one or two points which passed barely heeded at the time. Once while Helene was dressing her hair she looked up at the maid in the mirror and noticed a strange and rather horrible grin upon her face, which disappeared the moment their eyes met. Then again, Helene was extraordinarily slow and extraordinarily fastidious that evening. Nothing satisfied her, neither the hang of the girl's skirt, the folds of her sash, nor the arrangement of her hair.

"Come, Helene, be quick," said Celia. "You know how madame hates to be kept waiting at these times. You might be dressing me to go to meet my lover," she added, with a blush and a smile at her own pretty reflection in the glass; and a queer look came upon Helene Vauquier's face. For it was at creating just this very impression that she aimed.

"Very well, mademoiselle," said Helene. And even as she spoke Mme. Dauvray's voice rang shrill and irritable up the stairs.

"Celie! Celie!"

"Quick, Helene," said Celia. For she herself was now anxious to have the seance over and done with.

But Helene did not hurry. The more irritable Mme. Dauvray became, the more impatient with Mlle. Celie, the less would Mlle. Celie dare to refuse the tests Adele wished to impose upon her. But that was not all. She took a subtle and ironic pleasure to-night in decking out her victim's natural loveliness. Her face, her slender throat, her white shoulders, should look their prettiest, her grace of limb and figure should be more alluring than ever before. The same words, indeed, were running through both women's minds.

"For the last time," said Celia to herself, thinking of these horrible seances, of which to-night should see the end.

"For the last time," said Helene Vauquier too. For the last time she laced the girl's dress. There would be no more patient and careful service for Mlle. Celie after to-night. But she should have it and to spare to-night. She should be conscious that her beauty had never made so strong an appeal; that she was never so fit for life as at the moment when the end had come. One thing Helene regretted. She would have liked Celia-Celia, smiling at herself in the glass-to know suddenly what was in store for her! She saw in imagination the colour die from the cheeks, the eyes stare wide with terror.

"Celie! Celie!"

Again the impatient voice rang up the stairs, as Helene pinned the girl's hat upon her fair head. Celie sprang up, took a quick step or two towards the door, and stopped in dismay. The swish of her long satin train must betray her. She caught up the dress and tried again. Even so, the rustle of it was heard.

"I shall have to be very careful. You will help me, Helene?"

"Of course, mademoiselle. I will sit underneath the switch of the light in the salon. If madame, your visitor, makes the experiment too difficult, I will find a way to help you," said Helene Vauquier, and as she spoke she handed Celia a long pair of white gloves.

"I shall not want them," said Celia.

"Mme. Dauvray ordered me to give them to you," replied Helene.

Celia took them hurriedly, picked up a white scarf of tulle, and ran down the stairs. Helene Vauquier listened at the door and heard madame's voice in feverish anger.

"We have been waiting for you, Celie. You have been an age."

Helene Vauquier laughed softly to herself, took out Celia's white frock from the wardrobe, turned off the lights, and followed her down to the hall. She placed the cloak just outside the door of the salon. Then she carefully turned out all the lights in the hall and in the kitchen and went into the salon. The rest of the house was in darkness. This room was brightly lit; and it had been made ready.


## CHAPTER XVIII


## THE SEANCE

Helene Vauquier locked the door of the salon upon the inside and placed the key upon the mantel-shelf, as she had always done whenever a seance had been held. The curtains had been loosened at the sides of the arched recess in front of the glass doors, ready to be drawn across. Inside the recess, against one of the pillars which supported the arch, a high stool without a back, taken from the hall, had been placed, and the back legs of the stool had been lashed with cord firmly to the pillar, so that it could not be moved. The round table had been put in position, with three chairs about it. Mme. Dauvray waited impatiently. Celia stood apparently unconcerned, apparently lost to all that was going on. Her eyes saw no one. Adele looked up at Celia, and laughed maliciously.

"Mademoiselle, I see, is in the very mood to produce the most wonderful phenomena. But it will be better, I think, madame," she said, turning to Mme. Dauvray, "that Mlle. Celie should put on those gloves which I see she has thrown on to a chair. It will be a little more difficult for mademoiselle to loosen these cords, should she wish to do so."

The argument silenced Celia. If she refused this condition now she would excite Mme. Dauvray to a terrible suspicion. She drew on her gloves ruefully and slowly, smoothed them over her elbows, and buttoned them. To free her hands with her fingers and wrists already hampered in gloves would not be so easy a task. But there was no escape. Adele Rossignol was watching her with a satiric smile. Mme. Dauvray was urging her to be quick. Obeying a second order the girl raised her skirt and extended a slim foot in a pale-green silk stocking and a satin slipper to match. Adele was content. Celia was wearing the shoes she was meant to wear. They were made upon the very same last as those which Celia had just kicked off upstairs. An almost imperceptible nod from Helene Vauquier, moreover, assured her.

She took up a length of the thin cord.

"Now, how are we to begin?" she said awkwardly. "I think I will ask you, mademoiselle, to put your hands behind you."

Celia turned her back and crossed her wrists. She stood in her satin frock, with her white arms and shoulders bare, her slender throat supporting her small head with its heavy curls, her big hat —a picture of young grace and beauty. She would have had an easy task that night had there been men instead of women to put her to the test. But the women were intent upon their own ends: Mme. Dauvray eager for her seance, Adele Tace and Helene Vauquier for the climax of their plot.

Celia clenched her hands to make the muscles of her wrists rigid to resist the pressure of the cord. Adele quietly unclasped them and placed them palm to palm. And at once Celia became uneasy. It was not merely the action, significant though it was of Adele's alertness to thwart her, which troubled Celia. But she was extraordinarily receptive of impressions, extraordinarily quick to feel, from a touch, some dim sensation of the thought of the one who touched her. So now the touch of Adele's swift, strong, nervous hands caused her a queer, vague shock of discomfort. It was no more than that at the moment, but it was quite definite as that.

"Keep your hands so, please, mademoiselle," said Adele; "your fingers loose."

And the next moment Celia winced and had to bite her lip to prevent a cry. The thin cord was wound twice about her wrists, drawn cruelly tight and then cunningly knotted. For one second Celia was thankful for her gloves; the next, more than ever she regretted that she wore them. It would have been difficult enough for her to free her hands now, even without them. And upon that a worse thing befell her.

"I beg mademoiselle's pardon if I hurt her," said Adele.

And she tied the girl's thumbs and little fingers. To slacken the knots she must have the use of her fingers, even though her gloves made them fumble. Now she had lost the use of them altogether. She began to feel that she was in master-hands. She was sure of it the next instant. For Adele stood up, and, passing a cord round the upper part of her arms, drew her elbows back. To bring any strength to help her in wriggling her hands free she must be able to raise her elbows. With them trussed in the small of her back she was robbed entirely of her strength. And all the time her strange uneasiness grew. She made a movement of revolt, and at once the cord was loosened.

"Mlle. Celie objects to my tests," said Adele, with a laugh, to Mme. Dauvray. "And I do not wonder."

Celia saw upon the old woman's foolish and excited face a look of veritable consternation.

"Are you afraid, Celie?" she asked.

There was anger, there was menace in the voice, but above all these there was fear-fear that her illusions were to tumble about her. Celia heard that note and was quelled by it. This folly of belief, these seances, were the one touch of colour in Mme. Dauvray's life. And it was just that instinctive need of colour which had made her so easy to delude. How strong the need is, how seductive the proposal to supply it, Celia knew well. She knew it from the experience of her life when the Great Fortinbras was at the climax of his fortunes. She had travelled much amongst monotonous, drab towns without character or amusements. She had kept her eyes open. She had seen that it was from the denizens of the dull streets in these towns that the quack religions won their recruits. Mme. Dauvray's life had been a featureless sort of affair until these experiments had come to colour it. Madame Dauvray must at any rate preserve the memory of that colour.

"No," she said boldly; "I am not afraid," and after that she moved no more.

Her elbows were drawn firmly back and tightly bound. She was sure she could not free them. She glanced in despair at Helene Vauquier, and then some glimmer of hope sprang up. For Helene Vauquier gave her a look, a smile of reassurance. It was as if she said, "I will come to your help." Then, to make security still more sure, Adele turned the girl about as unceremoniously as if she had been a doll, and, passing a cord at the back of her arms, drew both ends round in front and knotted them at her waist.

"Now, Celie," said Adele, with a vibration in her voice which Celia had not remarked before.

Excitement was gaining upon her, as upon Mme. Dauvray. Her face was flushed and shiny, her manner peremptory and quick. Celia's uneasiness grew into fear. She could have used the words which Hanaud spoke the next day in that very room —"There is something here which I do not understand." The touch of Adele Tace's hands communicated something to her-something which filled her with a vague alarm. She could not have formulated it if she would; she dared not if she could. She had but to stand and submit.

"Now," said Adele.

She took the girl by the shoulders and set her in a clear space in the middle of the room, her back to the recess, her face to the mirror, where all could see her.

"Now, Celie" —she had dropped the "Mlle." and the ironic suavity of her manner —"try to free yourself."

For a moment the girl's shoulders worked, her hands fluttered. But they remained helplessly bound.

"Ah, you will be content, Adele, to-night," cried Mme. Dauvray eagerly.

But even in the midst of her eagerness-so thoroughly had she been prepared-there lingered a flavour of doubt, of suspicion. In Celia's mind there was still the one desperate resolve.

"I must succeed to-night," she said to herself—"I must!"

Adele Rossignol kneeled on the floor behind her. She gathered in carefully the girl's frock. Then she picked up the long train, wound it tightly round her limbs, pinioning and swathing them in the folds of satin, and secured the folds with a cord about the knees.

She stood up again.

"Can you walk, Celie?" she asked. "Try!"

With Helene Vauquier to support her if she fell, Celia took a tiny shuffling step forward, feeling supremely ridiculous. No one, however, of her audience was inclined to laugh. To Mme. Dauvray the whole business was as serious as the most solemn ceremonial. Adele was intent upon making her knots secure. Helene Vauquier was the well-bred servant who knew her place. It was not for her to laugh at her young mistress, in however ludicrous a situation she might be.

"Now," said Adele, "we will tie mademoiselle's ankles, and then we shall be ready for Mme. de Montespan."

The raillery in her voice had a note of savagery in it now. Celia's vague terror grew. She had a feeling that a beast was waking in the woman, and with it came a growing premonition of failure. Vainly she cried to herself, "I must not fail to-night." But she felt instinctively that there was a stronger personality than her own in that room, taming her, condemning her to failure, influencing the others.

She was placed in a chair. Adele passed a cord round her ankles, and the mere touch of it quickened Celia to a spasm of revolt. Her last little remnant of liberty was being taken from her. She raised herself, or rather would have raised herself. But Helene with gentle hands held her in the chair, and whispered under her breath:

"Have no fear! Madame is watching."

Adele looked fiercely up into the girl's face.

"Keep still, HEIN, LA PETITE!" she cried. And the epithet —"little one" —was a light to Celia. Till now, upon these occasions, with her black ceremonial dress, her air of aloofness, her vague eyes, and the dignity of her carriage, she had already produced some part of their effect before the seance had begun. She had been wont to sail into the room, distant, mystical. She had her audience already expectant of mysteries, prepared for marvels. Her work was already half done. But now of all that help she was deprived. She was no longer a person aloof, a prophetess, a seer of visions; she was simply a smartly-dressed girl of to-day, trussed up in a ridiculous and painful position-that was all. The dignity was gone. And the more she realised that, the more she was hindered from influencing her audience, the less able she was to concentrate her mind upon them, to will them to favour her. Mme. Dauvray's suspicions, she was sure, were still awake. She could not quell them. There was a stronger personality than hers at work in the room. The cord bit through her thin stockings into her ankles. She dared not complain. It was savagely tied. She made no remonstrance. And then Helene Vauquier raised her up from the chair and lifted her easily off the ground. For a moment she held her so. If Celia had felt ridiculous before, she knew that she was ten times more so now. She could see herself as she hung in Helene Vauquier's arms, with her delicate frock ludicrously swathed and swaddled about her legs. But, again, of those who watched her no one smiled.

"We have had no such tests as these," Mme. Dauvray explained, half in fear, half in hope.

Adele Rossignol looked the girl over and nodded her head with satisfaction. She had no animosity towards Celia; she had really no feeling of any kind for her or against her. Fortunately she was unaware at this time that Harry Wethermill had been paying his court to her or it would have gone worse with Mlle. Celie before the night was out. Mlle. Celie was just a pawn in a very dangerous game which she happened to be playing, and she had succeeded in engineering her pawn into the desired condition of helplessness. She was content.

"Mademoiselle," she said, with a smile, "you wish me to believe. You have now your opportunity."

Opportunity! And she was helpless. She knew very well that she could never free herself from these cords without Helene's help. She would fail, miserably and shamefully fail.

"It was madame who wished you to believe," she stammered.

And Adele Rossignol laughed suddenly—a short, loud, harsh laugh, which jarred upon the quiet of the room. It turned Celia's vague alarm into a definite terror. Some magnetic current brought her grave messages of fear. The air about her seemed to tingle with strange menaces. She looked at Adele. Did they emanate from her? And her terror answered her "Yes." She made her mistake in that. The strong personality in the room was not Adele Rossignol, but Helene Vauquier, who held her like a child in her arms. But she was definitely aware of danger, and too late aware of it. She struggled vainly. From her head to her feet she was powerless. She cried out hysterically to her patron:

"Madame! Madame! There is something—a presence here-some one who means harm! I know it!"

And upon the old woman's face there came a look, not of alarm, but of extraordinary relief. The genuine, heartfelt cry restored her confidence in Celia.

"Some one-who means harm!" she whispered, trembling with excitement.

"Ah, mademoiselle is already under control," said Helene, using the jargon which she had learnt from Celia's lips.

Adele Rossignol grinned.

"Yes, LA PETITE is under control," she repeated, with a sneer; and all the elegance of her velvet gown was unable to hide her any longer from Celia's knowledge. Her grin had betrayed her. She was of the dregs. But Helene Vauquier whispered:

"Keep still, mademoiselle. I shall help you."

Vauquier carried the girl into the recess and placed her upon the stool. With a long cord Adele bound her by the arms and the waist to the pillar, and her ankles she fastened to the rung of the stool, so that they could not touch the ground.

"Thus we shall be sure that when we hear rapping it will be the spirits, and not the heels, which rap," she said. "Yes, I am contented now." And she added, with a smile, "Celie may even have her scarf," and, picking up a white scarf of tulle which Celia had brought down with her, she placed it carelessly round her shoulders.

"Wait!" Helene Vauquier whispered in Celia's ear.

To the cord about Celia's waist Adele was fastening a longer line.

"I shall keep my foot on the other end of this," she said, "when the lights are out, and I shall know then if our little one frees herself."

The three women went out of the recess. And the next moment the heavy silk curtains swung across the opening, leaving Celia in darkness. Quickly and noiselessly the poor girl began to twist and work her hands. But she only bruised her wrists. This was to be the last of the seances. But it must succeed! So much of Mme. Dauvray's happiness, so much of her own, hung upon its success. Let her fail to-night, she would be surely turned from the door. The story of her trickery and her exposure would run through Aix. And she had not told Harry! It would reach his ears from others. He would never forgive her. To face the old, difficult life of poverty and perhaps starvation again, and again alone, would be hard enough; but to face it with Harry Wethermill's contempt added to its burdens-as the poor girl believed she surely would have to do-no, that would be impossible! Not this time would she turn away from the Seine, because it was so terrible and cold. If she had had the courage to tell him yesterday, he would have forgiven, surely he would! The tears gathered in her eyes and rolled down her cheeks. What would become of her now? She was in pain besides. The cords about her arms and ankles tortured her. And she feared-yes, desperately she feared the effect of the exposure upon Mme. Dauvray. She had been treated as a daughter; now she was in return to rob Mme. Dauvray of the belief which had become the passion of her life.

"Let us take our seats at the table," she heard Mme. Dauvray say. "Helene, you are by the switch of the electric light. Will you turn it off?" And upon that Helene whispered, yet so that the whisper reached to Celia and awakened hope:

"Wait! I will see what she is doing."

The curtains opened, and Helene Vauquier slipped to the girl's side.

Celia checked her tears. She smiled imploringly, gratefully.

"What shall I do?" asked Helene, in a voice so low that the movement of her mouth rather than the words made the question clear.

Celia raised her head to answer. And then a thing incomprehensible to her happened. As she opened her lips Helene Vauquier swiftly forced a handkerchief in between the girl's teeth, and lifting the scarf from her shoulders wound it tightly twice across her mouth, binding her lips, and made it fast under the brim of her hat behind her head. Celia tried to scream; she could not utter a sound. She stared at Helene with incredulous, horror-stricken eyes. Helene nodded at her with a cruel grin of satisfaction, and Celia realised, though she did not understand, something of the rancour and the hatred which seethed against her in the heart of the woman whom she had supplanted. Helene Vauquier meant to expose her to-night; Celia had not a doubt of it. That was her explanation of Helene Vauquier's treachery; and believing that error, she believed yet another-that she had reached the terrible climax of her troubles. She was only at the beginning of them.

"Helene!" cried Mme. Dauvray sharply. "What are you doing?"

The maid instantly slid back into the room.

"Mademoiselle has not moved," she said.

Celia heard the women settle in their chairs about the table.

"Is madame ready?" asked Helene; and then there was the sound of the snap of a switch. In the salon darkness had come.

If only she had not been wearing her gloves, Celia thought, she might possibly have just been able to free her fingers and her supple hands from their bonds. But as it was she was helpless. She could only sit and wait until the audience in the salon grew tired of waiting and came to her. She closed her eyes, pondering if by any chance she could excuse her failure. But her heart sank within her as she thought of Mme. Rossignol's raillery. No, it was all over for her....

She opened her eyes, and she wondered. It seemed to her that there was more light in the recess than there had been when she closed them. Very likely her eyes were growing used to the darkness. Yet-yet-she ought not to be able to distinguish quite so clearly the white pillar opposite to her. She looked towards the glass doors and understood. The wooden shutters outside the doors were not quite closed. They had been carelessly left unbolted. A chink from lintel to floor let in a grey thread of light. Celia heard the women whispering in the salon, and turned her head to catch the words.

"Do you hear any sound?"

"No."

"Was that a hand which touched me?"

"No."

"We must wait."

And so silence came again, and suddenly there was quite a rush of light into the recess. Celia was startled. She turned her head back again towards the window. The wooden door had swung a little more open. There was a wider chink to let the twilight of that starlit darkness through. And as she looked, the chink slowly broadened and broadened, the door swung slowly back on hinges which were strangely silent. Celia stared at the widening panel of grey light with a vague terror. It was strange that she could hear no whisper of wind in the garden. Why, oh, why was that latticed door opening so noiselessly? Almost she believed that the spirits after all...And suddenly the recess darkened again, and Celia sat with her heart leaping and shivering in her breast. There was something black against the glass doors —a man. He had appeared as silently, as suddenly, as any apparition. He stood blocking out the light, pressing his face against the glass, peering into the room. For a moment the shock of horror stunned her. Then she tore frantically at the cords. All thought of failure, of exposure, of dismissal had fled from her. The three poor women-that was her thought-were sitting unwarned, unsuspecting, defenceless in the pitch-blackness of the salon. A few feet away a man, a thief, was peering in. They were waiting for strange things to happen in the darkness. Strange and terrible things would happen unless she could free herself, unless she could warn them. And she could not. Her struggles were mere efforts to struggle, futile, a shiver from head to foot, and noiseless as a shiver. Adele Rossignol had done her work well and thoroughly. Celia's arms, her waist, her ankles were pinioned; only the bandage over her mouth seemed to be loosening. Then upon horror, horror was added. The man touched the glass doors, and they swung silently inwards. They, too, had been carelessly left unbolted. The man stepped without a sound over the sill into the room. And, as he stepped, fear for herself drove out for the moment from Celia's thoughts fear for the three women in the black room. If only he did not see her! She pressed herself against the pillar. He might overlook her, perhaps! His eyes would not be so accustomed to the darkness of the recess as hers. He might pass her unnoticed-if only he did not touch some fold of her dress.

And then, in the midst of her terror, she experienced so great a revulsion from despair to joy that a faintness came upon her, and she almost swooned. She saw who the intruder was. For when he stepped into the recess he turned towards her, and the dim light struck upon him and showed her the contour of his face. It was her lover, Harry Wethermill. Why he had come at this hour, and in this strange way, she did not consider. Now she must attract his eyes, now her fear was lest he should not see her.

But he came at once straight towards her. He stood in front of her, looking into her eyes. But he uttered no cry. He made no movement of surprise. Celia did not understand it. His face was in the shadow now and she could not see it. Of course, he was stunned, amazed. But-but-he stood almost as if he had expected to find her there and just in that helpless attitude. It was absurd, of course, but he seemed to look upon her helplessness as nothing out of the ordinary way. And he raised no hand to set her free. A chill struck through her. But the next moment he did raise his hand and the blood flowed again, at her heart. Of course, she was in the darkness. He had not seen her plight. Even now he was only beginning to be aware of it. For his hand touched the bandage over her mouth-tentatively. He felt for the knot under the broad brim of her hat at the back of her head. He found it. In a moment she would be free. She kept her head quite still, and then-why was he so long? she asked herself. Oh, it was not possible! But her heart seemed to stop, and she knew that it was not only possible-it was true: he was tightening the scarf, not loosening it. The folds bound her lips more surely. She felt the ends drawn close at the back of her head. In a frenzy she tried to shake her head free. But he held her face firmly and finished his work. He was wearing gloves, she noticed with horror, just as thieves do. Then his hands slid down her trembling arms and tested the cord about her wrists. There was something horribly deliberate about his movements. Celia, even at that moment, even with him, had the sensation which had possessed her in the salon. It was the personal equation on which she was used to rely. But neither Adele nor this-this STRANGER was considering her as even a human being. She was a pawn in their game, and they used her, careless of her terror, her beauty, her pain. Then he freed from her waist the long cord which ran beneath the curtain to Adele Rossignol's foot. Celia's first thought was one of relief. He would jerk the cord unwittingly. They would come into the recess and see him. And then the real truth flashed in upon her blindingly. He had jerked the cord, but he had jerked it deliberately. He was already winding it up in a coil as it slid noiselessly across the polished floor beneath the curtains towards him. He had given a signal to Adele Rossignol. All that woman's scepticism and precaution against trickery had been a mere blind, under cover of which she had been able to pack the girl away securely without arousing her suspicions. Helene Vauquier was in the plot, too. The scarf at Celia's mouth was proof of that. As if to add proof to proof, she heard Adele Rossignol speak in answer to the signal.

"Are we all ready? Have you got Mme. Dauvray's left hand, Helene?"

"Yes, madame," answered the maid.

"And I have her right hand. Now give me yours, and thus we are in a circle about the table."

Celia, in her mind, could see them sitting about the round table in the darkness, Mme. Dauvray between the two women, securely held by them. And she herself could not utter a cry-could not move a muscle to help her.

Wethermill crept back on noiseless feet to the window, closed the wooden doors, and slid the bolts into their sockets. Yes, Helene Vauquier was in the plot. The bolts and the hinges would not have worked so smoothly but for her. Darkness again filled the recess instead of the grey twilight. But in a moment a faint breath of wind played upon Celia's forehead, and she knew that the man had parted the curtains and slipped into the room. Celia let her head fall towards her shoulder. She was sick and faint with terror. Her lover was in this plot-the lover in whom she had felt so much pride, for whose sake she had taken herself so bitterly to task. He was the associate of Adele Rossignol, of Helene Vauquier. He had used her, Celia, as an instrument for his crime. All their hours together at the Villa des Fleurs-here to-night was their culmination. The blood buzzed in her ears and hammered in the veins of her temples. In front of her eyes the darkness whirled, flecked with fire. She would have fallen, but she could not fall. Then, in the silence, a tambourine jangled. There was to be a seance to-night, then, and the seance had begun. In a dreadful suspense she heard Mme. Dauvray speak.


## CHAPTER XIX


## HELENE EXPLAINS

And what she heard made her blood run cold.

Mme. Dauvray spoke in a hushed, awestruck voice.

"There is a presence in the room."

It was horrible to Celia that the poor woman was speaking the jargon which she herself had taught to her.

"I will speak to it," said Mme. Dauvray, and raising her voice a little, she asked: "Who are you that come to us from the spirit-world?"

No answer came, but all the while Celia knew that Wethermill was stealing noiselessly across the floor towards that voice which spoke this professional patter with so simple a solemnity.

"Answer!" she said. And the next moment she uttered a little shrill cry —a cry of enthusiasm. "Fingers touch my forehead-now they touch my cheek-now they touch my throat!"

And upon that the voice ceased. But a dry, choking sound was heard, and a horrible scuffling and tapping of feet upon the polished floor, a sound most dreadful. They were murdering her-murdering an old, kind woman silently and methodically in the darkness. The girl strained and twisted against the pillar furiously, like an animal in a trap. But the coils of rope held her; the scarf suffocated her. The scuffling became a spasmodic sound, with intervals between, and then ceased altogether. A voice spoke —a man's voice-Wethermill's. But Celia would never have recognised it-it had so shrill and fearful an intonation.

"That's horrible," he said, and his voice suddenly rose to a scream.

"Hush!" Helene Vauquier whispered sharply. "What's the matter?"

"She fell against me-her whole weight. Oh!"

"You are afraid of her!"

"Yes, yes!" And in the darkness Wethermill's voice came querulously between long breaths. "Yes, NOW I am afraid of her!"

Helene Vauquier replied again contemptuously. She spoke aloud and quite indifferently. Nothing of any importance whatever, one would have gathered, had occurred.

"I will turn on the light," she said. And through the chinks in the curtain the bright light shone. Celia heard a loud rattle upon the table, and then fainter sounds of the same kind. And as a kind of horrible accompaniment there ran the laboured breathing of the man, which broke now and then with a sobbing sound. They were stripping Mme. Dauvray of her pearl necklace, her bracelets, and her rings. Celia had a sudden importunate vision of the old woman's fat, podgy hands loaded with brilliants. A jingle of keys followed.

"That's all," Helene Vauquier said. She might have just turned out the pocket of an old dress.

There was the sound of something heavy and inert falling with a dull crash upon the floor. A woman laughed, and again it was Helene Vauquier.

"Which is the key of the safe?" asked Adele.

And Helene Vauquier replied: —

"That one."

Celia heard some one drop heavily into a chair. It was Wethermill, and he buried his face in his hands. Helene went over to him and laid her hand upon his shoulder and shook him.

"Do you go and get her jewels out of the safe," she said, and she spoke with a rough friendliness.

"You promised you would blindfold the girl," he cried hoarsely.

Helene Vauquier laughed.

"Did I?" she said. "Well, what does it matter?"

"There would have been no need to —" And his voice broke off shudderingly.

"Wouldn't there? And what of us-Adele and me? She knows certainly that we are here. Come, go and get the jewels. The key of the door's on the mantelshelf. While you are away we two will arrange the pretty baby in there."

She pointed to the recess; her voice rang with contempt. Wethermill staggered across the room like a drunkard, and picked up the key in trembling fingers. Celia heard it turn in the lock, and the door bang. Wethermill had gone upstairs.

Celia leaned back, her heart fainting within her. Arrange! It was her turn now. She was to be "arranged." She had no doubt what sinister meaning that innocent word concealed. The dry, choking sound, the horrid scuffling of feet upon the floor, were in her ears. And it had taken so long-so terribly long!

She heard the door open again and shut again. Then steps approached the recess. The curtains were flung back, and the two women stood in front of her-the tall Adele Rossignol with her red hair and her coarse good looks and her sapphire dress, and the hard-featured, sallow maid. The maid was carrying Celia's white coat. They did not mean to murder her, then. They meant to take her away, and even then a spark of hope lit up in the girl's bosom. For even with her illusions crushed she still clung to life with all the passion of her young soul.

The two women stood and looked at her; and then Adele Rossignol burst out laughing. Vauquier approached the girl, and Celia had a moment's hope that she meant to free her altogether, but she only loosed the cords which fixed her to the pillar and the high stool.

"Mademoiselle will pardon me for laughing," said Adele Rossignol politely; "but it was mademoiselle who invited me to try my hand. And really, for so smart a young lady, mademoiselle looks too ridiculous."

She lifted the girl up and carried her back writhing and struggling into the salon. The whole of the pretty room was within view, but in the embrasure of a window something lay dreadfully still and quiet. Celia held her head averted. But it was there, and, though it was there, all the while the women joked and laughed, Adele Rossignol feverishly, Helene Vauquier with a real glee most horrible to see.

"I beg mademoiselle not to listen to what Adele is saying," exclaimed Helene. And she began to ape in a mincing, extravagant fashion the manner of a saleswoman in a shop. "Mademoiselle has never looked so ravishing. This style is the last word of fashion. It is what there is of most

CHIC. Of course, mademoiselle understands that the costume is not intended for playing the piano. Nor, indeed, for the ballroom. It leaps to one's eyes that dancing would be difficult. Nor is it intended for much conversation. It is a costume for a mood of quiet reflection. But I assure mademoiselle that for pretty young ladies who are the favourites of rich old women it is the style most recommended by the criminal classes."

All the woman's bitter rancour against Celia, hidden for months beneath a mask of humility, burst out and ran riot now. She went to Adele Rossignol's help, and they flung the girl face downwards upon the sofa. Her face struck the cushion at one end, her feet the cushion at the other. The breath was struck out of her body. She lay with her bosom heaving.

Helene Vauquier watched her for a moment with a grin, paying herself now for her respectful speeches and attendance.

"Yes, lie quietly and reflect, little fool!" she said savagely. "Were you wise to come here and interfere with Helene Vauquier? Hadn't you better have stayed and danced in your rags at Montmartre? Are the smart frocks and the pretty hats and the good dinners worth the price? Ask yourself these questions, my dainty little friend!"

She drew up a chair to Celia's side, and sat down upon it comfortably.

"I will tell you what we are going to do with you, Mlle. Celie. Adele Rossignol and that kind gentleman, M. Wethermill, are going to take you away with them. You will be glad to go, won't you, dearie? For you love M. Wethermill, don't you? Oh, they won't keep you long enough for you to get tired of them. Do not fear! But you will not come back, Mile. Celie. No; you have seen too much to-night. And every one will think that Mlle. Celie helped to murder and rob her benefactress. They are certain to suspect some one, so why not you, pretty one?"

Celia made no movement. She lay trying to believe that no crime had been committed, that that lifeless body did not lie against the wall. And then she heard in the room above a bed wheeled roughly from its place.

The two women heard it too, and looked at one another.

"He should look in the safe," said Vauquier. "Go and see what he is doing."

And Adele Rossignol ran from the room.

As soon as she was gone Vauquier followed to the door, listened, closed it gently, and came back. She stooped down.

"Mlle. Celie," she said, in a smooth, silky voice, which terrified the girl more than her harsh tones, "there is just one little thing wrong in your appearance, one tiny little piece of bad taste, if mademoiselle will pardon a poor servant the expression. I did not mention it before Adele Rossignol; she is so severe in her criticism, is she not? But since we are alone, I will presume to point out to mademoiselle that those diamond eardrops which I see peeping out under the scarf are a little ostentatious in her present predicament. They are a provocation to thieves. Will mademoiselle permit me to remove them?"

She caught her by the neck and lifted her up. She pushed the lace scarf up at the side of Celia's head. Celia began to struggle furiously, convulsively. She kicked and writhed, and a little tearing sound was heard. One of her shoe-buckles had caught in the thin silk covering of the cushion and slit it. Helene Vauquier let her fall. She felt composedly in her pocket, and drew from it an aluminium flask-the same flask which Lemerre was afterward to snatch up in the bedroom in Geneva. Celia stared at her in dread. She saw the flask flashing in the light. She shrank from it. She wondered what new horror was to grip her. Helene unscrewed the top and laughed pleasantly.

"Mlle. Celie is under control," she said. "We shall have to teach her that it is not polite in young ladies to kick." She pressed Celia down with a hand upon her back, and her voice changed. "Lie still," she commanded savagely. "Do you hear? Do you know what this is, Mlle. Celie?" And she held the flask towards the girl's face. "This is vitriol, my pretty one. Move, and I'll spoil these smooth white shoulders for you. How would you like that?"

Celia shuddered from head to foot, and, burying her face in the cushion, lay trembling. She would have begged for death upon her knees rather than suffer this horror. She felt Vauquier's fingers lingering with a dreadful caressing touch upon her shoulders and about her throat. She was within an ace of the torture, the disfigurement, and she knew it. She could not pray for mercy. She could only lie quite still, as she was bidden, trying to control the shuddering of her limbs and body.

"It would be a good lesson for Mlle. Celie," Helene continued slowly. "I think that if Mlle. Celie will forgive the liberty I ought to inflict it. One little tilt of the flask and the satin of these pretty shoulders —"

She broke off suddenly and listened. Some sound heard outside had given Celia a respite, perhaps more than a respite. Helene set the flask down upon the table. Her avarice had got the better of her hatred. She roughly plucked the earrings out of the girl's ears. She hid them quickly in the bosom of her dress with her eye upon the door. She did not see a drop of blood gather on the lobe of Celia's ear and fall into the cushion on which her face was pressed. She had hardly hidden them away before the door opened and Adele Rossignol burst into the room.

"What is the matter?" asked Vauquier.

"The safe's empty. We have searched the room. We have found nothing," she cried.

"Everything is in the safe," Helene insisted.

"No."

The two women ran out of the room and up the stairs. Celia, lying on the settee, heard all the quiet of the house change to noise and confusion. It was as though a tornado raged in the room overhead. Furniture was tossed about and over the room, feet stamped and ran, locks were smashed in with heavy blows. For many minutes the storm raged. Then it ceased, and she heard the accomplices clattering down the stairs without a thought of the noise they made. They burst into the room. Harry Wethermill was laughing hysterically, like a man off his head. He had been wearing a long dark overcoat when he entered the house; now he carried the coat over his arm. He was in a dinner-jacket, and his black clothes were dusty and disordered.

"It's all for nothing!" he screamed rather than cried. "Nothing but the one necklace and a handful of rings!"

In a frenzy he actually stooped over the dead woman and questioned her.

"Tell us-where did you hide them?" he cried.

"The girl will know," said Helene.

Wethermill rose up and looked wildly at Celia.

"Yes, yes," he said.

He had no scruple, no pity any longer for the girl. There was no gain from the crime unless she spoke. He would have placed his head in the guillotine for nothing. He ran to the writing-table, tore off half a sheet of paper, and brought it over with a pencil to the sofa. He gave them to Vauquier to hold, and drawing out the sofa from the wall slipped in behind. He lifted up Celia with Rossignol's help, and made her sit in the middle of the sofa with her feet upon the ground. He unbound her wrists and fingers, and Vauquier placed the writing-pad and the paper on the girl's knees. Her arms were still pinioned above the elbows; she could not raise her hands high enough to snatch the scarf from her lips. But with the pad held up to her she could write.

"Where did she keep her jewels! Quick! Take the pencil and write," said Wethermill, holding her left wrist.

Vauquier thrust the pencil into her right hand, and awkwardly and slowly her gloved fingers moved across the page.

"I do not know," she wrote; and, with an oath, Wethermill snatched the paper up, tore it into pieces, and threw it down.

"You have got to know," he said, his face purple with passion, and he flung out his arm as though he would dash his fist into her face. But as he stood with his arm poised there came a singular change upon his face.

"Did you hear anything?" he asked in a whisper.

All listened, and all heard in the quiet of the night a faint click, and after an interval they heard it again, and after another but shorter interval yet once more.

"That's the gate," said Wethermill in a whisper of fear, and a pulse of hope stirred within Celia.

He seized her wrists, crushed them together behind her, and swiftly fastened them once more. Adele Rossignol sat down upon the floor, took the girl's feet upon her lap, and quietly wrenched off her shoes.

"The light," cried Wethermill in an agonised voice, and Helena Vauquier flew across the room and turned it off.

All three stood holding their breath, straining their ears in the dark room. On the hard gravel of the drive outside footsteps became faintly audible, and grew louder and came near. Adele whispered to Vauquier:

"Has the girl a lover?"

And Helene Vauquier, even at that moment, laughed quietly.

All Celia's heart and youth rose in revolt against her extremity. If she could only free her lips! The footsteps came round the corner of the house, they sounded on the drive outside the very window of this room. One cry, and she would be saved. She tossed back her head and tried to force the handkerchief out from between her teeth. But Wethermill's hand covered her mouth and held it closed. The footsteps stopped, a light shone for a moment outside. The very handle of the door was tried. Within a few yards help was there-help and life. Just a frail latticed wooden door stood between her and them. She tried to rise to her feet. Adele Rossignol held her legs firmly. She was powerless. She sat with one desperate hope that, whoever it was who was in the garden, he would break in. Were it even another murderer, he might have more pity than the callous brutes who held her now; he could have no less. But the footsteps moved away. It was the withdrawal of all hope. Celia heard Wethermill behind her draw a long breath of relief. That seemed to Celia almost the cruellest part of the whole tragedy. They waited in the darkness until the faint click of the gate was heard once more. Then the light was turned up again.

"We must go," said Wethermill. All the three of them were shaken. They stood looking at one another, white and trembling. They spoke in whispers. To get out of the room, to have done with the business-that had suddenly become their chief necessity.

Adele picked up the necklace and the rings from the satin-wood table and put them into a pocket-bag which was slung at her waist.

"Hippolyte shall turn these things into money," she said. "He shall set about it to-morrow. We shall have to keep the girl now-until she tells us where the rest is hidden."

"Yes, keep her," said Helene. "We will come over to Geneva in a few days, as soon as we can. We will persuade her to tell." She glanced darkly at the girl. Celia shivered.

"Yes, that's it," said Wethermill. "But don't harm her. She will tell of her own will. You will see. The delay won't hurt now. We can't come back and search for a little while."

He was speaking in a quick, agitated voice. And Adele agreed. The desire to be gone had killed even their fury at the loss of their prize. Some time they would come back, but they would not search now-they were too unnerved.

"Helene," said Wethermill, "get to bed. I'll come up with the chloroform and put you to sleep."

Helene Vauquier hurried upstairs. It was part of her plan that she should be left alone in the villa chloroformed. Thus only could suspicion be averted from herself. She did not shrink from the completion of the plan now. She went, the strange woman, without a tremor to her ordeal. Wethermill took the length of rope which had fixed Celia to the pillar.

"I'll follow," he said, and as he turned he stumbled over the body of Mme. Dauvray. With a shrill cry he kicked it out of his way and crept up the stairs. Adele Rossignol quickly set the room in order. She removed the stool from its position in the recess, and carried it to its place in the hall. She put Celia's shoes upon her feet, loosening the cord from her ankles. Then she looked about the floor and picked up here and there a scrap of cord. In the silence the clock upon the mantelshelf chimed the quarter past eleven. She screwed the stopper on the flask of vitriol very carefully, and put the flask away in her pocket. She went into the kitchen and fetched the key of the garage. She put her hat on her head. She even picked up and drew on her gloves, afraid lest she should leave them behind; and then Wethermill came down again. Adele looked at him inquiringly.

"It is all done," he said, with a nod of the head. "I will bring the car down to the door. Then I'll drive you to Geneva and come back with the car here."

He cautiously opened the latticed door of the window, listened for a moment, and ran silently down the drive. Adele closed the door again, but she did not bolt it. She came back into the room; she looked at Celia, as she lay back upon the settee, with a long glance of indecision. And then, to Celia's surprise-for she had given up all hope-the indecision in her eyes became pity. She suddenly ran across the room and knelt down before Celia. With quick and feverish hands she untied the cord which fastened the train of her skirt about her knees.

At first Celia shrank away, fearing some new cruelty. But Adele's voice came to her ears, speaking-and speaking with remorse.

"I can't endure it!" she whispered. "You are so young-too young to be killed."

The tears were rolling down Celia's cheeks. Her face was pitiful and beseeching.

"Don't look at me like that, for God's sake, child!" Adele went on, and she chafed the girl's ankles for a moment.

"Can you stand?" she asked.

Celia nodded her head gratefully. After all, then, she was not to die. It seemed to her hardly possible. But before she could rise a subdued whirr of machinery penetrated into the room, and the motor-car came slowly to the front of the villa.

"Keep still!" said Adele hurriedly, and she placed herself in front of Celia.

Wethermill opened the wooden door, while Celia's heart raced in her bosom.

"I will go down and open the gate," he whispered. "Are you ready?"

"Yes."

Wethermill disappeared; and this time he left the door open. Adele helped Celia to her feet. For a moment she tottered; then she stood firm.

"Now run!" whispered Adele. "Run, child, for your life!"

Celia did not stop to think whither she should run, or how she should escape from Wethermill's search. She could not ask that her lips and her hands might be freed. She had but a few seconds. She had one thought-to hide herself in the darkness of the garden. Celia fled across the room, sprang wildly over the sill, ran, tripped over her skirt, steadied herself, and was swung off the ground by the arms of Harry Wethermill.

"There we are," he said, with his shrill, wavering laugh. "I opened the gate before." And suddenly Celia hung inert in his arms.

The light went out in the salon. Adele Rossignol, carrying Celia's cloak, stepped out at the side of the window.

"She has fainted," said Wethermill. "Wipe the mould off her shoes and off yours too-carefully. I don't want them to think this car has been out of the garage at all."

Adele stooped and obeyed. Wethermill opened the door of the car and flung Celia into a seat. Adele followed and took her seat opposite the girl. Wethermill stepped carefully again on to the grass, and with the toe of his shoe scraped up and ploughed the impressions which he and Adele Rossignol had made on the ground, leaving those which Celia had made. He came back to the window.

"She has left her footmarks clear enough," he whispered. "There will be no doubt in the morning that she went of her own free will."

Then he took the chauffeur's seat, and the car glided silently down the drive and out by the gate. As soon as it was on the road it stopped. In an instant Adele Rossignol's head was out of the window.

"What is it?" she exclaimed in fear.

Wethermill pointed to the roof. He had left the light burning in Helene Vauquier's room.

"We can't go back now," said Adele in a frantic whisper. "No; it is over. I daren't go back."
And Wethermill jammed down the lever. The car sprang forward, and humming steadily over
the white road devoured the miles. But they had made their one mistake.


## CHAPTER XX


## THE GENEVA ROAD

The car had nearly reached Annecy before Celia woke to consciousness. And even then she
was dazed. She was only aware that she was in the motor-car and travelling at a great speed.
She lay back, drinking in the fresh air. Then she moved, and with the movement came to her
recollection and the sense of pain. Her arms and wrists were still bound behind her, and the
cords hurt her like hot wires. Her mouth, however, and her feet were free. She started forward,
and Adele Rossignol spoke sternly from the seat opposite.

"Keep still. I am holding the flask in my hand. If you scream, if you make a movement to
escape, I shall fling the vitriol in your face," she said.

Celia shrank back, shivering.

"I won't! I won't!" she whispered piteously. Her spirit was broken by the horrors of the
night's adventure. She lay back and cried quietly in the darkness of the carriage. The car dashed
through Annecy. It seemed incredible to Celia that less than six hours ago she had been dining
with Mme. Dauvray and the woman opposite, who was now her jailer. Mme. Dauvray lay dead
in the little salon, and she herself-she dared not think what lay in front of her. She was to be
persuaded-that was the word-to tell what she did not know. Meanwhile her name would be
execrated through Aix as the murderess of the woman who had saved her. Then suddenly the
car stopped. There were lights outside. Celia heard voices. A man was speaking to Wethermill.
She started and saw Adele Tace's arm flash upwards. She sank back in terror; and the car rolled
on into the darkness. Adele Tace drew a breath of relief. The one point of danger had been
passed. They had crossed the Pont de la Caille, they were in Switzerland.

Some long while afterwards the car slackened its speed. By the side of it Celia heard the
sound of wheels and of the hooves of a horse. A single-horsed closed landau had been caught
up as it jogged along the road. The motor-car stopped; close by the side of it the driver of
the landau reined in his horse. Wethermill jumped down from the chauffeur's seat, opened the
door of the landau, and then put his head in at the window of the car.

"Are you ready? Be quick!"

Adele turned to Celia.

"Not a word, remember!"

Wethermill flung open the door of the car. Adele took the girl's feet and drew them down
to the step of the car. Then she pushed her out. Wethermill caught her in his arms and carried
her to the landau. Celia dared not cry out. Her hands were helpless, her face at the mercy of
that grim flask. Just ahead of them the lights of Geneva were visible, and from the lights a
silver radiance overspread a patch of sky. Wethermill placed her in the landau; Adele sprang in
behind her and closed the door. The transfer had taken no more than a few seconds. The landau
jogged into Geneva; the motor turned and sped back over the fifty miles of empty road to Aix.

As the motor-car rolled away, courage returned for a moment to Celia. The man-the mur-
derer-had gone. She was alone with Adele Rossignol in a carriage moving no faster than an
ordinary trot. Her ankles were free, the gag had been taken from her lips. If only she could free
her hands and choose a moment when Adele was off her guard she might open the door and
spring out on to the road. She saw Adele draw down the blinds of the carriage, and very carefully, very secretly, Celia began to work her hands behind her. She was an adept; no movement

was visible, but, on the other hand, no success was obtained. The knots had been too cunningly tied. And then Mme. Rossignol touched a button at her side in the leather of the carriage.

The touch turned on a tiny lamp in the roof of the carriage, and she raised a warning hand to Celia.

"Now keep very quiet."

Right through the empty streets of Geneva the landau was quietly driven. Adele had peeped from time to time under the blind. There were few people in the streets. Once or twice a sergent-de-ville was seen under the light of a lamp. Celia dared not cry out. Over against her, persistently watching her, Adele Rossignol sat with the open flask clenched in her hand, and from the vitriol Celia shrank with an overwhelming terror. The carriage drove out from the town along the western edge of the lake.

"Now listen," said Adele. "As soon as the landau stops the door of the house opposite to which it stops will open. I shall open the carriage door myself and you will get out. You must stand close by the carriage door until I have got out. I shall hold this flask ready in my hand. As soon as I am out you will run across the pavement into the house. You won't speak or scream."

Adele Rossignol turned out the lamp and ten minutes later the carriage passed down the little street and attracted Mme. Gobin's notice. Marthe Gobin had lit no light in her room. Adele Rossignol peered out of the carriage. She saw the houses in darkness. She could not see the busybody's face watching the landau from a dark window. She cut the cords which fastened the girl's hands. The carriage stopped. She opened the door. Celia sprang out on to the pavement. She sprang so quickly that Adele Rossignol caught and held the train of her dress. But it was the fear of the vitriol which had made her spring so nimbly. It was that, too, which made her run so lightly and quickly into the house. The old woman who acted as servant, Jeanne Tace, received her. Celia offered no resistance. The fear of vitriol had made her supple as a glove. Jeanne hurried her down the stairs into the little parlour at the back of the house, where supper was laid, and pushed her into a chair. Celia let her arms fall forward on the table. She had no hope now. She was friendless and alone in a den of murderers, who meant first to torture, then to kill her. She would be held up to execration as a murderess. No one would know how she had died or what she had suffered. She was in pain, and her throat burned. She buried her face in her arms and sobbed. All her body shook with her sobbing. Jeanne Rossignol took no notice. She treated Celie just as the others had done. Celia was LA PETITE, against whom she had no animosity, by whom she was not to be touched to any tenderness. LA PETITE had unconsciously played her useful part in their crime. But her use was ended now, and they would deal with her accordingly. She removed the girl's hat and cloak and tossed them aside.

"Now stay quiet until we are ready for you," she said. And Celia, lifting her head, said in a whisper:

"Water!"

The old woman poured some from a jug and held the glass to Celia's lips.

"Thank you," whispered Celia gratefully, and Adele came into the room. She told the story of the night to Jeanne, and afterwards to Hippolyte when he joined them.

"And nothing gained!" cried the older woman furiously. "And we have hardly a five-franc piece in the house."

"Yes, something," said Adele. "A necklace —a good one-some good rings, and bracelets. And we shall find out where the rest is hid-from her." And she nodded at Celia.

The three people ate their supper, and, while they ate it, discussed Celia's fate. She was lying with her head bowed upon her arms at the same table, within a foot of them. But they made no more of her presence than if she had been an old shoe. Only once did one of them speak to her.

"Stop your whimpering," said Hippolyte roughly. "We can hardly hear ourselves talk."

He was for finishing with the business altogether to-night.

"It's a mistake," he said. "There's been a bungle, and the sooner we are rid of it the better. There's a boat at the bottom of the garden."

Celia listened and shuddered. He would have no more compunction over drowning her than he would have had over drowning a blind kitten.

"It's cursed luck," he said. "But we have got the necklace-that's something. That's our share, do you see? The young spark can look for the rest."

But Helene Vauquier's wish prevailed. She was the leader. They would keep the girl until she came to Geneva.

They took her upstairs into the big bedroom overlooking the lake. Adele opened the door of the closet, where a truckle-bed stood, and thrust the girl in.

"This is my room," she said warningly, pointing to the bedroom. "Take care I hear no noise. You might shout yourself hoarse, my pretty one; no one else would hear you. But I should, and afterwards-we should no longer be able to call you 'my pretty one,' eh?"

And with a horrible playfulness she pinched the girl's cheek.

Then with old Jeanne's help she stripped Celia and told her to get into bed.

"I'll give her something to keep her quiet," said Adele, and she fetched her morphia-needle and injected a dose into Celia's arm.

Then they took her clothes away and left her in the darkness. She heard the key turn in the lock, and a moment after the sound of the bedstead being drawn across the doorway. But she heard no more, for almost immediately she fell asleep.

She was awakened some time the next day by the door opening. Old Jeanne Tace brought her in a jug of water and a roll of bread, and locked her up again. And a long time afterwards she brought her another supply. Yet another day had gone, but in that dark cupboard Celia had no means of judging time. In the afternoon the newspaper came out with the announcement that Mme. Dauvray's jewellery had been discovered under the boards. Hippolyte brought in the newspaper, and, cursing their stupidity, they sat down to decide upon Celia's fate. That, however, was soon arranged. They would dress her in everything which she wore when she came, so that no trace of her might be discovered. They would give her another dose of morphia, sew her up in a sack as soon as she was unconscious, row her far out on to the lake, and sink her with a weight attached. They dragged her out from the cupboard, always with the threat of that bright aluminium flask before her eyes. She fell upon her knees, imploring their pity with the tears running down her cheeks; but they sewed the strip of sacking over her face so that she should see nothing of their preparations. They flung her on the sofa, secured her as Hanaud had found her, and, leaving her in the old woman's charge, sent down Adele for her needle and Hippolyte to get ready the boat. As Hippolyte opened the door he saw the launch of the Chef de la Surete glide along the bank.


## CHAPTER XXI


## HANAUD EXPLAINS

This is the story as Mr. Ricardo wrote it out from the statement of Celia herself and the confession of Adele Rossignol. Obscurities which had puzzled him were made clear. But he was still unaware how Hanaud had worked out the solution.

"You promised me that you would explain," he said, when they were both together after the trial was over at Aix. The two men had just finished luncheon at the Cercle and were sitting over their coffee. Hanaud lighted a cigar.

"There were difficulties, of course," he said; "the crime was so carefully planned. The little details, such as the footprints, the absence of any mud from the girl's shoes in the carriage of the motor-car, the dinner at Annecy, the purchase of the cord, the want of any sign of a struggle in the little salon, were all carefully thought out. Had not one little accident happened, and one little mistake been made in consequence, I doubt if we should have laid our hands upon one of the gang. We might have suspected Wethermill; we should hardly have secured him, and we should very likely never have known of the Tace family. That mistake was, as you no doubt are fully aware —"

"The failure of Wethermill to discover Mme. Dauvray's jewels," said Ricardo at once.

"No, my friend," answered Hanaud. "That made them keep Mlle. Celie alive. It enabled us to save her when we had discovered the whereabouts of the gang. It did not help us very much to lay our hands upon them. No; the little accident which happened was the entrance of our friend Perrichet into the garden while the murderers were still in the room. Imagine that scene, M. Ricardo. The rage of the murderers at their inability to discover the plunder for which they had risked their necks, the old woman crumpled up on the floor against the wall, the girl writing laboriously with fettered arms 'I do not know' under threats of torture, and then in the stillness of the night the clear, tiny click of the gate and the measured, relentless footsteps. No wonder they were terrified in that dark room. What would be their one thought? Why, to get away-to come back perhaps later, when Mlle. Celie should have told them what, by the way, she did not know, but in any case to get away now. So they made their little mistake, and in their hurry they left the light burning in the room of Helene Vauquier, and the murder was discovered seven hours too soon for them."

"Seven hours!" said Mr. Ricardo.

"Yes. The household did not rise early. It was not until seven that the charwoman came. It was she who was meant to discover the crime. By that time the motor-car would have been back three hours ago in its garage. Servettaz, the chauffeur, would have returned from Chambery some time in the morning, he would have cleaned the car, he would have noticed that there was very little petrol in the tank, as there had been when he had left it on the day before. He would not have noticed that some of his many tins which had been full yesterday were empty to-day. We should not have discovered that about four in the morning the car was close to the Villa Rose and that it had travelled, between midnight and five in the morning, a hundred and fifty kilometres."

"But you had already guessed 'Geneva,'" said Ricardo. "At luncheon, before the news came that the car was found, you had guessed it."

"It was a shot," said Hanaud. "The absence of the car helped me to make it. It is a large city and not very far away, a likely place for people with the police at their heels to run to earth in. But if the car had been discovered in the garage I should not have made that shot. Even then I had no particular conviction about Geneva. I really wished to see how Wethermill would take it. He was wonderful."

"He sprang up."

"He betrayed nothing but surprise. You showed no less surprise than he did, my good friend. What I was looking for was one glance of fear. I did not get it."

"Yet you suspected him-even then you spoke of brains and audacity. You told him enough to hinder him from communicating with the red-haired woman in Geneva. You isolated him. Yes, you suspected him."

"Let us take the case from the beginning. When you first came to me, as I told you, the Commissaire had already been with me. There was an interesting piece of evidence already in his possession. Adolphe Ruel-who saw Wethermill and Vauquier together close by the Casino and overheard that cry of Wethermill's, 'It is true: I must have money!' —had already been with his story to the Commissaire. I knew it when Harry Wethermill came into the room to ask me to take up the case. That was a bold stroke, my friend. The chances were a hundred to one that I should not interrupt my holiday to take up a case because of your little dinner-party in London. Indeed, I should not have interrupted it had I not known Adolphe Ruel's story. As it was I could not resist. Wethermill's very audacity charmed me. Oh yes, I felt that I must pit myself against him. So few criminals have spirit, M. Ricardo. It is deplorable how few. But Wethermill! See in what a fine position he would have been if only I had refused. He himself had been the first to call upon the first detective in France. And his argument! He loved Mlle. Celie. Therefore she must be innocent! How he stuck to it! People would have said, 'Love is blind,' and all the more they would have suspected Mlle. Celie. Yes, but they love the blind lover. Therefore all the more would it have been impossible for them to believe Harry Wethermill had any share in that grim crime."

Mr. Ricardo drew his chair closer in to the table.

"I will confess to you," he said, "that I thought Mlle. Celie was an accomplice."

"It is not surprising," said Hanaud. "Some one within the house was an accomplice-we start with that fact. The house had not been broken into. There was Mlle. Celie's record as Helene Vauquier gave it to us, and a record obviously true. There was the fact that she had got rid of Servettaz. There was the maid upstairs very ill from the chloroform. What more likely than that Mlle. Celie had arranged a seance, and then when the lights were out had admitted the murderer through that convenient glass door?"

"There were, besides, the definite imprints of her shoes," said Mr. Ricardo.

"Yes, but that is precisely where I began to feel sure that she was innocent," replied Hanaud dryly. "All the other footmarks had been so carefully scored and ploughed up that nothing could be made of them. Yet those little ones remained so definite, so easily identified, and I began to wonder why these, too, had not been cut up and stamped over. The murderers had taken, you see, an excess of precaution to throw the presumption of guilt upon Mlle. Celie rather than upon Vauquier. However, there the footsteps were. Mlle. Celie had sprung from the room as I described to Wethermill. But I was puzzled. Then in the room I found the torn-up sheet of notepaper with the words, 'Je ne sais pas,' in mademoiselle's handwriting. The words might have been spirit-writing, they might have meant anything. I put them away in my mind. But in the room the settee puzzled me. And again I was troubled-greatly troubled."

"Yes, I saw that."

"And not you alone," said Hanaud, with a smile. "Do you remember that loud cry Wethermill gave when we returned to the room and once more I stood before the settee? Oh, he turned it off very well. I had said that our criminals in France were not very gentle with their victims, and he pretended that it was in fear of what Mlle. Celie might be suffering which had torn that cry from his heart. But it was not so. He was afraid-deadly afraid-not for Mlle. Celie, but for himself. He was afraid that I had understood what these cushions had to tell me."

"What did they tell you?" asked Ricardo.

"You know now," said Hanaud. "They were two cushions, both indented, and indented in different ways. The one at the head was irregularly indented-something shaped had pressed upon it. It might have been a face-it might not; and there was a little brown stain which was fresh and which was blood. The second cushion had two separate impressions, and between them the cushion was forced up in a thin ridge; and these impressions were more definite. I measured the distance between the two cushions, and I found this: that supposing-and it was a large supposition-the cushions had not been moved since those impressions were made, a girl of Mlle. Celie's height lying stretched out upon the sofa would have her face pressing down upon one cushion and her feet and insteps upon the other. Now, the impressions upon the second cushion and the thin ridge between them were just the impressions which might have been made by a pair of shoes held close together. But that would not be a natural attitude for any one, and the mark upon the head cushion was very deep. Supposing that my conjectures were true, then a woman would only lie like that because she was helpless, because she had been flung there, because she could not lift herself-because, in a word, her hands were tied behind her back and her feet fastened together. Well, then, follow this train of reasoning, my friend! Suppose my conjectures-and we had nothing but conjectures to build upon-were true, the woman flung upon the sofa could not be Helene Vauquier, for she would have said so; she could have had no reason for concealment. But it must be Mlle. Celie. There was the slit in the one cushion and the stain on the other which, of course, I had not accounted for. There was still, too, the puzzle of the footsteps outside the glass doors. If Mlle. Celie had been bound upon the sofa, how came she to run with her limbs free from the house? There was a question —a question not easy to answer."

"Yes," said Mr. Ricardo.

"Yes; but there was also another question. Suppose that Mlle. Celie was, after all, the victim, not the accomplice; suppose she had been flung tied upon the sofa; suppose that somehow the imprint of her shoes upon the ground had been made, and that she had afterwards been carried away, so that the maid might be cleared of all complicity-in that case it became intelligible why the other footprints were scored out and hers left. The presumption of guilt would fall upon her. There would be proof that she ran hurriedly from the room and sprang into a motor-car of her own free will. But, again, if that theory were true, then Helene Vauquier was the accomplice and not Mlle. Celie."

"I follow that."

"Then I found an interesting piece of evidence with regard to the strange woman who came: I picked up a long red hair —a very important piece of evidence about which I thought it best to say nothing at all. It was not Mlle. Celie's hair, which is fair; nor Vauquier's, which is black; nor Mme. Dauvray's, which is dyed brown; nor the charwoman's, which is grey. It was, therefore, the visitor's. Well, we went upstairs to Mile. Celie's room."

"Yes," said Mr. Ricardo eagerly. "We are coming to the pot of cream."

"In that room we learnt that Helene Vauquier, at her own request, had already paid it a visit. It is true the Commissaire said that he had kept his eye on her the whole time. But none the less from the window he saw me coming down the road, and that he could not have done, as I made sure, unless he had turned his back upon Vauquier and leaned out of the window. Now at the time I had an open mind about Vauquier. On the whole I was inclined to think she had no share in the affair. But either she or Mlle. Celie had, and perhaps both. But one of them-yes. That was sure. Therefore I asked what drawers she touched after the Commissaire had leaned out of the window. For if she had any motive in wishing to visit the room she would have satisfied it when the Commissaire's back was turned. He pointed to a drawer, and I took out a dress and shook it, thinking that she may have wished to hide something. But nothing fell out. On the other hand, however, I saw some quite fresh grease-marks, made by fingers, and the marks were wet. I began to ask myself how it was that Helene Vauquier, who had just been helped to dress by the nurse, had grease upon her fingers. Then I looked at a drawer which she had examined first of all. There were no grease-marks on the clothes she had turned over before the Commissaire leaned out of the window. Therefore it followed that during the few seconds when he was watching me she had touched grease. I looked about the room, and there on the dressing-table close by the chest of drawers was a pot of cold cream. That was the grease Helene Vauquier had touched. And why-if not to hide some small thing in it which, firstly, she dared not keep in her own room; which, secondly, she wished to hide in the room of Mlle. Celie; and which, thirdly, she had not had an opportunity to hide before? Now bear those three conditions in mind, and tell me what the small thing was."

Mr. Ricardo nodded his head.

"I know now," he said. "You told me. The earrings of Mlle. Celie. But I should not have guessed it at the time."

"Nor could I —at the time," said Hanaud. "I kept my open mind about Helene Vauquier; but I locked the door and took the key. Then we went and heard Vauquier's story. The story was clever, because so much of it was obviously, indisputably true. The account of the seances, of Mme. Dauvray's superstitions, her desire for an interview with Mme. de Montespan-such details are not invented. It was interesting, too, to know that there had been a seance planned for that night! The method of the murder began to be clear. So far she spoke the truth. But then she lied. Yes, she lied, and it was a bad lie, my friend. She told us that the strange woman Adele had black hair. Now I carried in my pocket-book proof that that woman's hair was red. Why did she lie, except to make impossible the identification of that strange visitor? That was the first false step taken by Helene Vauquier.

"Now let us take the second. I thought nothing of her rancour against Mlle. Celie. To me it was all very natural. She-the hard peasant woman no longer young, who had been for years the confidential servant of Mme. Dauvray, and no doubt had taken her levy from the impostors who preyed upon her credulous mistress-certainly she would hate this young and pretty outcast whom she has to wait upon, whose hair she has to dress. Vauquier-she would hate her. But if by any chance she were in the plot-and the lie seemed to show she was-then the seances showed me new possibilities. For Helene used to help Mlle. Celie. Suppose that the seance had taken place, that this sceptical visitor with the red hair professed herself dissatisfied with Vauquier's method of testing the medium, had suggested another way, Mlle. Celie could not object, and there she would be neatly and securely packed up beyond the power of offering any resistance, before she could have a suspicion that things were wrong. It would be an easy little comedy to play. And if that were true-why, there were my sofa cushions partly explained."

"Yes, I see!" cried Ricardo, with enthusiasm. "You are wonderful."

Hanaud was not displeased with his companion's enthusiasm.

"But wait a moment. We have only conjectures so far, and one fact that Helene Vauquier lied about the colour of the strange woman's hair. Now we get another fact. Mlle. Celie was wearing buckles on her shoes. And there is my slit in the sofa cushions. For when she is flung on to the sofa, what will she do? She will kick, she will struggle. Of course it is conjecture. I do not as yet hold pigheadedly to it. I am not yet sure that Mlle. Celie is innocent. I am willing at any moment to admit that the facts contradict my theory. But, on the contrary, each fact that I discover helps it to take shape.

"Now I come to Helene Vauquier's second mistake. On the evening when you saw Mlle. Celie in the garden behind the baccarat-rooms you noticed that she wore no jewellery except a pair of diamond eardrops. In the photograph of her which Wethermill showed me, again she was wearing them. Is it not, therefore, probable that she usually wore them? When I examined her room I found the case for those earrings-the case was empty. It was natural, then, to infer that she was wearing them when she came down to the seance."

"Yes."

"Well, I read a description —a carefully written description-of the missing girl, made by Helene Vauquier after an examination of the girl's wardrobe. There is no mention of the earrings. So I asked her —'Was she not wearing them?' Helene Vauquier was taken by surprise. How should I know anything of Mlle. Celie's earrings? She hesitated. She did not quite know what answer to make. Now, why? Since she herself dressed Mile. Celie, and remembers so very well all she wore, why does she hesitate? Well, there is a reason. She does not know how much I know about those diamond eardrops. She is not sure whether we have not dipped into that pot of cold cream and found them. Yet without knowing she cannot answer. So now we come back to our pot of cold cream."

"Yes!" cried Mr. Ricardo. "They were there."

"Wait a bit," said Hanaud. "Let us see how it works out. Remember the conditions. Vauquier has some small thing which she must hide, and which she wishes to hide in Mlle. Celie's room. For she admitted that it was her suggestion that she should look through mademoiselle's wardrobe. For what reason does she choose the girl's room, except that if the thing were discovered that would be the natural place for it? It is, then, something belonging to Mlle. Celie. There was a second condition we laid down. It was something Vauquier had not been able to hide before. It came, then, into her possession last night. Why could she not hide it last night? Because she was not alone. There were the man and the woman, her accomplices. It was something, then, which she was concerned in hiding from them. It is not rash to guess, then, that it was some piece of the plunder of which the other two would have claimed their share-and a piece of plunder belonging to Mlle. Celie. Well, she has nothing but the diamond eardrops. Suppose Vauquier is left alone to guard Mlle. Celie while the other two ransack Mme. Dauvray's room. She sees her chance. The girl cannot stir hand or foot to save herself. Vauquier tears the eardrops in a hurry from her ears-and there I have my drop of blood just where I should expect it to be. But now follow this! Vauquier hides the earrings in her pocket. She goes to bed in order to be chloroformed. She knows that it is very possible that her room will be searched before she regains consciousness, or before she is well enough to move. There is only one place to hide them in, only one place where they will be safe. In bed with her. But in the morning she must get rid of them, and a nurse is with her. Hence the excuse to go to Mlle. Celie's room. If the eardrops are found in the pot of cold cream, it would only be thought that Mlle. Celie had herself hidden them there for safety. Again it is conjecture, and I wish to make sure. So I tell Vauquier she can go away, and I leave her unwatched. I have her driven to the depot instead of to her friends, and searched. Upon her is found the pot of cream, and in the cream Mlle. Celie's eardrops. She has slipped into Mlle. Celie's room, as, if my theory was correct, she would be sure to do, and put the pot of cream into her pocket. So I am now fairly sure that she is concerned in the murder.

"We then went to Mme. Dauvray's room and discovered her brilliants and her ornaments. At once the meaning of that agitated piece of hand-writing of Mlle. Celie's becomes clear. She is asked where the jewels are hidden. She cannot answer, for her mouth, of course, is stopped. She has to write. Thus my conjectures get more and more support. And, mind this, one of the two women is guilty-Celie or Vauquier. My discoveries all fit in with the theory of Celie's innocence. But there remain the footprints, for which I found no explanation.

"You will remember I made you all promise silence as to the finding of Mme. Dauvray's jewellery. For I thought, if they have taken the girl away so that suspicion may fall on her and not on Vauquier, they mean to dispose of her. But they may keep her so long as they have a chance of finding out from her Mme. Dauvray's hiding-place. It was a small chance but our only one. The moment the discovery of the jewellery was published the girl's fate was sealed, were my theory true.

"Then came our advertisement and Mme. Gobin's written testimony. There was one small point of interest which I will take first: her statement that Adele was the Christian name of the woman with the red hair, that the old woman who was the servant in that house in the suburb of Geneva called her Adele, just simply Adele. That interested me, for Helene Vauquier had called her Adele too when she was describing to us the unknown visitor. 'Adele' was what Mme. Dauvray called her."

"Yes," said Ricardo. "Helene Vauquier made a slip there. She should have given her a false name."

Hanaud nodded.

"It is the one slip she made in the whole of the business. Nor did she recover herself very cleverly. For when the Commissaire pounced upon the name, she at once modified her words. She only thought now that the name was Adele, or something like it. But when I went on to suggest that the name in any case would be a false one, at once she went back upon her modifications. And now she was sure that Adele was the name used. I remembered her hesitation when I read Marthe Gobin's letter. They helped to confirm me in my theory that she was in the plot; and they made me very sure that it was an Adele for whom we had to look. So far well. But other statements in the letter puzzled me. For instance, 'She ran lightly and quickly across the pavement into the house, as though she were afraid to be seen.' Those were the words, and the woman was obviously honest. What became of my theory then? The girl was free to run, free to stoop and pick up the train of her gown in her hand, free to shout for help in the open street if she wanted help. No; that I could not explain until that afternoon, when I saw Mlle. Celie's terror-stricken eyes fixed upon that flask, as Lemerre poured a little out and burnt a hole in the sack. Then I understood well enough. The fear of vitriol!" Hanaud gave an uneasy shudder. "And it is enough to make any one afraid! That I can tell you. No wonder she lay still as a mouse upon the sofa in the bedroom. No wonder she ran quickly into the house. Well, there you have the explanation. I had only my theory to work upon even after Mme. Gobin's evidence. But as it happened it was the right one. Meanwhile, of course, I made my inquiries into Wethermill's circumstances. My good friends in England helped me. They were precarious. He owed money in Aix, money at his hotel. We knew from the motor-car that the man we were searching for had returned to Aix. Things began to look black for Wethermill. Then you gave me a little piece of information."

"I!" exclaimed Ricardo, with a start.

"Yes. You told me that you walked up to the hotel with Harry Wethermill on the night of the murder and separated just before ten. A glance into his rooms which I had-you will remember that when we had discovered the motor-car I suggested that we should go to Harry Wethermill's rooms and talk it over-that glance enabled me to see that he could very easily have got out of his room on to the verandah below and escaped from the hotel by the garden quite unseen. For you will remember that whereas your rooms look out to the front and on to the slope of Mont Revard, Wethermill's look out over the garden and the town of Aix. In a quarter of an hour or twenty minutes he could have reached the Villa Rose. He could have been in the salon before half-past ten, and that is just the hour which suited me perfectly. And, as he got out unnoticed, so he could return. So he did return! My friend, there are some interesting marks upon the window-sill of Wethermill's room and upon the pillar just beneath it. Take a look, M. Ricardo, when you return to your hotel. But that was not all. We talked of Geneva in Mr. Wethermill's room, and of the distance between Geneva and Aix. Do you remember that?"

"Yes," replied Ricardo.

"Do you remember too that I asked him for a road-book?"

"Yes; to make sure of the distance. I do."

"Ah, but it was not to make sure of the distance that I asked for the road-book, my friend. I asked in order to find out whether Harry Wethermill had a road-book at all which gave a plan of the roads between here and Geneva. And he had. He handed it to me at once and quite naturally. I hope that I took it calmly, but I was not at all calm inside. For it was a new road-book, which, by the way, he bought a week before, and I was asking myself all the while-now what was I asking myself, M. Ricardo?"

"No," said Ricardo, with a smile. "I am growing wary. I will not tell you what you were asking yourself, M. Hanaud. For even were I right you would make out that I was wrong, and leap upon me with injuries and gibes. No, you shall drink your coffee and tell me of your own accord."

"Well," said Hanaud, laughing, "I will tell you. I was asking myself: 'Why does a man who owns no motor-car, who hires no motor-car, go out into Aix and buy an automobilist's road-map? With what object?' And I found it an interesting question. M. Harry Wethermill was not the man to go upon a walking tour, eh? Oh, I was obtaining evidence. But then came an overwhelming thing-the murder of Marthe Gobin. We know now how he did it. He walked beside the cab, put his head in at the window, asked, 'Have you come in answer to the advertisement?' and stabbed her straight to the heart through her dress. The dress and the weapon which he used would save him from being stained with her blood. He was in your room that morning, when we were at the station. As I told you, he left his glove behind. He was searching for a telegram in answer to your advertisement. Or he came to sound you. He had already received his telegram from Hippolyte. He was like a fox in a cage, snapping at every one, twisting vainly this way and that way, risking everything and every one to save his precious neck. Marthe Gobin was in the way. She is killed. Mlle. Celie is a danger. So Mile. Celie must be suppressed. And off goes a telegram to the Geneva paper, handed in by a waiter from the cafe at the station of Chambery before five o'clock. Wethermill went to Chambery that afternoon when we went to Geneva. Once we could get him on the run, once we could so harry and bustle him that he must take risks-why, we had him. And that afternoon he had to take them."

"So that even before Marthe Gobin was killed you were sure that Wethermill was the murderer?"

Hanaud's face clouded over.

"You put your finger on a sore place, M. Ricardo. I was sure, but I still wanted evidence to convict. I left him free, hoping for that evidence. I left him free, hoping that he would commit himself. He did, but-well, let us talk of some one else. What of Mlle. Celie?"

Ricardo drew a letter from his pocket.

"I have a sister in London, a widow," he said. "She is kind. I, too, have been thinking of what will become of Mlle. Celie. I wrote to my sister, and here is her reply. Mlle. Celie will be very welcome."

Hanaud stretched out his hand and shook Ricardo's warmly.

"She will not, I think, be for very long a burden. She is young. She will recover from this shock. She is very pretty, very gentle. If-if no one comes forward whom she loves and who loves her —I —yes, I myself, who was her papa for one night, will be her husband forever."

He laughed inordinately at his own joke; it was a habit of M. Hanaud's. Then he said gravely:

"But I am glad, M. Ricardo, for Mlle. Celie's sake that I came to your amusing dinner-party in London."

Mr. Ricardo was silent for a moment. Then he asked:

"And what will happen to the condemned?"

"To the women? Imprisonment for life."

"And to the man?"

Hanaud shrugged his shoulders.

"Perhaps the guillotine. Perhaps New Caledonia. How can I say? I am not the President of the Republic."

# The Affair at the Semiramis Hotel

Mr. Ricardo, when the excitements of the Villa Rose were done with, returned to Grosvenor Square and resumed the busy, unnecessary life of an amateur. But the studios had lost their savour, artists their attractiveness, and even the Russian opera seemed a trifle flat. Life was altogether a disappointment; Fate, like an actress at a restaurant, had taken the wooden pestle in her hand and stirred all the sparkle out of the champagne; Mr. Ricardo languished--until one unforgettable morning.

He was sitting disconsolately at his breakfast-table when the door was burst open and a square, stout man, with the blue, shaven face of a French comedian, flung himself into the room. Ricardo sprang towards the new-comer with a cry of delight.

"My dear Hanaud!"

He seized his visitor by the arm, feeling it to make sure that here, in flesh and blood, stood the man who had introduced him to the acutest sensations of his life. He turned towards his butler, who was still bleating expostulations in the doorway at the unceremonious irruption of the French detective.

"Another place, Burton, at once," he cried, and as soon as he and Hanaud were alone: "What good wind blows you to London?"

"Business, my friend. The disappearance of bullion somewhere on the line between Paris and London. But it is finished. Yes, I take a holiday."

A light had suddenly flashed in Mr. Ricardo's eyes, and was now no less suddenly extinguished. Hanaud paid no attention whatever to his friend's disappointment. He pounced upon a piece of silver which adorned the tablecloth and took it over to the window.

"Everything is as it should be, my friend," he exclaimed, with a grin. "Grosvenor Square, the *Times* open at the money column, and a false antique upon the table. Thus I have dreamed of you. All Mr. Ricardo is in that sentence."

Ricardo laughed nervously. Recollection made him wary of Hanaud's sarcasms. He was shy even to protest the genuineness of his silver. But, indeed, he had not the time. For the door opened again and once more the butler appeared. On this occasion, however, he was alone.

"Mr. Calladine would like to speak to you, sir," he said.

"Calladine!" cried Ricardo in an extreme surprise. "That is the most extraordinary thing." He looked at the clock upon his mantelpiece. It was barely half-past eight. "At this hour, too?"

"Mr. Calladine is still wearing evening dress," the butler remarked.

Ricardo started in his chair. He began to dream of possibilities; and here was Hanaud miraculously at his side.

"Where is Mr. Calladine?" he asked.

"I have shown him into the library."

"Good," said Mr. Ricardo. "I will come to him."

But he was in no hurry. He sat and let his thoughts play with this incident of Calladine's early visit.

"It is very odd," he said. "I have not seen Calladine for months--no, nor has anyone. Yet, a little while ago, no one was more often seen."

He fell apparently into a muse, but he was merely seeking to provoke Hanaud's curiosity. In this attempt, however, he failed. Hanaud continued placidly to eat his breakfast, so that Mr. Ricardo was compelled to volunteer the story which he was burning to tell.

"Drink your coffee, Hanaud, and you shall hear about Calladine."

Hanaud grunted with resignation, and Mr. Ricardo flowed on:

"Calladine was one of England's young men. Everybody said so. He was going to do very wonderful things as soon as he had made up his mind exactly what sort of wonderful things he was going to do. Meanwhile, you met him in Scotland, at Newmarket, at Ascot, at Cowes, in the box of some great lady at the Opera--not before half-past ten in the evening *there*--in any fine house where the candles that night happened to be lit. He went everywhere, and then a day came and he went nowhere. There was no scandal, no trouble, not a whisper against his good name. He simply vanished. For a little while a few people asked: 'What has become of Calladine?' But there never was any answer, and London has no time for unanswered questions. Other promising young men dined in his place. Calladine had joined the huge legion of the Come-to-nothings. No one even seemed to pass him in the street. Now unexpectedly, at half-past eight in the morning, and in evening dress, he calls upon me. 'Why?' I ask myself."

Mr. Ricardo sank once more into a reverie. Hanaud watched him with a broadening smile of pure enjoyment.

"And in time, I suppose," he remarked casually, "you will perhaps ask him?"

Mr. Ricardo sprang out of his pose to his feet.

"Before I discuss serious things with an acquaintance," he said with a scathing dignity, "I make it a rule to revive my impressions of his personality. The cigarettes are in the crystal box."

"They would be," said Hanaud, unabashed, as Ricardo stalked from the room. But in five minutes Mr. Ricardo came running back, all his composure gone.

"It is the greatest good fortune that you, my friend, should have chosen this morning to visit me," he cried, and Hanaud nodded with a little grimace of resignation.

"There goes my holiday. You shall command me now and always. I will make the acquaintance of your young friend."

He rose up and followed Ricardo into his study, where a young man was nervously pacing the floor.

"Mr. Calladine," said Ricardo. "This is Mr. Hanaud."

The young man turned eagerly. He was tall, with a noticeable elegance and distinction, and the face which he showed to Hanaud was, in spite of its agitation, remarkably handsome.

"I am very glad," he said. "You are not an official of this country. You can advise--without yourself taking action, if you'll be so good."

Hanaud frowned. He bent his eyes uncompromisingly upon Calladine.

"What does that mean?" he asked, with a note of sternness in his voice.

"It means that I must tell someone," Calladine burst out in quivering tones. "That I don't know what to do. I am in a difficulty too big for me. That's the truth."

Hanaud looked at the young man keenly. It seemed to Ricardo that he took in every excited gesture, every twitching feature, in one comprehensive glance. Then he said in a friendlier voice:

"Sit down and tell me"--and he himself drew up a chair to the table.

"I was at the Semiramis last night," said Calladine, naming one of the great hotels upon the Embankment. "There was a fancy-dress ball."

All this happened, by the way, in those far-off days before the war--nearly, in fact, three years ago today--when London, flinging aside its reticence, its shy self-consciousness, had become a city of carnivals and masquerades, rivalling its neighbours on the Continent in the spirit of its gaiety, and exceeding them by its stupendous luxury. "I went by the merest chance. My rooms are in the Adelphi Terrace."

"There!" cried Mr. Ricardo in surprise, and Hanaud lifted a hand to check his interruptions.

"Yes," continued Calladine. "The night was warm, the music floated through my open windows and stirred old memories. I happened to have a ticket. I went."

Calladine drew up a chair opposite to Hanaud and, seating himself, told, with many nervous starts and in troubled tones, a story which, to Mr. Ricardo's thinking, was as fabulous as any out of the "Arabian Nights."

"I had a ticket," he began, "but no domino. I was consequently stopped by an attendant in the lounge at the top of the staircase leading down to the ballroom.

"'You can hire a domino in the cloakroom, Mr. Calladine,' he said to me. I had already begun to regret the impulse which had brought me, and I welcomed the excuse with which the absence of a costume provided me. I was, indeed, turning back to the door, when a girl who had at that moment run down from the stairs of the hotel into the lounge, cried gaily: 'That's not necessary'; and at the same moment she flung to me a long scarlet cloak which she had been wearing over her own dress. She was young, fair, rather tall, slim, and very pretty; her hair was drawn back from her face with a ribbon, and rippled down her shoulders in heavy curls; and she was dressed in a satin coat and knee-breeches of pale green and gold, with a white waistcoat and silk stockings and scarlet heels to her satin shoes. She was as straight-limbed as a boy, and exquisite like a figure in Dresden china. I caught the cloak and turned to thank her. But she did not wait. With a laugh she ran down the stairs a supple and shining figure, and was lost in the throng at the doorway of the ballroom. I was stirred by the prospect of an adventure. I ran down after her. She was standing just inside the room alone, and she was gazing at the scene with parted lips and dancing eyes. She laughed again as she saw the cloak about my shoulders, a delicious gurgle of amusement, and I said to her:

"'May I dance with you?'

"'Oh, do!' she cried, with a little jump, and clasping her hands. She was of a high and joyous spirit and not difficult in the matter of an introduction. 'This gentleman will do very well to present us,' she said, leading me in front of a bust of the God Pan which stood in a niche of the wall. 'I am, as you see, straight out of an opera. My name is Celymène or anything with an eighteenth century sound to it. You are--what you will. For this evening we are friends.'

"'And for to-morrow?' I asked.

"'I will tell you about that later on,' she replied, and she began to dance with a light step and a passion in her dancing which earned me many an envious glance from the other men. I was in luck, for Celymène knew no one, and though, of course, I saw the faces of a great many people whom I remembered, I kept them all at a distance. We had been dancing for about half an hour when the first queerish thing happened. She stopped suddenly in the midst of a sentence with a little gasp. I spoke to her, but she did not hear. She was gazing past me, her eyes wide open, and such a rapt look upon her face as I had never seen. She was lost in a miraculous vision. I followed the direction of her eyes and, to my astonishment, I saw nothing more than a stout, short, middle-aged woman, egregiously over-dressed as Marie Antoinette.

"'So you do know someone here?' I said, and I had to repeat the words sharply before my friend withdrew her eyes. But even then she was not aware of me. It was as if a voice had spoken to her whilst she was asleep and had disturbed, but not wakened her. Then she came to--there's really no other word I can think of which describes her at that moment--she came to with a deep sigh.

"'No,' she answered. 'She is a Mrs. Blumenstein from Chicago, a widow with ambitions and a great deal of money. But I don't know her.'

"'Yet you know all about her,' I remarked.

"'She crossed in the same boat with me,' Celymène replied. 'Did I tell you that I landed at Liverpool this morning? She is staying at the Semiramis too. Oh, let us dance!'

"She twitched my sleeve impatiently, and danced with a kind of violence and wildness as if she wished to banish some sinister thought. And she did undoubtedly banish it. We supped together and grew confidential, as under such conditions people will. She told me her real name. It was Joan Carew.

"'I have come over to get an engagement if I can at Covent Garden. I am supposed to sing all right. But I don't know anyone. I have been brought up in Italy.'

"'You have some letters of introduction, I suppose?' I asked.

"'Oh, yes. One from my teacher in Milan. One from an American manager.'

"In my turn I told her my name and where I lived, and I gave her my card. I thought, you see, that since I used to know a good many operatic people, I might be able to help her.

"'Thank you,' she said, and at that moment Mrs. Blumenstein, followed by a party, chiefly those lap-dog young men who always seem to gather about that kind of person, came into the supper-room and took a table close to us. There was at once an end of all confidences--indeed, of all conversation. Joan Carew lost all the lightness of her spirit; she talked at random, and her eyes were drawn again and again to the grotesque slander on Marie Antoinette. Finally I became annoyed.

"'Shall we go?' I suggested impatiently, and to my surprise she whispered passionately:

"'Yes. Please! Let us go.'

"Her voice was actually shaking, her small hands clenched. We went back to the ballroom, but Joan Carew did not recover her gaiety, and half-way through a dance, when we were near to the door, she stopped abruptly--extraordinarily abruptly.

"'I shall go,' she said abruptly. 'I am tired. I have grown dull.'

"I protested, but she made a little grimace.

"'You'll hate me in half an hour. Let's be wise and stop now while we are friends,' she said, and whilst I removed the domino from my shoulders she stooped very quickly. It seemed to me that she picked up something which had lain hidden beneath the sole of her slipper. She certainly moved her foot, and I certainly saw something small and bright flash in the palm of her glove as she raised herself again. But I imagined merely that it was some object which she had dropped.

"'Yes, we'll go,' she said, and we went up the stairs into the lobby. Certainly all the sparkle had gone out of our adventure. I recognized her wisdom.

"'But I shall meet you again?' I asked.

"'Yes. I have your address. I'll write and fix a time when you will be sure to find me in. Good-night, and a thousand thanks. I should have been bored to tears if you hadn't come without a domino.'

"She was speaking lightly as she held out her hand, but her grip tightened a little and--clung. Her eyes darkened and grew troubled, her mouth trembled. The shadow of a great trouble had suddenly closed about her. She shivered.

"'I am half inclined to ask you to stay, however dull I am; and dance with me till daylight--the safe daylight,' she said.

"It was an extraordinary phrase for her to use, and it moved me.

"'Let us go back then!' I urged. She gave me an impression suddenly of someone quite forlorn. But Joan Carew recovered her courage. 'No, no,' she answered quickly. She snatched her hand away and ran lightly up the staircase, turning at the corner to wave her hand and smile. It was then half-past one in the morning."

So far Calladine had spoken without an interruption. Mr. Ricardo, it is true, was bursting to break in with the most important questions, but a salutary fear of Hanaud restrained him. Now, however, he had an opportunity, for Calladine paused.

"Half-past one," he said sagely. "Ah!"

"And when did you go home?" Hanaud asked of Calladine.

"True," said Mr. Ricardo. "It is of the greatest consequence."

Calladine was not sure. His partner had left behind her the strangest medley of sensations in his breast. He was puzzled, haunted, and charmed. He had to think about her; he was a trifle uplifted; sleep was impossible. He wandered for a while about the ballroom. Then he walked to his chambers along the echoing streets and sat at his window; and some time afterwards the hoot of a motor-horn broke the silence and a car stopped and whirred in the street below. A moment later his bell rang.

He ran down the stairs in a queer excitement, unlocked the street door and opened it. Joan Carew, still in her masquerade dress with her scarlet cloak about her shoulders, slipped through the opening.

"Shut the door," she whispered, drawing herself apart in a corner.

"Your cab?" asked Calladine.

"It has gone."

Calladine latched the door. Above, in the well of the stairs, the light spread out from the open door of his flat. Down here all was dark. He could just see the glimmer of her white face, the glitter of her dress, but she drew her breath like one who has run far. They mounted the stairs cautiously. He did not say a word until they were both safely in his parlour; and even then it was in a low voice.

"What has happened?"

"You remember the woman I stared at? You didn't know why I stared, but any girl would have understood. She was wearing the loveliest pearls I ever saw in my life."

Joan was standing by the edge of the table. She was tracing with her finger a pattern on the cloth as she spoke. Calladine started with a horrible presentiment.

"Yes," she said. "I worship pearls. I always have done. For one thing, they improve on me. I haven't got any, of course. I have no money. But friends of mine who do own pearls have sometimes given theirs to me to wear when they were going sick, and they have always got back their lustre. I think that has had a little to do with my love of them. Oh, I have always longed for them--just a little string. Sometimes I have felt that I would have given my soul for them."

She was speaking in a dull, monotonous voice. But Calladine recalled the ecstasy which had shone in her face when her eyes first had fallen on the pearls, the longing which had swept her quite into another world, the passion with which she had danced to throw the obsession off.

"And I never noticed them at all," he said.

"Yet they were wonderful. The colour! The lustre! All the evening they tempted me. I was furious that a fat, coarse creature like that should have such exquisite things. Oh, I was mad."

She covered her face suddenly with her hands and swayed. Calladine sprang towards her. But she held out her hand.

"No, I am all right." And though he asked her to sit down she would not. "You remember when I stopped dancing suddenly?"

"Yes. You had something hidden under your foot?"

The girl nodded.

"Her key!" And under his breath Calladine uttered a startled cry.

For the first time since she had entered the room Joan Carew raised her head and looked at him. Her eyes were full of terror, and with the terror was mixed an incredulity as though she could not possibly believe that that had happened which she knew had happened.

"A little Yale key," the girl continued. "I saw Mrs. Blumenstein looking on the floor for something, and then I saw it shining on the very spot. Mrs. Blumenstein's suite was on the same floor as mine, and her maid slept above. All the maids do. I knew that. Oh, it seemed to me as if I had sold my soul and was being paid."

Now Calladine understood what she had meant by her strange phrase--"the safe daylight."

"I went up to my little suite," Joan Carew continued. "I sat there with the key burning through my glove until I had given her time enough to fall asleep"--and though she hesitated before she spoke the words, she did speak them, not looking at Calladine, and with a shudder of remorse making her confession complete. "Then I crept out. The corridor was dimly lit. Far away below the music was throbbing. Up here it was as silent as the grave. I opened the door--her door. I found myself in a lobby. The suite, though bigger, was arranged like mine. I slipped in and closed the door behind me. I listened in the darkness. I couldn't hear a sound. I crept forward to the door in front of me. I stood with my fingers on the handle and my heart beating fast enough to choke me. I had still time to turn back. But I couldn't. There were those pearls in front of my eyes, lustrous and wonderful. I opened the door gently an inch or so--and then--it all happened in a second."

Joan Carew faltered. The night was too near to her, its memory too poignant with terror. She shut her eyes tightly and cowered down in a chair. With the movement her cloak slipped from her shoulders and dropped on to the ground. Calladine leaned forward with an exclamation of horror; Joan Carew started up.

"What is it?" she asked.

"Nothing. Go on."

"I found myself inside the room with the door shut behind me. I had shut it myself in a spasm of terror. And I dared not turn round to open it. I was helpless."

"What do you mean? She was awake?"

Joan Carew shook her head.

"There were others in the room before me, and on the same errand--men!"

Calladine drew back, his eyes searching the girl's face.

"Yes?" he said slowly.

"I didn't see them at first. I didn't hear them. The room was quite dark except for one jet of fierce white light which beat upon the door of a safe. And as I shut the door the jet moved swiftly and the light reached me and stopped. I was blinded. I stood in the full glare of it, drawn up against the panels of the door, shivering, sick with fear. Then I heard a quiet laugh, and someone moved softly towards me. Oh, it was terrible! I recovered the use of my limbs; in a panic I turned to the door, but I was too late. Whilst I fumbled with the handle I was seized; a hand covered my mouth. I was lifted to the centre of the room. The jet went out, the electric lights were turned on. There were two men dressed as apaches in velvet trousers and red scarves, like a hundred others in the ballroom below, and both were masked. I struggled furiously; but, of course, I was like a child in their grasp. 'Tie her legs,' the man whispered who was holding me; 'she's making too much noise.' I kicked and fought, but the other man stooped and tied my ankles, and I fainted."

Calladine nodded his head.

"Yes?" he said.

"When I came to, the lights were still burning, the door of the safe was open, the room empty; I had been flung on to a couch at the foot of the bed. I was lying there quite free."

"Was the safe empty?" asked Calladine suddenly.

"I didn't look," she answered. "Oh!"--and she covered her face spasmodically with her hands. "I looked at the bed. Someone was lying there--under a sheet and quite still. There was a clock ticking in the room; it was the only sound. I was terrified. I was going mad with fear. If I didn't get out of the room at once I felt that I should go mad, that I should scream and bring everyone to find me alone with--what was under the sheet in the bed. I ran to the door and looked out through a slit into the corridor. It was still quite empty, and below the music still throbbed in the ballroom. I crept down the stairs, meeting no one until I reached the hall. I looked into the ballroom as if I was searching for someone. I stayed long enough to show myself. Then I got a cab and came to you."

A short silence followed. Joan Carew looked at her companion in appeal. "You are the only one I could come to," she added. "I know no one else."

Calladine sat watching the girl in silence. Then he asked, and his voice was hard:

"And is that all you have to tell me?"

"Yes."

"You are quite sure?"

Joan Carew looked at him perplexed by the urgency of his question. She reflected for a moment or two.

"Quite."

Calladine rose to his feet and stood beside her.

"Then how do you come to be wearing this?" he asked, and he lifted a chain of platinum and diamonds which she was wearing about her shoulders. "You weren't wearing it when you danced with me."

Joan Carew stared at the chain.

"No. It's not mine. I have never seen it before." Then a light came into her eyes. "The two men--they must have thrown it over my head when I was on the couch--before they went." She looked at it more closely. "That's it. The chain's not very valuable. They could spare it, and--it would accuse me--of what they did."

"Yes, that's very good reasoning," said Calladine coldly.

Joan Carew looked quickly up into his face.

"Oh, you don't believe me," she cried. "You think--oh, it's impossible." And, holding him by the edge of his coat, she burst into a storm of passionate denials.

"But you went to steal, you know," he said gently, and she answered him at once:

"Yes, I did, but not this." And she held up the necklace. "Should I have stolen this, should I have come to you wearing it, if I had stolen the pearls, if I had"–and she stopped--"if my story were not true?"

Calladine weighed her argument, and it affected him.

"No, I think you wouldn't," he said frankly.

Most crimes, no doubt, were brought home because the criminal had made some incomprehensibly stupid mistake; incomprehensibly stupid, that is, by the standards of normal life. Nevertheless, Calladine was inclined to believe her. He looked at her. That she should have murdered was absurd. Moreover, she was not making a parade of remorse, she was not playing the unctuous penitent; she had yielded to a temptation, had got herself into desperate straits, and was at her wits' ends how to escape from them. She was frank about herself.

Calladine looked at the clock. It was nearly five o'clock in the morning, and though the music could still be heard from the ballroom in the Semiramis, the night had begun to wane upon the river.

"You must go back," he said. "I'll walk with you."

They crept silently down the stairs and into the street. It was only a step to the Semiramis. They met no one until they reached the Strand. There many, like Joan Carew in masquerade, were standing about, or walking hither and thither in search of carriages and cabs. The whole street was in a bustle, what with drivers shouting and people coming away.

"You can slip in unnoticed," said Calladine as he looked into the thronged courtyard. "I'll telephone to you in the morning."

"You will?" she cried eagerly, clinging for a moment to his arm.

"Yes, for certain," he replied. "Wait in until you hear from me. I'll think it over. I'll do what I can."

"Thank you," she said fervently.

He watched her scarlet cloak flitting here and there in the crowd until it vanished through the doorway. Then, for the second time, he walked back to his chambers, while the morning crept up the river from the sea.

* * * * *

This was the story which Calladine told in Mr. Ricardo's library. Mr. Ricardo heard it out with varying emotions. He began with a thrill of expectation like a man on a dark threshold of great excitements. The setting of the story appealed to him, too, by a sort of brilliant bizarrerie which he found in it. But, as it went on, he grew puzzled and a trifle disheartened. There were flaws and chinks; he began to bubble with unspoken criticisms, then swift and clever thrusts which he dared not deliver. He looked upon the young man with disfavour, as upon one who had half opened a door upon a theatre of great promise and shown him a spectacle not up to the mark. Hanaud, on the other hand, listened imperturbably, without an expression upon his face, until the end. Then he pointed a finger at Calladine and asked him what to Ricardo's mind was a most irrelevant question.

"You got back to your rooms, then, before five, Mr. Calladine, and it is now nine o'clock less a few minutes."

"Yes."

"Yet you have not changed your clothes. Explain to me that. What did you do between five and half-past eight?"

Calladine looked down at his rumpled shirt front.

"Upon my word, I never thought of it," he cried. "I was worried out of my mind. I couldn't decide what to do. Finally, I determined to talk to Mr. Ricardo, and after I had come to that conclusion I just waited impatiently until I could come round with decency."

Hanaud rose from his chair. His manner was grave, but conveyed no single hint of an opinion. He turned to Ricardo.

"Let us go round to your young friend's rooms in the Adelphi," he said; and the three men drove thither at once.


## II

Calladine lodged in a corner house and upon the first floor. His rooms, large and square and lofty, with Adams mantelpieces and a delicate tracery upon their ceilings, breathed the grace of the eighteenth century. Broad high windows, embrasured in thick walls, overlooked the river and took in all the sunshine and the air which the river had to give. And they were furnished fittingly. When the three men entered the parlour, Mr. Ricardo was astounded. He had expected the untidy litter of a man run to seed, the neglect and the dust of the recluse. But the room was as clean as the deck of a yacht; an Aubusson carpet made the floor luxurious underfoot; a few coloured prints of real value decorated the walls; and the mahogany furniture was polished so that a lady could have used it as a mirror. There was even by the newspapers upon the round table a china bowl full of fresh red roses. If Calladine had turned hermit, he was a hermit of an unusually fastidious type. Indeed, as he stood with his two companions in his dishevelled dress he seemed quite out of keeping with his rooms.

"So you live here, Mr. Calladine?" said Hanaud, taking off his hat and laying it down.

"Yes."

"With your servants, of course?"

"They come in during the day," said Calladine, and Hanaud looked at him curiously.

"Do you mean that you sleep here alone?"

"Yes."

"But your valet?"

"I don't keep a valet," said Calladine; and again the curious look came into Hanaud's eyes.

"Yet," he suggested gently, "there are rooms enough in your set of chambers to house a family."

Calladine coloured and shifted uncomfortably from one foot to the other.

"I prefer at night not to be disturbed," he said, stumbling a little over the words. "I mean, I have a liking for quiet."

Gabriel Hanaud nodded his head with sympathy.

"Yes, yes. And it is a difficult thing to get--as difficult as my holiday," he said ruefully, with a smile for Mr. Ricardo. "However"--he turned towards Calladine--"no doubt, now that you are at home, you would like a bath and a change of clothes. And when you are dressed, perhaps you will telephone to the Semiramis and ask Miss Carew to come round here. Meanwhile, we will read your newspapers and smoke your cigarettes."

Hanaud shut the door upon Calladine, but he turned neither to the papers nor the cigarettes. He crossed the room to Mr. Ricardo, who, seated at the open window, was plunged deep in reflections.

"You have an idea, my friend," cried Hanaud. "It demands to express itself. That sees itself in your face. Let me hear it, I pray."

Mr. Ricardo started out of an absorption which was altogether assumed.

"I was thinking," he said, with a faraway smile, "that you might disappear in the forests of Africa, and at once everyone would be very busy about your disappearance. You might leave your village in Leicestershire and live in the fogs of Glasgow, and within a week the whole village would know your postal address. But London--what a city! How different! How indifferent! Turn out of St. James's into the Adelphi Terrace and not a soul will say to you: 'Dr. Livingstone, I presume?'"

"But why should they," asked Hanaud, "if your name isn't Dr. Livingstone?"

Mr. Ricardo smiled indulgently.

"Scoffer!" he said. "You understand me very well," and he sought to turn the tables on his companion. "And you--does this room suggest nothing to you? Have you no ideas?" But he knew very well that Hanaud had. Ever since Hanaud had crossed the threshold he had been like a man stimulated by a drug. His eyes were bright and active, his body alert.

"Yes," he said, "I have."

He was standing now by Ricardo's side with his hands in his pockets, looking out at the trees on the Embankment and the barges swinging down the river.

"You are thinking of the strange scene which took place in this room such a very few hours ago," said Ricardo. "The girl in her masquerade dress making her confession with the stolen chain about her throat--—"

Hanaud looked backwards carelessly. "No, I wasn't giving it a thought," he said, and in a moment or two he began to walk about the room with that curiously light step which Ricardo was never able to reconcile with his cumbersome figure. With the heaviness of a bear he still padded. He went from corner to corner, opened a cupboard here, a drawer of the bureau there, and--stooped suddenly. He stood erect again with a small box of morocco leather in his hand. His body from head to foot seemed to Ricardo to be expressing the question, "Have I found it?" He pressed a spring and the lid of the box flew open. Hanaud emptied its contents into the palm of his hand. There were two or three sticks of sealing-wax and a seal. With a shrug of the shoulders he replaced them and shut the box.

"You are looking for something," Ricardo announced with sagacity.

"I am," replied Hanaud; and it seemed that in a second or two he found it. Yet--yet--he found it with his hands in his pockets, if he had found it. Mr. Ricardo saw him stop in that attitude in front of the mantelshelf, and heard him utter a long, low whistle. Upon the mantelshelf some photographs were arranged, a box of cigars stood at one end, a book or two lay between some delicate ornaments of china, and a small engraving in a thin gilt frame was propped at the back against the wall. Ricardo surveyed the shelf from his seat in the window, but he could not imagine which it was of these objects that so drew and held Hanaud's eyes.

Hanaud, however, stepped forward. He looked into a vase and turned it upside down. Then he removed the lid of a porcelain cup, and from the very look of his great shoulders Ricardo knew that he had discovered what he sought. He was holding something in his hands, turning it over, examining it. When he was satisfied he moved swiftly to the door and opened it cautiously. Both men could hear the splashing of water in a bath. Hanaud closed the door again with a nod of contentment and crossed once more to the window.

"Yes, it is all very strange and curious," he said, "and I do not regret that you dragged me into the affair. You were quite right, my friend, this morning. It is the personality of your young Mr. Calladine which is the interesting thing. For instance, here we are in London in the early summer. The trees out, freshly green, lilac and flowers in the gardens, and I don't know what tingle of hope and expectation in the sunlight and the air. I am middle-aged--yet there's a riot in my blood, a recapture of youth, a belief that just round the corner, beyond the reach of my eyes, wonders wait for me. Don't you, too, feel something like that? Well, then--" and he heaved his shoulders in astonishment.

"Can you understand a young man with money, with fastidious tastes, good-looking, hiding himself in a corner at such a time--except for some overpowering reason? No. Nor can I. There is another thing--I put a question or two to Calladine."

"Yes," said Ricardo.

"He has no servants here at night. He is quite alone and--here is what I find interesting--he has no valet. That seems a small thing to you?" Hanaud asked at a movement from Ricardo. "Well, it is no doubt a trifle, but it's a significant trifle in the case of a young rich man. It is generally a sign that there is something strange, perhaps even something sinister, in his life. Mr. Calladine, some months ago, turned out of St. James's into the Adelphi. Can you tell me why?"

"No," replied Mr. Ricardo. "Can you?"

Hanaud stretched out a hand. In his open palm lay a small round hairy bulb about the size of a big button and of a colour between green and brown.

"Look!" he said. "What is that?"

Mr. Ricardo took the bulb wonderingly.

"It looks to me like the fruit of some kind of cactus."

Hanaud nodded.

"It is. You will see some pots of it in the hothouses of any really good botanical gardens. Kew has them, I have no doubt. Paris certainly has. They are labelled. 'Anhalonium Luinii.' But amongst the Indians of Yucatan the plant has a simpler name."

"What name?" asked Ricardo.

"Mescal."

Mr. Ricardo repeated the name. It conveyed nothing to him whatever.

"There are a good many bulbs just like that in the cup upon the mantelshelf," said Hanaud.

Ricardo looked quickly up.

"Why?" he asked.

"Mescal is a drug."

Ricardo started.

"Yes, you are beginning to understand now," Hanaud continued, "why your young friend Calladine turned out of St. James's into the Adelphi Terrace."

Ricardo turned the little bulb over in his fingers.

"You make a decoction of it, I suppose?" he said.

"Or you can use it as the Indians do in Yucatan," replied Hanaud. "Mescal enters into their religious ceremonies. They sit at night in a circle about a fire built in the forest and chew it, whilst one of their number beats perpetually upon a drum."

Hanaud looked round the room and took notes of its luxurious carpet, its delicate appointments. Outside the window there was a thunder in the streets, a clamour of voices. Boats went swiftly down the river on the ebb. Beyond the mass of the Semiramis rose the great grey-white dome of St. Paul's. Opposite, upon the Southwark bank, the giant sky-signs, the big Highlander drinking whisky, and the rest of them waited, gaunt skeletons, for the night to limn them in fire and give them life. Below the trees in the gardens rustled and waved. In the air were the uplift and the sparkle of the young summer.

"It's a long way from the forests of Yucatan to the Adelphi Terrace of London," said Hanaud. "Yet here, I think, in these rooms, when the servants are all gone and the house is very quiet, there is a little corner of wild Mexico."

A look of pity came into Mr. Ricardo's face. He had seen more than one young man of great promise slacken his hold and let go, just for this reason. Calladine, it seemed, was another.

"It's like bhang and kieff and the rest of the devilish things, I suppose," he said, indignantly tossing the button upon the table.

Hanaud picked it up.

"No," he replied. "It's not quite like any other drug. It has a quality of its own which just now is of particular importance to you and me. Yes, my friend"—and he nodded his head very seriously--"we must watch that we do not make the big fools of ourselves in this affair."

"There," Mr. Ricardo agreed with an ineffable air of wisdom, "I am entirely with you."

"Now, why?" Hanaud asked. Mr. Ricardo was at a loss for a reason, but Hanaud did not wait. "I will tell you. Mescal intoxicates, yes--but it does more--it gives to the man who eats of it colour-dreams."

"Colour-dreams?" Mr. Ricardo repeated in a wondering voice.

"Yes, strange heated charms, in which violent things happen vividly amongst bright colours. Colour is the gift of this little prosaic brown button." He spun the bulb in the air like a coin, and catching it again, took it over to the mantelpiece and dropped it into the porcelain cup.

"Are you sure of this?" Ricardo cried excitedly, and Hanaud raised his hand in warning. He went to the door, opened it for an inch or so, and closed it again.

"I am quite sure," he returned. "I have for a friend a very learned chemist in the Collège de France. He is one of those enthusiasts who must experiment upon themselves. He tried this drug."

"Yes," Ricardo said in a quieter voice. "And what did he see?"

"He had a vision of a wonderful garden bathed in sunlight, an old garden of gorgeous flowers and emerald lawns, ponds with golden lilies and thick yew hedges--a garden where peacocks stepped indolently and groups of gay people fantastically dressed quarrelled and fought with swords. That is what he saw. And he saw it so vividly that, when the vapours of the drug passed from his brain and he waked, he seemed to be coming out of the real world into a world of shifting illusions."

Hanaud's strong quiet voice stopped, and for a while there was a complete silence in the room. Neither of the two men stirred so much as a finger. Mr. Ricardo once more was conscious of the thrill of strange sensations. He looked round the room. He could hardly believe that a room which had been--nay was--the home and shrine of mysteries in the dark hours could wear so bright and innocent a freshness in the sunlight of the morning. There should be something sinister which leaped to the eyes as you crossed the threshold.

"Out of the real world," Mr. Ricardo quoted. "I begin to see."

"Yes, you begin to see, my friend, that we must be very careful not to make the big fools of ourselves. My friend of the Collège de France saw a garden. But had he been sitting alone in the window-seat where you are, listening through a summer night to the music of the masquerade at the Semiramis, might he not have seen the ballroom, the dancers, the scarlet cloak, and the rest of this story?"

"You mean," cried Ricardo, now fairly startled, "that Calladine came to us with the fumes of mescal still working in his brain, that the false world was the real one still for him."

"I do not know," said Hanaud. "At present I only put questions. I ask them of you. I wish to hear how they sound. Let us reason this problem out. Calladine, let us say, takes a great deal more of the drug than my professor. It will have on him a more powerful effect while it lasts, and it will last longer. Fancy dress balls are familiar things to Calladine. The music floating from the Semiramis will revive old memories. He sits here, the pageant takes shape before him, he sees himself taking his part in it. Oh, he is happier here sitting quietly in his window-seat than if he was actually at the Semiramis. For he is there more intensely, more vividly, more really, than if he had actually descended this staircase. He lives his story through, the story of a heated brain, the scene of it changes in the way dreams have, it becomes tragic and sinister, it oppresses him with horror, and in the morning, so obsessed with it that he does not think to change his clothes, he is knocking at your door."

Mr. Ricardo raised his eyebrows and moved.

"Ah! You see a flaw in my argument," said Hanaud. But Mr. Ricardo was wary. Too often in other days he had been leaped upon and trounced for a careless remark.

"Let me hear the end of your argument," he said. "There was then to your thinking no temptation of jewels, no theft, no murder--in a word, no Celymène? She was born of recollections and the music of the Semiramis."

"No!" cried Hanaud. "Come with me, my friend. I am not so sure that there was no Celymène."

With a smile upon his face, Hanaud led the way across the room. He had the dramatic instinct, and rejoiced in it. He was going to produce a surprise for his companion and, savouring the moment in advance, he managed his effects. He walked towards the mantelpiece and stopped a few paces away from it.

"Look!"

Mr. Ricardo looked and saw a broad Adams mantelpiece. He turned a bewildered face to his friend.

"You see nothing?" Hanaud asked.

"Nothing!"

"Look again! I am not sure--but is it not that Celymène is posing before you?"

Mr. Ricardo looked again. There was nothing to fix his eyes. He saw a book or two, a cup, a vase or two, and nothing else really expect a very pretty and apparently valuable piece of--and suddenly Mr. Ricardo understood. Straight in front of him, in the very centre of the mantelpiece, a figure in painted china was leaning against a china stile. It was the figure of a perfectly impossible courtier, feminine and exquisite as could be, and apparelled also even to the scarlet heels exactly as Calladine had described Joan Carew.

Hanaud chuckled with satisfaction when he saw the expression upon Mr. Ricardo's face.

"Ah, you understand," he said. "Do you dream, my friend? At times--yes, like the rest of us. Then recollect your dreams? Things, people, which you have seen perhaps that day, perhaps months ago, pop in and out of them without making themselves prayed for. You cannot understand why. Yet sometimes they cut their strange capers there, logically, too, through subtle associations which the dreamer, once awake, does not apprehend. Thus, our friend here sits in the window, intoxicated by his drug, the music plays in the Semiramis, the curtain goes up in the heated theatre of his brain. He sees himself step upon the stage, and who else meets him but the china figure from his mantelpiece?"

Mr. Ricardo for a moment was all enthusiasm. Then his doubt returned to him.

"What you say, my dear Hanaud, is very ingenious. The figure upon the mantelpiece is also extremely convincing. And I should be absolutely convinced but for one thing."

"Yes?" said Hanaud, watching his friend closely.

"I am--I may say it, I think, a man of the world. And I ask myself"--Mr. Ricardo never could ask himself anything without assuming a manner of extreme pomposity--"I ask myself, whether a young man who has given up his social ties, who has become a hermit, and still more who has become the slave of a drug, would retain that scrupulous carefulness of his body which is indicated by dressing for dinner when alone?"

Hanaud struck the table with the palm of his hand and sat down in a chair.

"Yes. That is the weak point in my theory. You have hit it. I knew it was there--that weak point, and I wondered whether you would seize it. Yes, the consumers of drugs are careless, untidy--even unclean as a rule. But not always. We must be careful. We must wait."

"For what?" asked Ricardo, beaming with pride.

"For the answer to a telephone message," replied Hanaud, with a nod towards the door.

Both men waited impatiently until Calladine came into the room. He wore now a suit of blue serge, he had a clearer eye, his skin a healthier look; he was altogether a more reputable person. But he was plainly very ill at ease. He offered his visitors cigarettes, he proposed refreshments, he avoided entirely and awkwardly the object of their visit. Hanaud smiled. His theory was working out. Sobered by his bath, Calladine had realised the foolishness of which he had been guilty.

"You telephone, to the Semiramis, of course?" said Hanaud cheerfully.

Calladine grew red.

"Yes," he stammered.

"Yet I did not hear that volume of 'Hallos' which precedes telephonic connection in your country of leisure," Hanaud continued.

"I telephoned from my bedroom. You would not hear anything in this room."

"Yes, yes; the walls of these old houses are solid." Hanaud was playing with his victim. "And when may we expect Miss Carew?"

"I can't say," replied Calladine. "It's very strange. She is not in the hotel. I am afraid that she has gone away, fled."

Mr. Ricardo and Hanaud exchanged a look. They were both satisfied now. There was no word of truth in Calladine's story.

"Then there is no reason for us to wait," said Hanaud. "I shall have my holiday after all." And while he was yet speaking the voice of a newsboy calling out the first edition of an evening paper became distantly audible. Hanaud broke off his farewell. For a moment he listened, with his head bent. Then the voice was heard again, confused, indistinct; Hanaud picked up his hat and cane and, without another word to Calladine, raced down the stairs. Mr. Ricardo followed him, but when he reached the pavement, Hanaud was half down the little street. At the corner, however, he stopped, and Ricardo joined him, coughing and out of breath.

"What's the matter?" he gasped.

"Listen," said Hanaud.

At the bottom of Duke Street, by Charing Cross Station, the newsboy was shouting his wares. Both men listened, and now the words came to them mispronounced but decipherable.

"Mysterious crime at the Semiramis Hotel."

Ricardo stared at his companion.

"You were wrong then!" he cried. "Calladine's story was true."

For once in a way Hanaud was quite disconcerted.

"I don't know yet," he said. "We will buy a paper."

But before he could move a step a taxi-cab turned into the Adelphi from the Strand, and wheeling in front of their faces, stopped at Calladine's door. From the cab a girl descended.

"Let us go back," said Hanaud.


## III

Mr. Ricardo could no longer complain. It was half-past eight when Calladine had first disturbed the formalities of his house in Grosvenor Square. It was barely ten now, and during that short time he had been flung from surprise to surprise, he had looked underground on a morning of fresh summer, and had been thrilled by the contrast between the queer, sinister life below and within and the open call to joy of the green world above. He had passed from incredulity to belief, from belief to incredulity, and when at last incredulity was firmly established, and the story to which he had listened proved the emanation of a drugged and heated brain, lo! the facts buffeted him in the face, and the story was shown to be true.

"I am alive once more," Mr. Ricardo thought as he turned back with Hanaud, and in his excitement he cried his thought aloud.

"Are you?" said Hanaud. "And what is life without a newspaper? If you will buy one from that remarkably raucous boy at the bottom of the street I will keep an eye upon Calladine's house till you come back."

Mr. Ricardo sped down to Charing Cross and brought back a copy of the fourth edition of the *Star*. He handed it to Hanaud, who stared at it doubtfully, folded as it was.

"Shall we see what it says?" Ricardo asked impatiently.

"By no means," Hanaud answered, waking from his reverie and tucking briskly away the paper into the tail pocket of his coat. "We will hear what Miss Joan Carew has to say, with our minds undisturbed by any discoveries. I was wondering about something totally different."

"Yes?" Mr. Ricardo encouraged him. "What was it?"

"I was wondering, since it is only ten o'clock, at what hour the first editions of the evening papers appear."

"It is a question," Mr. Ricardo replied sententiously, "which the greatest minds have failed to answer."

And they walked along the street to the house. The front door stood open during the day like the front door of any other house which is let off in sets of rooms. Hanaud and Ricardo went up the staircase and rang the bell of Calladine's door. A middle-aged woman opened it.

"Mr. Calladine is in?" said Hanaud.

"I will ask," replied the woman. "What name shall I say?"

"It does not matter. I will go straight in," said Hanaud quietly. "I was here with my friend but a minute ago."

He went straight forward and into Calladine's parlour. Mr. Ricardo looked over his shoulder as he opened the door and saw a girl turn to them suddenly a white face of terror, and flinch as though already she felt the hand of a constable upon her shoulder. Calladine, on the other hand, uttered a cry of relief.

"These are my friends," he exclaimed to the girl, "the friends of whom I spoke to you"; and to Hanaud he said: "This is Miss Carew."

Hanaud bowed.

"You shall tell me your story, mademoiselle," he said very gently, and a little colour returned to the girl's cheeks, a little courage revived in her.

"But you have heard it," she answered.

"Not from you," said Hanaud.

So for a second time in that room she told the history of that night. Only this time the sunlight was warm upon the world, the comfortable sounds of life's routine were borne through the windows, and the girl herself wore the inconspicuous blue serge of a thousand other girls afoot that morning. These trifles of circumstance took the edge of sheer horror off her narrative, so that, to tell the truth, Mr. Ricardo was a trifle disappointed. He wanted a crescendo motive in his music, whereas it had begun at its fortissimo. Hanaud, however, was the perfect listener. He listened without stirring and with most compassionate eyes, so that Joan Carew spoke only to him, and to him, each moment that passed, with greater confidence. The life and sparkle of her had gone altogether. There was nothing in her manner now to suggest the waywardness, the gay irresponsibility, the radiance, which had attracted Calladine the night before. She was just a very young and very pretty girl, telling in a low and remorseful voice of the tragic dilemma to which she had brought herself. Of Celymène all that remained was something exquisite and fragile in her beauty, in the slimness of her figure, in her daintiness of hand and foot-- something almost of the hot-house. But the story she told was, detail for detail, the same which Calladine had already related.

"Thank you," said Hanaud when she had done. "Now I must ask you two questions."

"I will answer them."

Mr. Ricardo sat up. He began to think of a third question which he might put himself, something uncommonly subtle and searching, which Hanaud would never have thought of. But Hanaud put his questions, and Ricardo almost jumped out of his chair.

"You will forgive me. Miss Carew. But have you ever stolen before?"

Joan Carew turned upon Hanaud with spirit. Then a change swept over her face.

"You have a right to ask," she answered. "Never." She looked into his eyes as she answered. Hanaud did not move. He sat with a hand upon each knee and led to his second question.

"Early this morning, when you left this room, you told Mr. Calladine that you would wait at the Semiramis until he telephoned to you?"

"Yes."

"Yet when he telephoned, you had gone out?"

"Yes."

"Why?"

"I will tell you," said Joan Carew. "I could not bear to keep the little diamond chain in my room."

For a moment even Hanaud was surprised. He had lost sight of that complication. Now he leaned forward anxiously; indeed, with a greater anxiety than he had yet shown in all this affair.

"I was terrified," continued Joan Carew. "I kept thinking: 'They must have found out by now. They will search everywhere.' I didn't reason. I lay in bed expecting to hear every moment a loud knocking on the door. Besides--the chain itself being there in my bedroom--her chain--the dead woman's chain--no, I couldn't endure it. I felt as if I had stolen it. Then my maid brought in my tea."

"You had locked it away?" cried Hanaud.

"Yes. My maid did not see it."

Joan Carew explained how she had risen, dressed, wrapped the chain in a pad of cotton-wool and enclosed it in an envelope. The envelope had not the stamp of the hotel upon it. It was a rather large envelope, one of a packet which she had bought in a crowded shop in Oxford Street on her way from Euston to the Semiramis. She had bought the envelopes of that particular size in order that when she sent her letter of introduction to the Director of the Opera at Covent Garden she might enclose with it a photograph.

"And to whom did you send it?" asked Mr. Ricardo.

"To Mrs. Blumenstein at the Semiramis. I printed the address carefully. Then I went out and posted it."

"Where?" Hanaud inquired.

"In the big letter-box of the Post Office at the corner of Trafalgar Square."

Hanaud looked at the girl sharply.

"You had your wits about you, I see," he said.

"What if the envelope gets lost?" said Ricardo.

Hanaud laughed grimly.

"If one envelope is delivered at its address in London to-day, it will be that one," he said. "The news of the crime is published, you see," and he swung round to Joan.

"Did you know that, Miss Carew?"

"No," she answered in an awe-stricken voice.

"Well, then, it is. Let us see what the special investigator has to say about it." And Hanaud, with a deliberation which Mr. Ricardo found quite excruciating, spread out the newspaper on the table in front of him.


## IV

There was only one new fact in the couple of columns devoted to the mystery. Mrs. Blumenstein had died from chloroform poisoning. She was of a stout habit, and the thieves were not skilled in the administration of the anæsthetic.

"It's murder none the less," said Hanaud, and he gazed straight at Joan, asking her by the direct summons of his eyes what she was going to do.

"I must tell my story to the police," she replied painfully and slowly. But she did not hesitate; she was announcing a meditated plan.

Hanaud neither agreed nor differed. His face was blank, and when he spoke there was no cordiality in his voice. "Well," he asked, "and what is it that you have to say to the police, miss? That you went into the room to steal, and that you were attacked by two strangers, dressed as apaches, and masked? That is all?"

"Yes."

"And how many men at the Semiramis ball were dressed as apaches and wore masks? Come! Make a guess. A hundred at the least?"

"I should think so."

"Then what will your confession do beyond--I quote your English idiom--putting you in the coach?"

Mr. Ricardo now smiled with relief. Hanaud was taking a definite line. His knowledge of idiomatic English might be incomplete, but his heart was in the right place. The girl traced a vague pattern on the tablecloth with her fingers.

"Yet I think I must tell the police," she repeated, looking up and dropping her eyes again. Mr. Ricardo noticed that her eyelashes were very long. For the first time Hanaud's face relaxed.

"And I think you are quite right," he cried heartily, to Mr. Ricardo's surprise. "Tell them the truth before they suspect it, and they will help you out of the affair if they can. Not a doubt of it. Come, I will go with you myself to Scotland Yard."

"Thank you," said Joan, and the pair drove away in a cab together.

Hanaud returned to Grosvenor Square alone and lunched with Ricardo.

"It was all right," he said. "The police were very kind. Miss Joan Carew told her story to them as she had told it to us. Fortunately, the envelope with the aluminium chain had already been delivered, and was in their hands. They were much mystified about it, but Miss Joan's story gave them a reasonable explanation. I think they are inclined to believe her; and, if she is speaking the truth, they will keep her out of the witness-box if they can."

"She is to stay here in London, then?" asked Ricardo.

"Oh, yes; she is not to go. She will present her letters at the Opera House and secure an engagement, if she can. The criminals might be lulled thereby into a belief that the girl had kept the whole strange incident to herself, and that there was nowhere even a knowledge of the disguise which they had used." Hanaud spoke as carelessly as if the matter was not very important; and Ricardo, with an unusual flash of shrewdness, said:

"It is clear, my friend, that you do not think those two men will ever be caught at all."

Hanaud shrugged his shoulders.

"There is always a chance. But listen. There is a room with a hundred guns, one of which is loaded. Outside the room there are a hundred pigeons, one of which is white. You are taken into the room blind-fold. You choose the loaded gun and you shoot the one white pigeon. That is the value of the chance."

"But," exclaimed Ricardo, "those pearls were of great value, and I have heard at a trial expert evidence given by pearl merchants. All agree that the pearls of great value are known; so, when they come upon the market-—"

"That is true," Hanaud interrupted imperturbably. "But how are they known?"

"By their weight," said Mr. Ricardo.

"Exactly," replied Hanaud. "But did you not also hear at this trial of yours that pearls can be peeled like an onion? No? It is true. Remove a skin, two skins, the weight is altered, the pearl is a trifle smaller. It has lost a little of its value, yes--but you can no longer identify it as the so-and-so pearl which belonged to this or that sultan, was stolen by the vizier, bought by Messrs. Lustre and Steinopolis, of Hatton Garden, and subsequently sold to the wealthy Mrs. Blumenstein. No, your pearl has vanished altogether. There is a new pearl which can be traded." He looked at Ricardo. "Who shall say that those pearls are not already in one of the queer little back streets of Amsterdam, undergoing their transformation?"

Mr. Ricardo was not persuaded because he would not be. "I have some experience in these matters," he said loftily to Hanaud. "I am sure that we shall lay our hands upon the criminals. We have never failed."

Hanaud grinned from ear to ear. The only experience which Mr. Ricardo had ever had was gained on the shores of Geneva and at Aix under Hanaud's tuition. But Hanaud did not argue, and there the matter rested.

The days flew by. It was London's play-time. The green and gold of early summer deepened and darkened; wondrous warm nights under England's pale blue sky, when the streets rang with the joyous feet of youth, led in clear dawns and lovely glowing days. Hanaud made acquaintance with the wooded reaches of the Thames; Joan Carew sang "Louise" at Covent Garden with notable success; and the affair of the Semiramis Hotel, in the minds of the few who remembered it, was already added to the long list of unfathomed mysteries.

But towards the end of May there occurred a startling development. Joan Carew wrote to Mr. Ricardo that she would call upon him in the afternoon, and she begged him to secure the presence of Hanaud. She came as the clock struck; she was pale and agitated; and in the room where Calladine had first told the story of her visit she told another story which, to Mr. Ricardo's thinking, was yet more strange and--yes--yet more suspicious.

"It has been going on for some time," she began. "I thought of coming to you at once. Then I wondered whether, if I waited--oh, you'll never believe me!"

"Let us hear!" said Hanaud patiently.

"I began to dream of that room, the two men disguised and masked, the still figure in the bed. Night after night! I was terrified to go to sleep. I felt the hand upon my mouth. I used to catch myself falling asleep, and walk about the room with all the lights up to keep myself awake."

"But you couldn't," said Hanaud with a smile. "Only the old can do that."

"No, I couldn't," she admitted; "and--oh, my nights were horrible until"--she paused and looked at her companions doubtfully--"until one night the mask slipped."

"What--?" cried Hanaud, and a note of sternness rang suddenly in his voice. "What are you saying?"

With a desperate rush of words, and the colour staining her forehead and cheeks, Joan Carew continued:

"It is true. The mask slipped on the face of one of the men--of the man who held me. Only a little way; it just left his forehead visible--no more."

"Well?" asked Hanaud, and Mr. Ricardo leaned forward, swaying between the austerity of criticism and the desire to believe so thrilling a revelation.

"I waked up," the girl continued, "in the darkness, and for a moment the whole scene remained vividly with me--for just long enough for me to fix clearly in my mind the figure of the apache with the white forehead showing above the mask."

"When was that?" asked Ricardo.

"A fortnight ago."

"Why didn't you come with your story then?"

"I waited," said Joan. "What I had to tell wasn't yet helpful. I thought that another night the mask might slip lower still. Besides, I--it is difficult to describe just what I felt. I felt it important just to keep that photograph in my mind, not to think about it, not to talk about it, not even to look at it too often lest I should begin to imagine the rest of the face and find something familiar in the man's carriage and shape when there was nothing really familiar to me at all. Do you understand that?" she asked, with her eyes fixed in appeal on Hanaud's face.

"Yes," replied Hanaud. "I follow your thought."

"I thought there was a chance now--the strangest chance--that the truth might be reached. I did not wish to spoil it," and she turned eagerly to Ricardo, as if, having persuaded Hanaud, she would now turn her batteries on his companion. "My whole point of view was changed. I was no longer afraid of falling asleep lest I should dream. I wished to dream, but--—"

"But you could not," suggested Hanaud.

"No, that is the truth," replied Joan Carew. "Whereas before I was anxious to keep awake and yet must sleep from sheer fatigue, now that I tried consciously to put myself to sleep I remained awake all through the night, and only towards morning, when the light was coming through the blinds, dropped off into a heavy, dreamless slumber."

Hanaud nodded.

"It is a very perverse world, Miss Carew, and things go by contraries."

Ricardo listened for some note of irony in Hanaud's voice, some look of disbelief in his face. But there was neither the one nor the other. Hanaud was listening patiently.

"Then came my rehearsals," Joan Carew continued, "and that wonderful opera drove everything else out of my head. I had such a chance, if only I could make use of it! When I went to bed now, I went with that haunting music in my ears--the call of Paris--oh, you must remember it. But can you realise what it must mean to a girl who is going to sing it for the first time in Covent Garden?"

Mr. Ricardo saw his opportunity. He, the connoisseur, to whom the psychology of the green room was as an open book, could answer that question.

"It is true, my friend," he informed Hanaud with quiet authority. "The great march of events leaves the artist cold. He lives aloof. While the tumbrils thunder in the streets he adds a delicate tint to the picture he is engaged upon or recalls his triumph in his last great part."

"Thank you," said Hanaud gravely. "And now Miss Carew may perhaps resume her story."

"It was the very night of my début," she continued. "I had supper with some friends. A great artist. Carmen Valeri, honoured me with her presence. I went home excited, and that night I dreamed again."

"Yes?"

"This time the chin, the lips, the eyes were visible. There was only a black strip across the middle of the face. And I thought--nay, I was sure--that if that strip vanished I should know the man."

"And it did vanish?"

"Three nights afterwards."

"And you did know the man?"

The girl's face became troubled. She frowned.

"I knew the face, that was all," she answered. "I was disappointed. I had never spoken to the man. I am sure of that still. But somewhere I have seen him."

"You don't even remember when?" asked Hanaud.

"No." Joan Carew reflected for a moment with her eyes upon the carpet, and then flung up her head with a gesture of despair. "No. I try all the time to remember. But it is no good."

Mr. Ricardo could not restrain a movement of indignation. He was being played with. The girl with her fantastic story had worked him up to a real pitch of excitement only to make a fool of him. All his earlier suspicions flowed back into his mind. What if, after all, she was implicated in the murder and the theft? What if, with a perverse cunning, she had told Hanaud and himself just enough of what she knew, just enough of the truth, to persuade them to protect her? What if her frank confession of her own overpowering impulse to steal the necklace was nothing more than a subtle appeal to the sentimental pity of men, an appeal based upon a wider knowledge of men's weaknesses than a girl of nineteen or twenty ought to have? Mr. Ricardo cleared his throat and sat forward in his chair. He was girding himself for a singularly searching interrogatory when Hanaud asked the most irrelevant of questions:

"How did you pass the evening of that night when you first dreamed complete the face of your assailant?"

Joan Carew reflected. Then her face cleared.

"I know," she exclaimed. "I was at the opera."

"And what was being given?"

*The Jewels of the Madonna.*"

Hanaud nodded his head. To Ricardo it seemed that he had expected precisely that answer.

"Now," he continued, "you are sure that you have seen this man?"

"Yes."

"Very well," said Hanaud. "There is a game you play at children's parties--is there not?-- animal, vegetable, or mineral, and always you get the answer. Let us play that game for a few minutes, you and I."

Joan Carew drew up her chair to the table and sat with her chin propped upon her hands and her eyes fixed on Hanaud's face. As he put each question she pondered on it and answered. If she answered doubtfully he pressed it.

"You crossed on the *Lucania* from New York?"

"Yes."

"Picture to yourself the dining-room, the tables. You have the picture quite clear?"

"Yes."

"Was it at breakfast that you saw him?"

"No."

"At luncheon?"

"No."

"At dinner?"

She paused for a moment, summoning before her eyes the travellers at the tables.

"No."

"Not in the dining-table at all, then?"

"No."

"In the library, when you were writing letters, did you not one day lift your head and see him?"

"No."

"On the promenade deck? Did he pass you when you sat in your deck-chair, or did you pass him when he sat in his chair?"

"No."

Step by step Hanaud took her back to New York to her hotel, to journeys in the train. Then he carried her to Milan where she had studied. It was extraordinary to Ricardo to realise how much Hanaud knew of the curriculum of a student aspiring to grand opera. From Milan he brought her again to New York, and at the last, with a start of joy, she cried: "Yes, it was there."

Hanaud took his handkerchief from his pocket and wiped his forehead.

"Ouf!" he grunted. "To concentrate the mind on a day like this, it makes one hot, I can tell you. Now, Miss Carew, let us hear."

It was at a concert at the house of a Mrs. Starlingshield in Fifth Avenue and in the afternoon. Joan Carew sang. She was a stranger to New York and very nervous. She saw nothing but a mist of faces whilst she sang, but when she had finished the mist cleared, and as she left the improvised stage she saw the man. He was standing against the wall in a line of men. There was no particular reason why her eyes should single him out, except that he was paying no attention to her singing, and, indeed, she forgot him altogether afterwards.

"I just happened to see him clearly and distinctly," she said. "He was tall, clean-shaven, rather dark, not particularly young--thirty-five or so, I should say--a man with a heavy face and beginning to grow stout. He moved away whilst I was bowing to the audience, and I noticed him afterwards walking about, talking to people."

"Do you remember to whom?"

"No."

"Did he notice you, do you think?"

"I am sure he didn't," the girl replied emphatically. "He never looked at the stage where I was singing, and he never looked towards me afterwards."

She gave, so far as she could remember, the names of such guests and singers as she knew at that party. "And that is all," she said.

"Thank you," said Hanaud. "It is perhaps a good deal. But it is perhaps nothing at all."

"You will let me hear from you?" she cried, as she rose to her feet.

"Miss Carew, I am at your service," he returned. She gave him her hand timidly and he took it cordially. For Mr. Ricardo she had merely a bow, a bow which recognised that he distrusted her and that she had no right to be offended. Then she went, and Hanaud smiled across the table at Ricardo.

"Yes," he said, "all that you are thinking is true enough. A man who slips out of society to indulge a passion for a drug in greater peace, a girl who, on her own confession, tried to steal, and, to crown all, this fantastic story. It is natural to disbelieve every word of it. But we disbelieved before, when we left Calladine's lodging in the Adelphi, and we were wrong. Let us be warned."

"You have an idea?" exclaimed Ricardo.

"Perhaps!" said Hanaud. And he looked down the theatre column of the *Times*. "Let us distract ourselves by going to the theatre."

"You are the most irritating man!" Mr. Ricardo broke out impulsively. "If I had to paint your portrait, I should paint you with your finger against the side of your nose, saying mysteriously: '*I* know,' when you know nothing at all."

Hanaud made a schoolboy's grimace. "We will go and sit in your box at the opera to-night," he said, "and you shall explain to me all through the beautiful music the theory of the tonic sol-fa."

They reached Covent Garden before the curtain rose. Mr. Ricardo's box was on the lowest tier and next to the omnibus box.

"We are near the stage," said Hanaud, as he took his seat in the corner and so arranged the curtain that he could see and yet was hidden from view. "I like that."

The theatre was full; stalls and boxes shimmered with jewels and satin, and all that was famous that season for beauty and distinction had made its tryst there that night.

"Yes, this is wonderful," said Hanaud. "What opera do they play?" He glanced at his programme and cried, with a little start of surprise: "We are in luck. It is *The Jewels of the Madonna.*"

"Do you believe in omens?" Mr. Ricardo asked coldly. He had not yet recovered from his rebuff of the afternoon.

"No, but I believe that Carmen Valeri is at her best in this part," said Hanaud.

Mr. Ricardo belonged to that body of critics which must needs spoil your enjoyment by comparisons and recollections of other great artists. He was at a disadvantage certainly to-night, for the opera was new. But he did his best. He imagined others in the part, and when the great scene came at the end of the second act, and Carmen Valeri, on obtaining from her lover the jewels stolen from the sacred image, gave such a display of passion as fairly enthralled that audience, Mr. Ricardo sighed quietly and patiently.

"How Calvé would have brought out the psychological value of that scene!" he murmured; and he was quite vexed with Hanaud, who sat with his opera glasses held to his eyes, and every sense apparently concentrated on the stage. The curtains rose and rose again when the act was concluded, and still Hanaud sat motionless as the Sphynx, staring through his glasses.

"That is all," said Ricardo when the curtains fell for the fifth time.

"They will come out," said Hanaud. "Wait!" And from between the curtains Carmen Valeri was led out into the full glare of the footlights with the panoply of jewels flashing on her breast. Then at last Hanaud put down his glasses and turned to Ricardo with a look of exultation and genuine delight upon his face which filled that season-worn dilettante with envy.

"What a night!" said Hanaud. "What a wonderful night!" And he applauded until he split his gloves. At the end of the opera he cried: "We will go and take supper at the Semiramis. Yes, my friend, we will finish our evening like gallant gentlemen. Come! Let us not think of the morning." And boisterously he slapped Ricardo in the small of the back.

In spite of his boast, however, Hanaud hardly touched his supper, and he played with, rather than drank, his brandy and soda. He had a little table to which he was accustomed beside a glass screen in the depths of the room, and he sat with his back to the wall watching the groups which poured in. Suddenly his face lighted up.

"Here is Carmen Valeri!" he cried. "Once more we are in luck. Is it not that she is beautiful?"

Mr. Ricardo turned languidly about in his chair and put up his eyeglass.

"So, so," he said.

"Ah!" returned Hanaud. "Then her companion will interest you still more. For he is the man who murdered Mrs. Blumenstein."

Mr. Ricardo jumped so that his eyeglass fell down and tinkled on its cord against the buttons of his waistcoat.

"What!" he exclaimed. "It's impossible!" He looked again. "Certainly the man fits Joan Carew's description. But--" He turned back to Hanaud utterly astounded. And as he looked at the Frenchman all his earlier recollections of him, of his swift deductions, of the subtle imagination which his heavy body so well concealed, crowded in upon Ricardo and convinced him.

"How long have you known?" he asked in a whisper of awe.

"Since ten o'clock to-night."

"But you will have to find the necklace before you can prove it."

"The necklace!" said Hanaud carelessly. "That is already found."

Mr. Ricardo had been longing for a thrill. He had it now. He felt it in his very spine.

"It's found?" he said in a startled whisper.

"Yes."

Ricardo turned again, with as much indifference as he could assume, towards the couple who were settling down at their table, the man with a surly indifference, Carmen Valeri with the radiance of a woman who has just achieved a triumph and is now free to enjoy the fruits of it. Confusedly, recollections returned to Ricardo of questions put that afternoon by Hanaud to Joan Carew--subtle questions into which the name of Carmen Valeri was continually entering. She was a woman of thirty, certainly beautiful, with a clear, pale face and eyes like the night.

"Then she is implicated too!" he said. What a change for her, he thought, from the stage of Covent Garden to the felon's cell, from the gay supper-room of the Semiramis, with its bright frocks and its babel of laughter, to the silence and the ignominious garb of the workrooms in Aylesbury Prison!

"She!" exclaimed Hanaud; and in his passion for the contrasts of drama Ricardo was almost disappointed. "She has nothing whatever to do with it. She knows nothing. André Favart there--yes. But Carmen Valeri! She's as stupid as an owl, and loves him beyond words. Do you want to know how stupid she is? You shall know. I asked Mr. Clements, the director of the opera house, to take supper with us, and here he is."

Hanaud stood up and shook hands with the director. He was of the world of business rather than of art, and long experience of the ways of tenors and prima-donnas had given him a good-humoured cynicism.

"They are spoilt children, all tantrums and vanity," he said, "and they would ruin you to keep a rival out of the theatre."

He told them anecdote upon anecdote.

"And Carmen Valeri," Hanaud asked in a pause; "is she troublesome this season?"

"Has been," replied Clements dryly. "At present she is playing at being good. But she gave me a turn some weeks ago." He turned to Ricardo. "Superstition's her trouble, and André Favart knows it. She left him behind in America this spring."

"America!" suddenly cried Ricardo; so suddenly that Clements looked at him in surprise.

"She was singing in New York, of course, during the winter," he returned. "Well, she left him behind, and I was shaking hands with myself when he began to deal the cards over there. She came to me in a panic. She had just had a cable. She couldn't sing on Friday night. There was a black knave next to the nine of diamonds. She wouldn't sing for worlds. And it was the first night of *The Jewels of the Madonna!* Imagine the fix I was in!"

"What did you do?" asked Ricardo.

"The only thing there was to do," replied Clements with a shrug of the shoulders. "I cabled Favart some money and he dealt the cards again. She came to me beaming. Oh, she had been so distressed to put me in the cart! But what could she do? Now there was a red queen next to the ace of hearts, so she could sing without a scruple so long, of course, as she didn't pass a funeral on the way down to the opera house. Luckily she didn't. But my money brought Favart over here, and now I'm living on a volcano. For he's the greatest scoundrel unhung. He never has a farthing, however much she gives him; he's a blackmailer, he's a swindler, he has no manners and no graces, he looks like a butcher and treats her as if she were dirt, he never goes near the opera except when she is singing in this part, and she worships the ground he walks on. Well, I suppose it's time to go."

The lights had been turned off, the great room was emptying. Mr. Ricardo and his friends rose to go, but at the door Hanaud detained Mr. Clements, and they talked together alone for some little while, greatly to Mr. Ricardo's annoyance. Hanaud's good humour, however, when he rejoined his friend, was enough for two.

"I apologise, my friend, with my hand on my heart. But it was for your sake that I stayed behind. You have a meretricious taste for melodrama which I deeply deplore, but which I mean to gratify. I ought to leave for Paris to-morrow, but I shall not. I shall stay until Thursday." And he skipped upon the pavement as they walked home to Grosvenor Square.

Mr. Ricardo bubbled with questions, but he knew his man. He would get no answer to any one of them to-night. So he worked out the problem for himself as he lay awake in his bed, and he came down to breakfast next morning fatigued but triumphant. Hanaud was already chipping off the top of his egg at the table.

"So I see you have found it all out, my friend," he said.

"Not all," replied Ricardo modestly, "and you will not mind, I am sure, if I follow the usual custom and wish you a good morning."

"Not at all," said Hanaud. "I am all for good manners myself."

He dipped his spoon into his egg.

"But I am longing to hear the line of your reasoning."

Mr. Ricardo did not need much pressing.

"Joan Carew saw André Favart at Mrs. Starlingshield's party, and saw him with Carmen Valeri. For Carmen Valeri was there. I remember that you asked Joan for the names of the artists who sang, and Carmen Valeri was amongst them."

Hanaud nodded his head.

"Exactly."

"No doubt Joan Carew noticed Carmen Valeri particularly, and so took unconsciously into her mind an impression of the man who was with her, André Favart--of his build, of his walk, of his type."

Again Hanaud agreed.

"She forgets the man altogether, but the picture remains latent in her mind--an undeveloped film."

Hanaud looked up in surprise, and the surprise flattered Mr. Ricardo. Not for nothing had he tossed about in his bed for the greater part of the night.

"Then came the tragic night at the Semiramis. She does not consciously recognise her assailant, but she dreams the scene again and again, and by a process of unconscious cerebration the figure of the man becomes familiar. Finally she makes her début, is entertained at supper afterwards, and meets once more Carmen Valeri."

"Yes, for the first time since Mrs. Starlingshield's party," interjected Hanaud.

"She dreams again, she remembers asleep more than she remembers when awake. The presence of Carmen Valeri at her supper-party has its effect. By a process of association, she recalls Favart, and the mask slips on the face of her assailant. Some days later she goes to the opera. She hears Carmen Valeri sing in *The Jewels of the Madonna*. No doubt the passion of her acting, which I am more prepared to acknowledge this morning than I was last night, affects Joan Carew powerfully, emotionally. She goes to bed with her head full of Carmen Valeri, and she dreams not of Carmen Valeri, but of the man who is unconsciously associated with Carmen Valeri in her thoughts. The mask vanishes altogether. She sees her assailant now, has his portrait limned in her mind, would know him if she met him in the street, though she does not know by what means she identified him."

"Yes," said Hanaud. "It is curious the brain working while the body sleeps, the dream revealing what thought cannot recall."

Mr. Ricardo was delighted. He was taken seriously.

"But of course," he said, "I could not have worked the problem out but for you. You knew of André Favart and the kind of man he was."

Hanaud laughed.

"Yes. That is always my one little advantage. I know all the cosmopolitan blackguards of Europe." His laughter ceased suddenly, and he brought his clenched fist heavily down upon the table. "Here is one of them who will be very well out of the world, my friend," he said very quietly, but there was a look of force in his face and a hard light in his eyes which made Mr. Ricardo shiver.

For a few moments there was silence. Then Ricardo asked: "But have you evidence enough?"

"Yes."

"Your two chief witnesses, Calladine and Joan Carew--you said it yourself--there are facts to discredit them. Will they be believed?"

"But they won't appear in the case at all," Hanaud said. "Wait, wait!" and once more he smiled. "By the way, what is the number of Calladine's house?"

Ricardo gave it, and Hanaud therefore wrote a letter. "It is all for your sake, my friend," he said with a chuckle.

"Nonsense," said Ricardo. "You have the spirit of the theatre in your bones."

"Well, I shall not deny it," said Hanaud, and he sent out the letter to the nearest pillar-box.

Mr. Ricardo waited in a fever of impatience until Thursday came. At breakfast Hanaud would talk of nothing but the news of the day. At luncheon he was no better. The affair of the Semiramis Hotel seemed a thousand miles from any of his thoughts. But at five o'clock he said as he drank his tea:

"You know, of course, that we go to the opera to-night?"

"Yes. Do we?"

"Yes. Your young friend Calladine, by the way, will join us in your box."

"That is very kind of him, I am sure," said Mr. Ricardo.

The two men arrived before the rising of the curtain, and in the crowded lobby a stranger spoke a few words to Hanaud, but what he said Ricardo could not hear. They took their seats in the box, and Hanaud looked at his programme.

"Ah! It is *Il Ballo de Maschera* to-night. We always seem to hit upon something appropriate, don't we?"

Then he raised his eyebrows.

"Oh-o! Do you see that our pretty young friend, Joan Carew, is singing in the rôle of the page? It is a showy part. There is a particular melody with a long-sustained trill in it, as far as I remember."

Mr. Ricardo was not deceived by Hanaud's apparent ignorance of the opera to be given that night and of the part Joan Carew was to take. He was, therefore, not surprised when Hanaud added:

"By the way, I should let Calladine find it all out for himself."

Mr. Ricardo nodded sagely.

"Yes. That is wise. I had thought of it myself." But he had done nothing of the kind. He was only aware that the elaborate stage-management in which Hanaud delighted was working out to the desired climax, whatever that climax might be. Calladine entered the box a few minutes later and shook hands with them awkwardly.

"It was kind of you to invite me," he said and, very ill at ease, he took a seat between them and concentrated his attention on the house as it filled up.

"There's the overture," said Hanaud. The curtains divided and were festooned on either side of the stage. The singers came on in their turn; the page appeared to a burst of delicate applause (Joan Carew had made a small name for herself that season), and with a stifled cry Calladine shot back in the box as if he had been struck. Even then Mr. Ricardo did not understand. He only realised that Joan Carew was looking extraordinarily trim and smart in her boy's dress. He had to look from his programme to the stage and back again several times before the reason of Calladine's exclamation dawned on him. When it did, he was horrified. Hanaud, in his craving for dramatic effects, must have lost his head altogether. Joan Carew was wearing, from the ribbon in her hair to the scarlet heels of her buckled satin shoes, the same dress as she had worn on the tragic night at the Semiramis Hotel. He leaned forward in his agitation to Hanaud.

"You must be mad. Suppose Favart is in the theatre and sees her. He'll be over on the Continent by one in the morning."

"No, he won't," replied Hanaud. "For one thing, he never comes to Covent Garden unless one opera, with Carmen Valeri in the chief part, is being played, as you heard the other night at supper. For a second thing, he isn't in the house. I know where he is. He is gambling in Dean Street, Soho. For a third thing, my friend, he couldn't leave by the nine o'clock train for the Continent if he wanted to. Arrangements have been made. For a fourth thing, he wouldn't wish to. He has really remarkable reasons for desiring to stay in London. But he will come to the theatre later. Clements will send him an urgent message, with the result that he will go straight to Clements' office. Meanwhile, we can enjoy ourselves, eh?"

Never was the difference between the amateur dilettante and the genuine professional more clearly exhibited than by the behaviour of the two men during the rest of the performance. Mr. Ricardo might have been sitting on a coal fire from his jumps and twistings; Hanaud stolidly enjoyed the music, and when Joan Carew sang her famous solo his hands clamoured for an encore louder than anyone's in the boxes. Certainly, whether excitement was keeping her up or no, Joan Carew had never sung better in her life. Her voice was clear and fresh as a bird's--a bird with a soul inspiring its song. Even Calladine drew his chair forward again and sat with his eyes fixed upon the stage and quite carried out of himself. He drew a deep breath at the end.

"She is wonderful," he said, like a man waking up.

"She is very good," replied Mr. Ricardo, correcting Calladine's transports.

"We will go round to the back of the stage," said Hanaud.

They passed through the iron door and across the stage to a long corridor with a row of doors on one side. There were two or three men standing about in evening dress, as if waiting for friends in the dressing-rooms. At the third door Hanaud stopped and knocked. The door was opened by Joan Carew, still dressed in her green and gold. Her face was troubled, her eyes afraid.

"Courage, little one," said Hanaud, and he slipped past her into the room. "It is as well that my ugly, familiar face should not be seen too soon."

The door closed and one of the strangers loitered along the corridor and spoke to a call-boy. The call-boy ran off. For five minutes more Mr. Ricardo waited with a beating heart. He had the joy of a man in the centre of things. All those people driving homewards in their motor-cars along the Strand--how he pitied them! Then, at the end of the corridor, he saw Clements and André Favart. They approached, discussing the possibility of Carmen Valeri's appearance in London opera during the next season.

"We have to look ahead, my dear friend," said Clements, "and though I should be extremely sorry——"

At that moment they were exactly opposite Joan Carew's door. It opened, she came out; with a nervous movement she shut the door behind her. At the sound André Favart turned, and he saw drawn up against the panels of the door, with a look of terror in her face, the same gay figure which had interrupted him in Mrs. Blumenstein's bedroom. There was no need for Joan to act. In the presence of this man her fear was as real as it had been on the night of the Semiramis ball. She trembled from head to foot. Her eyes closed; she seemed about to swoon.

Favart stared and uttered an oath. His face turned white; he staggered back as if he had seen a ghost. Then he made a wild dash along the corridor, and was seized and held by two of the men in evening dress. Favart recovered his wits. He ceased to struggle.

"What does this outrage mean?" he asked, and one of the men drew a warrant and notebook from his pocket.

"You are arrested for the murder of Mrs. Blumenstein in the Semiramis Hotel," he said, "and I have to warn you that anything you may say will be taken down and may be used in evidence against you."

"Preposterous!" exclaimed Favart. "There's a mistake. We will go along to the police and put it right. Where's your evidence against me?"

Hanaud stepped out of the doorway of the dressing-room.

"In the property-room of the theatre," he said.

At the sight of him Favart uttered a violent cry of rage. "You are here, too, are you?" he screamed, and he sprang at Hanaud's throat. Hanaud stepped lightly aside. Favart was borne down to the ground, and when he stood up again the handcuffs were on his wrists.

Favart was led away, and Hanaud turned to Mr. Ricardo and Clements.

"Let us go to the property-room," he said. They passed along the corridor, and Ricardo noticed that Calladine was no longer with them. He turned and saw him standing outside Joan Carew's dressing-room.

"He would like to come, of course," said Ricardo.

"Would he?" asked Hanaud. "Then why doesn't he? He's quite grown up, you know," and he slipped his arm through Ricardo's and led him back across the stage. In the property-room there was already a detective in plain clothes. Mr. Ricardo had still not as yet guessed the truth.

"What is it you really want, sir?" the property-master asked of the director.

"Only the jewels of the Madonna," Hanaud answered.

The property-master unlocked a cupboard and took from it the sparkling cuirass. Hanaud pointed to it, and there, lost amongst the huge glittering stones of paste and false pearls, Mrs. Blumenstein's necklace was entwined.

"Then that is why Favart came always to Covent Garden when *The Jewels of the Madonna* was being performed!" exclaimed Ricardo.

Hanaud nodded.

"He came to watch over his treasure."

Ricardo was piecing together the sections of the puzzle.

"No doubt he knew of the necklace in America. No doubt he followed it to England."

Hanaud agreed.

"Mrs. Blumenstein's jewels were quite famous in New York."

"But to hide them here!" cried Mr. Clements. "He must have been mad."

"Why?" asked Hanaud. "Can you imagine a safer hiding-place? Who is going to burgle the property-room of Covent Garden? Who is going to look for a priceless string of pearls amongst the stage jewels of an opera house?"

"You did," said Mr. Ricardo.

"I?" replied Hanaud, shrugging his shoulders. "Joan Carew's dreams led me to André Favart. The first time we came here and saw the pearls of the Madonna, I was on the look-out, naturally. I noticed Favart at the back of the stalls. But it was a stroke of luck that I noticed those pearls through my opera glasses."

"At the end of the second act?" cried Ricardo suddenly. "I remember now."

"Yes," replied Hanaud. "But for that second act the pearls would have stayed comfortably here all through the season. Carmen Valeri--a fool as I told you--would have tossed them about in her dressing-room without a notion of their value, and at the end of July, when the murder at the Semiramis Hotel had been forgotten, Favart would have taken them to Amsterdam and made his bargain."

"Shall we go?"

They left the theatre together and walked down to the grill-room of the Semiramis. But as Hanaud looked through the glass door he drew back.

"We will not go in, I think, eh?"

"Why?" asked Ricardo.

Hanaud pointed to a table. Calladine and Joan Carew were seated at it taking their supper.

"Perhaps," said Hanaud with a smile, "perhaps, my friend--what? Who shall say that the rooms in the Adelphi will not be given up?"

They turned away from the hotel. But Hanaud was right, and before the season was over Mr. Ricardo had to put his hand in his pocket for a wedding present.

9 788802 279357